MISSION ABANDONED

DEFENDER SERIES

MISSION ABANDONED

DEFENDER SERIES
BOOK 5

REGGI BROACH

DEFENDER CHRISTIAN
PUBLICATIONS

Published by Defender Christian Publications, Harrison, TN, USA

ISBN: 9780998962047

PUBLISHERS NOTE:

This is a work of fiction. Names, characters, places, and incidents either are a product of the author's imagination or are used fictitiously, and any resemblance to actual persons, living or dead, business establishments, events, or locales is entirely coincidental. The publisher does not have any control over and does not assume any responsibility for author or third-party web sites or their content.

Defender Publications books are available at special discounts for bulk purchases, for sales promotions, or corporate use. Special editions, including personalized covers, excerpts of existing books, or books with corporate logos, can be created for some titles. For more information, contact R. B. Enterprises at: Special-Sales@RBEnterprises.info

But if serving the Lord seems undesirable to you, then choose for yourselves this day whom you will serve, whether the gods your ancestors served..., or the gods... in whose land you are living. But as for me and my household, we will serve the Lord."

Joshua 24:15

ACKNOWLEDGMENTS

God is good, all the time; and all the time, God is good. God continues daily to lead me and sculpt my life into something really awesome. I am not yet the finished product but watching him work amazes me.

I am thankful for his guidance in writing the fifth book in this series. I pray that each one will be true to who he is and how he works. I am doing my best to emulate the ways I have seen him work time and again. Yes, this is a fiction book, but there is *so much* truth in it.

Thank you, God, for allowing me to write. I am having so much FUN!

Thanks to my husband, Ron for all the tedious work you have done in formatting, uploading, promoting, critiquing, etc., etc., etc., this book and all the others. (I know one etc. is supposed to be sufficient, but the list really is expansive.)

Thanks to my friends, family, co-workers, and fans for their encouragement and for reading the books and giving their feedback.

Thank you, Janelle, for your editing and your genuine interest in the storyline. Thank you Jake Wallin for being the face of Capt. David Alexander.

Thank you, Jesus, for giving me a reason to write and a unique ministry.

TABLE OF CONTENTS

COMMONWEALTH INTERSTELLAR FORCE

SS EVANGELINE
Explorer Class Ship with atmospheric capabilities

- Drive Capabilities
  - Tachyon
  - Matter/Antimatter
- Weapons Capabilities
  - minimal laser
  - EMP and tachyon defensive weaponry
  - electromagnetic shields and deflectors
- Personnel Accommodations
  - 14

Mission

To establish a Commonwealth presence on all technologically undeveloped worlds, or worlds that have not chosen to ally with the Commonwealth despite non-spatial developments. To report any world where the invasive forces of the Liontari have a foothold.

CREW MANIFEST

The crew is to consist of two teams. The primary team is the ship's crew; the secondary team is the diplomatic mission team. Each team is to act as support personnel for the opposing team as needed.

- Captain David Alexander (Ship's Captain)
- Commander Brynna Alexander (First Officer & Diplomatic leader)
- Lt. Commander Braxton Flint (Architectural Engineer & Second Officer)
- Lt. Commander Lazaro Dominick (Chief Engineer)
- Lt. Commander Jason Adams (Physician & relief Pilot)
- Lt. Thane Ryder (Primary Pilot)
- Lt. Alexia Flint (Ship's Psychologist & relief Engineer)
- Lt. JG Marissa Holden (Navigation & security)
- Lt. JG Laura Adams (Nurse & Botanist)
- Ensign Aulani Ryder (Communications & Computer Technology)
- Ensign Cheyenne Dominick (Linguistics & Computer Specialist)
- Chief Petty Officer Jake Holden (Security Officer)

COMMONWEALTH INTERSTELLAR FORCE

SS EMISSARY
Explorer Class Ship with atmospheric capabilities

- Drive Capabilities
  - Tachyon
  - Matter/Antimatter
- Weapons Capabilities
  - minimal laser
  - EMP and tachyon defensive weaponry
  - electromagnetic shields and deflectors
- Personnel Accommodations
  - 14

Mission

To establish a Commonwealth presence on all technologically undeveloped worlds, or worlds that have not chosen to ally with the Commonwealth despite non-spatial developments. To report any world where the invasive forces of the Liontari have a foothold.

CREW MANIFEST

The crew is to consist of two teams. The primary team is the ship's crew; the secondary team is the diplomatic mission team. Each team is to act as support personnel for the opposing team as needed.

- Captain Nathaniel Weiseman (Ship's Captain)
- Commander Silas Asher (First Officer & Diplomatic leader)
- Lt. Commander Elize Davu (Architectural Engineer & Second Officer)
- Lt. Commander Claire Asher (Chief Engineer)
- Lt. Commander Stephanie Weiseman (Physician)
- Ensign Maya Evans (Primary Pilot)
- Lt. Commander Henry Oliver (Ship's Psychologist)
- Lt. JG Deka Davu (Navigation & security)
- Chief Petty Officer (CPO) Noah Evans (Medical Support)
- Chief Warrant Officer (CWO) Luna Oliver (Communications & Computer Technology)
- Ensign Genevieve Griffin (Linguistics & Computer Specialist)
- Chief Warrant Officer (CWO) Milo Griffin (Security Officer)

A NEW MISSION

Ensign Aulani Ryder sat at the comms station. Her task was to lock the ship up tight so no one could access its computers. The comm panel chirped. "Captain, the *Valiant* is hailing us. Should I answer it?"

The Captain moved to his station. Glancing around at the bridge crew, Captain David Alexander made sure everyone was paying attention. "The *Valiant* and Admiral Robert Deacons are our enemies. Be very careful what you say and do concerning them. Don't even allow your facial expressions to be read. My Uncle Rob is not our enemy. Know the difference. Ensign, make sure that carrier wave detection program is active. I need to know if they try to slip a signal through under the radar. Bounce the signal a couple times and put it through."

Admiral Deacons' face appeared on the screen. "Captain Alexander, where is your security officer?"

David glanced at Jake. Security Chief Jake Holden was calmly sitting at his security station. "He's here on the bridge where he belongs."

Admiral Deacons glared. "You would do well to watch that man carefully. He's not to be trusted."

David squinted at his uncle. "Why is that any concern of yours?" He challenged.

Admiral Deacons continued to glare at Jake's image on the corner of his screen. "He's responsible for the deaths of every soldier and civilian on the CIF military base on Romajin. There were ten thousand men and women on that base. They are ALL DEAD because of his actions."

Jake looked up, startled. He looked back at the Captain. "I—I don't understand. I didn't do anything to—to the base."

The Captain gave a reassuring glance to Jake, then turned his attention back to the Admiral. "Is this your way of trying to track us down, Admiral? If it is, I can assure you, by the time you get here, we'll be long gone."

"You would be foolish to think I'm not tracking your signal. I am. I just thought you should know there is no place in this galaxy for you to hide. You might as well turn yourselves in so you can receive a merciful execution. After Mr. Holden's actions, the entire Commonwealth Interstellar Force is out for blood... his and yours." The Admiral's face was deadly serious although his eyes showed concern.

David folded his arms across his chest. "Why do you think Chief Holden is responsible for anything happening on the Romajin CIF Base? What happened? This is the first we've heard of it."

"The self-destruct mechanism was triggered just as your ships left the planetary system. Your security chief gained enough trust on Romajin to be given access to the computer. Commodore Vardin, and nearly his entire command, are dead. There were a few who were off base, and those guarding the perimeter who survived. They tracked the signal coming from your ship... CAPTAIN."

Jake stood slowly. He turned halfway between the Captain and Admiral. Looking back and forth between the two, "I swear... I didn't do this. We walked out of there clean... no casualties. I would never do anything like this. Captain... please believe me."

David nodded for Jake to sit back down. "Admiral... I know the Chief betrayed this crew, but he did it so that no one got hurt. Mr. Holden is incapable of cold-blooded murder. I think the Supreme Executor orchestrated this to frame us and I don't really care whether you believe me. I will do some investigating on my own to clear my man to my satisfaction, and then I'll move on. You can let the Supreme Executor know his days of murdering the innocent are coming to an end."

"Captain, you've sealed your own fate and the fate of the other eleven ships. You've proven this mission is too dangerous. The other ships will be recalled, and their crews dealt with... permanently."

"Does this mean all twelve ships have encountered Pateras?"

The look on the Admiral's face was intense. He seemed intent on making a point without revealing too much information. "Captain, you did your best to hide your own involvement with Pateras. Do you really think we can trust any of the other crews? This is on you, Captain."

"This isn't on me. Supreme Executor Hale is responsible. Uncle Rob, why do you still support him like this? He's a mass murderer. Why can't you see that?"

David and his uncle stared at each other for a moment. The Admiral wasn't about to blink. David finally did for both their sake's.

David turned around and sat down in his chair. "On a personal note, neither you nor he can use my family against me again. I hope you aren't too disappointed." This was David's way of discreetly telling the Admiral their family was safe.

The Admiral's face remained perfectly neutral. "You seem to have a very negative view of me, the Supreme Executor, and the Commonwealth. I would never put our family in danger and neither would the Supreme Executor. I thought, for a brief period, your man had killed our family when he destroyed the base. Lucky for you scans revealed they were no longer there, or I would have hunted him down myself. The safest thing for you is to disappear with them. You know I still care about what happens to you, right?"

"Based on the things you let Executor Hale do to me, I'm not sure I believe that. Admiral, I think we're done here. Let the war commence."

Admiral Deacons reached for his controls to end the communication. "So be it then."

The screen went dark.

Admiral Deacons' face faded from the screen. The bridge crew of the *Evangeline* sat there in stunned silence.

Security Chief Jake Holden was paler than his colleagues. He swallowed hard, then turned to face the Captain. "Captain, I swear... I didn't destroy the Commonwealth Base on Romajin. I had nothing to do with... with whatever happened down there. You have to believe me."

Captain Alexander's eyes moved slowly until they locked on Jake's. "Chief, regardless of what I choose to believe, this has to be investigated. You are relieved of duty until further notice. Your computer access is denied pending the outcome of the investigation."

"Captain... please... I didn't do this."

Captain Alexander stood up. "My office, Chief. Ensign Ryder, block his computer access—all levels. Restrict the rest of the crew, including me, to view only access of all log entries and surveillance feeds from the last two weeks."

Ensign Aulani Ryder was still in shock. News of the destruction of ten thousand troops would rattle anyone. She had to despise those same troops, but not badly enough to wish them dead. Her mouth felt like cotton. She tried fruitlessly to swallow. "Y-yes, Captain." Her shaking hand moved toward the controls on her terminal to follow his orders.

David waved Jake to a chair in front of his desk.

Jake's body language reflected his feelings of loss. He knew his relationship with the crew was tenuous at best. This news only stretched their relations even tighter.

David sat down at his desk across from Jake. The two sat in silence for a moment. David finally spoke first. "Chief, I'm—"

Jake interrupted him. "Captain, I swear to you, I had nothing to do with this. Arni ordered me to provide you and the crew with water and get you out of your prison cells. That's it! That's all I did! I programmed a redundant diagnostics program on their communications and tracking systems just before we left, but I never touched the self-destruct sequence. I never got clearance of that level."

"I know, Chief. I believe you." David responded.

During his proclamation of innocence, Jake sat on the edge of his seat. Hearing the Captain's response caused him to slump resolutely back into his chair. "I don't understand. If you believe me, why did you relieve me of duty?"

"Chief, the crew don't fully trust you. We need to prove your innocence beyond a reasonable doubt."

"Captain, if you trust me, shouldn't they?"

"I'm afraid not. Someone gave them cause to doubt my allegiance." David eyed Jake.

Jake looked up guiltily. "They know I lied about that, Captain."

"Jake—right now they aren't sure what to believe. At first, they thought it was you who betrayed them. You and Executor Hale were very convincing. Some of the crew believed I was really the one who betrayed them. Now that I'm defending you, they have reason to suspect we were together in all of this."

Jake was on the edge of his seat again. "Both of us? What was that supposed to accomplish?"

David shook his head. "They have no idea... yet."

"Yet? Captain, I'm confused. I'm not doing anything."

"Jake, I'm going to get Commander Alexander and Lt. Flint to see what they can do to prove your innocence." The Captain wasn't certain anyone could defend the security chief with sufficient voracity. He thought perhaps between Lt. Lexi Flint, the ship's psychologist, and Commander Brynna Alexander, the Captain's own wife, Commander Brynna Alexander would come the closest. They would hopefully do it because of their trust in him, even if they didn't trust Jake.

"I still don't understand. You just took away their access to the very files we need."

David tried to pull the complete picture together for the young security chief. "They still have access to view the information we need. I'm going to put Lt. Ryder, Lt. Commander Dominick, and Ensign Ryder in charge of the investigation. If they find sufficient evidence of your guilt, they'll present it to Lt. Commander Adams, Ensign Dominick, and Lt. Commander Flint. Essentially, you'll be court-martialled. In the meantime, the Commander, Lt. Flint, and I will look for proof of your innocence. We still have limited access to those files."

Jake rolled his eyes. "Great! You might as well execute me now. Those three are going to do everything in their power to find evidence against me." Jake stared straight ahead as he considered the possibility. His fate was now in question. What would happen to him? Jake looked back at the Captain. "What will happen to me if they find me guilty?"

"That will be decided by the panel of judges."

"So why did you choose Lazaro and Thane to prosecute? You know they've been gunning for me since we left Romajin."

"I chose them for precisely that reason; because they are gunning for you."

Jake was on the edge of his seat again. "What? Are you wanting to get me convicted? Is this retribution for what I did to you?"

As soon as Jake asked, he regretted it. He deserved to pay for what he had done to the Captain and crew. There was no vengeance or malice on the Captain's face, only worry and concern. "No, Chief, of course not. Because of their anger, they'll be thorough, and the rest of the crew will trust whatever they find or don't find."

Jake slumped back down in his chair again. "I'm sorry. I shouldn't have asked that question. I trust you to do what's best. So, who's going to actually defend me? Can you do it?"

"As much as I would like to, I think Lexi or Brynna would be a better choice. It would be best if I recuse myself from this." David's voice and face reflected genuine regret.

"What if they decline?"

David's head shook slowly from side to side. "Chief, are you looking for trouble? If neither one will agree to it, then I'll do it. I won't leave you hanging... no pun intended."

"Thank you, sir. What do I do now that I don't have a job to go to?"

"I'm not confining you to quarters, but I strongly suggest you keep a low profile. Go to the gym if you need to, but spend as much time in your own quarters as possible. I don't want you to give even the most remote appearance of trying to sway anyone's opinion."

"You want me to just hang out by myself in my quarters? Marissa and I are still trying to work through our own issues. We're already arguing all the time. How's my irate, pregnant, hormonal wife going to handle having me around all the time? We'll both go crazy!"

"Chief, you still have me, Lexi, and Brynna on your side."

Jake shook his head. "You don't know that for sure."

"It'll be alright. We'll get you out of this. I promise."

Jake slumped back into his seat. "How long will this take?"

"I don't know for certain. I doubt it will take more than a few days. Just be patient. I think if this works out, you will regain the crew's trust. Spend some time talking to Arni. He can help you through this. I'll also make sure your data pad has access to reading material." David offered.

Jake looked skeptical. "I'm just not used to that yet. Can you talk to him for me? Can I use him as a witness for me? He knows what I did and didn't do."

"Jake, you need to get accustomed to talking to Arni yourself. I know the entire concept of supernatural beings is... different. We all have to get used to the idea. We also have to put it into practice. Arni's not going to hurt you." David laughed to himself. If he had heard himself say that a year ago, he would have checked himself into the nearest mental hospital.

Jake winced at his own thoughts. "Are you sure about that? He asked you to go through a world of hurt on my account. I know it was all my fault, but he asked you to do it."

David rubbed his face with his hands and sighed. The man had a valid point. "You're right. He may ask some very painful things of you. He wouldn't do it lightly, though. If he were to ask you to do something similar, it would be for a good cause. I allowed the crew and myself to be captured to reach you. I would have done the same thing for any of the crew. Even knowing now what I had to face, I would do it again if I had to. Trust Pateras enough to ask for his help—and accept his answer. He knows what he's doing."

Jake leaned forward, resting his forearms on his knees. "Yes sir, I trust him, and I want to do whatever he asks, but... he scares me sometimes."

David smiled. "Me too." He paused a minute before changing the subject. "I'll get with Brynna and Lexi at the end of the shift. I'm going to make assignments for the entire court-martial process. I really hope we won't need it, but I need to get started on this, so if you don't mind..."

Jake stood to leave. Pausing, he added, "Thanks for believing in me, Captain."

David nodded his acknowledgment. "You're welcome, Jake. Hang in there."

Jake headed back to his quarters to be alone with his thoughts for a while.

David sent messages to Commander Brynna Alexander and Lt. Lexi Flint asking them to report to him as soon as they were able. He sent similar messages to Lt. Commander Braxton Flint, Lt. Commander Jason Adams, and Ensign Cheyenne Dominick. David returned to the bridge to hand out the new assignments to those who were awake and on duty. "Lt. Ryder, Ensign Ryder, I want the two of you to work with Lt. Commander Dominick and investigate this incident. I don't want you pursuing a private vendetta. I want you to get at the truth. If you determine there's sufficient evidence to charge Chief Holden, then bring your charges to Lt. Commander Flint. In the event we are found by the Commonwealth, this goes on hold. Are we clear?"

Thane and Aulani glanced at each other before Thane responded with the question on both their minds. "Sir, why aren't you handling the court-martial?"

"Because I'm biased. I already have an opinion. I am recusing myself on those grounds. You should be thorough in your investigation. Any other questions?"

"You don't think he did it, do you?" Aulani queried.

"My opinion—is not relevant to your investigation," David responded as nonchalantly as possible.

Hearing no other questions, he excused himself to head down to engineering to talk to the ship's chief engineer, Lt. Commander Lazaro Dominick.

Lt. Commander Dominick wasn't pleased with his new assignment. His feelings about Jake, although more subdued, mirrored Thane's. Lazaro preferred to block his feelings rather than dredge them up again. This was going to force everyone to relive their six days of torture all over again. The first few days after escaping the Commonwealth military base on Romajin, tempers had been at an all-time high. The last two weeks served to slowly ease the tension between the crewmembers. As much as Lazaro distrusted Jake, he didn't like the potential of stirring things up again.

Lazaro did his best to change the Captain's mind about assigning him to this duty. "Captain, why me? I'm not sure I could be fair and impartial. Personally, I'd love to see Jake pay, and pay dearly for what he put us through on Romajin."

David sat down and stroked his chin thoughtfully. "Laz, please tell me the name of one crew member who doesn't have that opinion."

The Lt. Commander had no choice but to throw his hands up. The Chief's best chances would be at the hands of his own wife, Lazaro's wife, and the Captain. The Captain had confessed his forgiveness of Jake's betrayal. Jake's wife's feelings were mitigated by her love for her husband, but just barely. Lazaro's wife, Cheyenne, was just the forgiving type.

The Captain explained what he was looking for. "I need crew members with the technical expertise to research the files, the energy signatures, the communication logs, the computer routines, and sub-routines. I'm looking for knowledgeable and thorough, not unbiased. This isn't a witch hunt. I expect you to find facts and truths, not vengeance."

Over the last ten days, Lazaro had learned they had tortured the Captain beyond belief. The ship's psychologist, Lt. Lexi Flint, had conducted numerous group therapy sessions where each person was given the opportunity to share their experiences as prisoners of the Commonwealth. The crew had served the Commonwealth all their lives. To discover the true nature of the Commonwealth and reject their mission was enough to warrant therapy sessions for the crew. Being held prisoner by their former government, forced to endure the rigorous re-education process on a diet of only bread and water, then finally neither bread nor water, with the intention of a slow execution mandated a psychological resolution. The Captain had been reluctant to share his experiences. Lexi was forced to pull the Captain aside and pressure him to share at least part of what he was forced to endure. She heard Jake's side of the account and knew the magnitude of what the Captain had faced.

Lazaro had gotten a sick feeling in the pit of his stomach when the Captain finally divulged his predicament. Initially, the Captain had given a cold, clinical description of his situation. He had been dosed with pain enhancing and hallucinogenic drugs, beaten, and tortured. Over the course of the six days the crew had been imprisoned, David was taken to the base infirmary, his injuries healed, and then the cycle of drugs and torture would begin again. The news of Jake's active participation in the Captain's torturing made him even sicker. The Captain hadn't mentioned it himself. Jake had volunteered the information over the Captain's objections. Lazaro remembered the Captain getting agitated when pressured to go into detail about his feelings and emotions. The surprise came when the Captain laid all the blame squarely on the Supreme Executor of the Commonwealth, not on Jake.

Jake and the Captain also laid out the Supreme Executor's plan to discredit the Captain. Commander Alexander was nearly convinced her own husband had betrayed the crew and their marriage. Jake attempted to repair the damage he had done by divulging everything he had been privy to. The crewmembers were supposed to forgive their security chief's betrayal. At this point, they were finding new reasons to despise him.

David shared his intentions for those who would prosecute, try, and defend the Chief if necessary. He reiterated his expectation. "Lt. Commander, I expect you to conduct a thorough investigation. Find whatever evidence either for or against the Chief and present it to the Board of Judges. I'm not asking you to get Jake off the hook or get him hung. Just find out what happened."

Lazaro nodded reluctantly. "Yes sir." He still wasn't happy. Somehow the Captain had a way of making things seem better than they were.

David headed back to his office. This had the potential to severely compromise his plans for their upcoming mission. This was one tiny, tiny ship, and they were being hunted by—well—everyone. His plan was to leave this part of space and reach out to the other eleven ships sent on the same mission as the *Evangeline*. Having the entire Commonwealth desperate for their blood for destroying the military base on Romajin would not make any place safe. Taking the time to prove Jake's innocence was an annoyance at best, and a dangerous distraction at worst. David supposed this was the Supreme Executor's goal.

Jake stepped into his quarters. He stood there for a moment staring at his living room. He desperately wanted to change clothes and hit the gym to work out some of his frustrations. Jake's wife, Marissa, was sleeping in the next room. One thing he didn't want to do was wake his pregnant wife who was already trying to deal with deep-seated anger toward him in the middle of her sleep cycle with bad news. He wasn't sure what else to do with his free time. Jake took a step toward the desk when he remembered his computer access was restricted. He finally sat down in the chair closest to the door. He sat there looking forlorn as he contemplated his situation. Should he ask Arni for help? The ridiculous nature of the situation seemed too trite a thing to call on one so powerful. Surely this was beneath the station of a Supreme Being. If this was such a small thing, why was it bugging him like this? Maybe a nap would help clear his head. Jake reclined on the sofa. In a minute he was tossing and turning restlessly. Five minutes later, he rolled to his feet. He took off his uniform jacket and headed toward the gym despite his attire.

"So, you really aren't going to ask Pateras for help?"

The voice sent an icy chill up Jake's spine. He stopped just short of the door and turned around slowly. The Supreme Executor of the Commonwealth was sitting on the sofa he had just vacated. A year ago, Jake's first question would have been, "How did you get in here?" The question would have been emphasized by drawing a weapon with lightning fast reflexes. Today, knowing what he did now, it seemed like a rather pointless question. One didn't need to ask superior beings with supernatural powers how they achieved anything. Jake chose a more relevant question followed by a command he knew he couldn't enforce. "Why are you here? Get out! I no longer serve you."

"First, answer my question. Why haven't you asked Pateras for help with this?"

"If I answer your question, will you leave?" Jake countered.

"You know, I underestimated you. I think your crew has done the same thing. I would've expected them to be thanking you for saving them, singing your praises, and patting you on the back. I know you were the one who got them caught, which was bound to happen eventually, anyway. You clearly paid your debt to them by helping them escape again."

The Executor paused to let his words sink in a moment before continuing. "I tell you what, Mr. Holden. I'll make you a deal. Answer my question and give me the chance to present you with a counter-offer. If you choose to decline my offer, then I will waste no time in leaving."

Jake pondered his terms for a moment. He decided there wasn't any harm in listening. He knew he wouldn't accept anything the Supreme Executor offered. If it would convince him to leave, then so be it. "Fine, but for the record, I didn't help them escape. Arni did that. I was just the messenger or escort. He would have gotten them out even if I hadn't participated."

"According to your Captain, I put the crew through this torture to convince you to change sides. If you hadn't changed when you did, are you certain he would have gotten them out? Perhaps he would have allowed it to continue another day... maybe two days... just long enough for you to start seeing your friends die?"

Luciano watched Jake's face closely. There it was. A tiny flicker of doubt crossed his face. Even if he thought about the facts of the situation later and reassured himself, the doubt would still linger in the back of his mind. Luciano smiled. He could work with that.

Jake didn't like the smile on the Executor's face. He suddenly felt defeated, but he wasn't sure why. It was time to end this confabulation. "I decided it was unnecessary to ask Pateras for help because I didn't do anything wrong... this time. Why bother him when the facts will clear me? If you don't mind, present your offer so I can refuse it. I don't want to keep you from... whatever it is you do."

"Let me get to the point then. I can see how busy you are." Executor Hale taunted. "I left sufficient evidence for your crew to find you guilty. I doubt Pateras is going to pay much attention to the squabbles of one small ship's crew when the fate of the entire galaxy is at stake. My offer is this. I'll get you off the hook with your crew. You can stay here with them as long as you like. All I want you to do is report back to me, everything your Captain is doing. I will leave you and your crew alone, no jail, no traps, and no arrests. I can even steer trouble away from you and your little ship. When you decide you're ready to get off this tiny ship, just let me know. You and your family will get an entire planet to yourselves. I still can't allow your wife to contaminate others, so you will have a rather lonely existence. I can send in whatever supplies you need and build whatever house or other structures you want. What do you think?"

Jake had questions about the offer, which he quickly stifled. "Are you done?"

Executor Hale stood and walked toward Jake. "Mostly. Are you interested?"

"No, you can leave now."

Executor Hale sighed. "Very well then." He turned as if to walk away then stopped. Glancing over his shoulder he added, "My offer is still open if you should ever change your mind. You know, I can be more convincing... if I need to be."

Executor Hale walked away again, and his visage faded as he reached the wall.

Jake stared at the spot where the Dark Lord had faded. Why had he faded instead of simply vanishing? What did he mean by being more convincing? Realization hit him hard and fast. His wife was sleeping on the other side of that very wall. Alarm bells went off in Jake's head as he heard his wife scream. Jake rushed through the door in time to see Marissa's body slam against the wall near him and collapse onto the floor. As Jake moved to his wife's side, he looked the direction she had come from. He saw an image of himself with bloody scratches across his face, grinning evilly. His sadistic twin morphed back into the Supreme Executor then vanished.

Jake hastily knelt beside Marissa to evaluate her. She was still alive, although unconscious. The entire crew was trained as field medics. Despite his desire to pick her up and cradle her in his arms, Jake's training kicked in, and he refrained from moving her. He hailed Ensign Ryder on the bridge with the comm unit on his bracelet. "Ensign Ryder, I have a medical emergency in my quarters. I need the doc, a med kit, and stretcher, right away... please... hurry!"

Aulani hastily notified Dr. Jason Adams and his wife Lt. Laura Adams of the emergency. Thane, hearing her call out to the doc, hailed the Captain with the information.

Jason and Laura were off duty and sleeping so it took them a couple minutes to throw on a minimal amount of clothing and head for the Infirmary to collect the needed supplies. The Captain made it down two levels from his office and into the Infirmary before Jason. He collected the stretcher and med kit as Jason stepped out of his quarters.

Jason followed David directly to Jake's cabin. Taking the scanner from the Captain, Jason curtly asked, "What happened?"

Fear didn't generally paralyze a trained security officer. This time it did. Commonwealth Security officers weren't trained to handle the supernatural. Jake sat there at Marissa's side staring at her. His mind was still trying to process everything he had just seen without succumbing to the fear of losing his wife and child. The war in his mind blocked everything else off.

When Jason realized Jake would not be much help, he focused on Marissa. Laura had gone directly to the Infirmary to prepare to receive the patient. She surmised if Jake made the call, it must be Marissa who needed help and planned accordingly.

Jake finally managed to ask, "Are they going to be okay?"

David had similar questions including the one Jason asked. David pulled Jake to his feet and moved him a few feet away from Marissa. "Chief... Chief... look at me. What happened to Marissa?"

The look on Jake's face indicated he was caught between shock and terror. David wondered if Jake were reliving the day about six months ago when Marissa had actually been killed. Arni had brought her back to them, but was he willing to do that again if necessary? David slapped his comm unit and ordered Ensign Ryder to summon Lt. Flint to Jake's quarters. While waiting for the ship's psychologist, he did the only thing he knew he could to get answers from his rattled security officer. David assumed his most imposing stance and belted, "Security Chief Holden, report!"

David saw a shaky wall go up between Jake's emotions and cognitive functions. He slowly stood at attention and reported, "L-Lt. Holden was th-thrown against the... wall."

David and Jason exchanged concerned glances. David asked the question that had crossed both their minds. "How was she thrown against the wall, Chief?" David was trying hard not to assume the only other person present had thrown her.

Jake nervously looked down at his wife's motionless body. "Um... she... it was..." Jake started to get a handle on himself. "Captain, I didn't do this. Can we talk in the other room?"

The Captain knew he wasn't going to like whatever Jake said. If the ship had taken a hit or the artificial gravity had failed, everyone would have known about it. An isolated failure of the artificial gravity could have happened and would show up on a diagnostic readout. The thing it wouldn't do is scare the Chief this badly. It was not a gravity failure. "Chief, wait for me in my office while I help the doc get Marissa to the Infirmary."

More alarm bells went off in the Chief's head. "No! Please, Captain, I can't be alone right now. I can't leave Marissa alone either. She has to be protected. Captain, please don't make me leave."

Protected from what, he wondered. David wasn't sure what to make of the situation, but Marissa was the priority right now. He nodded his approval then moved to help the doctor load Marissa onto the stretcher. The two rushed her to the Infirmary and into a bed. Jason turned to the Captain and Jake. "I need to work, Jake. Marissa will be fine. I don't know about the baby yet. I don't need you in here distracting me. Please go someplace else, so I can concentrate."

David escorted Jake out and back to his quarters. The second the door closed behind them, David demanded some answers. "Jake! Did you do this to her?"

Jake stood there still looking dazed and scared. He didn't have a clue how to explain what he had seen to the Captain. He was already in so much trouble, and the Captain was sticking his neck out for Jake as it was. "No... not exactly."

David grabbed Jake by his shirt and slammed him against the nearest wall. "What is that supposed to mean?"

Jake swallowed hard. He had never been afraid of the Captain until today. The look on the Captain's face gave him reason to be afraid, more than he already was. "I think... I think I want to wait for Lexi."

Now the Captain was even more worried. He relaxed his grip. Jake would never willingly seek professional counseling. Something had spooked the man beyond belief.

"Tell me what happened to Marissa. Why don't you want to be alone? I saw the look on your face, Chief. It wasn't grief. It was fear. What could possibly scare you like this?" The Captain released his grip on Jake and backed away from him.

Jake slid down the wall onto the floor looking up at David with tears in his eyes. "He—He was here. He told me he was framing me for what happened on Romajin and now this. He—He wants me to work for him again. He wants me to report everything you're doing to him. He—He's willing to hurt my family to get what he wants."

David asked the question he already knew the answer to, "Who? Who did this?" David really just needed to hear Jake say it.

Jake wiped away his tears only to have them replaced by more. "Executor Hale. He was here. He tried to get me to rejoin him. When I told him to leave, he attacked Marissa."

Despite the far-fetched nature of the story, David was relieved to hear it. He relaxed as it reassured him his Security Chief had not gone off the deep end and attacked his own wife and child. "So, Marissa can back you up?"

Jake's tears abated and were replaced by fear. "No, she can't. She thinks I did this. He—He changed his appearance. I ran into the bedroom when I heard her scream. I saw myself standing by the bed. When she wakes up, she's going to think I hurt her. Captain, I would never harm her or the baby. What do I do?"

David offered Jake a hand up off the floor. "We'll figure this out as soon as we get Lexi in here."

Jake sat down dejectedly in the nearest chair.

David watched him closely. He wondered why he was finding it so easy to trust the one who had betrayed them all, just three weeks ago. Something about him seemed very different since leaving Romajin. A hail at the door interrupted his thoughts. It was Lexi. David invited her in and explained the situation. He started his explanation with the detonation of the self-destruct mechanism on Romajin and the Admiral's accusations against Jake. When David finished talking, he grew concerned about the obvious skepticism on Lexi's face.

Even through the fog in his mind, Jake could see Lexi was having a hard time swallowing his story. Jake was looking desperate. "Captain, Lexi, I know how this looks. This isn't one of those psycho-babble things where I can't admit some horrible thing I've done, so I create a story where somebody else who looks just like me did it."

The two looked at each other, unsure of what to say next. David broke the awkward silence. "Jake, I have to admit, I have a few doubts, but I'm strongly leaning toward believing you."

Lexi seemed more disturbed by the Captain's admission. "Captain, can we discuss this privately for a moment?"

Captain Alexander stood up. "Let's talk in the corridor. Jake, we'll be right outside this door if you need us."

Jake stood as well. "Captain, could I go check on Marissa?"

Before he could respond, Lexi answered. "Jake, that's not a good idea right now. This has no bearing on your guilt or innocence and whether or not I believe you. If your story is true, Marissa is going to believe you hurt her. If your story is false, she's going to think the same thing. When she wakes up, she's likely to react badly, especially if you're present. Somebody needs to prepare her for this before you see her."

Jake gave a reluctant nod. Sadly, Lexi's reasoning was sound. "Captain, may I at least have access to the surveillance feed?"

David agreed to the request and contacted Aulani to get Jake the access. He and Lexi stepped into the corridor.

Lexi expressed her concerns. "Captain, I'm really not sure what to make of this. The stress Jake's been under could have caused him to snap. Under normal circumstances, there's no way he would have hurt Marissa, but Pateras has rewritten everything we've ever known to be true. Jake took the longest and fought the hardest before accepting Pateras. It may have been too much for him with the added stress of the Romajin accusation."

The Captain shook his head. "I don't buy it. Jake's been a changed man since we left Romajin. He's a better man now. The entire crew has been quite—uh—forthcoming about their anger toward him. Surprisingly, Jake hasn't lost his temper even once. He isn't a calm person by nature."

Lexi persisted with her argument, "Captain, that's exactly what I'm saying. If he's been internalizing all that hostility, he may have reached his limit and exploded."

David shifted his weight from one foot to the other. "Lieutenant, I don't think he's been internalizing anything. He's accepted the blame and the anger. It seemed like there were times he even welcomed it. It feels like he's taking it on as penance for the harm he caused the crew. To be completely honest, I believe him. Think about it. Luciano Hale isn't human. We have no idea exactly what he's capable of. I have seen Luciano Hale change his appearance myself. I've seen him appear and disappear at will."

Lexi countered. "That also makes him the perfect fall guy. Captain, I admit his story could be true, but how do we know that for certain?"

David thought for a moment. "We can investigate and see if there's any evidence to support his claim. We can simply choose to believe him, or not. We can ask Arni to shed some light on the situation. He may or may not tell us what we need to know."

Lexi agreed, "You're right about that. Sometimes Arni doesn't always give us the answers we want."

As the two continued to discuss the situation, Jake watched the feed coming in from the Infirmary. Jason was updating Laura. "I've got the internal bleeding stopped, and her concussion is well on its way to mending…"

Hearing the concern in his voice, Laura asked, "But…?"

Jason scowled. "… but I can't get the baby stabilized. Her body is still shunting blood to her vital organs and away from the uterus. If I can't get that stopped, she could lose the baby."

Jake heard the two discussing treatment options. He didn't really understand what was happening. He reached a point where he couldn't stand watching anymore. Standing abruptly, he headed for the door.

A voice in his head added to his frustration. "This is all your fault. You should have accepted the Supreme Executor's offer. It's not too late. He can still help her."

The voice permeated his being, tying his stomach in knots. Jake stopped short of the door. It was time to ask for help, perhaps past time. He turned back to face the empty room. "Pateras, I assume you can hear me. I need help. I don't want to betray anyone else—ever. Please save my baby's life. I'll do anything. Take my life, take anything, just protect my wife and son."

Jake stood there waiting for a response. The room remained empty and silent. He walked out the door interrupting David and Lexi.

David scowled. "What is it, Jake? Has something happened?"

Jake's heavy heart slowed his responses. "Marissa's fine, but the baby's still in danger. I—I asked Pateras for help. He didn't answer me. Captain, I need a favor."

David glanced at Lexi. It only took a split second for him to see her concern was growing. He assumed Jake was going to ask for his help in contacting Arni. He guessed wrong.

"Captain, Executor Hale seems to think I'm a weak link. The crew doesn't trust me. My wife and child are suffering on account of me."

"What is it you need from me?"

Jake knew what he was about to ask wouldn't be received well. He had trouble making eye contact with either of them. "I want you to put me in stasis."

Lexi's jaw dropped. "What? Jake, why?"

"It... uh... It's best for everyone."

David folded his arms across his chest. "I'm going to need a better explanation than that."

"Captain, we're on the front lines in a war like we've never seen before. Whatever you do in this war is going to be of paramount importance. I don't want to interfere with that. This is too important."

Lexi still looked disturbed, "Jake, how is putting you in stasis supposed to help?"

"For one, the crew will feel safer if I'm out of the way and..." Jake hesitated.

David knew they were about to get to the heart of the matter. "What's the real reason, Jake?"

"I don't want to be his weak link. I don't want to be the chink in your armor. Captain, if you put me in stasis, he can't use me against you. He also would have no reason to harm Marissa or the baby."

Although Lexi still carried some unresolved anger toward Jake, she still cared about his well-being. "Jake, locking yourself away in a stasis chamber will not solve this. It's just running away."

Jake agreed to some extent, but he didn't have any better ideas. "Lexi, Captain, I'm a security chief. It's my job to protect this crew. If I've become a liability, then I have to step out of that position. I can't just stay here on the ship and remain inactive."

Visions of Jake going stir crazy flashed through their minds. With his temper, it was not a pleasant thought. Jake continued. "Think about it. If I stay aboard the ship, he could just keep pushing my buttons until one day it works, or he could push to the point where I lose Marissa and our son."

David shook his head. "We've all got pressure points, Jake. Do you expect me to confine the rest of the crew one at a time until no one is left?"

"No, Captain, of course not. The rest of you haven't proven yourselves capable of betrayal. I have."

David shook his head. "That doesn't track, Jake. We all betrayed the Commonwealth."

Jake was losing patience. His fear for his son's life was growing with each passing moment. "Captain, I betrayed the crew to the Commonwealth, and then I betrayed the Commonwealth. I'm twice as capable of betrayal. Captain, my son is dying, and this may be his only chance for survival. My only other options are to betray you again, leave the ship, or face my own execution. I would prefer the option of remaining alive, so I can return as an active crew member someday."

David glanced at Lexi who returned an incredulous look. "Captain, you can't seriously be considering this, can you?"

David shrugged. "He's right. He would still be here and able to return to active duty at some point."

Lexi was becoming exasperated. "Just how long do you intend to keep him in stasis? A day? A week? A year? Twenty years?"

David looked back at Jake. "Chief, what are you thinking?"

"Until my wife and son are out of danger, and my name's been cleared. I can't return to active duty until the crew knows they can trust me."

David nodded. "Fair enough. Any other requests?"

"Just one. Wake me up in time to see my son be born. I want to hold him for a moment before you return me to stasis."

David paced in the corridor as he considered Jake's request. Jake's patience was nearly gone by this time. "So, are we agreed?"

David turned back to face Jake. "I have one condition and one addendum."

Jake's heart skipped a beat. He wondered what the Captain could possibly stipulate. "Yes sir?"

"You're going to be the one to tell Marissa, and you come out of stasis the second Arni says so, even if your other conditions aren't met."

Jake swallowed hard. "Captain, Marissa will not want to see me. She thinks I threw her against a wall. I'd rather you explain it to her after it's done."

The Captain shook his head. "Those are my conditions, Chief. I can put you in restraints and stay at your side while you explain it to her."

Jake saw the resolve on his Captain's face. There would be no more discussion. He finally nodded. Pulling a pair of restraints from his own belt, he handed them to the Captain. He turned around, so the Captain could place them on him.

Lexi stood there in shock watching them. She couldn't believe her eyes. How could the Captain agree to this madness? Tears welled up in her eyes. She caught herself actually pitying Jake. Anger slowly replaced her tears. She was angry with herself for pitying Jake, angry with Jake for playing the part of the martyr, angry with Jake for giving up, and angry with the Captain for giving in to Jake's ridiculous request.

David watched the array of emotions wash over her face. The look he gave her in return clearly told her to remain silent.

Lexi decided to push her luck. "Captain!"

David kept one hand on Jake's arm preventing him from turning around to see Lexi. David whisked himself around to face the distraught psychologist. He raised his free hand and pointed his finger at her. "Lt. Flint, I would appreciate it if you would join us in the infirmary. Lt. Holden may need your counsel. I, however, do not at this precise moment." His harsh tone put to rest any other thoughts of voicing her objections.

Lexi stiffened as she replied, "Yes SIR!" She followed silently behind the two as they walked into the Infirmary.

Jason was standing at Marissa's bedside when the three entered. The concern on his face had not changed since Jake had seen him on the monitor in his quarters. That was at least partially good news. If the look had changed to one of sorrow, Jake would have noticed instantly. "Chief, I was just about to contact you with an update. I've got Marissa sedated and was about to engage a temporary stasis field. She had a concussion, several minor fractures, and some internal bleeding. I have all the damage repaired, there's just one problem. Her body, in trying to protect itself, started shunting blood to the primary vital organs. Which means..."

Jake interrupted the doctor to ease his attempt to relay bad news. "Her body was sacrificing the baby to protect her own life. I know. I saw it on the monitor. Is the baby still alive?"

"Yes, he's still alive. Her body, for some reason, isn't returning to normal. Even though she's out of danger, her body hasn't realized the danger is over. I want to put them in stasis. Sometimes it causes the body to reset. It forgets about being in crisis mode and returns to normal." Jason reached toward the stasis controls.

Jake stepped forward. "Wait! I need to talk to her first."

Jason frowned more than he already was. "Jake, we don't have a lot of time here. Every second we waste…"

"I got that. I'm going to do whatever I can to save my son. Please wake her for me, I need to talk to her."

Jason looked over at the Captain. "Captain, what's going on?"

David glanced at Marissa then at Jake before answering. Jake looked as though his heart were breaking. "Doc do whatever you have to do to wake her without further endangering her or the baby. This is crucial."

"Captain, the longer I wait to put her in stasis endangers the baby. Can't this wait?" The stress level in Jason's voice was increasing.

Laura moved over beside Jason. She had been quietly watching the exchanges and the anguish on each face. She whispered to her husband. She didn't know the extent of the situation, but she could tell it was of grave importance. "Jason, I think we need to let them do this."

Now his wife and nurse had joined the assault on his medical expertise. After looking at her sternly, Jason picked up a hypo-spray. He placed a neural inhibitor on her spine and activated it then injected her with just enough of a stimulant to wake her. He leaned over her and softly called her name. "Marissa, I need you to wake up and listen to me for a minute. Jake wants to talk to you, but your baby is in danger. You aren't going to be able to move. Whatever you do, just remain calm. Don't get uptight, okay? Do you understand?"

Marissa's eyelids felt incredibly heavy. She fought hard to keep them open. The doctor's words seemed far away. She wished he would stop talking so she could sleep. The stimulant kicked in, and his words started making sense. Somehow saying "stay calm" seemed to mean instant panic. She forced herself to focus. The doctor was standing on her left. She slowly moved her gaze around to the others. She saw Lexi looking angry at the foot of her bed. She wondered who made her angry. Her eyes moved on to see the Captain holding Jake's arm, and Jake's arms were behind him. The Captain stepped forward bringing Jake with him. The Captain spoke first. "Marissa, Jake can't hurt you, but he needs to talk to you. Do you remember what happened?"

The look on Marissa's face changed as she recalled the recent events. Her face moved from drowsy to frightened. Jason stepped closer to her as he saw her heart rate increase. Jake knew Jason was about to interfere, so he jumped quickly to the point. "Marissa, I swear I didn't do this to you. Executor Hale did this. He wants me to betray the Captain. I refused, and he tried to hurt you. I won't let him do this again. The Captain's putting me into stasis until the danger is over. I'm sorry I couldn't protect you. This is the only thing I can do. Please don't hate me. I love you." Jake kissed her on the forehead and backed away. He nodded at Jason to continue his intended treatment.

Marissa blinked back tears. She wished her arms could move to wipe them away. Jason picked up his hypo-spray to sedate her again when she reacted abruptly. "No! Wait!" Her tears flowed freely. "Captain, Jake couldn't have done this. It's not possible. I saw him… but… something wasn't right. I thought it was Jake… at first. Captain, he couldn't have picked me up and thrown me like that. Someone or something that looked like Jake picked me up. He held me over his head and threw me across the room. I… I tried to grab onto him. I scratched his face… Jake has no scratches. Captain, help me…"

David moved over to Marissa. "I'll take care of it. Everything is going to be fine. You have my word, rest for now."

David nodded at Jason who quickly sedated her and engaged the stasis field. As soon as Marissa was out of danger, Jason looked up. "You two put my patients in danger for that? All you wanted to do was apologize? What is wrong with both of you?"

As Jason continued his rant, Lexi saw Laura reviewing the medical data for the last few seconds before the stasis field was engaged. Lexi had very little actual medical training except what applied to her own field of expertise. She thought she understood what Laura was seeing. "Laura is that showing what I think it is?"

Laura backed it up and watched it again. "Maybe... Jason?"

Jason finished his rant and turned to see what had the women's attention. Laura replayed the data again. The anger faded from Jason's face, "Well, I'll be..."

Jake watched anxiously. "What is it?"

Jason moved over and turned the stasis field off, then watched the data. The new data supported the last few seconds of data recorded prior to establishing the stasis field. Marissa's circulatory system had rerouted blood back to her extremities and her uterus. Jason looked at Jake in awe. "Her circulation is returning to normal."

Jake was clearly relieved. "The stasis field worked? How could you tell so quickly?"

Laura jumped in before Jason could answer. "No, Jake, it was changing before the stasis field went up. Jason was distracted by her vital signs and getting her into the stasis field. He didn't notice the subtle changes."

"So, is the baby going to be alright?" Jake asked anxiously.

Jason nodded. "It would appear so. I'll have to keep a close eye on them for a couple days, but yeah, he looks like he's going to be fine."

Lexi glanced skeptically at the Captain. "So, what made the difference? Why did her condition change so suddenly?"

David's mouth twitched almost imperceptibly. "Why are you looking at me? I'm not the doctor."

Lexi was glaring again. "You knew if Jake spoke to her, it could change her perception and thereby her body's reaction."

Jason glanced back and forth at the two. "That's entirely possible. If she thought Jake had done this, it could cause her to subconsciously reject his child. Setting the record straight could have changed her perspective enough to relieve the stress in her body."

Laura looked at Jake's face. "What did she mean about scratching his face? Jake doesn't have any scratches on his face."

Jason grabbed his scanner and scanned Marissa's fingertips. "There's foreign skin tissue and DNA under her nails. It doesn't match Jake's. I don't have the Supreme

Executor's DNA on file, and I doubt the Commonwealth would provide us with that information." Jason moved over and scanned Jake's face. "Scans don't indicate any tissue damage at all. Chief let me see your forearms."

Jake turned around, so the doctor could scan his arms. "What's this? Why are you wearing binders?"

The Captain unlocked the binders and released Jake. "It was so Marissa would feel secure."

Jason scanned Jake and found nothing. "Marissa scratched someone, but it wasn't Jake."

Laura stood there looking confused. Was there was a reason to think Jake did this? Lexi gave her a brief explanation. Laura shook her head in amazement. She knew how much Jake loved Marissa, and the extent of Marissa's injuries indicated very drastic violence. She didn't doubt Jake could kill if necessary, but not Marissa, and certainly not like this.

Jake took one last look at Marissa then turned to the Captain. "I met your condition. Let's get this over with."

Jason looked at the two men. Somehow, part of his message to Marissa had gotten overlooked by the doctor. "Get what over with?"

"Jake wants the Captain to put him into stasis until this whole mess is cleared up." Lexi spat venomously.

The Captain gave her a disapproving look. "That's enough, Lieutenant. Doc, do you have a preference to which chamber to put him in?"

Jason blinked. "Uh... No, I guess not. They're all the same."

The Captain walked over to the chamber closest to Marissa and slid it out of its berth in the wall. Opening the lid to the chamber, he turned back to Jake. "Are you sure you want to do this?"

Jake scowled. "No, I don't want to do this. I just don't want to be the weak link. I want the crew and my family to be safe. I can't do my job effectively with all of this hanging over me." Jake climbed into the chamber and laid down mumbling to himself. "I hate these things."

David looked down at his security chief. "You know I trust you. Right?"

Jake nodded. "I know, sir. I appreciate you saying so, but it's not enough. Can you close this thing and activate it before I get claustrophobic?"

David nodded. "Just remember Chief, the second Arni says so, you're out of here no matter what else is going on."

"If Arni wants me out, then so be it. I'll deal with whatever he requires of me. I just need to know it's what he's asking."

Jake settled in and shut his eyes. David started to close the lid when Lexi stopped him. "Jake, wait. I trust you too."

Jake opened his eyes and tried to keep from looking annoyed. "Thank you, Lexi. If you really believe in me, then prove me innocent of the deaths on Romajin. Captain, if I'm found guilty, carry out my sentence without waking me."

Lexi was back to looking distraught. "Jake, I'll get you out of this. There won't be any sentence to carry out."

The Captain nodded his agreement to carrying out Jake's sentence without waking him, although his opinion aligned with Lexi's for once. Jason and Laura looked like they were close to joining their voices in with Lexi's to avow their trust in Jake. The two had looks of doubt and regret on their faces.

David started to lower the lid again when something stopped it from closing. Standing at Jake's head was Arni with his hand on the lid stopping its descent. "Arni!"

Jake opened his eyes and hastily located the man. He waited anxiously for Arni's next words. He sincerely hoped his message meant he could get out of the stasis chamber. Even though Arni had not ordered him into the chamber, he had already decided he wasn't coming out of it without Arni's express instruction.

"Jake, you don't belong in there. You have work to do out here."

David lifted the lid and moved aside for Jake to get out. Jake wasted no time in climbing out of his "casket." David hastily closed the chamber and slid it back into the wall.

"Pateras has seen what you're willing to give up protecting others. He's pleased with the devotion you have shown to him. He has a wall of protection around you and your family. Luciano can no longer touch them physically. They are safe." Arni placed his hand on Jake's shoulder in a reassuring manner.

The tension and fear immediately left him. The fear had gripped him so, and when it left, his knees grew weak. "I need to sit down," he responded. He moved over to a nearby chair to regain his strength. His hands were visibly trembling. "Arni, I have never felt so alone and so scared in all my life. When I saw what he could do—the power he had—I felt completely helpless. I was so afraid of losing her again. I couldn't let him use me to betray the crew. When you didn't answer, I didn't know what else to do."

Arni stood in front of him. "As I told your Captain a few weeks ago, you need to entrust their care to me. You may not understand what I am doing. You may not like what I'm doing. Everything I do has a purpose and will always be for the best. Just remember, this place is only temporary. The rest of your lives will be lived out in the realm of Pateras. When you ask something of me, know that I will always answer. My answer may not come in the timing you expect, but it will come. I will always be with you just as I am always with Pateras and with the rest of the crew. Don't doubt yourself. Your crimes against Pateras have been forgiven. You are a valued part of his family now." As he spoke, those present and conscious hung on his every word. Although his words were meant for Jake, they all gleaned from his message.

"What about Romajin? I didn't hurt anyone on Romajin... except the Captain... and the crew."

Arni smiled and spoke low enough for only Jake to hear. "I know you didn't. Let this play out. Be prepared to face this court-martial head on. My father has the situation under his control. Can you do that?"

Jake nodded. A court-martial was a walk in the park compared to losing his family. Arni helped Jake to his feet. Jake wasn't one for showing affection to anyone except Marissa. Knowing this, Arni offered Jake his hand to shake. Jake took Arni's hand. His relief was so great Jake could not stop with a simple handshake. He pulled Arni in for a quick hug across their handshake to express his profound appreciation and relief.

Jason didn't want to interrupt, but in keeping with true medical professionalism, wanted the best possible care for his patients. "Arni, about Marissa and the baby…"

Arni smiled knowing Jason's desire. He stepped to Marissa's side. He took her hand in his, "Marissa, it's time to wake up."

The sedatives dissolved from her bloodstream, her eyes fluttered, and she smiled at the sight of Arni. Realizing he was holding her hand she squeezed it tightly. "Arni…"

Marissa remembered her talk with Jake. She scrambled to get upright. "Jake? The baby? Are they okay?"

Jake moved over to Marissa. "I'm here."

Jason glanced at his scanner again. "The baby's fine too."

Marissa turned her attention back to Arni. "I was afraid for a moment my baby and I were going to be with your father… permanently. It's not that I don't like your father, but I wasn't ready to be done here. I hope you aren't offended by that."

Arni smiled even bigger. "Neither of us is offended. You're right. Your work here isn't done."

Arni turned to the Captain. "Captain Alexander, I need a favor."

David was surprised by Arni's statement. The man had unlimited power at his disposal, so what could he possibly need from him. "Sure, anything. What do you need?"

"I need to spend some time with your crew to teach and train them. May I stay in your guest quarters for a while?"

David blinked, such a mundane request startled him. "Uh… yes, of course. Do you… need to… uh… eat and sleep?"

Arni smiled knowing the Captain's anxiety about asking. "Yes, I do eat and sleep—although since Pateras restored me after my death on Drea, they are no longer necessities. This is a human body, though it is now enhanced by Pateras beyond its human limitations. I asked to use your guest quarters for the crew's comfort, not my own."

Jake felt a new-found energy surge through him. "So, the reason Luciano Hale can't touch us now is because you'll be staying on board the ship?"

Arni always seemed to smile the way a parent does when he watches a small child try something new. That smile appeared on his face again. "Not quite. Jake, I have been here the whole time. I need to teach you how to fight him. He is considerably more powerful than you are, but you have access to my power. Alone, you couldn't fight him. With access to me and my Father, he cannot stop you."

An excitement filled the room. This one small ship with a twelve-person crew was trying to stand up to an entire galaxy. It was overwhelming. For the first time in two weeks, they had hope.

LOOSE ENDS

David called the staff meeting to order. Arni's presence had the crew both nervous and excited.

Before the staff meeting, Brynna pulled David aside. "Captain, are you going to give me a head's up about what's going on?"

David sighed. "Not this time, Commander. I apologize for that, but there's too much ground to cover, and we need to get to work. Just try not to look too surprised by anything. I don't want the crew to lose confidence in me."

Brynna wasn't amused. She placed a blank expression on her face and entered the dining hall behind the last of the crew. She was suddenly alarmed. All twelve crew members were present in addition to Arni. Who was flying the ship and monitoring the tachyon and matter/anti-matter levels? Computer screens on the walls were programmed to display readouts from the external scanners and the engineering information. Brynna scowled. Even with Arni present, this was too dangerous. Knowing her concerns, Arni took her hand and gave it a squeeze. He pulled her in for a hug and whispered, "I created you, and I know how you're going to end. This isn't it." He pulled back and smiled at her. She returned a weak smile. She still thought it was a dangerous precedent to set. As she took her place near David, she expressed her delight in seeing Arni again. Despite Arni's reassurance, she still positioned herself where she could see the monitors.

David started the meeting by telling them why Arni was present. It seemed the best place to start since few would pay attention to anything else he said until that particular topic was covered.

"Settle down, people. We've got work to do and a lot of topics to cover."

The crew moved slowly to their seats. They had heard the captain, but they were clearly distracted. David was fast losing patience. "Room! A-ten-TION!"

The crew dropped whatever they were doing and snapped to attention. "Ladies and Gentlemen, although this is no longer a Commonwealth vessel, it still operates under strict military protocols. I expect you to conduct yourselves accordingly. We're going up against insurmountable odds. We took a vote. You agreed to stay aboard this ship and serve under my leadership. I can't lead if you don't follow. If you don't pay attention to my orders, we could all pay the price. Do you understand?"

The crew responded in unison, "Yes sir!"

"Seats! Now!" He paused for a few seconds to allow them to scramble into their places and get settled. He followed up with one brief warning before starting his briefing. "Do not let that happen again."

"The first thing I want to go over with you relates to Arni's presence. Arni has requested to stay aboard the *Evangeline* to spend some time with us. He will stay in the guest quarters for the duration of his visit. We are up against some difficult odds, and as several of us have seen today, we don't have a clue how to fight back."

As per military protocol, Commander Alexander raised her hand to question the Captain. "May I ask, what's happened?"

"I was just getting there. Security Chief Holden and Lt. Holden were paid a visit by Luciano Hale. He tried to entice and threaten the chief to rejoin his cause. In so doing, he threw the chief's wife against a wall. Marissa and the baby are fine, but according to the doc, it was a seriously close call. Arni says we have weapons at our disposal. We need to know what they are, and how to use them."

David informed the crew about the destruction of the CIF base on Romajin and Admiral Deacons' accusation. David worded the next part of his explanation carefully. "Regardless of whether I believe Mr. Holden is or is not responsible for this tragedy, we need evidence. If he's guilty, he will be punished appropriately. If he's innocent, the crew needs to know it to restore some lost trust. The rest of the galaxy needs to know we aren't terrorists or monsters. If we expect to present our case against the Commonwealth to the rest of the galaxy, we don't need this hanging over our heads."

David paused to field any questions. The crew was conspicuously quiet. Hearing none, he moved on.

"The last thing on the agenda is our next move. We're going to need to lay low until we resolve this situation with Mr. Holden. What I don't want to happen is for Executor Hale to recall the other ships and execute those crews while we keep our heads down. Admiral Deacons basically gave us our next target. He undoubtedly gave it to us with the Supreme Executor's knowledge. Which means the Supreme Executor intends to use it to set a trap for us and any other crews who are sympathetic."

Braxton interrupted with a disturbing question. "Sir, exactly whose side is the Admiral on?"

Before David could respond, Arni answered. "Robert serves my father. He is in a position of power and knowledge. The day will come when he can serve me openly, but for now, he must remain silent."

Jake was quick to add, "If it weren't for the Admiral, we wouldn't be alive. He's the one who told me what the Supreme Executor was planning for the crew. His ship was the lead ship when we escaped. He's the only one who was capable of shooting us down. He didn't. He's limited in what he can do, but he would die to protect us if he had to."

David was glad for the support. His speech at the beginning of the briefing was a strong effort to keep the crew focused. At this point in time, they could easily walk off the job without fear of punitive action. Like it or not, this was now a voluntary position, and David was at their mercy. David laid out his plans for contacting and locating the other eleven ships. It was going to take a great deal of stealth and craftiness to find them without being tracked themselves.

David closed out his briefing with a small pep talk. "Whatever lies ahead of us is going to be difficult and tricky. You are a good crew, but you aren't that good."

"Captain are you supposed to be encouraging us?" Lt. Lexi Flint quipped. "As your ship's psychologist, I have to say, it's not working for me."

Captain Alexander let the comment go and continued. "I want to make sure we all understand what we're up against. I can't command this ship alone. Without you, I can't do it. We have a new mission and the heat of the entire galaxy raining down on us. We are not equipped to accomplish this new mission. We need him and his father." David pointed at Arni. "We also have to put the past behind us. As soon as we get this business with Chief Holden settled, we need to move forward and trust each other implicitly. So, let's get moving. Check the duty roster for your schedules. Don't let yourselves get too tired. We could find ourselves in a critical situation at any point in time. We're going to have to live in a battle-ready status at all times. Take this time to learn all that you can from Arni. Pateras is the only way we will survive this. We will survive this so long as we stick together and stick with the plan." David turned his briefing over to Arni.

Arni greeted them warmly. "I'm glad to be here. I am both grateful and relieved you have all chosen to follow my father. My father wants you to know he loves and cares for each of you dearly."

Thane and Lazaro cast sideways glances at each other along with concerned glances at Jake. Had they been wrong about Jake? Could Jake fool Arni? They weren't ready to drop their grudges just yet. It would take a little more convincing.

Arni smiled knowing what the two were thinking as he made eye contact with them. He said nothing but continued his address. "I know you want to meet my father. Meeting him face to face is not possible right now. I assure you though, my Father and I are the same. If you know me, you know him. We are of the same mind. I know our relationship is going to be difficult for you to understand.

We share the same plans and goals. I am my father in human form. We are separate, but the same."

Quizzical looks populated the faces of the crew. How to explain this concept to those with limited minds was like trying to explain color to one who was blind. One day they would understand, but today they would just have to accept it.

"We are one being, manifested in different forms. I will only be with you for a short time. After I am done teaching you, I will return to my father. I won't leave you alone and unprotected though. David could not see me in prison on Romajin, but I was always at his side. There is another who will come. He is also equally a part of my father. He will teach you, guide you, reveal things to you. You will not see him as you see me. His presence will not leave you. He is your Intercessor and Advocate. When you speak to him, it is the same as speaking to my father and me. His resources are at your disposal. We will provide whatever you need."

The crew believed in and trusted Pateras El Liontari despite only two of them having met him. They had no idea where his home base was located, or how he operated. There was no comm channel to reach him on. They had learned from his son, Arni, early on that Pateras could read their minds and knew their thoughts. Before they even trusted Arni, they knew this was true. Arni also quickly taught them to simply speak his name, and he would hear them. Now they were learning about a third person.

Arni spent the next several days visiting with the crew, talking with them, teaching and encouraging them. His goal was to enable them to face the overwhelming task ahead. The crew needed Arni's words of wisdom, now more than ever. In less than a year most of the crew had met and married their spouses, started their latest Commonwealth assignment of first contact situations, discovered mythical supernatural beings capable of incredible power, learned some of the Commonwealth's deep dark secrets, and the thing of greatest impact, committed treason against the Commonwealth. Despite having the power of the Liontari household behind them, the crew still felt very much alone and outnumbered.

Twelve men and women against an estimated twenty-four quintillion people could have an emotionally crushing impact.

Arni wasn't just about business. He hung out with the crew during their times of rest and relaxation, meal times, and even visited them while they worked.

One such time Arni sat next to Marissa watching Jake and the Captain play a one-on-one game of Zone. Zone was a popular ball game among the crew. Marissa enjoyed watching it more than playing which was probably for the best as she was nearly six months pregnant. Jake and the Captain could be quite competitive. Their verbal banter during the game was equally amusing. Arni and Marissa laughed heartily at the two as they tried to one up each other with every attempt at scoring. The final buzzer sounded ending the game. The Captain had scored the winning point in the nick of time. For once, Jake took his loss well. He cordially shook the Captain's hand and offered him a sincere congratulation.

Marissa marveled at the changes in her husband's demeanor over the past few weeks. He seemed genuinely relaxed and happy. She knew he harbored some painful scars from his childhood. A part of him never seemed to be happy—until now.

As the four talked about the highlights of the game, Lazaro approached slowly. His visage was that of a man laden with bad news. David spotted his approach. Seeing the solemn look on his face, he metaphorically donned his Captain's hat. "What is it, Lt. Commander Dominick?"

Lazaro glanced nervously at the others present. He would have preferred talking to the Captain privately although they all needed to know what he had to say. "Captain, we've completed our investigation of the allegations against the chief. There's... uh... there's sufficient evidence to believe the chief sent the self-destruct signal to Romajin. We're recommending an immediate court martial. Here's a copy of the evidence we found. Will there be anything else, sir?"

"I see." David took the data crystal from Lazaro. He wiped his face off again with his towel. There wasn't any additional sweat on his face, just frustration. "Have you notified Lt. Commander Flint of your intentions?"

"My intentions? I don't understand, sir."

David handed the data crystal back to the Lt. Commander. "I thought I made myself perfectly clear. If you believe he's guilty, you and the investigation team are prosecuting him. Lt. Commander Flint and the team assigned to him will try the case. Lt. Flint and Commander Alexander are his defense counsel. I'm totally recusing myself from this. I appreciate the notification, but you need to present your evidence to Lt. Commander Flint. See that the chief's defense counsel gets a copy of your evidence so they can prepare a defense."

"Captain, I don't understand why you aren't handling this. It's your responsibility." Lazaro wouldn't normally challenge the captain, but his anger toward Jake fueled his insubordination.

David allowed the matter to pass. If he fought the anger they felt toward Jake, it would only generate more hard feelings. He knew it was simply going to have to burn itself out. "I can't be impartial. The only way he gets a fair trial is if I stay out of it. If you must know, even in light of whatever evidence you have there, I think he's innocent. That isn't satisfactory. We need evidence the rest of the galaxy will believe. This has to be legitimate. My opinion will not even satisfy the rest of the crew."

Lazaro stood there in shock. He knew the Captain seemed to be Jake's only friend right now, but he assumed it was because the Captain was trying to be noble. Every member of the crew had an ax to grind with Jake. Surely the Captain had a bigger ax than anyone. The things he suffered were considerably worse than what the others suffered. How could he just excuse Jake like that? Lazaro snapped out of his stupor and finally responded. "Yes sir, I'll take care of it, sir." He stepped back and saluted the Captain. The shock had so rattled him, he failed to wait for the appropriate counter salute. He turned and promptly left the gymnasium.

After the exchange, Jake walked back onto the Zone court away from his three companions. He picked up the ball lying on the floor. He held it in his hands for a moment and spun it around in his hands several times. His emotions got the best of him. He swung around and pelted the ball at one of the goals. The ball bounced aggressively off the sideboard. It continued to bounce around the playing area until it lost momentum. His anger was apparent when he turned back around. "Why?!? Arni, why is he doing this to me? I didn't do this!"

Marissa stood and walked slowly to her husband. She had the hardest struggle among the crew to accept Jake back. Her own husband had betrayed her along with the rest of the crew. She reached up and took his hand gently. "Jake, we believe you. I believe you."

Jake looked into her eyes. His intent was to give her a patronizing retort. He saw her pain and could no longer follow through with it. Instead, he wrapped his arms around her and held her tightly.

David and Arni moved toward the couple. As their hug seemed to reach a conclusion, David added his support to them. "Jake, Marissa, we have to do this by the book. We'll get to work on your defense right away. Jake, I believe you, too. You wouldn't have intentionally murdered one person, let alone ten thousand."

David turned to go talk to Jake's defense team. He gave Arni a polite nod as he turned to go. David knew if Arni said Jake was innocent, the crew would accept it. He also knew for that very reason, Arni would say nothing. They both knew the crew needed definitive evidence.

Lexi and Brynna were serving as the defense counsel.

It was near the end of the shift, so David had no qualms about waking either of them. He sent both women messages to meet him in his office as soon as possible.

When the two women received the message, they showered, dressed, and grabbed something to eat. They took their meals with them to the Captain's office. David invited Jake and Marissa to join them. As David sat at the table in his office thinking and sipping on a cup of coffee, he decided he needed one more thing. "Computer notify... never mind, belay that order. Arni, I need you to talk to the defense team." The room was empty, but David knew Arni would hear him.

In a moment, his guests trickled into the room. Jake and Marissa were the first to arrive. Jake had showered and had a little time to calm down. He appeared apprehensive but contrite. Lexi and Brynna arrived next with their meal trays. David stalled for a moment hoping Arni would join them. When he didn't arrive, David moved forward. He brought Lexi and Brynna up to speed. They were told what their responsibilities were. He finally asked the most important question. "Chief Holden has adamantly proclaimed his innocence on this matter. I need to hear from both of you. Can you two, in good conscience, represent Jake?"

Lexi looked Jake in the eye. "Yes sir, I can. I told him the day Marissa was attacked I trust him. I still have some hard feelings, but they won't stop me from doing my best for him." Lexi gave Jake and Marissa a reassuring smile.

The Captain turned his attention to his wife and First Officer. "Commander, tell me honestly, can you represent Jake? Are you confident in his claim of innocence?"

Brynna turned her visual focus to David. "Of course, I can represent the chief." Her answer seemed positive to all those in the room.

David saw something else in her eyes. Glancing at the door, he was still hoping Arni would show up. "Alright then, review the evidence they have and see what else you can find. The three of you will need to work together to find some serious proof to clear him. Leave me out of it, if at all possible. My opinion bears unnecessary weight and influence. Any questions?"

A deafening silence filled the small office prompting David to dismiss the meeting. Lexi, Jake, and Marissa sensed something wasn't right when David kept looking

41

toward the door. "Alright everyone, you are dismissed. Commander, if you don't mind, hang back so I can brief you on the shift logs."

The room cleared rather quickly. As the door closed behind the last departing crewmen, David blasted his Commander. "Just what was that?"

His demand startled Brynna. "What was what?" Her tone instinctively matched his.

"That was no answer to my question. If you can't represent the chief in good conscience, then you should have spoken up."

Brynna snapped back at him, "I said I could do it and I will."

"How do you expect to give him sufficient representation if you're still holding onto a grudge against him?"

"My feelings don't enter into this. You asked me to do a job. I intend to do it with all the professionalism required for me to do it right!" Her anger was now written all over her face.

David stood and paced. He had long passed the point of concern and was well into frustration. "Exactly what are your feelings about Jake?"

"I told you it isn't relevant! I'll do my job. What are you so worried about? I know how to follow orders, and I know how to do my job. Nothing else is necessary."

David opened his mouth to respond when his office door chimed. Instead of blasting Brynna again, David blasted the unknown visitor. "Who is it, and what do you want?!?"

The door opened to reveal Arni. "You wanted to see me?"

David's face flushed with embarrassment. "I'm sorry, Arni. I didn't mean to yell at you. Please forgive me."

Arni smiled gently. "This isn't the first time I've been yelled at. I get blamed for a lot of things. Sometimes I'm actually responsible for the things I'm blamed for."

"I—uh, I was hoping you would talk to the defense team in support of Jake. I've already dismissed the meeting." Brynna's obvious distaste for the task at hand distracted David. It didn't occur to him, Arni had come at precisely the right time.

"Only one member of the defense team needs to hear from me." Arni looked purposefully at Brynna who shook her head slowly.

"Oh, no. Don't you start on me, too." Brynna was ready to bolt from the office. She stood up as Arni sat down.

David was about to order her to take her seat when Arni waved him off. "Captain, if you don't mind, please have a seat. Commander, please sit down. Tell me what's going on."

David and Brynna were both caught off guard when Arni called them by their rank. He had always deferred to their names, even in the most formal of circumstances.

The two took their seats as requested. Brynna was still steaming from David's inferred accusation that she was incapable of doing her job. "Arni, I'm trained as an officer. Not every job is pleasant. I can handle Chief Holden's defense. My opinion doesn't matter."

Arni leaned forward and took Brynna's hand. "Your opinion may not matter regarding Jake's defense. It does matter to Jake and Marissa. It also matters to David, and to me."

Brynna held onto one small portion of Arni's message. "Do you really think I care about Jake's feelings?"

Arni took Brynna's free hand in his. He turned her toward him. "Brynna, I know, right at this moment, you really don't care about Jake's feelings. What is it you think needs to happen to him?"

"Everything he did to us needs to be done to him! Every beating David endured, every missed meal, every hour we spent drugged and restrained in the re-education chairs, he should have to go through every minute of it. Every time they hit us with the disciplinary rods, he should have to feel it. He should have to feel the pain of believing Marissa left him for another man. He should suffer everything we did." She spat venomously.

Her answer pained Arni, although he wasn't surprised by it. "Most people wouldn't wish any of that on their worst enemy."

"He is my worst enemy!" Brynna unequivocally stated.

David leaned forward. "No, he isn't."

"David, I seriously don't see how you can forgive him so easily. You suffered more than any of us. All of this is his fault." Brynna was getting close to tears.

David started pacing again. Arni waited quietly for what he knew David was about to say. "Brynna, you heard what I told the crew. This wasn't Jake's fault. It's mine. I could have stopped it. I didn't. Arni told me what was about to happen. I had a way to contact the crew and send them into hiding. I didn't do it. Everything you just said, should happen to me, not to Jake. Jake was doing his job. He was trained and ordered to protect the Commonwealth from Pateras. He was doing what every one of us was supposed to do, including you."

"David, you didn't betray us to the Commonwealth!"

"Yes... I did." David sat back down dejectedly. "I'm sorry I hurt you this badly. I let this happen to try to reach Jake and bring him around. It's my fault you had to suffer. I suppose I had no right to take the entire crew down with me. Please forgive me. More importantly, forgive Jake."

"I can never forgive him!" Brynna's blood ran cold. "I suppose I could have forgiven him for what he did to me and the rest of the crew. I can't forgive him for what he did to you."

"Brynna..." Arni spoke gently. "If you don't forgive Jake, my father can't forgive you."

Brynna suddenly looked lost. "Forgive me? For what?"

"For anything. Have you forgotten already? Every human owes their lives to my father for the crimes against him."

"But you said you forgave us. Have you changed your mind?"

Arni shook his head. "All of your crimes before today have been forgiven as I promised. The crime you're committing right now, has not yet been forgiven."

"What crime?" Brynna was alarmed and confused.

Arni continued to hold her hands in a firm and reassuring manner. He spoke even more softly and gently. "The crime of unforgiveness."

Tears streamed slowly and quietly down her face. "But, you don't understand. He's caused so much pain. You don't know what we've suffered because of him."

Arni gave Brynna a look she couldn't comprehend. The look on David's face was similar. The two gave her a moment to reconsider what she had just said. David finally spoke up in defense of Arni. "Brynna, if he knows our every thought, don't you think he knows our feelings and pain too."

Arni let go of one of Brynna's hands. He gently lifted her chin until her eyes met his. "How much have I suffered because of you, Brynna?"

For a moment Brynna's mind flashed back to the day on Drea when the crew was supposed to be executed for their role in the deaths of all the inhabitants of Galat III. The crew sat there helplessly as they watched Arni die in their place. His body convulsing violently with every energy pulse. Captain Parker, the prison warden, called the name of each crew member just prior to each jolt, the jolt intended for the crew member named. At the time, Brynna thought David was the one receiving the lethal pulses. It was minutes after they declared the prisoner dead, they discovered Arni had taken David's place. Brynna heard Captain Parker call her name just as clearly as she heard it nearly five months ago.

Arni watched her try to put the pieces together. Brynna pulled her hands away from him. She stood and moved to the corner of the room. She crossed her arms in front of her and turned her back to the two men. Still facing away from them, she tried to argue one last time. "But... that isn't the same thing. David took my place. You took David's place."

"Brynna, even if you had never set foot on Drea, if I had taken someone else's place, if you had been the only person alive, I would have taken your place. I took this pain for you. I did this for you. I did it for David. I did it for the six men who nearly killed David. I did it... for Jake. If you have to be angry with someone, be angry with me, not Jake. My father and I orchestrated this because Jake is a man who deserves a second chance. We know all there is to know about him. If we can do that and still believe he's worth giving a second chance, can't you give him that?"

Brynna turned toward David. "You really knew this was going to happen and did it anyway?"

45

"Yes... and Brynna, even looking at it through hindsight, I would do it again. Jake isn't the same man."

"You've really forgiven him? This isn't just you, putting up a front?"

"I've really forgiven him," David reassured her.

Brynna searched his face for any hint of doubt. His eyes returned nothing, but true forgiveness.

"All those things he did to you... I—I couldn't bear to hear..." Brynna sobbed.

David moved to wrap his arms around her and hold her. He quietly reassured her as Arni waited patiently.

Brynna finally understood why David was so upset. He had put himself and the entire crew through a painful ordeal for the sole purpose of convincing Jake to change sides. By rejecting Jake, she was essentially saying he had gone through all that pain for nothing. Brynna's crying eased, and she apologized several times to David. As her conscience eased, she released him and turned to Arni. She had done the same thing to him. "Arni, I'm so sorry. I am eternally grateful for everything you did to save our lives. I'm sorry I took it for granted. I was wrong. I will forgive Jake. It may take a little time to get past the anger, but I'll get there. You have my word."

Arni smiled and stood. "You'll get there... and it won't take long."

Brynna hugged Arni then excused herself to go talk to Jake.

Jake was alone in his quarters when Brynna reached his door.

He invited the Commander in. "Please have a seat. Did you come to talk about my case?"

"No, Jake I didn't, not directly anyway." Brynna was both ashamed and embarrassed by what she was about to say. "Jake, I hate to say this, but I came to apologize to you."

Jake scooted forward in his seat. "Apologize? For what?" Her response to the captain came back to him. The realization hit him. "Oh, I see."

Jake stood and took a few steps away from her. "You aren't comfortable defending me. I understand, Commander. There's no need to apologize. Thank you for your candor."

"Jake… I came to apologize for being angry with you and holding a grudge against you." Before she could finish, Jake tried to dismiss her.

"It's fine, really. I guess I should have taken Marissa back to Drea. I don't know why I thought I could ever fit in here again. I don't really deserve to fit in. You're right to hate me. What I did was unforgivable. You don't have to go on, Commander. I understand."

"No, Jake, you don't understand. I was wrong to hate you. I came here to ask you to forgive me. I'm not refusing to represent you. I would like you to forgive me for not forgiving you. I was wrong."

Jake turned around to face Brynna. "You're right. I don't understand. I don't deserve forgiveness. You've got every reason to hate me. Why are you asking for forgiveness?"

Brynna hung her head. "I talked to Arni and David. They showed me, none of us actually deserves a second chance. Arni gave us all a second chance. We owe it to him to forgive each other. David was right. You did what any Commonwealth soldier would have done and what I should have done. You arranged to get us caught. We knew the risks we were taking by committing treason. We chose to follow Arni and we knew you hadn't."

"Are you trying to justify what I did? There's no justification for betrayal. I should have walked away or turned myself in, not set a trap for the crew." Jake paced restlessly, hanging his head in shame.

"No, that isn't what I'm trying to do. I'm trying to say there's plenty of blame to go around. You don't get to lay claim to all of it. David said he knew what it would take to win you over. He allowed all of us to be captured. Don't you see, Arni and Pateras planned this, David accepted it on your behalf. They said you were worth rescuing. I was looking at the pain we all suffered and holding you accountable."

Jake grew more restless. "I am accountable."

"No, Jake, you aren't. Luciano Hale started this. Your job was to execute us. You saved our lives, and I just wasn't seeing it that way. You saved us several times over." Brynna teared up again. "Even if you hadn't saved our lives, Arni forgave you, David forgave you, how can I do any less? None of us deserve forgiveness. The feelings I have had against you..."

Brynna shook her head slowly as she considered her thoughts and feelings. The tears she had been blinking back, overran their boundaries. Jake had stopped pacing near her chair. She looked up at him slowly. "Jake, I'm so sorry for the—the things I thought and felt, the anger, the hatred. I wanted to hurt you as badly as you hurt us. Please forgive me." Brynna reached up and grabbed his hand.

Jake stood there in shock thinking he should have been the one asking for forgiveness. In a moment he realized he was only prolonging her pain. Jake sat down on the coffee table in front of her without releasing her hand. "Commander, by all means—I forgive you. You... uh... are good at hiding your feelings. I'm sure I deserve whatever you wished on me, at least in thought if not in actuality. I never knew you felt so strongly. Commander, please don't feel obligated to..."

"Chief, I'm not doing this out of obligation or duty. I want to do this. I need to do this, for you and for me."

The two continued to talk for nearly an hour as Brynna explained her grief, pain, and desire to forgive him. Before she left, the two had begun to rebuild their bridges.

COURT MARTIAL

"All rise." Lt. Commander Braxton Flint called the room to order. "The court-martial proceedings against Chief Petty Officer Jacob Holden are hereby called to order. Chief Holden, you have been charged with multiple counts of first degree murder and acts of terrorism. How do you plead?"

The crew had assembled in the gymnasium for the court martial. Lt. Commander Adams and Ensign Dominick sat with Lt. Commander Flint serving as the Judicial Board. Lazaro was in engineering, but connected to the proceedings via a video link. The Captain was on duty on the bridge and linked in as well. The Captain was making every effort to distance himself from the proceedings despite his convictions that Jake was innocent.

Jake stood at attention. "Not guilty."

"Your plea has been entered. Everyone be seated. We will begin with the prosecution presenting their case. After the prosecution presents its case, the defense will present its case. After both sides have completed their arguments and rebuttals, the Judicial Panel will review the evidence and render its judgment. Are there any questions from either side?"

Lt. Thane Ryder was presenting the prosecution's case. He stood to address the Court. "Prosecution has no questions."

Lt. Lexi Flint followed suit. "Defense has no questions."

It had been three days since Lazaro had announced the intent to bring charges against the security chief. The mood aboard the *Evangeline* had already been subdued and somber. In the three days leading up to the trial, the tension soared. The captain had strongly advised the crew against discussing Jake among themselves. He knew making it an order was nearly pointless. It was a small ship and the crew consisted of married couples. Asking nicely seemed the best option. The one thing he hoped to achieve was to keep Jake's guilt from being decided in ship board gossip. The impending court martial pervaded everyone's thoughts and weighed down the mood on board.

Arni continued to visit with the crew. As the court martial began, he placed himself quietly in the background, refusing to give insights to Jake's guilt or innocence. He quietly advised them to base their assertions on the evidence of what actually was, not what they wanted it to be.

Thane called his wife, Aulani as his first witness. "Ensign Ryder, could you please explain to the court what you found when you examined the ship's logs?"

Aulani glanced nervously at Jake who remained expressionless. "After examining the ship's logs, we found a signal was transmitted from the *Evangeline* to the CIF base on Romajin. The time and date stamps coincide with the time and date of the explosion on Romajin. The signal sent were codes that would match a standard Commonwealth self-destruct sequence. We could not confirm it was the code specific to the base on Romajin. In reviewing the computer logs for the time in question, we discovered a number of new files sent to the ship's database. The files were sent to the ship using Chief Holden's log-in assigned to him on Romajin. The ID tag identifies the sender as Lt. Jake Holden."

Aulani glanced at Jake, who did little more than blink. Marissa sat behind her husband absently rubbing her belly and their unborn baby as she worried about the evidence against him.

Thane followed with a clarifying question. "What is the significance of the ID tag?"

Aulani looked at Jake again with more conviction. "Jake's rank before Romajin was Chief Petty Officer. When

Jake rejoined the crew as we left Romajin, he was wearing the rank insignia of a lieutenant. His rank could only have been changed by the appropriate Commonwealth officials."

"What sort of files did you find in the database?"

"Mostly surveillance files of the Supreme Executor's office and a few other places," Aulani answered.

"What potential uses could those files have?" Thane prodded.

Lexi stood quickly. "Objection. Her answer would be speculation."

Thane turned to the panel of judges. "I'm not asking her to speculate on the Chief's intentions, just the potential need and uses for those files."

Braxton leaned forward to issue his ruling on the point. "I will overrule the objection, but please be cautious Lt. Ryder. Ensign, you may answer the question."

Aulani nodded, "Yes sir, the files could be used as a source of information, extortion, or evidence for any number of things. The files explain a number of events that occurred on Romajin. They could incriminate the chief, the captain, the rest of the crew, or the Supreme Executor. Who the files incriminate depends on the individual's perspective. For instance, there is a data file of Executor Hale ordering the so-called accidental death of Lt. Marissa Holden. There's also a file mentioning the promotion of CPO Jake Holden to the rank of lieutenant."

"You mentioned a file ordering the death of Lt. Marissa Holden. I thought Supreme Executor Hale had an agreement with the chief to free him and his wife and child."

"Yes, that's my understanding of the situation."

"Were there files mentioning that arrangement?" Thane pressed.

"There were references to the agreement. There were no copies of the agreement. There is also the chief's confession once the crew reunited aboard the *Evangeline*. He openly admitted he made an agreement with Admiral Deacons and Admiral Garcia to turn in the crew. He also openly admitted the Supreme Executor reneged on the agreement. Several others can testify that Executor Hale held Marissa hostage in his office when the crew attempted to escape Romajin."

Thane played the confession surveillance video for the court. After the video played, Thane continued his line of questions. "So, CPO Holden had motive for revenge against Supreme Executor Hale."

"So it would seem," Aulani said simply.

Lexi stood. "Objection. Calls for speculation."

Thane quickly countered. "Ensign Ryder has degrees making her qualified to speculate on human behavior and motivation."

Lt. Commander Flint glanced at the prosecution and the defense then at Aulani. "I'll allow it. Please use caution Lt. Ryder."

Thane nodded. "Yes sir. Ensign Ryder, taking the Lt. Commander's advisement, what reasons, based on your training, would one have to destroy a military base like the one on Romajin?"

Aulani thought for a second. "Revenge, an act of warfare, I suppose there may be other reasons, but those are the ones that come to mind right away." Before Thane could ask the obvious next question, Aulani jumped in and answered it. "The *Evangeline* and the *Independence* were outnumbered and outgunned. The only advantages we had in our escape was whatever help Pateras provided and our greater speed and maneuverability. Since the Supreme Executor ordered the execution of Lt. Holden, Chief Holden had two motivating factors to destroy the base on Romajin. Destroying the base would provide a distraction to aid in our escape and revenge for Marissa."

Thane continued his questions. "To your knowledge, did anyone else have access to the Chief's Romajin access code?"

"I... I... uh... really couldn't say. Ensign Dominick and Lt. Holden were on the bridge of the *Evangeline* during our escape from Romajin. I was on board the *Independence* with you, Lt. Commander Dominick, and Lt. Adams. I don't think there was time once we were aboard ship for the Chief to give the codes to anyone or for anyone to locate and use them without knowing they were an option."

Thane pressed on again. "What about the surveillance footage? Did it show CPO Holden sending the self-destruct codes to Romajin?"

Aulani gave Jake an uncertain glance. She wanted to believe him, but the evidence didn't support his claims. "The surveillance footage for the time in question was deleted from the files and spliced together leaving a gap."

"How did you discover the files had been altered?"

"Before abandoning the SS *Independence* on Galat III, I transferred all files to the *Evangeline* and erased the memory on the *Independence*. The time stamps between messages on the two ships started out in agreement then as the two ships attempted to dock with each other, the time stamps were off by eight minutes." Aulani gave Jake another glance. She couldn't get a read on him. His face remained emotionless.

Thane continued to question his wife about the records. Nothing he covered was going to help Jake's case. It didn't take long for Thane to make a solid case against his shipmate.

Lexi took her turn to question Aulani about the records and her professional opinions. There was little to clarify since the evidence was clearly not in Jake's favor. "Ensign Ryder, since there was an eight-minute gap in the files, is it possible someone else could have tampered with the files and sent that signal to Romajin?"

"It is possible, just not probable. The logs indicated the files were altered using Chief Holden's shipboard identity code."

"We've already established the improbability of anyone having access to the chief's Romajin log-in. Who had access to his ship log-in? Who could have used his ID to erase the files?"

"I had access, the Captain, the Commander, and Ensign Dominick. The Captain and Commander, however, were in the Infirmaries on separate ships."

Lexi moved ahead, trying to plant some reasonable doubt. "Ensign, do you have the capabilities to delete the surveillance and alter the logs? Do the others you mentioned have those same abilities?"

Aulani frowned at the question knowing where it could lead. "Yes, to both questions, but..."

"That will be all, Ensign. No further questions."

Thane quickly stood. "Ensign Ryder, please finish your answer to the lieutenant's question. You seemed to have other pertinent information."

Lexi scowled. She didn't want any other information on the record.

Aulani answered. "The people with access and capabilities still didn't have access to Chief Holden's Romajin ID, nor would they have made the mistake of not keeping the time stamp synchronized. That's a rookie mistake."

Thane sat down and thanked Aulani for answering as she did. Lexi stood again and asked the court to indulge her with a redirect. Braxton granted her permission.

"Ensign Ryder, you said it was a rookie mistake. Could that sort of mistake happen to someone suffering from exhaustion and dehydration?"

This time it was Thane's turn to scowl as Aulani answered. "I'm no doctor, but yes, it could definitely factor into it. I might have made that kind of mistake on that particular day. I was in such rough shape, I doubt I would have even thought things out well enough to delete those files and try to hide my tracks."

Thane and Lexi finished with Aulani and dismissed her. Thane begged the court's indulgence as he asked the doctor to testify despite his position on the Judicial Board. He assured the Judicial Board his questions were merely regarding technical expertise, not personal witness accounts. Braxton allowed it. He wasn't sure what it could hurt given the unusual circumstances they were in.

Dr. Adams confirmed Aulani's belief that the crew did not have the mental capacity to execute such an intricate albeit flawed deception.

When Thane was satisfied, he smugly rested his case and sat down rather pleased with himself. Somehow this seemed to take the burden of trying to forgive Jake off him.

Lexi called Jake to the stand to speak in his own defense. She gave him a great deal of latitude in his testimony. It may not have been the wisest course of action from a legal standpoint, but she felt his willingness to incriminate himself accidentally would speak volumes. "Chief Holden, please tell the court, in your own words, what exactly transpired on the day the military base was destroyed."

Jake explained his part in helping the crew and the Captain's family escape the prison facilities on the Romajin military base. The plan was laid out by Arni and guided by his servant Gabe. Jake finished by adamantly denying sending any sort of signal to Romajin or altering the surveillance logs.

As he finished his dissertation, Lexi followed with her next question. "Chief, who had access to your Romajin ID codes?"

"I can't say for certain, but Admiral Garcia and Admiral Deacons gave me the codes. I can only assume Supreme Executor Hale has that access based on a number of reasons. I would also surmise the Romajin Command and Administrative Staff were privy to that information." Jake's demeanor remained calm.

"Among those you mentioned, who would have the most to gain by using those codes to frame you?"

Thane jumped to his feet. "Objection. Calls for speculation."

Lexi quickly countered. "I intend to back up the chief's answer with further evidence, and it is within his rights to provide an alternate theory to the crime in question."

Braxton really hated this job. He glanced back and forth at the two. It was clear they meant to fulfill their roles to the very end. "I'll allow it so long as you can back it up. You may answer the question, Chief."

Jake nodded calmly and looked back at Lexi. Despite his distaste for psychology, she had become a source of comfort for him. "There's no doubt in my mind about this. Although Admiral Garcia could profit from it, Supreme Executor Hale has the most to gain."

Lexi had been moving about the court floor as Jake testified. Now she moved back to her chair and simply asked, "Why?"

Jake shifted in his seat. "He blatantly told me so. He wants me to work for him again, and he told me he framed me for it. He said he could make it go away if I agreed to serve him again."

At Lexi's prompting, Jake reiterated his encounter with Executor Hale in his quarters a few days ago. As he concluded, Lexi followed up with questions of a more psychological nature. "Chief, what steps did you take to protect your wife, child, and this crew from… well, from yourself?"

"I asked Captain Alexander to put me in stasis. It guaranteed I couldn't be put in a position to harm the crew, and it kept my family from being used against me."

"So why aren't you in stasis now Chief?" Lexi continued.

Jake's eyes fell on Arni. "Arni stopped the Captain. He told me he would protect us. I trust him."

Lexi followed with one last question. "What will you do if you are found guilty?"

Jake's eyes remained fixed on Arni's. "I will accept the court's judgment and take whatever punishment it sets forth, no matter what it costs me."

Lexi put her data pad down. "No further questions."

Thane jumped up and approached Jake.

"This incident you say happened in your quarters, can anyone else testify to what happened? Did you record it? Did Marissa hear any of it?"

Jake shook his head. "No. No one was there. Marissa was asleep in the next room."

Thane quickly jumped on that. "So, all we have is your word on this. Haven't you lied to us before? Weren't you lying to us on Tudoren? Didn't you lie to us on Romajin? Why should we believe you now?"

Jake looked sorrowfully at the floor. His regrets piling on him so heavily, he felt as though he would suffocate. A seductive voice whispered to him, "I can still get you out of this, just accept my offer." Jake looked up at Arni. Arni had said nothing to him. His eyes were filled with compassion as he saw Jake's struggle.

Through his silence Thane continued to hammer him with a barrage of questions and accusations, daring him to answer. Jake felt distanced from the proceedings going on around him. In the background he heard Lexi strenuously objecting to Thane's attacks. He heard Braxton trying to regain control of the courtroom. So many voices, one finally broke through the anarchy. "Do you still trust me, Jake?"

Jake looked up again. Arni hadn't moved or spoken audibly, although it had clearly been his voice. Without speaking, Jake nodded at Arni. He sat up straighter in his chair. "Enough!" He shouted above all the other voices. Everyone got quiet.

"Yes, I lied many times. I am not lying now. Whether or not you believe me is the decision of this court. No, I did not send that self-destruct code to the Romajin military base. I did not have that code. Commodore Vardin would never have trusted me with that kind of information. If this court finds me guilty, then so be it. I'm guilty of enough other things, I deserve numerous other punishments. Regardless of whether I live or die, I will serve Pateras."

To ease the tension in the room, Braxton called for a one-hour recess. During the recess, Cheyenne realized certain proof might exist to exonerate the chief, but it had not been introduced and didn't look like it would. Knowing she couldn't discuss the case she found herself in a quandary. She went to the only person she thought could help.

"Arni, I think there may be evidence that hasn't been discovered in this case. I can't go digging into it and remain on the Judicial board, and I can't discuss it with anyone. What do I do?"

Arni smiled. "How will justice best be served?" He knew that she already knew the answer to her question. She was simply looking for someone to validate the ideas already in her head.

Cheyenne raced off to find her evidence which took only a few minutes. Once she found it, she knew she needed to tell someone. The young ensign went immediately to the bridge to find the Captain.

Bursting onto the bridge, Cheyenne blurted out her situation. "Captain, I need you to replace me on the Judicial Board."

"I can't do that Chey—Ensign. You have to see this through no matter what." David thought perhaps her distaste for the task had overwhelmed her.

Arni stepped onto the bridge knowing she needed a bit more support. The two looked his direction when they heard the door open on the bridge. Arni glanced at David then focused on Cheyenne who gathered strength from his presence. David felt his last statement lose ground immediately.

"Captain, I know I shouldn't have, but I checked the computer files and found evidence to present to the court. This evidence is crucial to Jake's defense and cannot be ignored. I can't remain on the Judicial Board in light of this evidence."

David's temper flared briefly. He slapped the comm button on his console, "Lt. Commander Braxton Flint, Lt. Lexi Flint, and Lt. Thane Ryder, report to the bridge."

The three reported in short order. David kept his information brief and pointed. "Ensign Dominick has compromised herself and will need to be replaced on the Judicial Review Board. Lt. Commander Flint replace her with Lt. Adams when you reconvene. Lieutenants Ryder and Flint file any grievances with Lt. Commander Flint on the record. After the court martial is complete, you may file for disciplinary action against Ensign Dominick if you decide it is warranted. Dismissed."

The group stood around looking at each other blankly for a moment, then decided leaving the bridge was in their best interests. Arni and Cheyenne remained a moment longer.

"Captain are you mad at me?" Cheyenne ventured cautiously.

David had been staring angrily off into the air. He forced himself to look her in the eyes. "Are you doing what's right?"

"Yes sir."

David relaxed. "Then no, I'm not mad at you. I'm just inconvenienced and annoyed that this wasn't handled some other way. What did you find, by the way?"

"Sir, when you were afraid your loyalty was being questioned you had the Commander and me to set up redundancy files for all the computer logs. Since you left the service of the Commonwealth, neither of you have been checking the files. There's evidence to exonerate the chief in those files. I had to do this, sir."

"Understood, Ensign. Take your evidence to Lt. Flint so she has time to prepare."

Cheyenne raced off the bridge to talk to Lexi. David turned around to express his gratitude to Arni. "Thank you, I really needed this to turn out right."

The court was slightly late resuming. Just before the proceedings began again, Jake cornered Lexi. "Lexi, I want to change my plea to guilty."

Lexi returned a look of shock. It took her a moment to speak. "Jake, are you saying you destroyed that base?"

Jake shook his head. Returning a look of disbelief, he quickly refuted her accusation. "No, Lexi, I didn't. I'm just saying, perhaps it would be best for all concerned if I took this hit. The Captain could turn me in and take some of the heat off the crew. I could pay for the wrongs I have committed, and the crew wouldn't need to learn how to trust me again. Besides, based on the case against me, they're going to find me guilty. Let's just save everybody a lot of trouble."

Lexi understood his reasoning. She didn't agree with it, but she understood. "No, Chief, we aren't doing that. I…"

"It's not your decision. It's mine. I want to do this."

"What about Marissa and the baby? You do this, and you'll never see your baby. Chief, I can win this case."

"Marissa and the baby will be safer without me. Let's make the plea change as soon as we start up again."

Lexi balked. "Chief, give me thirty more minutes in court. If you still want to change your plea, then I'll accept it. I can prove your innocence, but I need thirty minutes of testimony, maybe less. Your wife and baby are worth thirty minutes, aren't they?"

Jake gave a sullen nod. He took his place in the courtroom as Braxton called the court to order.

Braxton entered the change of judiciary members into the record along with a reprimand of Ensign Dominick. Laura had been present for the entire trial, so she was already familiar with the evidence. Braxton began the proceedings again by asking if either side had any further questions for the chief. Both sides declined any further questions at this time. Lexi reserved the right to recall him later if needed.

Lexi called Cheyenne to the stand. Before she could begin her interview, Jake grabbed Lexi's hand. "What's going on? Why the change in the Judicial Board and what information does Cheyenne have?"

Lexi leaned down and whispered. "I didn't have time to discuss this with you. This is how I can prove your innocence. Just be patient."

Braxton pushed Lexi to begin her questions. He wanted this to be over as soon as possible.

Lexi moved to stand a few feet directly in front of Cheyenne. "Ensign Dominick, tell the court what you told me earlier."

Cheyenne glanced at Braxton knowing she had inconvenienced him as well as the Captain. "I found proof in the ship's logs that Jake didn't send that code to Romajin. Several months ago, before defecting from the Commonwealth, Captain Alexander's loyalty came under question. The Commander and I created a computer program to keep a secondary log of all computer entries. It records any file duplications, deletions, creations, or transmissions, either incoming or outgoing."

Thane saw where this was going. His role as the prosecutor pushed him to object, his desire to know the truth kept him silent. Braxton caught Thane's anxious movements out of the corner of his eye. He glanced to see if Thane intended to object. Seeing his hesitation, Braxton returned his attention to Cheyenne.

Lexi prodded Cheyenne to continue. "I assume you've been into those files recently. What did you find?"

"I found records of a transmission coming from the SS *Independence*. It was a carrier wave attached to one of the regular transmissions. The message contained a file with a computer program. I analyzed the file and the program.

It contained the same information that went out in the transmission to Romajin."

Lexi pushed to clarify. "So, you're saying whoever sent that transmission was actually aboard the *Independence*?"

Cheyenne shook her head. "No, not exactly. It's possible, but not probable. The Captain wanted to make sure someone didn't slip in and use our own codes to shut us out of the computer or take control of the ship remotely. He had us set up this program specifically to detect those carrier waves. The *Evangeline* and the *Independence* were hailed numerous times by the three ships that were pursuing us. The log shows those same carrier waves were attached to the hails from the *Chimera*, Executor Hale's ship. The signals were not accepted by the *Evangeline* because its comm system was programmed to reject such signals. The *Independence* didn't have that programming. The Chief didn't know about the program. In his attempts to maintain contact with the *Independence*, he had me do everything I could to keep the channels open. I—I may have been more responsible than the Chief for the destruction of the base on Romajin. I kept the transmission protocols wide open. The logs show that five seconds after the net was full and the tachyon drive was engaged, a signal was sent to Romajin."

Lexi continued to push. "How does this prove the Chief didn't send the signal?"

Cheyenne scowled. "It's not conclusive proof that he didn't, just that it's highly unlikely. This was done using a computer program sent to the ship after we were in flight. It was sent from the comms station to the command console then to Romajin. When I broke down the program, I discovered it was meant to look like it came from the command console. I didn't have enough time to get into a lot of detail. There may be other proofs, and it's possible the Chief created the program and planted it while on Romajin. I would find that really hard to believe though."

"So, you're saying a computer program designed to send a self-destruct code using the Chief's ID and the command station, was sent from the *Chimera* to the *Independence* then to the *Evangeline*. It was just lying there waiting for someone to give the order to activate the tachyon drive."

Cheyenne had her data pad in her hand with a copy of the information she was testifying about displayed on it. Something caught her eye on the pad. She suddenly sent the data to the holographic imager in the center of the room. It projected the data on the empty walls around the room. Her disposition had been eager moments ago. She now reached a point of being excited. Her eyes sparkled. Highlighting a line of code, she explained. "No, look at this portion of code. This program was designed to send the self-destruct codes from whatever station the Chief was using. If he had been at the helm, command, or the dining hall, it would have sent from that location. This program was designed to search him out. This proves he was framed."

When Cheyenne started her testimony, Jake was slouching in his chair. The longer she testified, the more intrigued he became. By the end of her testimony, he was leaning forward thoroughly engrossed as hope welled up within him.

Lexi relinquished the floor to Thane for cross-examination. Thane debated about asking for a recess to process this new information. Braxton knew his debate and offered him some time. Thane stood slowly and moved around in front of his own table to answer Braxton's offer.

"Thank you for your consideration. I don't think I will need any extra time to consider this evidence. I have just a couple questions for Ensign Dominick. Is it possible for the Chief to write such an intricate program to make it appear he had been framed?"

Thane received several dirty looks from everyone in the room. It was clear to everyone, Jake had been framed. The one thing they didn't realize was Thane was in agreement with them. He took his responsibilities seriously. He wasn't about to ignore any other explanations.

Cheyenne was excited about her discovery and had trouble wrapping her brain around Thane's suggestion. "Uh... I don't... I don't know the extent of his computer training. As a sociologist, he is devious enough to do so, but..."

"That's all, Ensign. Thank you."

Lt. Flint came out of her chair in a heartbeat. "Redirect, Your Honor?" She continued without waiting for Braxton's approval, "but what, Ensign?"

"The Chief was grieving over his own poor choices, searching for a way to get us out of prison, supplying us with water, learning to follow Arni among many other things. This program is pretty intricate and the plan quite devious. I seriously doubt he could design it unless he had a month to plan, and he didn't know what his circumstances would be a month before that. I can't say he absolutely couldn't, but it's doubtful, really doubtful."

Lexi sat down next to Jake. "I have no further questions for this witness. The defense has only one other witness. If the prosecution wishes to acknowledge the presence of Supreme Executor Hale as being on board the ship and attacking Marissa, I won't bother calling on Lt. Holden to testify."

Thane stood. "What is that supposed to prove?"

Lexi turned toward Thane. "It establishes the Chief's story with credibility. It says at least part of his story is accurate."

Thane looked annoyed. "Fine, the prosecution acknowledges Supreme Executor Hale came aboard the ship and attacked Lt. Holden. The prosecution does not acknowledge the contents of their conversation nor the purpose of his visit."

Cheyenne started to step down from the stand when Thane stopped her. "One more question, Ensign. Who had access to these logs you presented?"

Cheyenne cocked her head slightly. "You, Ensign Ryder, and Lt. Commander Dominick had editorial capabilities. Everyone else had 'view only' privileges."

Lexi rested her case, and the court adjourned to deliberate. Jake and Marissa were relieved to have this part over. The two were elated with Cheyenne's discovery. Lexi was sure the three would be back with a verdict in Jake's favor in a matter of minutes. Three hours later, they were still waiting. The Captain was even showing signs of being edgy when they took so long. David was trying his best to keep a healthy distance away from the trial and influencing it. He wanted desperately to find out what was taking them so long. The case looked pretty clear cut to him.

One hour later the crew found themselves back in the gym turned courtroom. The faces of the Judicial Board remained deadly serious. The thing Jake found most disturbing was the Tri-EMP sitting on the table in front of him. David continued to watch from the bridge. He wasn't sure what was going on.

Braxton called the room to order. "Crew of the *Evangeline*, this board has made its decision. It has, however, chosen to withhold that information for the time being. This crew was profoundly affected when the Captain chose to follow Pateras alone. The destruction of the base on Romajin and the accusations against the Chief have even greater potential to affect the crew. I understand the Captain wanted to give the Chief a chance at a fair trial. The crew of the *Evangeline* is small and close knit. This board feels it is in the best interest for everyone involved to cast their votes as to the Chief's guilt or innocence. We will vote the same as we did before; when the Captain asked us to decide whether to continue to allow him to command this ship."

Before Braxton could finish, David attempted to interrupt him. Braxton promptly shut him down. "Captain, you told me to handle this, and I'm handling it. If the Chief did this, he brought the entire galaxy down on us. If the three of us decide he's guilty, we deprive his wife and child of a husband and father, this crew goes down one man, and we risk alienating anyone who believes he's innocent. If we decide he's innocent, we're forcing him to stay here with anyone who believes he deserves to be punished. This Judicial Board wants the entire crew to vote. We've already decided how we're going to handle the results of the vote."

David was ready to be done with his shift. He seriously needed to spend some time with the haggard punching bag in the gym. "Alright Lt. Commander, proceed."

Braxton pulled the ammunition clip out of the Tri-EMP. He slid eleven projectiles out of the clip and handed one to each person present. He took the two remaining shells and sent Laura to give one to Lt. Commander Dominick in Engineering and one to the Captain, on the bridge. Lt. Commander Adams brought two empty, non-translucent containers in from the infirmary and placed them on the judges' table. Braxton instructed the crew on how the vote would be conducted. "The container on the left means you believe the Chief is guilty, the one on the right means you think he's innocent. You will approach the table and place your hands in both bins simultaneously. Drop your shell in the appropriate bin. Commander, if you would begin the voting then switch places with the Captain so he can cast his vote. Lt. Flint, do the same for Lt. Commander Dominick. The rest of us will vote while the other two are in route. The votes won't be counted until you have returned, Lt. Flint. Any questions?"

Jake stared straight ahead as the voting commenced. His mind raced, and his body twitched visibly as he heard each pellet hit the bottom of the containers. He was so sure they were going to find him guilty until Cheyenne's testimony. Why were they doing this? He heard the words Braxton said to the Captain, but they made no sense.

The last pellet struck the bottom of its bin stirring Braxton to step forward. "Before the votes are revealed, I want you to know what the Judicial Board decided. Will the defense please rise?"

Jake and Lexi stood as ordered. As a courtesy, Thane stood as well.

"CPO Holden, this court determined there was insufficient evidence to find you guilty of the destruction of the Commonwealth base on Romajin. If these bins reveal a unanimous vote of guilt, you will be summarily executed, and your body will be returned to the Commonwealth with our apologies."

Jake, Marissa, and Lexi grew pale at the thought.

"It is highly unlikely, that will occur as this board has openly disagreed with the idea of your guilt. If the majority believe you are guilty, you will be put off this ship at the nearest and safest habitable planet. If the vote is in your favor, but not unanimous, you will be freed but under advisement to watch your back. If the crew votes you are unanimously not guilty, then you are free and safe."

Jake swallowed hard when Braxton paused. He nodded for Braxton to proceed. Braxton took the guilty bucket and turned it upside-down. For a moment there was dead silence in the room. Nothing fell out of the bin. Braxton picked up the second bin and flipped it over. Eleven projectiles fell out. Braxton breathed a sigh of relief along with the rest of the crew. He gladly announced, "Eleven not guilty votes, no abstentions. Chief, you are free to go. Court is adjourned."

Everyone breathed a sigh of relief. There were no resounding cheers, no applause, simply relief, and a few tears of joy. Marissa threw herself into Jake's arms. Jake was still numb with disbelief. Cheyenne stepped forward to offer her congratulations. Jake wasn't the type to hug anyone other than Marissa. Under the circumstances, he couldn't help himself. He hugged Cheyenne tightly and whispered, "Thank you."

Jake looked around to find Arni standing next to the Captain on the bridge just as the Captain shut off the comm feed. Jake made a mental note to thank Arni the next time he saw him.

The crew quietly made their way to Jake and Marissa to offer their support and congratulations. Jake was quick to thank Lexi for her help as his defense counsel.

Thane reached his hand out to congratulate Jake. "Chief, you have done some things that were clearly wrong, but this wasn't one of them. I'm glad we got this matter cleared up. Sorry if I pushed too hard."

Jake accepted the handshake. "You did your job, and I'm glad you pushed, even though I didn't care for it at the time. At least I know the verdict was real and I still have a small amount of trust from the crew. Thanks, Thane."

Braxton approached as the two were talking. "Chief, I hope you understand why we asked the entire crew to vote."

Jake nodded. "I didn't, to begin with, but I do now. Thanks, Lt. Commander. I think I needed that."

Braxton offered his congratulations then excused himself to go talk to the Captain. He knew the Captain wasn't amused at the vote. As providence would have it, Arni had already made the situation clear to him.

Brynna hugged Marissa then offered her congratulations to Jake. As they finished talking, Brynna ended with a tongue-in-cheek comment. "Now that you're back on the active duty list, help Lt. Commander Flint clean up the courtroom and report to the Captain to find out when your next duty shift is."

Jake blinked at her in surprise. He was glad to be back on the active duty list, although he hoped to spend a little time celebrating his victory, or release, from this terrible burden. He managed to at least acknowledge his orders. Brynna grinned and hailed the Captain to suggest the Chief have one more night off.

The Captain added his own congratulatory remarks to the others and ordered the Chief to take the first shift in the morning at the helm. The rest of the evening Jake spent celebrating with his wife.

COURT MARTIAL

TRUCE

Five days later, the ship was quietly tucked away in a canyon on the planet Ela Prime. The shuttle dropped its passengers and retreated to a cautious distance. The *Evangeline* had sent messages to the other eleven Explorer Class ships. A few responded. Most didn't.

David walked up behind Captain Nathaniel Weiseman. The two men had been friends since they entered the CIF Academy in high school. David quietly hoped their friendship would outweigh his own treason.

"Hello, Nate."

Nate's head raised slowly as he recognized the voice behind him. He had hoped this day would never come. Why had his friend done this? Why was he forcing his hand?

David watched Nate's reaction as he recognized David's voice. He held his breath, hoping for the best until he saw Nate reach surreptitiously for a weapon. Mentally David swore. Physically, he moved his hands away from his own weapons, keeping them clearly visible and non-threatening.

Captain Weiseman whipped around to face David with his sidearm pointed menacingly at the now well-known traitor and terrorist.

"Captain Alexander, you are under arrest."

David ignored his friend's declaration, "Nate, we need to talk."

"Shut up! I know how you followers of Pateras work. I'm loyal to the Commonwealth, and I'm going to stay that way. You won't take over my mind."

David looked around as he searched for the right words. He didn't want to get shot before he had his say. "Please—Nate—I'm not trying to take over your mind. Who you are loyal to, is your choice. I came here to warn you."

Nate's tension eased as David spoke.

David picked up his pace as the tension dissipated. "Executor Hale intends to execute all twelve Explorer teams. His recall orders are a ruse to get you back onto a CIF base. He's going to wipe out the entire program. The mission was a bust and loyal or not, he's getting rid of the evidence."

Captain Weiseman scoffed, "Nice try, I'm still taking you in."

David shook his head, "Not today you aren't."

"What makes you so sure about that?" Nate asked cautiously. His friend was just a little too comfortable.

"My security chief is at the top of the rise, with a laser rifle pointed at you."

Hearing the Captain's warning, Chief Holden turned the laser sight on and positioned the beam. A small red dot appeared on Captain Weiseman's chest. Nate looked down at the menacing spot. Setting his jaw firmly, he looked at David. "I see. You might as well shoot me, Captain. I'm not joining your cause or quest or whatever you want to call it."

Nate allowed his hand to relax. His weapon flipped upside down as he offered it to David.

David wisely kept his distance. He waved him off, "Just put it away. He's only here for my protection. I just came to talk."

Nate put his weapon away slowly, keeping a close eye on the conspicuous red dot on his shirt. Being careful to keep his hands clearly visible, Nate forced himself to ignore the laser sight. "Your protection, huh? So that means he won't shoot me if I walk away."

David folded his arms across his chest. "That's not... exactly what I said. I never said he wouldn't shoot you. He just won't kill you."

"So, you've stooped to shooting your friends. Is that it? What happened to you? How could you turn your back on the Commonwealth like this?"

"You drew on me, Nate. My weapon is still in my holster."

"You've betrayed everything you ever stood for. You betrayed your friends, your family, your oath as an officer." His words reflected anger and bitterness.

"Things aren't always what they seem to be. The Commonwealth isn't what they taught us to believe it was. Executor Hale isn't the peaceful, benevolent leader we thought he was." David calmly answered his friend's accusation.

"Would you just shoot me or speak your peace and get out! I have no interest in anything you have to say, traitor!"

The two were standing in a tent pavilion overlooking a mining work-site. Captain Weiseman had been leaning over a table covered with diagrams. Several other tables and chairs were scattered around the pavilion. David moved to an adjacent table and leaned against it.

"You know, if somebody were out to kill my crew and me, I'd want to know about it."

Nate folded his arms across his chest defiantly. "It doesn't matter how many times you say it. I'm still not going to believe you."

"Nate, we've been friends for years. Have I ever lied to you?"

"My friend David never lied to me. I don't know who you are." Nate retortcd.

"Ouch, that hurts. I'm the same man. I chose to walk away. I made a conscious decision to leave the Commonwealth. I can't work for anyone who would eradicate an entire planet's population. We found Pateras' followers on our very first stop. We left like we were supposed to when we discovered him. The population was a simple, peaceful society. They were a promising, intelligent people. I have proof the Pacification Fleet wiped the entire planet out. Supreme Executor Hale ordered it directly. Have you located any followers of Pateras in your travels?"

"What? Why do you want to know? Are you trying to put together an alliance of non-space-faring worlds? What good is that supposed to do? I'm not giving you any information." Nate spat angrily.

"I'm not asking you where these worlds are. It's better if I don't know. Any world you've reported as belonging to Pateras has probably been destroyed. Strabothon is within your assigned territory, isn't it? I know it's on the line between you and the *Concord*. Which one of you reported them? The Supreme Executor had the world destroyed. Did the CIF SS *Emissary* sign their death warrant or did the Captain of the CIF SS *Concord*?"

Nate grew angrier with every word. "Murder isn't my bag it's yours. You were the one who destroyed the military base on Romajin. How many people have you killed? Reports say you and your crew killed over ten thousand people."

David's posture stiffened. He paced aimlessly. When he finally was able to stomach the words, he whispered. "I'm responsible for the death of over six million people."

Nate's anger, assuaged by the magnitude and bluntness of David's answer, faded into shock. "What?!?"

His next words would have been, "You're kidding" except David's demeanor clearly indicated he wasn't.

David's back was turned to Nate. When he heard his friend's question, he turned slightly. Not wanting to look his friend in the eye, he spoke over his shoulder to answer.

"We aren't responsible for the deaths on Romajin. We didn't do that. Despite being warned, I reported the population of Galat III as being loyal to Pateras. There were over six million people on Galat III. I'm responsible for their deaths."

"I thought you said the Pacification Fleet wiped them out. You might want to get your story straight. It's got a few holes in it." Nate retorted bitterly.

Before David could respond, Jake's voice came through the Captain's ear piece. "Captain, I'm going to have to move. I've got company closing in on my position."

"Understood, Chief."

David turned around to face his friend straight on. His back-up was now gone, it was no longer safe to have his back to his friend. Mentally David laughed at the irony of feeling unsafe turning his back on a man he considered a friend. "The only holes in my story are in your understanding of it. I didn't pull the trigger, but I'm just as culpable as those who did." David's anger over the situation grew as the images of the past flooded his memory. "The Commonwealth SET ME UP TO KILL SIX MILLION... MEN... WOMEN... AND CHILDREN!"

David dropped his guard and paced around in his anger. "We saw their bodies when we revisited Galat III. The body of a boy my helmsman taught to make toy gliders, the bodies of a set of twins my doc delivered. The parents named those twins after the Doc and my linguistics officer. They never even got a proper burial. They died right where they were and were left there."

Nate still stood there defiantly. "They were our enemies—Captain."

David angrily grabbed Nate's jacket with his fists. "Babies and children? I found wild dogs chewing on their bones. They weren't our enemies! The people signed the agreement to join the Commonwealth. They didn't know what hit them or even why." David shook his friend hoping to shake some sense into him.

Seeing the opportunity, Nate swiftly broke David's grip on his jacket. Shoving his shoulder into David's abdomen, Nate took David to the ground. The two wrestled, each trying to best the other. The ensuing scuffle caused the tables and chairs to be thrown awry. Nate gained the upper hand for a moment, but David threw his rival off. The two quickly rolled to their feet and assumed defensive postures. Neither had reached for the weapons they both carried. They both seemed content to hold to their more basal instincts.

The two circled each other slowly looking for their next opening. David tried to dissuade his friend from attacking again. "You're taking quite a chance with my man out there."

Nate returned a chilling grin. "He's not out there anymore. You're smart enough to have a plan in place in case he was found. He hailed you a few minutes ago to tell you he had to relocate." Captain Weiseman charged

David again landing some solid hits into his friend's abdomen.

After David's imprisonment on Romajin, he was accustomed to taking hits. The fists to his abdomen hardly fazed him. David took Nate back to the ground. He punched Nate in return. Nate took several punches to the face before he slowed down. As Nate lost momentum, David backed off. He stepped away from his fellow Captain and dropped his hands down to his sides. "Are we done?" He asked cautiously.

Nate rolled over onto his hands and knees to catch his breath. He spat blood onto the ground and sat up on his heels. Taking another deep breath, he wiped blood from his nose onto his sleeve.

David's guilt over the pain he had caused his friend swelled. He was a trained soldier and fighting back was an instinct. David slowly approached his former comrade. He offered him a hand up. "I'm sorry. I shouldn't have fought back. I didn't mean to hurt you."

Nate glared at him. "Why are you here, really?"

"I'm really trying to save your life and your crew's lives. I swear it. Yes, I'd love to have you join me, but even if you don't, I'll be satisfied to get you out of this alive."

"Get me out of this alive? Is that why you just tried to kill me?" Nate argued.

"If I meant to kill you, you wouldn't be getting up." David still stood over Nate offering him a hand up.

Nate took his hand, stood, and slowly began putting the tables and chairs back into their proper places. He was also slowly putting distance between himself and David.

David tried to clean himself. He wiped sweat from his brow, dusted himself off and checked his face for bleeding. He was pleasantly surprised to realize for once he hadn't been punched in the mouth. As he straightened his uniform, he discovered his weapon was missing. He looked around to see if it had fallen on the ground. He was disappointed to discover it hadn't. He turned cautiously to face Nate again.

Nate was standing with his feet firmly planted and David's weapon in his hand. "Did you lose something?" The weapon was pointed directly at David.

"If you're going to use that on me, I suggest you make sure the setting is lethal. If Supreme Executor Hale finds out you've spoken to me, he'll kill you just to be sure I haven't infected you. That's the only chance you have at survival. I'm not even sure that will be enough."

Captain Weiseman stared at Captain Alexander as though he had lost his mind. "Do you want to die?"

"No, of course not. I—I'm just willing to if it means saving you and your crew. Supreme Executor Hale threatened to kill every person who heard me say anything on Romajin. It's an interesting coincidence, isn't it? That entire base is now gone." David's tone seemed to mock his friend now turned foe.

Nate had already been struggling with the message he received from Admiral Deacons regarding Captain Alexander and his crew. It caught him between sorrow, anger, and confusion. Captain Weiseman continued to stare at Captain Alexander before returning to his cold, detached and calculative self. "Where's your Security Chief, Captain? Have him stand down and come in, now."

The ominous red dot reappeared on Captain Weiseman's chest. Without moving, David addressed the Chief, "Stand down, Chief." David was silent for a moment clearly listening to the Chief speak.

Captain Weiseman took a menacing step forward. "Put him on speaker, Captain."

David reached down and pressed a control on his bracelet. "Chief, you have your orders. Stand down. If he shoots me, return to the ship and get out of here. No rescue attempts. No retribution. I belong to Pateras."

Angered and frustrated, Captain Weiseman retorted, "Chief, put your weapons down and walk in here now or I will shoot your Captain!"

There was silence for a moment then Jake's voice came through calmly and clearly. "Understood, Captain— Alexander. Pateras is in control." The red dot vanished.

"Some security chief you have there. He's willing to abandon his Captain? Or was that Pateras thing some kind of code?"

"No, it was pretty straightforward. I serve Pateras, and my fate is in his hands, not yours." David calmly responded. "Actually, serving Pateras has been good for

75

my security chief. He's much better at obeying orders and arguing less."

"Where's your security chief posted? What's his location?"

"Use your own scanners if you want to find him. I'm not helping you locate him." David's eerie calm was unnerving Nate.

"You'd like for me to take my eyes off you for even half a second, wouldn't you?" Nate goaded.

David smiled, held his arms out in a casual gesture of surrender then turned casually away from Nate. He slowly lowered himself to his knees and placed his hands behind his head. "Do what you need to, Nate. I'm done fighting."

Nate nervously searched the horizon to locate the elusive security chief. Before he could activate his own scanner, his comm unit beeped frantically at him. The thought ran through his mind that while David and the security chief were keeping him occupied, David's crew could have been rounding up the rest of the *Emissary's* crew. Glancing at the display on his bracelet, Nate saw the message was flagged as urgent. Nate took three long fast steps toward David. Pressing the barrel of his weapon forcefully against David's neck, he demanded, "What have you done to my crew?"

David was less calm when he answered. "I haven't done anything. My people are nowhere near here. I left them behind to keep them safe. You might want to find out what that is before you blame me."

Nate's bracelet continued to beep frantically with the programmed distress signal. Just as he started to answer, a rumble and a vibration shook the ground under them. Nate answered the call. An equally frantic voice came through the speaker. "Captain! There's been a cave-in! We've got a dozen or so villagers trapped and several crewmen in the mine. I'm still getting a head-count. Both of our engineers were in there and Captain—so was Stephanie. What are your orders, sir?"

Nate paused for a moment before answering. The voice on the other end again frantically asked, "Captain, what are your orders?"

"Get your head-count, get the shuttle in closer, but set her down easy. Get the Surf-ve and all available personnel to the mine entrance. I need Milo up here at the pavilion with me."

"Yes sir. Captain, Milo was in the mine as well. What's wrong?"

"Nothing, never mind, I'll be down there momentarily."

David stood carefully keeping his hands in plain sight. "Nate let my people help."

Nate raised his weapon higher. "Keep still or I swear I will shoot you."

"Nate, by my count you have at least a third of your crew trapped, injured or—worse. You need help. I can give you that help." David argued.

"You probably did this. I should shoot you and get it over with!" Nate threatened.

David sighed. "I didn't do this. Nate, let us help you. You've got more important things to worry about than my crew and me. After we get those people out of there, we'll go away and leave you alone."

Nate weighed the urgency of the situation against his former friend's promises.

Seeing his friend's dilemma, David offered one last entreaty. "Nate, we were friends. I want to help, for old time's sake?"

"Are you begging for your life?"

"No, shoot me if you must. I told you I'm done fighting for my life. Right now, I'm fighting for your wife and crew. I promise to keep my people in line, no recruiting for Pateras. If you want, I give you my word, after the rescue operation, we can pick up right where we left off. I'll send my crew away and I'll stay behind. It's your call, but you need the help. Please let me help. Steph was my friend too."

David, Nate, and Stephanie had been inseparable as teens. The three kept in touch while Stephanie went to medical school. David's duty assignments caused him to lose touch for a few years. Nate and Stephanie married three months before joining the Explorer Mission Project. The three renewed their friendship during the training program.

For the sake of his wife and their friendship, Nate slowly lowered the weapon. He powered it down and tossed it back to David. "I have your word?"

"You do. Let's get to work."

Nate motioned for David to follow him down the hill toward the base of the mountain in front of them. Nate paused a moment and turned back to David, "Wait here until I bring my crew up to speed on your offer to help."

"I'd rather not, if you don't mind. Trust cuts both ways. I need to know my crew isn't going to be harmed if I bring them out in the open. I'm willing to trust you. I'm not as sure about your crew's intentions." David wanted to trust his friend but was still wise enough to be cautious.

"I suppose I would do the same. Let's pick up the pace though." Nate commented.

The pavilion was sandwiched between several vantage points. It provided a decent vantage point to see the city to the East, the road to the mine which was located to the Northwest and the river to the South.

Nate took off at a trot, and David kept pace, a couple steps behind him. As they neared the mine entrance, the terrain became steeper, and the path narrowed. Nate got more nervous about his wife and crew and moved even quicker. David attempted to keep up with him. Being less familiar with the terrain, he lost a little ground.

Commander Silas Asher was getting anxious wondering why the Captain was taking so long getting to the mine. Hearing the sounds of running and pebbles scattering he looked up the side of the hill. He saw Captain Weiseman and another officer coming at nearly a dead run. It wasn't one of the *Emissary* crew members. Silas remembered the Captain's question about the Security Chief. It took only one more moment for Commander Asher to realize the man pursuing his Captain was none other than the traitorous fugitive Captain David Alexander of the *Evangeline*. Commander Asher drew his weapon and took off toward his Captain.

Captain Weiseman lost his footing and slid the last few feet down the embankment sending dust and gravel flying as he hit the ground. Commander Asher raced past his Captain. In a flash he had his feet planted, his weapon pointed at David and used his body as a shield to guard his fleeing Captain.

Captain Alexander realized his predicament and hastily put on his brakes sending another shower of dirt and gravel flying. Going back up the hill was not a viable option. The Commander's Tri-EMP would peg him in the back before he could get two steps away. David stood still yet poised to launch himself at the Commander if he decided it was necessary. His eyes darted back and forth between the Commander and Captain Weiseman. David's eyes finally landed on Captain Weiseman.

"Nate?"

Nate rolled to his feet. "Commander stand down!"

"But sir, he's..."

"I know who and what he is. He wants to help. Put your weapon down, Commander." Captain Weiseman ordered firmly.

A conspicuous red dot materialized on Commander Asher's right side. Neither Silas nor the rest of the *Emissary's* crew had seen the dot as yet. The two Captains saw it.

David remained still except for a brief glance to the direction the laser sight appeared to be coming from. "Everyone just needs to stand down and remain calm." His sentence was specifically aimed at his own security chief.

Captain Weiseman took one casual step forward which put the laser sight on his own back. Neither Captain wanted to give the Commander any additional reasons to doubt David's sincerity.

David continued trying to placate the nervous commander. "Commander Asher, I'm not here to take control of anyone's mind. I came to bring your Captain a message. As soon as I heard about the mine accident, I offered to bring my crew in to help. I'll go in peace as soon as your crew and those miners are safe."

Commander Asher knew David from the command portion of the training program. They didn't know each other very well, but they had gotten along well enough. Silas lowered his weapon and moved back. Weapon still in hand, he moved away from both men. "Captain, have you been compromised?"

Captain Weiseman was losing patience. "Commander, we are wasting precious time. I am a loyal Commonwealth soldier. Put your weapon away. We have work to do. People need our help, and Captain Alexander has given me his word he and his crew will behave themselves. My wife and I have known Captain Alexander for fifteen years. His word is good. We can take this up again once everyone is safe."

Commander Asher, the rest of the crew, and a handful of the locals stood there trying to make sense of the situation. Silas kept a firm grip on his weapon, unsure of who to trust. Nate looked helplessly at his Commander. "Silas, please, the crew's lives are at stake, but not from him."

Silas holstered his weapon. The look on his face didn't reflect his change of heart.

Nate glanced at David. "Would you like to invite your security chief to join us?"

David glanced up the hill. "Chief, care to join us or do you have more plans of your own?" The chief had disobeyed orders again. David wanted to be certain the chief knew he wasn't happy.

"On my way, sir. Do you want me to alert the crew?"

"Yes, have them bring the ship in but keep it at least one mile out. I don't want it rattling that mine when it lands. I need Braxton, Jason, and Laura to bring the Surf-ve out as soon as possible. Have the others on standby."

Several tents were scattered along the sides of the road in front of the mine entrance. A local from the nearby city talked to Captain Weiseman and the others while pointing at a map of the mine. They conducted the conversation in the local language. David scowled. "Care to translate, Nate?"

"Sorry, we've gotten so used to these nanites translating in our brains, I forget we don't actually know how to speak the language. This is Ensign Genevieve Griffin, our linguistics person. She can get the language files uploaded to your nanites."

David sheepishly explained. "We haven't started using the nanites. Admiral Deacons brought them to us after we—uh changed our loyalties. I was concerned they would present a security issue. I'm afraid my people will need to use the translators in our comm units."

Nate gave David an annoyed stare. "Fine, Gennie, transfer the files to Captain Alexander's comm unit. Commander Asher, how many people are in the mine and do we have any idea where they are? Have you been able to contact any of them?"

"There are five crew members in the mine. I can only locate four of them by their comm units. I'm still trying to get a head count on the locals. There are typically anywhere between ten and thirty people in there at any given time. I hailed all five crewmen, no one has answered as yet."

"This is Jo-Na-fandrassin. We've been calling him Jo-Na. He's the foreman for this job site. He thinks there are fifteen to twenty of his people in there."

Silas leaned over the map in front of them and spoke to Jo-Na while Ensign Griffin plugged a data crystal into the port on David's bracelet. A brief thought ran through David's mind. What if the ensign were giving him more than language files? He shook off the thought. If she were, he'd deal with it later. There were more important things to deal with now.

Jake trotted up, his laser rifle slung over his shoulder, and joined the group as Silas explained the layout of the mine. Several stern and resentful looks greeted him. David briefly introduced the newcomer to the others, "My security chief, Chief Petty Officer (CPO) Jake Holden."

The group muttered or nodded some semblance of a greeting then turned their attention back to Jo-Na and Silas. David's language files updated, and Jo-Na's voice came through David's ear piece translated into Intergalactic Standard (I.S.). David handed off the language data crystal to Jake who looked at it skeptically then plugged it into his own data port. Jake's translation program updated in time for him to catch part of Jo-Na's explanation.

"There are three main tunnels into the mine. The tunnels were originally natural formations. As we discovered the black rocks, we made the tunnels larger to get the deposits. I warned the King and his advisers we should not try to move so quickly. Their greed has proven deadly. There is something else you should all know. The King's son is here. He is somewhere in the mine. If we don't get him out alive and well, all our lives could be forfeit."

Commander Asher and the two Captains exchanged looks of concern. Commander Asher looked to Captain Weiseman, "So what's our plan of action, sir?"

Nate stared at the map in front of him. Several thoughts ran through his mind, although none were complete. He glanced at Gennie and Silas whose spouses were also trapped in the mine. Nate realized none of them could operate at maximum efficiency. Gennie's eyes pleaded for him to say—something—anything. Nate knew the only thing he could say wouldn't be popular.

David's eyes read Nate's. Trying to take the load off his friend, David suggested, "My architectural engineer is in route. Perhaps we should get some scans ready for him when he arrives. Who's your architectural engineer?"

Silas gave a sullen response, "Elize Davu, she's inside, along with my wife, our chief engineer."

Nate decided it was time to make some proper introductions so David would know what resources he had. He hadn't officially turned the operation over to him, but it was inevitable considering the circumstances. "Captain Alexander this is Ensign Maya Evans, my helmsman, Lieutenant Luna Oliver, my Comms Officer, Dr. Henry Oliver, ship's psychologist, CPO Noah Evans, medical support, and you know the others."

Nate took David's guidance and started making assignments. "Henry, Maya, get as close as you safely can and take scans of the debris, life signs, and tunnels. Luna, you and Noah try again to get through to our people. See what you can find out about physical injuries and the condition of the locals."

Nate stopped at that point. He knew there was more to be said, more to be done, but he didn't know the next step. He couldn't think of anything but his missing wife and crewmen.

David knew his struggle. Until Nate handed him the operation, he didn't want to appear to usurp the man's authority. "Jo-Na, we're probably going to need to bring in some support beams, ropes, equipment for hauling away debris. We'll also need people to haul equipment and supplies in, and debris out. What do you have access to?"

"I've sent a messenger into town to ask for help. I don't have nearly enough supplies for what you will need. There is a forest to the north where we have been bringing lumber in, but it will take far too long to get more from there."

David turned his focus back to Nate. "My shuttle can use its lasers to down trees and haul them in. We can use hand held lasers to cut them down to size. Nate, since you're short on people, my navigator could use your shuttle to help with that task, if that's okay with you."

Silas wasn't eager to let David's people anywhere near their ship. "Let me send Lt. Commander Oliver to do that," Silas urged. He could see his Captain losing control of the situation. "Your navigator can help in the mine."

David frowned. He knew Commander Asher felt threatened. "I'm sorry, Commander, my navigator can't do that. I'll put her in our shuttle and my pilot on the ground."

Nate and Silas gave David a questioning look. Nate decided he needed to know the stakes on David's side. "You sound like there's a problem. I need to know what's going on."

David looked away for a moment. "My... uh... navigator is six months pregnant."

Captain Weiseman straightened from leaning over the table. "Pregnant? How is that possible?" Captain Weiseman knew every woman on all twelve ships had been temporarily sterilized.

David glanced at Jake. "It's a long story. After this is over, I'll tell you about it. She's fine and healthy; I'm just not about to put her into that type of situation."

Nate stared at David for another moment. "Alright, I assume she's checked out on weapons?"

David nodded, "Absolutely."

"She and my helmsman can handle my shuttle. I'll let them hash out who wants to fly and who wants to shoot. Commander, take the Surf-ve back to the ship and drop Maya off. She can rendezvous with your people at the forest. I'd prefer your people stay off my ship. I'll let her on the shuttle, but that's it." Nate's voice had a tone of finality.

David nodded again. "Yes, Captain." He felt a twinge of pain in his spirit at his friend's lack of trust. He consoled himself with the thought that if their situations were reversed, David probably would've done the same.

The approaching Surf-ve from the *Evangeline* interrupted the awkward silence. "Is it okay with you if my Commander oversees the lumber harvest?"

Nate nodded despite Commander Asher's scowl.

David touched his comm unit to address his own people. "Commander Alexander, come in."

Brynna's voice was quick to respond, "This is Commander Alexander, go ahead."

"Commander, I'm assigning Lt. Holden to work with Ensign Maya Evans aboard the *Emissary's* shuttle. There's a forest to the north. We need lumber cut and hauled down here as fast as you can. Use whoever you need up there and send everyone else down here to the mine entrance. I'm sending you the linguistics files for the local population, get Ensign Dominick to distribute the file to the rest of the crew. The crew will need lasers in addition to standard arms." Not wanting to feed their fear, David kept his orders as close to standard CIF orders as possible. He knew they would be unnerved enough knowing David's crew was armed. They shouldn't be too concerned when he put the order into the perspective of a standard operating procedure.

David had put Brynna on an open speaker instead of through his ear piece to keep everything open and honest. Brynna took her cues from her Captain. "Yes Captain. Anything else?"

"One thing, our goal is to rescue people from this mine. Keep the sensors watching the skies for CIF ships and inform the crew, we aren't here to recruit for Pateras. I gave Nate my word."

"So, I shouldn't ask Arni for help?" Brynna asked carefully.

"That's a personal matter, Commander. Get moving, we've got lives at stake including Stephanie's." David closed the comm line and turned his attention to the crew members approaching them.

Nate called his people back who had been scanning the area. Before he could ask what they found, the *Emissary's* communications officer interrupted, "Captain, I've got Deka on comms!" Luna put him on speaker as well.

Nate bellowed, "Deka, report! What's your status?"

Deka coughed, and his voice was gravelly. "Captain, Elize and I are fine. We have only minor injuries. There are three other miners trapped with us." Deka coughed again. "We are in the upper chamber of the middle tunnel. Captain... my scanners show we're getting no air circulation. Do you know about the status of the others?"

"No, Deka, I don't. You're the first one I've heard from."

Noah Evans jumped in before the Captain could say anything more. "Deka, you and the others need to lie down and sleep if you can. You need to conserve your oxygen until we can get to you. The more you move around or talk, the more air you'll use up."

Deka responded calmly, but concisely. "Understood."

Nate added one more thing, "Stay strong, lieutenant. We've got help. We'll get to you. Captain, out." He cut the communication off quickly so Deka wouldn't waste energy and air asking questions, especially questions he didn't want to answer.

Luna tried the other crew members again. Claire Asher answered this time. The first sound coming from her comm unit was a moan. Hearing his wife's voice, Silas verbally pounced, "Claire! Claire! Lt. Commander Asher report! Claire, can you hear me? Claire, respond!"

"Please... stop yelling... my head... hurts." Claire mumbled.

Silas started to go at her again. Nate held his hand up to stop him. "Lt. Commander, I need a status report. What is your physical condition, your location, and who's with you?"

"I—I can't see anything... The lantern on my bracelet seems to be broken. Ahh! Oww! My ankle hurts... badly. I—I think it's broken,"

A voice in the background came through the translator. "Commander Claire, Commander Claire, light your lantern again."

They heard Claire tell her companion, her lantern was broken. Her companion could be heard again in the background begging her to turn her lantern on.

Jason had joined the group and was standing at David's elbow. He motioned for Luna to mute the sound on the comm unit. Her distrust of the *Evangeline* crew had momentarily left her, and she did as he instructed.

"Captain, if she took a blow to the head, she may have pressure on the occipital lobe of her brain. She may not be able to see. It's probably temporary and definitely repairable. If we can get her to turn her light on again and talk to her companion, he can tell us whatever she can't."

David nodded then motioned to Silas. "Doc, this is Commander Silas Asher, Claire's husband."

Jason realized he should have been slightly more sensitive in his approach. Jason took advantage of the situation. "Commander Asher, you know your wife better than the rest of us. How's she going to handle this and who should be the one to tell her? Would she handle it better coming from a medical professional, her Captain or you?"

Silas, for once, looked like a lost puppy. "Captain, I—I don't know."

Nate leaned forward across the table. Nodding at Luna, he ordered, "Put her back on."

"Captain... are you still there?"

"Claire... I'm sorry we had to put you on hold for a moment. We think there's another minor problem, but the medical professionals on this end say it's an easy fix once we get you out of there."

"What is it, sir?"

"Who's there beside you asking you to turn your lantern on?"

"I think it's Da-Batto. Da-Batto is that you?"

The group again heard the voice. "Yes, Commander Claire."

Nate spoke their native language into the comm unit. "Da-Batto, can you hear me?"

"Yes, Captain Weiseman, I can hear you."

"Da-Batto, I need you to do something for me in just a minute. Are you hurt?" The Captain's question almost came as an afterthought.

"No Captain Weiseman, I have some scrapes and bruises, but I am not hurt much. What do you need me to do?"

"Give me just a minute, Da-Batto. Claire, try to switch your lantern on one more time."

The group waited, breathlessly listening as Claire fumbled with the control on her bracelet. "Captain, it's still not working."

"Da-Batto, can you see Commander Claire's lantern?"

"Yes, Captain Weiseman. She thought it was broken. It is working again."

Captain Weiseman proceeded cautiously. "Claire, you can't see the light, can you?"

The group heard her breathe faster and a faint crack in her voice as she spoke. "N—No, I can't see it."

"It's going to be okay, Claire. The Doc says this is temporary. Take it easy, okay. We'll get you out of there and get your eyesight fixed." Silas jumped in to encourage his wife.

"The doc? She was in here with us. Why are you lying to me, Silas?"

Silas realized his mistake but wasn't sure how to deal with it. Nate was in no better shape. Jason jumped in, attempting to dig the two out of the hole they found themselves in. "Lt. Commander Asher, my name is Dr. Jason Adams. Our ship was bringing a very important personal message to your Captain when the mine collapsed. I can assure you, what your husband said is completely accurate. I can get your eyesight patched up as soon as we get you out of there."

Nate jumped in as soon as Jason stopped talking. "Claire, visual problems aside, I need to know where you are, what sort of injuries to be prepared for and how many civilians are with you. Most of all, where is Prince Ca-Litana? Is he near your location? Is he alive? Lt. Commander, you have work to do. Get me some information. If Da-Batto is well enough, get him to survey the area, get those head-counts and the status of everyone you have access to."

Claire sounded stronger and more accepting of her situation. "Yes sir, I'll get on it. Lt. Commander Asher, out." Claire gave Da-Batto his assignment, her bracelet, and waited for his report.

While they waited on Claire's report, Braxton reviewed the scans of the mine. The scans revealed the main tunnel and the two secondary tunnels had collapsed into one immense wall of debris. Braxton used the holographic data module to project the mine layout. As he studied and discussed the damage and barricades, Jason quietly added a life signs overlay on the projection. He stared at the display for a moment then tapped Noah on the arm. Noah saw Jason grab his med kit. Noah raced after Jason toward the mine entrance. The group looked at the two men quizzically.

David yelled, "Lt. Commander Adams, get back here!"

Braxton looked down at the display then up at David. "There's a survivor just inside the mine entrance. He's about twenty feet inside."

David was sorely tempted to chase after the two men and yank them back out himself.

Nate was equally angry with his own medic. He angrily looked at both crews and the mine foreman. "NOBODY goes into that mine until Lt. Commander Flint says it's SAFE! ARE WE CLEAR?!"

It pained Nate to say such a thing knowing his own wife was trapped in the mine along with several of his crew. His own personal desire was to throw every rock out of that cavern one at a time until the path was clear.

David backed Nate up. "That goes for my crew as well!"

Both crews soberly acknowledged their orders. David tapped his comm unit. "Lt. Commander Adams, report!"

The seven seconds it took for Jason to respond felt like an eternity. "This is Lt. Commander Adams, go ahead, Captain." The sound of his voice echoing from the cavern came through the comm unit.

"Get your backside out of there right now, mister or so help me…"

"Captain, we've got an injured man. We're bringing him out."

Thirty seconds later the two men emerged carrying a third man on their stretcher. Jo-Na, Nate, and David met the men near the entrance. Jo-Na looked eagerly at the man on the stretcher. He was clearly disappointed when he saw the man's face. He glanced at Nate. "This is the Prince's bodyguard. Is he alive?"

Jason and Noah were busy working on their patient. Jason wasn't too engrossed in his task to prevent him from answering the question. "He's alive. He has a concussion, multiple bruises, and contusions. Nothing appears to be broken. He should be able to talk to us in an hour or two. I need to get him back to the ship though."

David nodded, "Put him in the Surf-ve and run your patients through our ship. Nate, if it's okay with you, Chief Evans can triage here. I'll get one of my people to ferry patients back and forth as needed."

Nate gave his curt approval. The Captain was nearing a point of sensory overload.

Jo-Na shook his head. "Your healer shouldn't bother. If the prince is dead, he will be executed for failing to protect him. The King will take his anger out on us all if his son dies in that mine."

Nate grabbed the sullen foreman by the front of his tunic. "So, what do you propose we do? Run away and leave everyone to die? Is that what you want to do? What's stopping you? I'm not stopping you. Run away!" Nate released the man and shoved him away.

Jo-Na fell to the ground when Nate released him. He bolted up angrily. In a flash, he was back in Nate's face. "I take my responsibilities as seriously as you take yours! Those are my friends in there! Those men are my responsibility. This is my fault, and I will answer for my actions! Don't take me for a coward! I will stay here until every person in that mine is accounted for, dead or alive. I will face the King's wrath bravely. My anger and sorrow is in seeing good men die for nothing."

David and Jake stood ready to jump between the two men. Nate realized he had misunderstood the foreman's comments. He also realized they were wasting precious time. "David... I'm not in any shape to handle this operation. Please take over. Tell me what you want my people to do."

Those still present moved back to the image of the mine to hear Braxton's recommendations. In a few minutes, a strategy was in place. Jo-Na sent two men into town to commandeer as many wagons, buckets, wheelbarrows and volunteers as possible. As they finished briefing those present, the shuttles arrived with the first trees. Brynna dropped Cheyenne off along with more laser rifles to carve the trees into usable pieces of lumbar. Inside of an hour, the place became a hive of activity. Men, women, and children from the town poured out in droves to help with the rescue operation. Nate's crew helped Cheyenne work on the trees. David and Nate started toward the flurry of activity to do their part when Nate's security officer hailed him.

"Captain... Captain, it's Milo..."

Nate stopped in his tracks. David stopped with him. "What is it?"

Nate put the call on speaker. "Milo? What's your status? Why are you using Stephanie's comm unit?" Nate had one more question, but he couldn't bring himself to ask it.

"My comm unit... is busted. Da-Batto just found us. I was... unconscious. I'm here... beside Stephanie. She's alive, but she's unconscious. She's trapped under... under a pretty big pile of rubble. This doesn't look good, sir. I'm sorry. Her bracelet seems to function though. What... What are your orders, sir?"

Nate looked at David. David asked. "Do they have a fresh air supply?"

"Milo, Claire is in the same tunnel with you. She's injured and can't see. Do you have a scanner? Are you getting fresh air from anywhere?"

"Just a second."

The two heard scuffling noises. "No sir, I don't think so."

Nate's face looked pained. David muted Nate's comm unit before answering. "Have him treat whatever injuries he can, then get him to move everyone toward the center of the mountain, so they don't get hit with any debris when we try to punch through the outside wall. Tell them to sit tight and wait to be rescued. They have to conserve their air."

Nate passed the message along. Milo was quick to argue against leaving Stephanie alone. Nate made the tough call. "Milo, leave Da-Batto with her and see who else needs your help. Once you get everyone squared away, you can return to her side. That's an order, Chief!"

As Nate closed the comm line, he looked as though he was somewhere between crying and vomiting. David pitied his friend. Potentially sacrificing his wife was David's biggest fear about command. David tapped his friend on the arm. "Let's get her out of there."

David left Braxton in charge of the project as the only qualified structural engineer present. It seemed to help alleviate the stress among Nate's crew. They were clearly concerned about having their own Captain following the orders of a known traitor. Although Braxton was also considered a known traitor, he wasn't a captain, and his own commanding officer was sweating in the trenches with the other crew members. It allowed Nate's crew to work without fearing David's crew.

It only took a few minutes to get more trees than they needed to provide braces to put in the mine passageways. Braxton wanted to use the lasers on the shuttles to carve through the side of the mountain in two places, to get into two of the occupied caverns. The shuttles were too big to set down close enough to the mine. It forced him to use the two Surf-ves for the lower cavern.

The two surface vehicles positioned themselves at the coordinates Braxton provided. They burned rectangular and crisscross pattern into the side of the mountain stopping periodically to allow the volunteers to haul away the debris.

Thane and Jake took the shuttle to carve a hole into the upper cavern. This cavern was closer to the surface but was fraught with other dangers. The shuttle had to be held steady while Jake carefully guided the lasers.

Braxton positioned himself in the shuttle to watch the scanners closely. He wanted to have the best vantage point to detect problems before they happened.

Jason hailed the Captain. "Captain Alexander, my patient is awake. He says two people are trapped in a tunnel off to the left. He keeps asking about Prince Ca-Litana. The man is getting agitated."

David stopped working to concentrate on Jason's message. Jo-Na walked past him hauling away unneeded tree limbs. David stopped him. "Jo-Na, would the Prince's bodyguard harm himself if he thought the prince was dead?"

Jo-Na dropped his load and straightened up to rest his back a moment as he pondered David's question. "It's possible. If he fears the type of death the King may plan for him. The King is capable of creating deaths which are… most distressful."

David nodded his understanding. "Doc consider your patient to be potentially suicidal. If he thinks he failed his master, he may try to take his own life. Take whatever precautions you deem necessary to keep him alive. I'll pass that information about the men in the other tunnel to Lt. Commander Flint. Keep me posted on any other information that comes to light."

Braxton did a secondary scan of the indicated area based on the new information. "Captain, I have confirmed the two life signs in the cavern, but there seems to be some interference from the metallic substances in the mine. We need to scan every area closely and use multiple search parameters to be sure we don't miss anything."

"Acknowledged, Commander. If you think we're clear to get inside that main tunnel, I'll run additional scans and upload them to the shuttle and data module as we progress through the debris." The Captain responded.

Braxton cleared the Captain to excavate the debris in the main tunnel.

David organized the volunteers to haul debris and place the newly formed cross-braces. The group moved toward the mine opening to get started when Braxton frantically hailed all hands. The *Emissary's* comms were linked with the *Evangeline's*.

"All hands stand down! Move away from the mine. Shut down all lasers immediately!"

The ground began to rumble and shake. The men on the ground took off running away from the mine. The two surface vehicles stopped their lasers and backed their vehicles away cautiously. Rocks and dirt rolled and slid, a large boulder broke off and tumbled down the mountain narrowly missing one of the Surf-ves.

Braxton hadn't had time to separate his comm channels. The message had gone to all personnel, including those trapped inside the mine. Hearing the broad warning, those inside steeled themselves for whatever was about to happen. Inside the caverns, the ground shook. More rock and debris rained on those inside the tunnels.

Claire did what she could to curl up in a ball to protect herself. With her lack of vision and her broken ankle, she could do little else. Fear was quickly overtaking her. Even after the ground stopped moving and rocks stopped falling, Claire continued to shake and shiver. Tears formed in her eyes. Just before she reached the point of total panic, a hand touched her shoulder. "Claire, are you okay?"

"Milo? Is that you?"

Milo lifted her head. "The Captain sent me to check on you. Where are you hurt?"

Claire sniffed and wiped the tears from her face. "I've got a large knot on the back of my head. I think my ankle's broken and—um—I can't see anything. Other than a giant hole in my pride, that's about it."

Milo smiled weakly. He was attempting to cheer her up a little until he realized she couldn't see his attempt. He ran a scanner over her then offered a verbal reassurance. "According to the scanner, you're going to live. The one thing I don't think we can treat is the hole in your pride, I think you're stuck with that one."

Claire sniffed again and smiled back at him. "Understood, Chief. What do you suppose happened outside?"

"I'm guessing they were trying to reach us and had another rock slide or cave-in. Whose voice was that?" Milo hadn't been briefed on the presence of additional CIF personnel.

"Someone from the Commonwealth came to bring the Captain a message. They have a doctor with them. Maybe, it was their captain. Have you found the Doc? Wasn't she with you?"

Milo got quiet for a moment, not sure how much he should tell her. He decided it was better for Claire if she had something other than herself to worry about. "The doc is in the shaft. She's pinned under the debris and can't move right now. I won't lie to you, Claire. She's in bad shape. We have to get her out of here as soon as possible."

"Then let me help, Milo. I may not be able to walk or see, but I can help move smaller rocks." Claire tried to stand.

Milo held her in place. "Claire, we can't. We have to conserve our oxygen. I need to check on the miners. Stay put and try to get some rest."

Claire reached out and grabbed Milo's arm. "Chief they're also trying to locate Prince Ca-Litana. Tell the captain the minute you find him."

Chief Milo Griffin gave his superior a firm, "Yes ma'am."

Milo moved over to a couple miners to check on them. He kept a careful eye on his shipmate to be sure she wasn't going to fall apart without him. Claire appeared to be holding her own at this point. The other miners had non-life-threatening injuries similar to Claire's. Most were just afraid. Before Milo headed back to the Captain's wife, he let Claire know he was leaving the area, but he would check on her again in a little while.

Milo returned to find Stephanie regaining consciousness. She tried to speak but found the dust in her throat too thick to overcome. Milo gave her one small sip of water to clear her throat. Stephanie coughed then spoke in a coarse tone. "Judging by the look on your face, it's bad isn't it?"

Milo knew better than to lie to her. He pulled up the results of her scan and showed them to her.

Stephanie stared at them for a moment. She swallowed hard before trying to speak again. She looked at Milo. "Have a portable stasis field on standby. You'll have to put me in, the second I'm free from the rubble. I'll need to go to an advanced life support facility. It's the only way I'll survive. Do you understand me, Milo? Tell Noah to do exactly as I said."

Milo nodded. "Yes, ma'am. Do you need anything for pain? Do you want to talk to the Captain?"

Stephanie's answer was barely audible, "No, to both questions."

Milo was confused. "I don't understand."

"The captain has enough on his mind right now. I don't want to make things harder for him."

Milo swallowed hard. "I understand that. I don't understand why you don't need something for pain."

Stephanie pushed herself to remain cold and clinical. "The nerves are damaged. The only thing I can feel is being cold and a couple bruises on my upper body."

Milo quickly pulled off his over-shirt and laid it across her. Stephanie tried to push it away. "No Chief, you need to keep it. You're taking care of everyone in here. You need to keep yourself in top shape. Your over-shirt isn't going to keep me alive."

Milo refused to take it back. When she tried to order him to take it, he politely told her she was in no shape to be giving orders.

As soon as the landslide settled down,

Braxton took another scan of the area then hastily yanked on a harness and lowered himself from the shuttle to the ground.

Nate, David, and Jo-Na were back under the tent surveying the damage and updating their plans. Braxton joined the three to add the newest scans to the data module.

Deka hailed his captain. "Captain, we've had another cave-in! What's going on?"

Nate looked helplessly at David when he heard Lt. Davu's call. David calmly answered. "Find out if his situation has changed. If it hasn't, tell him to stand-down, and wait for orders."

Nate followed David's instructions feeling more helpless every moment.

David turned his attention back to Braxton and Jo-Na. Braxton decided trying to punch a hole through the upper side of the mountain was a bad idea. The area was proving too unstable. He didn't want to abandon the people in the upper cavern, but at the moment, he wasn't sure how to get them out without risking the ones in the lower caverns. After studying his scans for another minute, he told the Captain to resume removing debris from the main tunnel of the mine. He authorized the surf-ves to resume their tunneling although he cut their speed and cutting depth in half.

Captain Weiseman surveyed Lt. Commander Flint's change in strategy. "What about my people up top? How are you going to get them out?"

Braxton glanced up from his equipment briefly. "I don't know yet. I have some ideas, but I would feel better if we got the people out of the lower cavern before we try drilling through again. If we aren't careful, the mountain will fall in on all of them. I'm going to go up the side of the mountain and see if I can at least punch a small hole in the cavern, so they at least can get some air. That should buy them more time."

Nate grew angry and impatient. "You have some ideas? Should buy them more time? Exactly what is that supposed to mean?" Nate grabbed Braxton's jacket and jerked the Lt. Commander forward. David started to step in, but Braxton waved him off.

"Captain Weiseman, I'm doing everything possible to save your people—all of them. If we move too fast, it could get them killed and some of our people too. When I said it could buy them more time, I meant they can go several days without food or water. They won't last three more hours without air. If you don't mind, I need to get back to work. We're wasting precious time."

Nate released the Lt. Commander.

David pulled his friend away to return to the mine entrance. As they walked away, David looked over his shoulder at Braxton. "Be careful, Commander." David and Nate went back to work.

Braxton called for the shuttle to hoist him up the side of the mountain. Taking one of the laser rifles, he scanned the area and found one small, weak spot. He pulled on a set of goggles and lowered himself from the shuttle just short of the ground. He adjusted his harness to keep himself in a horizontal position. Using the targeting system in his goggles and the sight on the rifle he took careful aim into a crevice. The rocks popped and hissed as the laser burned through them. As his instruments detected his target depth was close to being penetrated, Braxton stopped firing and hailed Elize and Deka.

"Lt. Commander Davu, Lt. Davu, this is Lt. Commander Flint. I am about to breach the ceiling of your cavern. I need you to stay clear in case more debris falls. Do you copy?"

Deka looked at Elize. "Who's Lt. Commander Flint?"

Elize's brow furrowed for a moment. "Braxton? Is that you?"

Now Deka looked more concerned. "Who's Braxton, and why do you know him?"

Elize shook her head at him.

Braxton acknowledged her question. "Yes Elize, it's me. Use your scanners to find the safest spot away from my laser. I'm trying to at least get you an air hole. It's going to be awhile longer before I can get you out of there."

"Will do, Commander. Thanks for the help."

Elize scanned the area and moved everyone in the cavern away from the target. Once they were settled again, Deka pursued his line of questions again. "Elize, who is this man and how do you know him?"

Elize scowled at her jealous husband. "He's an engineer I met during training. How many female navigators did you meet during your training?"

The two continued some pointless banter until a small section of their ceiling crumbled and gave way. A small ray of light pierced the darkness. It was enough to lighten the mood tenfold. The amount of light coming in was smaller than the actual crevasse. The staleness they were breathing moments ago began to dissipate. The group's energy levels had waned quickly after the tunnel collapsed. Even though their energy was returning, there was still nowhere to go and nothing to do. For lack of anything better, Elize stood and walked over to the narrow beam of light. She stuck out her hand as if to catch the light. She took a deep breath and filled her lungs with the fresh air. It was the most exhilarating thing she had experienced in a long time.

Touching her comm unit, she hailed Braxton, using his rank to avoid irritating her husband any further. "Lt. Commander Flint, we have air. No additional injuries or cave-ins to report. Thanks, Commander."

Feeling slightly warmer with Milo's jacket on, Stephanie let herself fall asleep. She suddenly couldn't remember if it was better to stay awake or get some rest. The grave readings on the scanner suggested if they didn't get rescued soon, her choice wouldn't matter. Staying awake was hard work. Sleep won out. Milo did a quick scan when she nodded off to make sure nothing had changed. Her condition was stable. He picked up the med kit sitting beside them. There was very little in it to help her situation. He was trained to administer pain killers, neural inhibitors, blood volumizers, stimulants, and sedatives. His concern was using what little they had, too soon and running out before they could be rescued. He decided it was time to hail Noah.

"Da-Batto, I'm going to go check on the others. Keep an eye on the doc for me. Just push this button on the bracelet to call me to come back if you need to." Da-Batto still carried Claire's bracelet. He seemed quite content to stay near the doc and what should be the way out of the tunnel no matter how much debris stood between him and his escape. Da-Batto eagerly accepted his mission, especially if it meant staying put.

Milo headed back down the tunnel. His goal was to talk to Noah out of Stephanie's range of hearing. He would check on the others just as a precaution, but it wasn't his primary goal. Just before he rounded the last bend taking him into the wider cavern where the others waited, Milo hailed Noah. "Chief Griffin to Chief Evans, come in, please."

Noah was hauling away debris with the others as he waited for the patients trapped inside to be freed. When he heard his comm unit, he stopped and moved out of the way. "This is Chief Evans, go ahead."

Milo's voice came through softly. "Chief, the doc wanted me to tell you, you need to have a stasis field on standby. She said she'll need to go into it the second she's freed from the debris. Noah, this is assuming she makes it that long. This doesn't look good. When we pull these rocks off her, she's going to bleed out, into her gut. Claire said you have another doc out there?"

"Yes, it's Dr. Jason Adams from the *Evangeline*."

Milo started when he heard the name of the ship. "The *Evangeline*? Why are they here?"

Noah stepped a little further away from the traffic. "They said they came to bring some message to the Captain. I don't know what message, but they seem normal to me. Just so you know, their comms are tied into ours so you might want to keep that in mind."

Milo scowled. "I see."

Noah could tell his shipmate was not handling the news well. "The captain vouched for them. They're supposed to leave as soon as we rescue the miners. They've promised to behave themselves."

Milo tried to silence his inner alarm bells. "If I send the files to you, can you send the scans of Commander Weiseman to their doc to get his opinion?"

"Sure, push them through."

Milo sent the files and closed the comm link. He made the rounds and checked on the trapped miners and his other crew member. He thought about moving Claire back into the passageway with the doc, but decided it was safer further from the cave-in site.

Noah forwarded the information to Jason who concurred with Dr. Weiseman's assessment of her own status and plan of care. Jason gave strict orders not to extricate her from the rubble without his presence. He contacted Milo directly to give him guidance when to use the few medications at his disposal. He reiterated the orders not to dig her out without him. Milo gave a subdued acknowledgment of his orders then returned to Stephanie's side to check on her.

Claire sat there trying to get comfortable. Her ankle was swelling inside her boot and throbbing mercilessly. She thought about asking Milo to give her something to ease her discomfort. She decided Stephanie might need it worse than she did. The darkness closed in on her both physically and emotionally. The air was getting thick and stale. She knew the doc on the outside had assured her, he could repair her eyesight—but what if he was wrong? What if they didn't live long enough in the cavern to get treated? What if the men trapped in the cavern with her decided to take advantage of her blindness? Without her bracelet, she could no longer hail the security chief. If they survived and were rescued, how would she live without her sight? Engineers depended a great deal on their eyes. What about Stephanie? Was she going to live even if the others survived? Claire scolded herself for being selfish in her thoughts. She was not hurt that badly, but the doc was probably dying.

Tears slipped quietly down her face. A voice whispered to her. "Lt. Commander Asher?"

She quickly wiped away her tears. "Yes? Who's there? I can't see. Did you come from the other ship? Did they get the tunnel cleared?"

"Whoa, slow down. That's a lot of questions to answer at one time. No, the tunnel hasn't been cleared yet. Yes, I arrived on the other ship."

Claire didn't give him time to answer the rest of her questions before launching more at the strange voice coming from a few feet above her. "If you came on the other ship, how did you get in here? What are you doing here? Who are you?"

The kind voice responded. "Is it alright if I sit here with you?"

Claire tried to shift again to give the stranger room beside her. "Ow, my ankle... I'm sorry. My ankle is broken, it's swelling, and I can't get it to stop throbbing."

The stranger knelt beside her. She could hear some rustling. He lifted her arm gently and placed a folded piece of clothing in her hand. "Why don't you lie down and use this for a pillow? I'm going to elevate your feet to help relieve the swelling."

Claire was slightly unnerved at being left alone in a cavern full of men who were now contemplating their own demise. She continued to worry that they might try to take advantage of her. The man with her now spoke in clear Intergalactic Standard, so he must be a Commonwealth soldier even though he hadn't yet identified himself. Surely, she would be safe with him. She was still nervous about lying down.

"It's alright. I won't let anything happen to you, Lt. Commander." The man gently helped her get comfortable and lifted her injured leg gently onto his own lap.

Claire had to admit, his lap was more comfortable than the cold hard ground. When the man made no further moves toward her, she relaxed a little more. "My name is Claire. How did you get in here?"

"I was in here before the tunnel collapsed. Since we're on a first name basis, my name is Arni."

"Nice to meet you, Arni. Is it alright if we talk for a while? I really need a distraction about now."

"Sure, what would you like to talk about?"

The two talked softly and casually until fatigue won out and Claire nodded off.

TRUCE

MORE TROUBLE

"We're through!" Nate hollered.

A flurry of activity ensued. Noah dropped his load of rubble where it was and raced into the tunnel. Volunteers crowded around the tunnel entrance as they stopped their activities. The main tunnel into the mine was split into three separate shafts. The first one split off to the left into a small natural cavern. This shaft was close enough to the main entrance that it wasn't deeply buried.

The opening wasn't big enough to let anyone through yet. Noah got to the opening and yelled. "Who's in here? Are you hurt?"

The answer quickly came back. "There are only the two of us. We have only small cuts and bruises. We're fine—could use some water though."

Noah grabbed a canteen from his belt and passed it through the opening to the waiting occupants. He assured the two men they would have them out momentarily. He instructed the men to move to the back of their cavern until they could make a large enough hole to get them out.

Encouraged by the impending rescue of the first miners, the volunteers picked up their pace. Braxton and Jo-Na moved in and out of the shaft, making sure every effort was being made to keep the rescue workers safe.

Ten minutes later, the two rescued men walked out of the mine under their own power. A cheer of elation spread among the workers. Despite the cheers, David and Braxton looked at each other, knowing there were nineteen more still trapped. Fourteen of those were quickly running out of air.

Braxton shook his head knowing if the fourteen didn't get at least one small opening for air, they would be dead soon. "Captain, please... can't we ask Arni for help?"

David looked at Braxton guiltily. "I have been. I haven't seen or heard anything from him. We need to keep doing what we're doing until he tells us to do something different."

Despite hearing nothing from Arni, Braxton breathed a sigh of relief. "Thank goodness."

David frowned. "Thank goodness? I told you I haven't heard anything from him."

Braxton gave him a weak smile. "Yes, but you asked, so I know I'm not trying to do this on my own."

David's serious tone didn't change. "You know you don't have to wait for me. You can ask him for help on your own."

"You promised Capt. Weiseman we would behave ourselves. I wasn't really sure what that meant."

"I just meant we should focus on rescuing miners, not on convincing the crew of the *Emissary* to ally with Pateras." David stood upright and stretched some of the kinks out of his back. "I'm going to send those two back to the ship to get checked out. Can you spare one of the Surf-ves for a little while?"

Braxton nodded. "I'm going to change my strategy again. We need to get at least one small hole through that wall to get them some air. We can resume digging them out once we put a hole through that wall. The rock is denser and harder to punch through than I realized. It doesn't matter which vehicle you take."

David nodded and moved toward the pavilion where Nate, Jo-Na, and Noah had moved their rescued men. David told Nate his plan for the two men. Noah wanted to go with them long enough to retrieve the portable stasis generator. The three men climbed aboard one vehicle and headed down the road away from town to the landing site of the *Evangeline*. Braxton pulled the volunteers out of the first tunnel and advised them to rest until they were needed in the secondary tunnel.

David and Nate moved back to the tent where Braxton continued to study the scans of the ground and the drilling. Braxton ordered the remaining Surf-ve to fire a focused beam onto the weakest, thinnest point to get that one desperately needed air hole. This cavern was considerably larger than the other two and held a lot more air. The air would be consumed, but not for several more hours. The two vehicles together had drilled ten feet in. The cavern they were attempting to reach was carved out by a mountain spring to within eighteen feet of the surface before a previous cave-in forced the spring to reroute itself, leaving a large empty space.

The two vehicles had been firing lasers almost non-stop for several hours. With the one vehicle firing at the one spot, it didn't stop for breaks. Aulani was manning the vehicle. Since it was not moving and firing, only one person was needed for its operation. A warning flashed on the display in front of her. She was preoccupied with the depth displays and failed to notice the warning until it was too late. The laser shut down abruptly. The second it stopped, the three men looked up sharply. Braxton hit his comm unit. "Aulani, what's wrong? Why did you stop drilling?"

It took her a moment to realize what had happened. "Braxton, my laser overheated. It won't let me re-initialize it."

Braxton glanced around, looking for his own chief engineer, Lazaro. The silence had already gotten the man's attention. Lazaro was racing toward the vehicle. Braxton hastily moved toward it with him. Scans showed the oxygen in the lower cavern was reaching critical levels.

David slammed his fist on the table in front of him. "Arni! Please!" He stood there overwrought with fear and frustration for a moment until he heard the tiniest whisper. A wave of peace washed over him. He looked up, feeling a renewed hope, and breathed a sigh of relief. He offered a quick verbal, "Thank you." David slapped Nate's arm. "C'mon."

David raced toward the vehicle. He opened a rear side panel and pulled two laser rifles out. Nate was a mere half-step behind his friend. David handed one rifle to Nate then raced to the front of the vehicle. They focused their individual beams right where the Surf-ve had stopped.

Lazaro looked up to see the men blasting the rock wall. The men were standing quite close to the focal point. They had to keep their eyes on the precise spots of drilling to be effective in their efforts. The brightness of the laser and the bits of rock cracking and popping as they exploded away from the superheated surface threatened their vision. Lazaro frowned and glanced quickly at Aulani. "Get them some goggles!" He snapped.

Aulani jumped to do as he ordered. Knowing the urgency of the situation, she carefully placed the goggles on each of them so they didn't have to stop firing.

Brynna joined the group. Seeing the problem, she hailed the second Surf-ve. "Ensign Griffin, we need your Surf-ve back here as soon as possible. Get those wounded to the ship and get back here fast."

Ensign Griffin acknowledged her orders and picked up her speed. She and Noah wondered what had happened, but they knew they would find out soon enough.

Brynna looked up to see the local townspeople suddenly scampering away. She glanced the direction they were running away from. Several soldiers were escorting a caravan.

An order came from a high-ranking official traveling next to an ornate carriage. The soldiers pushed their horses to surround the area, corralling the fleeing civilians.

Brynna took the goggles off Nate's eyes and took the laser from him. "We've got company, and he looks important."

Aulani followed Brynna's example and took David's place.

David followed Nate's lead as they cautiously approached the carriage. Jo-Na swallowed hard and joined the two men. Nate spoke softly to David as they walked. "This is King De-Marion. Follow my lead. Don't look him in the eye. The man has a vile temper."

Jo-Na stepped as close as he dared to the carriage and knelt on one knee. Nate moved beside him, knelt, and lowered his head in subservience. David did as he was instructed. The town's people within sight of the King all knelt as well as the members of the *Emissary's* crew. The *Evangeline's* crew kept working.

The King stepped out of his carriage. His chief guards moved to flank him. The King paused a moment to survey the surrounding situation. His eyes landed on the two women who kept their backs to him and the two men working frantically on the laser. The King's anger flared. "Captain Weiseman, why do your people insult me and my kingdom by turning their backs and refusing to bow to me? I was told they had instructed you on proper etiquette."

Keeping his head down, Nate answered. "Forgive me King De-Marion, those are not my people. They have just arrived today, and due to the crisis in the mine, there has not been time to teach them. They are trying desperately to reach those trapped before it's too late. This man beside me is their leader. His name is Captain Alexander."

King De-Marion stepped in front of David. A snarl formed on his face. "If it were not for the concern for my son, I would punish you in front of your subordinates for their transgressions. Where is my son?"

Jo-Na spoke up. "Forgive me, your Highness. Prince Ca-Litana is trapped somewhere in the mine. That is the reason Captain Alexander's people continue to work. They are desperate to find him. Time is growing short. If we can't get a hole punched into the inner cavern, they will cease to breathe soon."

The King's face turned red with anger. He drew a dagger from his waistband and grabbed Jo-Na brutally by the hair. He pulled his head back, exposing his neck. The King swung the dagger menacingly, preparing to strike the foreman.

Before Nate could stop him, David was on his feet, ready to intervene. "King De-Marion, please wait! We need this man alive to help us find your son. He knows this mine better than anyone here." David was careful to keep his head bowed despite being on his feet.

Although King De-Marion ruled by fear and intimidation. He respected boldness. Still poised to slay the man in front of him, he held his position. "He is responsible for causing harm to my son."

David's communication with the man was taking what felt like a painfully long time since everything had to go through his comm unit to be translated. "If he is responsible for harm to your son, he can always be punished later. If he is dead and you find another is to blame, you can't unpunish him. Perhaps he is the only one who could save your son's life. Do you want to risk your son's life just to satisfy your desire to punish the guilty?"

The King slowly relaxed his grip on Jo-Na. "Very well, I give you back your life—for now. If you wish to keep it, find my son, unharmed."

Jo-Na had, as promised, faced the king and his own punishment bravely. His face had paled slightly, but he remained strong. "Your Highness, may we resume our duties? Perhaps you and your companions would care to wait under the first pavilion over there." Jo-Na pointed to the tent furthest from their work area.

"Very well. Return to your duties."

Jo-Na stood and backed away several steps before turning his back to the King. Nate and David followed Jo-Na's lead.

Before they could discuss this latest development, the second Surf-ve approached and came to a stop behind the king's guards who were blocking the road. Nate turned back toward the king. "King De-Marion, may our wagon be allowed to enter? We need it to continue our work."

The King looked at the wagon for a moment then nodded to his men to allow it to pass. Braxton pulled the first Surf-ve back to allow the second one to take its place. Lazaro continued working on the first one while Braxton took over working on the hole Brynna and Aulani were drilling. Just as Lazaro got the overheated laser working again, Braxton stopped firing.

Thinking the second laser had quit, Lazaro hailed Braxton, his frustration clear by his tone. "What happened? Don't tell me that one overheated!"

"No, Laz, we're almost through. I need to alert those inside to stand clear of the opening. Chief Griffin, come in please."

Milo was feeling the effects of the thinning oxygen. "Yes—this is—this is Chief Griffin. G-Go ahead."

"Chief, I'm sending you the coordinates of the spot we are drilling through into your cavern. Can you make sure everyone is clear of that location?"

Milo stood slowly. "Yeah... I'm going."

Braxton could hear him breathing fast and trying to take deep breaths. He started to urge him to move faster when he heard him pick up his pace. The man wasn't thinking clearly enough to shut off his borrowed comm unit. He heard Milo trying to rouse two of the miners. One miner was no longer conscious. Milo had little left in him. He got the one miner who was awake to help him pull the unconscious man away from the intended point of impact.

As soon as Braxton's scanner showed the men were clear, he powered the laser again and fired. The one quick blast blew a small hole the size of a fist in the cavern wall. Braxton stopped long enough to scan the area again for stress points. Satisfied no more disasters were pending, he lined up the next points of impact.

The two vehicles worked together for several hours until the sun dipped low onto the horizon. They cut a large rectangular chunk of solid rock ten to twelve feet long, six feet high, and six feet wide. Now able to breathe again and seeing their freedom was eminent, the miners who were able moved around inside the cavern as close to the drill site as they dared. Using some of the stripped tree branches, Jo-Na pushed cargo straps through to them. He told them to secure them around the end of the giant block. Nate and David organized the remaining volunteers who had not fled the area as the king arrived to haul some of the smaller, more round tree trunks to lay in the stone's path.

Everything now in place, Braxton paused for a moment and looked at the set-up, still feeling concerned. He paused long enough for David and Nate to check on him. "What's got you worried, Lt. Commander?" David asked.

Braxton was so deeply entangled in his thought processes, it took him a moment to realize the two men were standing beside him and they had asked him… something. "I'm sorry, sir. What did you say?"

David repeated his question, then followed with, "Are you okay, Commander?"

Braxton scowled. "It's been a long day. I'm tired and frustrated. I'm afraid of missing something, and I really hope those straps can hold the weight of that rock."

David and Nate were just as tired as Braxton, and they understood his fear. David's mind jumped back to their time on Tudoren when Admiral Deacons presented two new technologies to them. "Did you use those new anti-grav cylinders Admiral Deacons gave us?"

Braxton's eyes lit up. "No, I didn't, and that could definitely make a difference."

The anti-grav units were metallic and four inches long. Two cylinders placed equal distance apart on a man's belt were enough to make a man weightless. The Admiral had given the crew sixteen sets of cylinders. David and Lazaro agreed to split their supply between the Surf-ve and the shuttle. Nate had wisely made a similar arrangement, only he kept four sets aboard his ship. Nate pulled his six sets from his Surf-ve, and Lazaro pulled the eight sets from the *Evangeline's* Surf-ve.

The crew could only reach the first few inches of the stone. Not wanting to damage the cylinders, Braxton ordered the crew to cut notches and channels into the stone, place the cylinders, then carefully fixed them in place with a pliable polymer. He and Lazaro tied the cylinder controls into the Surf-ve's computer. The unfortunate problem with this approach was that the stone would now be heavy on the back end and light on the front.

Ensign Maya Evans took control of the *Emissary's* Surf-ve while Thane took control of their own vehicle. Lazaro and Commander Silas Asher joined Maya to monitor the scanners while Braxton watched from the other vehicle. Braxton warned everyone to stay clear of the area. He turned his comm unit on and broadcast to everyone.

A hush fell over the crowd as they heard Braxton giving a play-by-play announcement of his moves.

"Powering the anti-grav cylinders. Setting polarity to twenty-five percent... fifty percent... seventy-five percent. Helmsmen, power the Surf-ves, set to reverse. Power engines to ten percent on my mark... MARK."

The straps pulled taut, but nothing else moved. Braxton didn't expect anything to change just yet. He fully intended to ease into it.

"Increase reverse power to twenty percent... thirty percent... forty percent... now fifty..."

The engines were generally silent, but now they were whining under the strain. The straps still seemed to be holding, and the landscape showed no signs of collapse. Braxton pushed harder.

"Powering cylinders to one hundred percent. Increase engines to sixty percent."

The straps groaned, and the stone grated and scraped. The front end threatened to begin bouncing. Lazaro decreased the cylinder's power by five percent to prevent the stone from hitting the top of the channel they carved into the cavern.

"Increase engine power by five percent."

The two helmsmen did as instructed. The stone and Surf-ves slowly rolled away from the mountainside. As the stone reached the halfway point, Thane reported the engine was beginning to overheat although it could go a little longer before it reached a critical point. Not wanting to risk another setback, Braxton ordered a shut-down of both vehicles and the cylinders. He got out and started cutting new channels and notches to move half the cylinders further down the length of the stone. The others moved to help him. This gave the engines time to cool while they shifted the weight of the load. David and Nate brought in more logs to roll the stone across, making the move even easier.

Everything in place again, Thane and Maya powered their vehicles while Braxton re-powered the cylinders. Knowing the limits a little better this time, Braxton was slightly more aggressive.

"Cylinders powering to fifty percent... seventy-five percent... ninety percent... take vehicles to reverse power slowly increase power to forty percent and hold there."

The stone's weight was more balanced than it had been on the first try, but still had a distinct drag on the back end. The stone creaked and groaned. Braxton adjusted the cylinders so that the ones closer to the back of the stone were at full power, but kept the cylinders at the front at eighty percent. He ordered the engines to ease to sixty percent.

The engines heated more quickly this time as they had only a short amount of time to cool off. As the stone reached the end of the channel, Thane warned Braxton

111

the engines were nearing critical. Braxton acknowledged the information, then ordered them to take power to eighty percent. Commander Asher glanced out the window at Braxton. He scowled at the Lt. Commander although Braxton never knew it. Maya followed the order despite seeing the warnings on her own display.

Commander Asher was seconds away from ordering her to shut the engine down when the stone, now firmly rolling across the logs, slid free of the tunnel. The two pilots decreased the power and rolled the stone a few feet further before shutting everything down.

Braxton ordered Thane and Marissa to unhook the straps and take the Surf-ve to retrieve the shuttle. The guards around the mine were no longer concerned with the comings and goings of the large wagons. They simply moved aside and let it pass. Thane supposed the evidence that the Surf-ve could slice them up faster than any sword fueled their cooperative spirits. Braxton checked the scans for any instability. He allowed the crews and volunteers to enter the cavern and start tending or evacuating the trapped miners. He and Jo-Na conscripted some help to place support beams in the tunnel. The tunnel, being solid rock, appeared stable, but Braxton wasn't about to take chances. The wounded, including Claire, were loaded onto the remaining Surf-ve. Noah was already familiar with all the injuries. The only life-threatening injuries were Stephanie's. Nate was one of the first ones through the tunnel and headed immediately to his wife's side. Noah was on his heels.

Nate sat down beside her and stroked her head and face gently. He gave Noah a questioning glance. He was afraid Stephanie would lose her fighting spirit if the report wasn't good. The scanner's information was worse than the information Milo had transferred to him earlier. Noah stood and motioned Nate away from his wife. Stephanie continued to lie there unconscious, never knowing Nate had arrived or stepped away.

As David joined them in the tunnel inside the cavern, he heard Noah whisper to his Captain. "Captain, Stephanie said she would need to go into stasis the second she's free of the debris, and she's right. I'm not qualified to deal with this, and I'm not comfortable dealing with digging her out. We need a real doctor here at her side when we dig her out, or she could die before we get her into stasis."

David stepped forward. "Chief, can you handle the injuries that are about to head to the *Evangeline*?"

Noah nodded. "Most of them; the ones I can't handle aren't life threatening, and they can wait."

"Then go with the wounded back to the *Evangeline* and take over treating them. Send my doc back here."

Noah knew David's plan was the right one. He was still conflicted over leaving Stephanie's side, stepping foot onto the ship of a traitor, and obeying the orders of a known traitor. He looked to his own Captain for a response.

Nate gave Noah a tired nod. "Do as he says until he gives you reason not to trust him."

Noah nodded. He glanced at Stephanie, mentally wishing her well and fearing he may never see her alive again. Noah hastily left the cavern to make sure he got aboard the Surf-ve before it left.

David tapped his comm link. "Braxton, I need you in the tunnel to the left of the cavern. Lt. Commander Adams, I need you to switch places with Chief Evans to oversee extricating Dr. Weiseman from this tunnel."

Jason acknowledged the orders and prepared any additional equipment he thought he might need. Braxton acknowledged his order and headed the direction the Captain indicated once he saw no one near him needed his immediate attention.

David and Nate sat down beside Stephanie, each taking one of her hands in theirs. Nate stroked her face again. This time she stirred. Her eyes fluttered open. Seeing her husband's face, she smiled weakly. "I knew you'd get us out of here."

Nate smiled at her in return. "I'm not sure I can take credit for this rescue. This was mostly his endeavor." Nate nodded in David's direction.

Stephanie realized someone was holding her other hand and turned her head slowly. David's face was shrouded in darkness. Nate reached for the portable lantern he had carried in and moved it closer. The shadow dissolved. David's smile and worried eyes came into focus. "Davie… what are you doing here? They said… They said…" a fit of coughs smothered Her words. Nate grabbed his canteen and offered her a small sip of water.

David saved her the trouble of asking. "What they said is true, from a certain perspective. I can explain it all later when you're feeling better."

Stephanie swallowed and took a slow, deep breath. "You and I both know that's not... likely to happen. By the time I'm... better, you'll be long gone."

David smiled. "You never know. It may line up better than you think."

"Davie, why are you here?"

David squeezed her hand. "I just wanted to talk to some old friends."

Stephanie squinted at him. "Liar," she mumbled.

Nate came to David's rescue. "He's not lying about that. We talked this morning before the mine tunnels collapsed. He just didn't tell you the topic of conversation. It's a good thing he was here though. Without him and his crew, you would have died in here, along with a third of the crew."

Stephanie's eyes focused on her husband's face. "Were you in the tunnels when they collapsed? Your face is bruised."

David winced. "I'm afraid that's my fault. He tried to arrest me. I resisted. Sorry."

David felt the pulse in Stephanie's wrist get stronger for a moment as she processed what he said. Before the conversation could go any further, Braxton walked up. "Captain..."

"Commander, I know we have others who need to be rescued, but they will survive another couple of days if need be. Dr. Weiseman is in greater need. Getting her out of here is your top priority. Jason is on his way here now. Consult with him."

"NO! My son is your priority. Not this woman." King De-Marion had entered without anyone noticing.

The three men looked up, startled. In working with the locals, Braxton had left his translator running and ignored it when he wasn't talking with the locals. The group's I.S. conversation had been translated within King De-Marion's hearing.

Nate was now ready to deck the pompous, overgrown, spoiled child. He leaped to his feet and stared the man in the eyes. He was met by the King's bodyguards and the point of their spears firmly pressed against his neck.

David jumped to pull his friend back. Nate allowed David to pull him away and step in front of him. David placed his own neck in front of the spears. He bowed his head ever so slightly. Turning on his translator, David addressed the King. "King De-Marion, please forgive him. He cares for his wife as much as you care for your son. We have not forgotten your son, and we do not intend to stop looking for him. Jo-Na, Commander Asher and I will search for your son while Lt. Commander Flint attempts to rescue Captain Weiseman's wife. Lt. Commander Flint cannot plan a rescue until we know where the prince is. As soon as we have located him, we will break down whatever walls we must to reach him."

King De-Marion glared at the two men, then glanced down at the frightened and hurting Stephanie. "See that you do. If my son dies in this mine, not one of you will leave it alive. Bring him out alive, and you will come out alive."

Nate stepped out from behind David. "And what will you contribute toward the effort of finding your son? You sent him in here. The workers are growing tired. They have had very little rest, food, or water. Can you not provide replacement workers and some food and drink for those who continue to work?"

King De-Marion didn't like being challenged. If he refused to contribute to the search for his son, his people would surely judge him to be self-centered and uncaring. If he gave them what they asked for, they might judge him to be weak. He had no way of knowing his people already viewed him as self-centered and uncaring. "Very well. I will have fresh troops brought out from the city, along with food and water. When the fresh troops arrive, the guards currently standing watch can help you dig while the other workers rest."

Nate had little appetite, but he had forced himself to swallow an emergency field ration once or twice through the day. He couldn't really remember because he would take a bite of the small bar and shove it in his pocket. Two or three hours later he would remember it and take another bite and shove the rest in his pocket again. He gruffly thanked the king for his generosity, then walked away.

Just before he sat down, he reached into his pocket and pulled out two half-eaten nourishment bars. That explained why he couldn't remember how many he had eaten. His eyes moved from the two morsels in his hand to Stephanie's face. Her eyes showed understanding. "You should eat those," she spoke weakly.

He started to shove them back into his pocket as he sat down beside her again. "I don't want to eat in front of you. It's rude." He tried to joke in the face of their grave situation.

Stephanie smiled at his weak attempt at humor. "It's okay. I'm not really hungry right now. Nate, please eat them."

Nate opened his hand and looked at them again. He wasn't hungry either. He decided it would make Stephanie feel better to see him eat.

Brynna, Lazaro, and Aulani helped get the giant stone block hooked to the shuttle and hauled just far enough out of the way to keep the paths and roads clear. As soon as it dropped the stone, Thane flew back to the ship. David ordered him and Marissa to stay with the shuttle and take turns keeping watch with Cheyenne aboard the *Evangeline*.

Brynna walked up in time to hear the order. "What's that about?"

Nate patted Stephanie's hand, then excused himself for a moment. He recognized David's cautionary posturing. Braxton and Jo-Na were standing nearby, examining the debris. David called the two over. "Jo-Na, is there any other place the king's son might be? Are there any other openings, caverns, or crevices? Could he have gotten out somehow?"

Once the questions got through the Captain's translator, Jo-Na shook his head. "No. I suspect he's buried under the same debris Doctor Stephanie is trapped under. I appreciate you telling King De-Marion you needed my help to rescue his son, but I am afraid it was a useless endeavor. He could not survive under there."

"So why are you pulling some of your people back?" Nate was still stuck on David's cautionary move.

"King De-Marion threatened to kill everyone in here if his son doesn't leave this cave alive. I'm trying to pull as many people back out of harm's way as possible. I also want someone capable of pulling off an assault on the outside. I want to be ready if he tries something. When Jason gets back with the Surf-ve, Commander Asher, get into it discreetly and hide in one of the storage compartments. Brynna, take Ensign Evans, Ensign Griffin, and Lt. Oliver to get more equipment from the ships. Commander Asher, make sure your ship and people are secure while Brynna secures my ship and my people. I strongly advise you to get some rest. You may need it if you need to coordinate a rescue attempt."

Commander Asher balked. "Won't they get suspicious if we don't return? And forgive me for saying so, but I don't trust leaving you alone with my Captain."

Both crews were now gathered together, watching the men vying for control of the mission. David wasn't about to put Nate in the position of deciding who needed to control this next phase of the mission. Captain Alexander put it plainly for Silas. "I can leave if you like. Your Captain is compromised by grief and exhaustion. Half of your crew are trapped in the upper cavern, injured, or otherwise occupied. I can leave and wait for His Majesty to attack, or I can stay here. It's up to you."

Silas turned to Nate who was working hard to process information. "Captain…"

Nate's temper flared. "Silas! You heard what he said. It's your decision. One of you needs to leave. You decide who. I'm not leaving Stephanie. I turned this Op over to him for a reason. Do you really think my state of mind has improved?"

Silas was somewhat conflicted. He wanted to check on his wife. His worries kept him from focusing as well as he would like. "Alright, have it your way." Silas backed away angrily.

David knew it was late, everyone was tired, and tempers were going to flare. He let the matter drop and moved on quickly. "If you're worried about them noticing the Surf-ve not returning, then make multiple trips in and out. Bring equipment in and take people out. We need lasers, shields, and backup power packs for all our weapons. My concern is the later it gets, the less likely they are to let people out."

Silas realized David was probably right. "I'll take Commander Alexander out along with the other women and bring back the supplies you need. I may need to bring one of them back with me to avoid suspicion. Does the doc need anything to take care of Stephanie?"

David glanced at his doctor working diligently over his wounded friend. "I doubt it, but check with him anyway." David knew Jason wouldn't walk into this situation unprepared.

"Brynna and Silas, stay in touch and work together if we end up in trouble. Jake, stay on your toes and watch King De-Marion. If he does anything suspicious, sing out. Braxton, getting the rest of the trapped personnel free is your responsibility. What do you need from us?"

Braxton looked at the situation and considered his resources. "I'm going to split our workers into two groups. It's too tight in this tunnel to have a large number of people working in here. Trying to work around the Docs complicates matters. We have to be extremely careful not to cause further structural collapses."

Jake pulled the portable shield generator off his belt and handed it to Braxton. "This should provide sufficient protection for them. If you position a couple of logs on either side of them, it could give them a little more room and support."

Braxton took the device from him. "Good idea, Jake. I'll be supervising both dig sites, but each site will still need someone to keep a closer eye on things. Captain Alexander, can you handle the tunnel while Lazaro works on the other site?"

David nodded. "Just tell me how to get started."

Braxton quickly told the Captain to remove the debris from the top left side of the pile after Stephanie's position was secured. "Don't move anything directly off her until I'm here. I'll send volunteers in here with buckets, shovels, and wheelbarrows to cart away the debris as you pull it out. You might also want to scan for human remains."

Braxton hastily concluded the briefing and moved to advise Jo-Na and enlist his help with organizing the volunteers.

The two crews scattered to fulfill their assignments. Jake grabbed David, Nate, and Dr. Henry Oliver, the *Emissary's* psychologist, to help carry in two logs. The anti-grav cylinders made quick work of the task. They positioned the logs on either side of her. Jason sat down beside her and put the portable shield generator on his hand. The device slipped on like a wrist brace. When activated, it would project a large umbrella-like shield capable of deflecting projectiles and absorbing the energy of a laser. If removing the fallen debris caused a secondary cave-in or landslide, Jason could protect them using the logs and the shield.

Jake slung his laser rifle across his back and made frequent trips in and out of the cavern, keeping an eye on King De-Marion. The man seemed content to make himself comfortable in the tent. Jake watched the Surf-ve head slowly away from the cave. The guards didn't attempt to stop it. He breathed a sigh of relief and moved back inside.

The next two hours were a quiet repetition of drilling, hauling away rubble, and brief breaks. The king brought food and relief workers as promised. He also had more comfortable furniture brought out for his own use.

The work crews cleared enough of the debris to see that one large boulder pinned Stephanie. They moved to clear everything from around it without dislodging anything it might be propped on. Stephanie was clearly getting weaker with each passing hour.

David decided it was time to call Braxton in and pull Stephanie out. Braxton joined them in the tunnel and surveyed the situation. Seeing Stephanie's deteriorating condition, he pulled David, Jason, and Nate aside to tell them his plan.

"I want to drill into the rock and put the anti-grav cylinders into it. I'm going to bring the power up quickly on them. We'll need two people to pull her out and get her into the stasis field as fast as possible. As soon as that one rock is free, everyone needs to get clear. It's big enough to dislodge the debris and possibly cause it to shift and collapse again."

Jason was quick to second Braxton's desire to get Stephanie into the stasis field quickly. "I'm going to load her up with medications before we move her, but the second that rock is off her, she's going to bleed out internally. Her blood pressure is going to plummet. She hasn't felt much pain before now, but the second that rock comes off her, she'll start feeling pain again. Captain, can we have the Surf-ve standing by to get us back to the ship as soon as possible?"

"I'll hail Silas to get back in here at the last possible moment. I don't want his highness to know what we're doing until it's done. Let's give Nate a moment with Stephanie before we do this."

Nate gave David an appreciative nod. He moved to his wife's side and whispered to her. Stephanie was barely conscious. When Nate finished, the look on his face reflected how helpless he felt. He stepped away from her and pulled David aside.

"Davie, if you were telling the truth about the Commonwealth, where can we take Stephanie? Our ships don't have sufficient facilities to heal her. I can't keep her in stasis indefinitely. What can I do?"

David looked around, debating his answer. "Nate… I can think of three potential places to go; you won't like any of them."

"I certainly don't like the idea of living without her." Nate countered.

"I could ask Arni to help her. You could take her to a private hospital on Romajin. There's no longer a military base there. There's another place you could go, but you couldn't come back from there. It's the same place where I sent my family."

"You're right. I don't care for those options. Who is this Arni, and what would he do?"

David sighed, knowing Nate wouldn't care for the answer. "He's the son of Pateras. He's incredibly powerful. I've seen him heal people and even brought people back from death."

"Hmph… not interested. That's not even possible."

"A year ago, I would've agreed with you. Nate, I didn't just see it. I experienced it personally. Admiral Deacons saw me die. The day he left the planet we were on, Arni brought me back to life. And don't think it was a matter of a few minutes, it wasn't. It was the next day. He did the same for my navigator."

Nate scowled at his friend. "You gave me your word."

"I'm sorry. I'm not trying to… to sway your loyalty. I just know—it's what I would do if it were Brynna. You asked for my opinion."

Nate let the matter drop. "Let's concentrate on getting her out of here and back to your ship. We'll worry about the rest later."

David nodded. "Agreed. Are we ready to do this?"

Jason and Nate slid the stretcher as far under Stephanie as they could and attached the stasis field generators to each corner of the stretcher.

David called for Silas to bring the Surf-ve as close to the opening as possible. Silas acknowledged his orders. He had made a couple trips in and out without incident. The later it got, the more their risks increased. As soon as Noah had Milo patched up, Silas picked him up so he could have more back-up. On the way back to the mine, the two discussed the *Evangeline* and its crew. The two men agreed the crew's presence was appreciated, although they were quite concerned about the influence David clearly had over their own captain.

MORE TROUBLE

IMPASSE

Silas and Milo parked the Surf-ve at the newest mine entrance and made their way into the cavern carrying two data modules each like the one Braxton had been using to plan their rescue of the miners. The devices were large enough to look like an armload. They set the modules down in the tunnel near Stephanie.

David looked at the modules then back at Silas. "What are those for? Did Braxton send for them?"

Silas shook his head. "It was Milo's idea. We've brought in everything possible already. We thought it would look suspicious if we didn't bring in more equipment. They don't know what the things are, and it's not like we don't have thirty of them sitting in the cargo hold."

A quick laugh escaped David's mouth. If he weren't so tired and the circumstances so serious, he might've found it worthy of far more laughter. "Good idea. We're about to pull Stephanie out. Be ready to slip her out quietly, but don't waste any time."

Jason was kneeling next to Stephanie administering as much medication as he dared. As soon as he prepped her, Jason nodded to Nate and Braxton.

Nate knelt beside his unconscious wife and prepared to pull her mangled body from the debris as soon as she was free. A knot formed in his stomach. She shouldn't have been in this mine to begin with. He should never have allowed her or any of his crew inside, given Jo-Na's concerns about the mine's safety.

David stood ready with the shield. Braxton had the cylinders placed strategically in the rock pinning Stephanie down. Jo-Na and Jake had rods of their freshly hewn timber jammed under the edges of the boulder. They were preparing to leverage the stone away from her body the second the cylinders activated.

Braxton took one last quick look around to be sure he hadn't overlooked anything. One mistake could cost Stephanie her life or cause injury or death to the others. He glanced at David who gave him a reassuring nod. Braxton looked around as though he were searching for someone. Seeing no one in particular, he finished with a soft, "Arni, don't let this go wrong."

Lt. Commander Flint powered the cylinders up quickly to fifty percent power. The loose rubble slid as Jake and Jo-Na's levers loosened the boulder. Braxton ran the power up to seventy-five percent. Jake and Jo-Na jammed their levers further behind the stone and pushed down hard and fast. The stone lifted and wobbled dangerously.

Jason hollered to Nate. "Now!" The two grabbed Stephanie and pulled her the rest of the way onto the stretcher. Despite her unconscious state, they could hear her moan painfully. Jason had programmed the stasis field to activate on voice control. The second she was firmly on the stretcher, Jason and Nate grabbed the handles, "Computer, activate stasis field." They pulled her hastily out of the tunnel and back into the cavern.

As the rock tumbled aside, the debris shifted and slid down. Braxton yelled, "Get back! Everybody out!"

Jake and Jo-Na dropped their levers and bolted along with Braxton and David. The group reassembled in the cavern and waited for the dust to settle. David tapped Jake's arm. "Let's step outside and provide a distraction while they move Steph into the Surf-ve."

The two men trotted outside coughing and headed for a trough of water to splash on their faces. Their ruse was unsuccessful. King De-Marion was wide awake and growing impatient. He ordered his men to close ranks around the Surf-ve. The guards pulled their swords forcing the crew back into the tunnel. Several of the workers who had stepped outside were herded in with them. David and Nate called out to the angry monarch. "King De-Marion, what is the meaning of this? May we speak with you, Your Highness?"

The king granted them the audience they requested, although it was rather one-sided. "I warned you to find my son. No one else is to leave until my son is found... alive. If he is dead, all of you will die."

David tried to intervene. "Your Highness, you would hold your son's life to be equal to twenty men and women's lives?"

"My son's life is worth more than a hundred men and women."

"And if you destroy all those who serve you, will it relieve your pain? Will those who lost family members to your anger remain loyal to you, or will they learn to despise their King?"

The King stood there weighing David's words. "Someone must pay for my son's life. Do you have a better idea?"

"Allow the Surf-ve to take the woman back to our ship. I will offer you one life worth more than a thousand lives in return if we cannot bring your son out alive."

King De-Marion saw something odd in the Captain's demeanor. He didn't know the cause, but he wasn't ready to give in yet. "I deny your request. You and all the workers, save five, will return to the mine. I will keep five out here. Tomorrow morning by sunrise you will present me with my son. If he is dead, you will present his body along with the one worth many to pay for his death. I know you have magnificent weapons at your disposal. If you attack my troops or try to escape, we will slay the five before you can reach them. If there is bloodshed tonight, it will be on your own head."

David had abided by the customs and expected etiquette, but now he was done catering to this overgrown child. "And if this man's wife dies, I will personally see that you never rule over anything more than a flock of sheep! I will take everything you own and give it to the poor living in the streets. Your name will be dishonored, and you will be a laughingstock to everyone within a hundred miles of here."

King De-Marion turned away. He ordered his guards to escort the men back into the cavern and retrieve five of the volunteers.

Nate was both furious and afraid. He managed to keep quiet, allowing David to confront the king. Captain Weiseman knew his emotions were all over the place and he was incapable of doing nothing more than starting a war. The thing bothering him the most was that the idea of starting a war was uncharacteristically appealing.

David briefed the crew on the meeting with the King. Silas and Milo were now trapped in the cavern with them. Commander Asher was accustomed to speaking freely to his own captain and had no reservations about taking the same liberty with Captain Alexander. "If the king is expecting you to hand somebody over to him in the morning, who did you plan on sacrificing?"

Nate scowled at his first officer. "Silas, that's enough. Captain Alexander wasn't planning on sacrificing anyone. He was just trying to buy us some time."

David stood there looking around the cavern at the tired, dejected workers. Inwardly, he continued to ask Pateras for answers. So far, those answers had not come.

Braxton was torn between getting the last trapped group out of the upper cavern and waiting to hear the Captain's next plan. As he stood there, Braxton seemed to get a glimpse into David's soul. "Captain, you can't. There's no guarantee he'll stop at one death."

Nate looked at David then back at Braxton. "Can't what? What are you talking about?"

Jake stepped next to Braxton. "The Captain plans to offer his own life if there's no other way out of this."

Nate looked at his friend. "Is that right? David, are they right? Is that what you're planning?"

David finally made eye contact with Nate. Knowing he couldn't lie to his friend he laid his plan out for him. "That's not 'Plan A,' I assure you. I'm really hoping for a better option, but if everything else fails, I will. Stephanie's stable for now so we have time to find another way out of this. Let's get busy getting the rest of your crew and the other miners out of the upper cavern. Braxton how much further do we have to go?"

The group was tired and easily distracted by David's diversion. Braxton had Lazaro cutting through some softer rock into the upper part of the tunnel. The group moved to increase the previous efforts which were already nearing fruition. An hour later, they dug through into the upper tunnel. The occupants of the upper cavern had to crawl through the narrow opening one at a time. The miners went through first followed by Elize and then Deka. Jason quickly assessed and treated each one for injuries while Henry and Aulani brought them food and water.

Despite being tired and hungry, Elize gave Braxton a grateful hug for rescuing them. Deka eyed the two of them suspiciously. Elize pulled Braxton over to introduce him to her rivalrous husband.

After sufficient introductions and explanations, Nate and David ordered their crews to get some sleep. Jo-Na encouraged the miners and volunteers to get some sleep as well. The group was so tired, they all fell into a deep sleep.

The two Captains, along with Silas, Milo, Braxton, and Jake sat down to discuss their options. Silas grabbed one data module, that had been brought in as a ruse, to project a three-dimensional image of the area. The men discussed and argued the different escape and attack scenarios for the next two hours.

The best thing they could decide on was to continue scanning the area for any signs of Prince Ca-Litana. They spread out, conducted additional scans, and added the information to the data module. Finding nothing again, the men returned to their seats in the cavern. The crew of the *Evangeline* was weary and frustrated. The crew of the *Emissary* was weary, frustrated, and dejected.

The two Captains agreed they all needed at least a small amount of rest. The time until morning was growing short. Milo volunteered to stand watch first. Silas took second, and Jake took the third watch. Their watches only lasted about an hour and a half each.

Jake hailed Marissa as everyone settled down to get some sleep. Marissa was already asleep in preparation for whatever the morning might hold. She groggily answered his hail.

"Hey Honey, sorry to wake you."

Jake's comm unit was equipped with a small camera and screen. He looked at Marissa's sleepy face and smiled.

Marissa returned a sleepy smile. "What's wrong Jake?"

"Nothing, we're stuck sleeping here in the mine until morning, and I wanted to talk to you before I get some sleep."

"Why are you stuck there?"

"The royal pain won't let anybody leave until he gets his son back safely. Unfortunately, that probably won't happen, and the Captain has to come up with a plan to get us out of here safely." Jake's face displayed his annoyance.

Marissa scowled. "Oh no, Jake, his son's dead?"

"More than likely, and he wants somebody's head on a platter to pay for it," Jake replied wryly.

"Jake, consider how the king must feel. If it were our son how would you feel? Wouldn't you want somebody to pay if our son died needlessly?"

Jake thought about it for a moment. "I suppose you're right. I probably would. Actually, you are right. When Luciano Hale tried to harm you both, I was ready to take his head off personally." Jake got quiet for a moment. "Marissa, this may not really be the time to discuss this, but we need to talk about something."

Marissa shifted into a more upright position. "What is it?"

"We never expected to have children. Marissa, I'm a security officer, the first line of defense in a war we can't hope to win. Have you considered what you'll do if something happens to me?"

"Jake is there something you're not telling me?"

Jake looked away from the screen and around at his surroundings for a moment to gather his thoughts before responding. "Honey, I'm going to be a father, and this job is dangerous. What if something happens and I'm not there for our son?" Jake hoped he had dodged her question appropriately. He didn't want to lie to her. He was considering doing something he knew he shouldn't.

Marissa breathed a little easier. She thought perhaps Jake was merely coming to terms with his impending fatherhood. "Jake, I try not to think about losing you."

"But what if you did? I lost you once. This is a dangerous job. What if you lost me? There's no guarantee Pateras would return me to you. Would you be able to keep going? Would you be able to take care of our son?"

"Jake, I'm not sure I'm ready for this kind of talk. It's scaring me."

The worry on Jake's face softened. "I'm sorry. I wasn't trying to scare you. I just want to know that... if... if something happens... you'll be okay. Please, tell me you'll be okay. I want to know you'll tell our son, not to be a careless dope like his dad."

Marissa's tension eased when Jake began to tease. "Jake, you are NOT careless."

"I notice you left out the part where I'm not a dope." Jake baited his tired wife.

"Oh, you are a big dope. I don't have an argument with that part." Marissa grinned for a moment then her face got serious again. "Jake, what's this really about?"

Jake grinned weakly. "I think I'm just tired and missing you. Maybe it's just hormones."

"Hormones? What are you talking about? You aren't pregnant, I am."

Jake smiled more confidently. "I just thought if you could get away with blaming your moodiness on hormones I could to."

Marissa stuck her tongue out at him. "You know if you were here, I'd slap you upside the head."

Jake grinned again. "I know. It's why I decided it was safe to say it."

"You also know I'll just wait until you get home then slap you, right?"

"Nah, you wouldn't do that."

Marissa grinned back at him. "Wanna bet?"

Jake's grin got bigger and more impish. "Of course, you wouldn't. This is just another one of your pregnant dreams. We never had this discussion."

Marissa scowled at him. "You are so evil."

"Nu-uh, this is your wicked dream, not mine. I'm still your sweet, lovable, adoring husband."

"Jacob Holden!"

Jake laughed outright at her reaction. "I love you, Marissa. Tell Jake junior, daddy loves him, too."

"I think he heard you. The baby just kicked me. Wow, he's definitely your son. That felt like some of the moves I've seen you use when you're sparring."

Jake smiled, but his eyes reflected sorrow. Marissa saw it but dismissed it. She assumed it was because he wanted to be at home with her. The two said goodnight and Marissa rolled over to go back to sleep. Jake wasn't quite ready to go to sleep.

"Computer record a time delay message for Lt. Marissa Holden." He watched the indicator on his bracelet to know when to record. He was extremely tired, and his speech was slightly slurred, but he needed to record this one last message for his wife.

"Marissa, I'm sorry for this. I'm afraid the Captain is going to offer his life to pay for the Prince's life. I can't let him do that. I owe the Captain—I owe him a lot. He's too important to this mission. It's my job to protect you, the crew and the Captain. Dr. Weiseman's wife isn't going to survive if we don't get her out of here soon. The crew still doesn't trust me. At least this way, I can prove my loyalty is to Pateras, the Captain, and crew. I'm really hoping Pateras will make my plan work the way I want it to. If he doesn't... well... I might not... I'm sorry if I'm not there to see our son be born or help you raise him. Forgive me for that. I love you, both. Good bye, Marissa. Good bye, little man."

Jake sighed. His eyes were extremely heavy, and he expected to get little more than a nap. "Computer... set message delivery for... oh... six hours should be long enough."

The computer droned softly, "Setting delivery time for 0600 hours." Jake failed to notice the discrepancy in the time. He confirmed the current time, set the alarm for 0500 hours, then grabbed a brief nap.

Four hours later Jake started his watch.

After he was sure Silas was asleep, Jake woke Milo. "I need your help. We need to get Lt. Commander Weiseman and the Doc out of here right now. The power insufficiency alarm is going off on the stasis chamber. At the very least, we need to get it hooked to the power supply on the Surf-ve."

Milo woke with a start and jumped into crisis mode. His face went from tired and annoyed to "let's get to work." He jumped up and followed Jake. "What do you need me to do?" His next question should have been, "Have you notified the command staff?" but his lack of sleep and Jake's startling manner of waking him prevented him from thinking past the moment.

"Take a laser rifle and slip up the side of the mountain to get a good vantage point on those hostages. As soon as you're in place, the doc and I'll load the stretcher onto the Surf-ve. I'll escort them out then head up the hill to make sure those hostages get free. Just keep those guards away from the Surf-ve and the hostages."

Milo shook his head skeptically. Something felt wrong, but he was too tired to put the pieces together. "Got it!"

Jason woke with a start. Jake was standing over him shaking him. "What? What's wrong?"

Jake looked down at the stretcher. "The power supply is failing on the stasis field. We have to get the Commander out of here right now. Let's go, quietly."

Jason was also too sleepy to ask some rather obvious questions or notice the problems with Jake's story. He did as he was told without question. His primary concern was still getting his patient back to the ship.

The two quietly carried the stretcher out to the Surf-ve. They followed Milo to the entrance. The laser rifles Jake and Milo carried had dual capabilities. The lasers could be used as a laser cutter of varying intensities and configurations. It could also fire the Tri-EMP pellets using the laser as a targeting sight. As they reached the entrance, Milo knelt on one knee and expertly dropped the two nearby guards without getting the attention of the guards along the perimeter. After checking to make sure the coast was clear, he moved stealthily up the side of the mountain to a neat enclosure of rocks, a couple hundred feet up. Jake waited for the all-clear signal from Milo. Milo settled into his nest and scanned the area to see if anyone had noticed their movements. He hailed Jake quietly to give him a situation report.

Hearing Milo's approval, Jake and Jason moved Stephanie quickly and quietly into the waiting vehicle. Jake knew the second it powered up and started moving, they would get every guard's attention. He briefed Jason on the plan to get the Surf-ve out and rescue the five hostages. The two quietly got Stephanie settled and hooked up to the Surf-ve's power supply. Jake wanted to be sure the stasis field remained intact even if they were caught and chased back into the mine.

All the pieces now in place, Jake climbed on top of the vehicle and laid down with his laser rifle. Taking a deep breath, Jake knew he was about to cause a dangerous uproar, and if he survived, he would be due a serious berating from his wife and his Captain. Jake touched his comm unit. "Let's do this. Doc, start her up and proceed slowly and calmly. Don't rush it until you have no other choice. Milo, you ready?"

"Ready."

Jason gingerly pressed the power switch as though the pressure of his hand on the switch would affect the sound of the engines. The engines weren't loud, and the guards were drowsy. Jason gently pushed the vehicle forward. The rocks and gravel cracking and popping under the tires got the attention of the guards. Jake started firing from atop the moving vehicle dropping the guards closest to their escape route into unconscious heaps on the ground. One guard put himself directly in front of their path before Jake could stop him. Jake fired. The man collapsed blocking their escape. Jason had picked up speed the second he knew their escape had been detected. When the guard fell in front of the Surf-ve, he halted the vehicle causing Jake to clamor for a grip on the rails atop the vehicle. Jake realized Jason wasn't about to run the man over. He agilely hoisted himself over the rail. Landing on his feet beside the vehicle, he slung his rifle onto his back with the strap then grabbed the unconscious man's feet and drug him from the roadway. Jason advanced the vehicle slowly as his path was cleared. Jake jumped onto a running board on the side of the vehicle. He grabbed the railing on top of the vehicle and pulled his small sidearm from its holster to protect himself and their escape.

One extremely competent guard gave chase and was making progress in gaining on them. Jake carefully twisted around to fire on his pursuer. Taking aim was difficult as the Surf-ve bounced and twisted. Jake fired. His would-be attacker dodged at precisely the right moment. The man was getting close enough to reach the vehicle. Jake took aim again and fired twice this time. The man dodged the first shot but was caught by the second. He convulsed and collapsed. Jake breathed a sigh of relief.

The vehicle cleared the guarded perimeter and rounded the bend out of sight of the mine. Jason slowed down so Jake could jump off. Jake raced up the back side of the hill toward the position of the five hostages. As he ran up the hill, he mentally prayed Milo had taken out all the guards. He took cover behind a small close grouping of trees. Jake turned his scanner on and connected it to the display on his bracelet. He quietly hailed Milo to check his status. "Milo, what's your situation and the situation of those hostages?"

Milo softly responded. "I got all the guards around the hostages before they could react. My position is still secure for the moment. Your path appears to be clear from here."

"Acknowledged. I'm headed in to free the hostages. Watch my back until I give you the all clear. As soon as the hostages are free, get back in the mine. Jake, out." Jake hastily closed the channel before Milo could ask questions. It was only a matter of seconds before Milo figured out the command staff did not sanction Jake's actions. He also knew Jason would notify Brynna any moment of his arrival at the ship and she would contact the Captain.

Jake raced across an open area to the small group of prisoners. He jumped into the center of them and began slicing through their ropes with his knife. The group was tired and scared. Jake engaged his translator and quickly told them to head toward the river to the north then enter the city by the north gate. He hoped the guards would search for their prisoners between here and the closer eastern gate. He guarded them as they escaped for the first few hundred yards. As soon as he saw their path was clear, he hailed Milo. "They're clear, get back inside and report to the command staff. Chief Holden, out."

Milo stabbed at his bracelet, "Wait, Chief Holden, come in!" Milo wasn't sure what was wrong, but something was definitely out of place. Which direction was his counterpart headed? Back to his ship? Back to the mine? How did he plan on getting back in safely? Jake refused to answer his hail, another indication of trouble. Milo half ran, and half slid down the embankment. He slid just inside the mine entrance and fired at two more guards who were closing in on the mine. A larger contingent of off-duty guards moved to surround the entrance having been awakened by the commotion. Milo punched his comm unit and hailed Captain Weiseman. He swept his laser back and forth in front of the men to serve as a warning to any others who attempted to rush the mine entrance.

Seeing their adversary wasn't about to fire unless provoked, their commander ordered his troops to hold their positions. He pulled all but a handful of his men back and off to one side where Milo couldn't see them any longer. Milo cussed softly knowing these men were planning another avenue of attack. He was still waiting on Captain Weiseman to answer his hail. It had only been a few seconds. It felt like an eternity. He rolled to the opposite side of the mine entrance to see if he could find out what the missing guards were planning. He could see their heat signatures on his scanner moving into specific formations. Their goal still wasn't clear. Getting desperate, he slapped his comm unit again "Captain Weiseman, Commander Asher, Captain Alexander, I need help at the mine entrance! Come in, please!"

Captain Weiseman woke with a start and replayed the hail. Hearing the emergency in Milo's voice, he reached over and shook David and Silas. The two rolled over and looked at him questioningly. Nate grabbed his sidearm and headed for the mine entrance. "C'mon, something's wrong."

Silas and David grabbed their weapons and chased after Nate. Silas stayed a mere pace behind his Captain.

David got to the edge of the tunnel entrance and stopped. Jason had been sleeping next to the entrance with Stephanie and her temporary stasis chamber. Both were gone. David glanced around the dimly lit cavern for Jake. He punched a button on his bracelet. "Computer locate Security Chief Jake Holden."

Jake made his way stealthily down the hill watching his scanner display carefully. He moved to the back of the tent King De-Marion had made his temporary home. The King was awake again and watching the activity curiously. Two guards stood at either side of him. Jake took his rifle from his back and easily dispatched the two guards. The King glanced at his two unconscious guards coldly. "I assume you plan to force me to recall my guards and free your people."

King De-Marion never even looked in Jake's direction. Jake didn't care for the man's over-confidence. Jake brought his laser rifle into point-blank range at the King's back. "That's the plan, Your Highness. Order your men to stand down."

The King turned slowly. He folded his arms across his chest and never altered his posture. "I could give such an order, but you should know there are consequences to such an action. Do you have any children?"

Jake winced almost imperceptibly. He didn't know what the King was up to, but it was unnerving him.

The King caught Jake's wince. "A son, perhaps?"

Jake felt his face betray him again. He decided to come clean and perhaps unsettle the King. "My wife and I are expecting our first child, a son. Give the order."

"Don't you want to know the price? If I am captured or forced to give such an order, my troops have been ordered to go into the city and kill the first one hundred male children they encounter. Now, you can take me prisoner if you wish or I can order my troops to stand down. My troops will immediately ride into the city and not respond to any other orders. If you kill me, they are under orders

135

to slay all male children in the entire city. Drop your weapons and turn yourself over to me or I will give the order. The choice is yours. If you use your lightning stick on me, they will assume I am dead or captured and fulfill my last order."

Jake felt sick. His desire to change his Tri-EMP to a lethal setting welled up within him. This man truly was a monster. Mentally, Jake called out to Arni and begged for help while confessing his poor choices leading up to this moment. Jake toyed with the idea of stalling. It seemed as though King De-Marion knew his every thought.

"Your decision? I am not a patient man. Hand over your weapons or I give the order."

Jake had his rifle propped firmly against his shoulder. He fidgeted nervously. He called out again to Arni. This time he got an answer. Arni spoke quietly to Jake. "You should have trusted me earlier. Your life is in my hands. Submit to him."

Jake answered audibly. "That really wasn't the answer I was hoping for." He lowered his weapon, powered it down and locked it. The King and his men would not be able to use the weapon without the crew's help. Jake carefully laid it down then slowly removed his other weapons and laid them down beside his rifle. Before dropping the final weapon, he added a warning to the King who was looking confused at Jake's last statement. "King De-Marion, the one who I follow has ordered me to submit to your authority. He rules over everything including life and death. I'm following his orders, not yours. I know an evil man like you. His defeat is already written. His defeat, and yours, is nearer than you think."

King De-Marion sneered. "The rantings of a condemned man mean nothing to me." King De-Marion waved to the commander of his troops. The commander ran to the King's side along with four other guards. The guards grabbed Jake and stripped him of his bracelet, scanner, and utility belt. Jake heard the Captain hail him. His bracelet was no longer reachable.

Jason hailed the *Evangeline* as he approached.

Marissa had the early shift. She opened the cargo bay to receive the Surf-ve and notified the appropriate personnel.

After getting everyone settled, Brynna joined Marissa on the bridge to prepare for whatever she knew David might ask of the crew. The computer beeped at Marissa.

David joined the others at the mine entrance where Nate was getting a report from Milo when Brynna reported Jason had arrived with Stephanie in the Surf-ve.

David's computer displayed the location of Jake's bracelet. He felt his temper flare as he saw Jake was in the pavilion occupied by King De-Marion. David had Brynna monitor the conversation so he wouldn't have to relay the information twice. "Nate, what did I miss?"

Nate glanced outside. "Milo says he and Jake got the Docs out on the Surf-ve and the hostages freed. He doesn't know what happened to Jake though. The troops outside are using the leftover trees and rocks to build some sort of protective barriers. Where's your security chief?"

"He's apparently decided to pay the King a visit." David groused.

In the background, he heard Marissa cry out, "Jake! NO!"

"Captain, standby. Marissa, what is it?"

Marissa played back the message Jake sent her. Brynna gritted her teeth for a moment then turned her attention back to David. "Captain, Chief Holden sent a farewell message to Lt. Holden. I believe he intends to sacrifice himself to save you and the rest of the crew."

David clenched his jaw tightly. "Commander, standby for now. Tell Lt. Holden I'm going after him, but I'm not bringing him back in one piece. I'm going to tear him apart myself, the second I get my hands on him."

The sun lit the sky as dawn approached. Nate got a quick scan of the area before the group fell back into the larger cavern leaving Milo to guard the entrance. Hearing the raucous, Jo-Na, Lazaro and Braxton wearily got up and joined the group.

Silas looked back and forth at the two Captains. Despite hearing Milo's report, Silas was confused by what just happened. "Somebody want to explain this to me?" His eyes landed on David with an accusatory stare.

"Jake... Jake has been through a lot recently. He knows he caused all of us, especially me, a lot of pain. My crew is having trouble trusting him again. I think Jake's giving his own life to save the crew and prove his loyalty to Pateras. I'm sorry, Nate. I didn't authorize his actions."

Braxton and Lazaro glanced at each other. Their guilt etched clearly in their own faces. Braxton swallowed his pride. "Captain, how do we get him back?"

David shook his head. "I don't know. Give me a minute to think." He turned to walk away for a moment.

Silas offered a sarcastic, "Your new boss isn't going to rescue him for you?"

Nate gave Silas an annoyed stare.

David silently called out to Arni for help. He was quietly reminded that Jake belonged to Pateras. In a moment, David turned back around and rejoined the waiting men. "Let's go see if his Highness will grant us an audience. I'll go alone, just in case."

Nate shook his head. "I'm going with you. Your people risked their lives to rescue my people, it's the least I can do."

David shook his head. "No, you need to stay here to coordinate a counter offensive if he doesn't let the miners and the rest of the crew out of here."

Nate folded his arms across his chest resolutely. "Silas and Milo can handle that. I'm going and that's final. You can't give me orders. Remember?"

Jo-Na stepped forward. "I will go too."

David wasn't willing to put any more lives at risk. "No, Jo-Na, stay here and help my men continue to search for the Prince. If anyone can stop the King at this point, it's Prince Ca-Litana. Braxton, Lazaro, run more scans of the collapsed areas. He's got to be here somewhere. Commander Asher, if we don't return, please do whatever you have to get my people out of here safely."

Hearing David's skepticism, Silas debated about taking Nate's place. "Captain, diplomacy is my side of the mission. Let me go with him instead."

Nate rebutted his request immediately. "We're way past diplomacy, Silas. The crew's safety is my responsibility."

Silas countered. "Which is why you should stay here and organize the counterstrike. To be honest, it's his crew member in trouble, not ours."

Nate's temper flared. "Yes, it's his crewman in danger, but it's because he risked his life to save my WIFE! That will be all, Mr. Asher."

David didn't want to interfere with their internal difference of opinion. He also didn't want to risk more lives. "Nate, I really should go alone. Don't risk yourself or your people."

"I know more about this man and their customs than you do. I'm going. Let's get moving before those troops finish building their project outside." Nate moved toward the mine entrance without waiting for the others to concede to him.

Milo gave a yell. "Captain, something's happening."

Nate, Silas, and David hastened to the end of the tunnel. Lazaro and Braxton wanted to join them. They knew their orders of finding the Prince took precedence over their curiosity and worry. They headed into the tunnel where Stephanie had been and started running more scans.

Nate, Silas, Milo, and David peered out into the morning light. The guards brought Jake to the base of the hill a mere hundred yards from the mine entrance. They watched as the guards stripped Jake of his shirt and boots then stretched him out on the ground. Four posts were driven into the ground. The guards secured each of his limbs to a post. David held his hands out to his side keeping them visible. "We seek an audience with King De-Marion." David's bracelet relayed the translation. The time waiting for the translation to go through seemed interminable.

Nate shook his head. "You really should use those nanites."

David glanced at him. "Sorry my friend, I have too much at stake. Once I'm sure they're safe, I'll reconsider."

The Commander of the Guards sent a man off to report their request to King De-Marion. Several guards had taken shelter behind their newly constructed barricades. They watched the two Captains and the mine entrance cautiously. Their Commander had prudently placed archers behind the nearest trees and behind the barricades. If anyone started firing, injuries were now a certainty.

The messenger returned and spoke to his commander. The man nodded and yelled out new orders. The translators didn't pick up enough to decipher. David's anxiety level climbed as he saw the results of those orders. The archers armed their bows, drew back and aimed their arrows at Jake. The commander approached the two Captains and gave them King De-Marion's answer. "King De-Marion has agreed to meet with you. You may even carry your weapons. If you attempt to use those weapons to free your man or harm the King, your man will be killed instantly. Do you agree to this temporary truce?"

Nate stepped forward. "We agree. Our men in the mine will remain in the mine and will not fire on anyone. We will not draw our weapons except in our own defense."

"You may follow me." The commander led the men to face the King.

David and Nate entered the King's pavilion and knelt reverently. "King De-Marion, forgive us for asking, but why have you taken my friend's crew member prisoner?" Nate asked gingerly.

King De-Marion was casually eating breakfast. He looked up from his plate and answered coldly. "He sought to attack me first, then challenged my authority as the Supreme Ruler. I could not afford to let him usurp my authority. My subjects would lose respect for me. I am doing to him and to you what he tried to do to me."

David stared at the ground in front of the king. "What is that? What do you intend to do to him?" It was apparent they had put Jake on display, and the outcome would not be a good one.

The troops continued working around Jake. They erected a framework above him and wrapped a rope around the center cross beam with the ends hanging on either side of the beam. Jake hadn't been told what was going to happen to him. He couldn't quite make sense of the preparations.

King De-Marion's anger flared. Throwing his food down on the plate in front of him, he stood and moved directly in front of the two men kneeling before him. "I sought only to redeem the loss of my son. Your man came out of the darkness and attempted to embarrass and humiliate me. He tried to place himself as one who rules over me. He attempted to force my hand. You are his leader. I hold you responsible for his actions. I will now force your hand."

David forced himself to keep his head down. The King was now close enough to touch, which had his guards shifting nervously. King De-Marion reached down and lifted David's chin with his staff until he could look him in the eye.

David calmly appealed to the sadistic monarch, "King De-Marion, you are right. You should hold me responsible for his actions. Whatever you have planned for him, do it to me instead. I'm the one who should suffer, not him."

The King glared at David. "You are the one who will suffer. Your man will die. Here is the weapon he sought to use against me. I return it to you. How he dies is up to you. I have arranged a slow, painful death for him. If you wish to spare him such a death, you can use this weapon and kill him yourself, quickly."

David stood abruptly. "If you want someone dead, then take my life, not his."

"The matter is decided. I have ordered my men to return to the city and kill the male children in every household as payment for the death of my son. They will follow this order if your people attack me, or my guards. You may stop some of them from following my orders, but you cannot stop all of them. My son will need servants in the land of the dead. The children will become his slaves in the next life. It is also tradition to slay the concubines when a man of power dies. My son was young and had only four concubines and two wives. My guards will slay his concubines. They will slay all unmarried women of marrying age so that he has as many women

141

as his heart desires. I will see that my son is fully cared for in the next life. His wives both carry children. They will be spared as one of them will bear the next heir to the throne. So, I force your hand. Allow your one man to die and I will spare the lives of the young women and male children in the city. Submit to me and the only lives lost will be that of his concubines and your servant. Fight me and many lives will be lost. You are already responsible for your own man's death. I give you the choice as to how he dies."

An eerie calm settled over David. He had faced similar circumstances once before on Tudoren. His face changed to reflect peace. "King De-Marion, I knew another man who tried to bend others to his will by killing children. Pateras challenged him, and he fell… to his death. Pateras controls me, and my man. If he allows either of us to fall, then we do so, gladly in his service. Your schemes mean nothing to me. Be warned, Pateras can destroy you too, if he chooses."

"Brave words, Captain Alexander. I doubt you will feel so brave when your man is screaming in pain and terror," King De-Marion retorted as he returned to his plate of food. "Take them back to the mine entrance. If he fires his lightning stick at his own man, then so be it. If he fires at anyone else, have the archers kill his man, then get to the city and carry out my orders."

Nate glared at King De-Marion and wondered how David could be so calm. "Why are you doing this? It's your fault your son was in the mine. It's your fault the mine collapsed. Did you send him in there on purpose? Did you want him to die?"

The guards pushed the men back toward the mine as Nate continued to accuse the King. "Your greed killed your son! You are not a worthy ruler of these people."

David broke away from the guards. "King De-Marion, may I speak to my man for a moment?"

The King had been ignoring Nate's accusations. He stopped and listened as David's bracelet conveyed the translation. He called out to the guards, "Allow him a moment with his servant. He cannot accuse me of being without compassion."

David and Nate approached Jake. The guards had established a perimeter of wood scraps and brush around Jake. The guards stopped them just outside the perimeter. Jake raised his head off the ground to talk to his Captain. "Captain, I'm sorry. I didn't mean for this to happen."

David looked around at nothing in particular, trying to decide what to say to his condemned crewman. "Jake… I know you didn't, and as soon as we find a way out of this, you're going to get an earful."

"Yes sir, I know I deserve it. Forgive me for taking matters into my own hands. Arni's not too happy with me either. Captain… exactly what's going to happen to me? I know it's nothing good."

David stopped looking around and faced Jake straight on. "King De-Marion is arranging a slow, painful death of some sort for you. His intention is to force me to choose between allowing you to die slowly and painfully, or to shoot you myself."

Jake laid his head slowly back down on the ground. As the gravity of his predicament, and the Captain's, sank in, Jake raised his head to speak again. "Captain do whatever you think is best. I'll accept whatever you choose."

"Jake, I'm hoping Arni intends to get you out of this. I'll wait as long as I can for him, but I won't let you suffer needlessly." David promised sadly. He wasn't sure he would have the strength to kill his own security chief. Killing in the heat of battle was one thing. This was something else entirely. "I would ask you if you have any messages for your wife, but it appears you've already taken care of that."

Jake strained against his bonds, "What? She got the message already? I thought I timed it so I could cancel delivery if everything went like it was supposed to. I wanted it to be a source of comfort for her if I was already gone. How did she find out?"

David scowled. "You weren't thinking clearly, Chief. You programmed delivery for 0600 hours this morning."

Jake's head dropped back onto the ground roughly. "Oh man, I really screwed up."

"Just what were you thinking, Chief?" David asked. He needed to know Jake's motivation for his actions.

"Initially, I was going to offer myself to King De-Marion to pay for his son's death. When I took over the watch, I saw Stephanie's stasis field reach critically low energy levels and had to change my plan. I knew the King wasn't about to let her out of here, so I grabbed Milo to help me get her out and protect those hostages. Once the Doc was safely away, I freed the hostages so they wouldn't face any retribution then I tried to take the King into custody. I underestimated him."

"Jake, why didn't you take some back-up with you? Why do this with just Milo?" David continued to press him for details.

"Captain, the crew's walking on tiptoes around me. I just wanted them to trust me again. I thought I could prove my loyalty or die trying. I'm sorry I disappointed you again."

"You've frustrated me, Chief. You haven't disappointed me. Any last requests, Jake?"

"Take care of Marissa and my son."

David looked over at Nate then back at Jake. "You know I will, but that was supposed to be your job."

"Yes sir, thank you, sir." Jake laid his head back down and pulled at the ropes holding him again.

David and Nate moved back into the mine to discuss their options with the rest of the crew.

Silas pulled Jo-Na and the remaining crew members together as soon as he saw the two Captains heading back. Between the two crews, there were ten crewmen including the Captains. Nate filled them in on their talk with the King while David continued his mental distress call to Pateras.

Aulani moved over near the Captain. "Captain, please tell me you've got a plan to rescue him."

David looked down at Aulani. She was only a few inches shorter than him, but somehow, she was dwarfed by their circumstances. David gave her arm a quick reassuring rub. "This one's in Pateras' hands, not mine."

Silas watched the two sullen Captains for a moment before asking. "What if we send the ships and shuttles to take out anyone trying to reach the city?"

Nate shook his head. "Chief Holden will be the first person killed if we fire on any of the King's men. I also would prefer not to cause more bloodshed."

A wagon arrived from the city. Two men unloaded two clay jars and carefully placed them on the ground on either side of Jake. Jake watched them with morbid curiosity. He hadn't been enlightened to what sort of death to anticipate. Closed clay jars did nothing but reinforce the idea that his death would be anything besides quick and painless. The two clay jars were gently hoisted and rested against each other on opposite sides of the scaffold.

Nate looked at David. It was his crew member and his call. David looked at Braxton, "Any sign of the Prince?"

Braxton shook his head. "I'm sorry, Captain. No sign of life or human remains. I didn't even find a speck of unidentified DNA. It's like he was never even in here."

"What if he wasn't? Jo-Na are you positive he was in the mine?" Silas asked.

Jo-Na nodded. "I watched him and his guard enter the mine right before it collapsed. There's no doubt he went in and he never came out."

Nate turned back to David. "What's your plan, Davie?"

David turned to walk away. "I need a minute to speak to Arni."

Silas glowered at him. "You can't do anything without your new puppet master's blessing?"

David whipped back around and was in Silas's face in a few quick steps. "Oh, I'm quite capable of making a decision on my own. I've seen what happens when I call the shots and when he calls the shots. His plans are better than mine. No matter what I choose, there will be bodies on the ground. I'm asking him for a better option. Do you have a better option, Commander?"

Silas wanted to shove the Captain back out of his personal space. He was torn between Captain Alexander's treason and his duly appointed rank of "Captain." He settled for continuing to glare at him.

Nate broke the tension, "Silas, please, Captain Alexander has the right and the responsibility to use whatever resources are at his disposal. It's his man in danger. I don't care how you feel about him personally. If you can't be helpful, then just keep a lid on it."

Silas backed down. "Sorry, Captain… Weiseman. Sorry, Captain Alexander."

David walked away again. Aulani slid off a rock she had been sitting on. She followed the Captain to an open area in the cavern where he knelt on one knee. Sensing he wasn't alone, he looked over his shoulder to see Aulani watching him curiously. "Yes, Ensign?"

"Captain, I know I saw the Galatans kneel when they spoke to Pateras, but why do you kneel? We were only taught about kneeling in deference to local customs. "

David stood and turned to face her. He weighed her question carefully. "In some ways it just started feeling natural, like it's what I'm supposed to do. Who do you think Pateras is, Ensign?"

"A supreme being capable of great power."

David folded his arms across his chest and nodded. "I have no argument there. Those do apply. Aulani, he's more than that. He created every single planet, every star, every galaxy, and every single human being. He knows the thoughts and desires of every man, woman, and child who has already existed and those yet to be born. He's that big and powerful. Who am I in relation to all of that? If he wanted to, he could squash me and not think about it. He doesn't look at me like a bug though. He claims me as a child. I kneel because I owe him my very existence. He didn't have to care what happens to me, but he does. He cares about what happens to Jake. I kneel because of my amazement at everything he does, just because he wants to. Silas was partly right. I don't want to make a move without consulting Pateras. He knows the future, I don't. Does that answer your question?"

Aulani blinked back tears, "Yes sir, I think I understand. Captain, can I kneel with you?"

David smiled. "Sure, I'd love the company."

The waiting Commonwealth officers watched the exchange curiously. They couldn't hear the conversation, but Lazaro and Braxton deduced the gist of it. Lazaro had been hesitant to join the others in following Pateras. His wife had been far more eager and enthusiastic. Lazaro tapped Braxton with the back of his hand then headed toward the Captain and Aulani. Braxton followed him. The two knelt on either side of David and Aulani.

Silas rolled his eyes at the sight. "Captain, this is ridiculous. He's not going to get any answers by talking to the air. What are we going to do?"

Nate stared at the strange behavior of the trained Commonwealth soldiers. "Put the shuttle on standby. We don't need to let even one of those troops get back into the city or people are going to die."

Silas slapped his bracelet angrily. "Finally." He hailed his crew and gave the orders.

In a moment, David and his crew stood and returned to join the others. David hailed Brynna. "Commander have the shuttle on emergency standby. DO NOT lift off until you hear from me personally. The King has ordered his troops to head into the city and start killing people. If things don't go the way he wants, he may retaliate against his own subjects. Be ready to protect the city if necessary."

Brynna acknowledged the orders and sent Thane and Marissa to prep the shuttle.

David didn't wait for the awkward questions to come. "I don't know what Pateras has planned, but it's in his hands, and we will wait for him."

Remembering his Captain's orders, Silas muttered under his breath. "That was helpful."

It was loud enough for David to hear. David glanced at Silas and added. "Nobody fires a weapon, except in their own defense or on my command. Remember, this is my op."

Milo was still guarding the front entrance. He had kept his comm link open to keep track of the briefing. He hailed Captain Weiseman. "Captain, the King is approaching. He's demanding that everyone exit the mine and assemble outside for the Chief's execution."

David led both crews and the miners outside. David had slung Jake's laser rifle on his back when King De-Marion returned it to him. The strap rested across his chest. David anxiously gripped the strap and waited for his instructions.

King De-Marion moved closer to the waiting crowd near the mine entrance. "You who live and walk among the stars think you are gods to be worshiped. You are mere

147

men. My people will see just how helpless and weak you truly are. They will know I do not fear you. This man will either die a slow and painful death, or you will kill him yourselves. My people will know you are not gods and that I RULE HERE."

"King De-Marion, we never claimed to be gods. We told you we were men when we arrived here a month ago." Nate argued.

"You displayed your magnificent machines and powers to my people. They believed you were more powerful than I am. They worshiped you. Even my son became enamored with your fancy tools and gifts, and it has cost him his life. Now it will cost you one of your own. When the people hear this man cry out in pain as the ants fill him with their venom, they will see you as pathetic weaklings like I do."

The translation was picked up and relayed to Jake's ear piece. Jake raised his head and looked at the King. "Ants?! My wife hates bugs. Can't you just run me through with a sword?" This was a humiliating way for a security chief to die and a horrible way for his wife to lose him.

Without his bracelet, the king heard nothing but gibberish from Jake. The King looked at Jake with nothing but contempt. David took a deep breath then shouted one last warning to the King. "King De-Marion, Pateras is a far greater ruler than you. He will reveal himself and his power to you."

"Not before you see MY POWER. Break the jars and light the fire." The King retorted. Four men pulled the two heavy jars apart with ropes until several feet separated them, then released the two ropes. The two jars fell back into place, crashing into each other. The clay jars shattered, sending a cascade of pottery shards, sand, and angry ants falling onto Jake. The men hastily pulled back and set the brush on fire.

Jo-Na stepped up beside David. "Quickly, use your weapon and end his suffering. The fire will excite the ants, and they will bite him more ferociously."

Aulani's eyes widened in fear. Instinctively she cried out. "Jake! Captain do something!"

David pulled the laser rifle off his back. He fingered the rifle in his hands.

Jake wriggled and twitched as the ants crawled frantically across his skin. Jake's heart rate reflexively increased as his fight-or-flight instincts kicked in. The feel of the ants wriggling and running all over his body was distasteful enough. The fear of their bites and the anticipation of the associated pain added to his fear. Jake was used to fighting men in combat, not insects.

David raised the rifle. The rifle seemed immensely heavier than the last time he picked it up. He took aim at Jake's chest. One piercing blast to Jake's heart would stop his suffering. Jake saw David take aim at him. He gave his Captain an affirming nod then forced himself to lie still. He knew if he moved at the wrong time, David might miss and cause him greater pain. Jake closed his eyes, trying to ignore the crawling sensation.

David focused the guide beam and tried to shut out the feelings of nausea and regret washing over him. His distaste for killing, even for a good cause, weighed him down. He had killed men before with this very weapon. It had left him feeling cold and empty for a long time after the incident. Pateras had forgiven him, but this was different. Jake had been a thorn in his side in the beginning. He had betrayed the Captain and crew to the Commonwealth, now he was offering his life to save those same people. David desperately wanted another alternative. He made one last silent impassioned plea to Arni. This time he got his answer. A quiet voice whispered to him. "Wait for me. I've got this."

David lowered the rifle. Nate stared at him in disbelief. He volunteered, "Do you need me to do it?"

David watched Jake carefully. He pointed the rifle at him again and watched the targeting display. David zoomed the scope in as close as he could get it, then abruptly lowered the rifle. Milo scowled at Captain Alexander's perceived weakness. He raised his own rifle and took aim at Jake. David hastily blocked his shot. "No, Chief, don't."

Milo tried to move the Captain out of his way. "If you aren't going to show him some mercy, at least let me."

Nate jumped in to support his security chief. "Davie, if you can't do this, let the Chief help. Don't put your man through this."

David continued to block the shot. "Put my man through what? Look at him through the targeting display."

Milo lifted the rifle gently. He advanced the display and looked closely at the chief. There were no signs of bites on his skin. The ants were quickly leaving his body and swarming onto the ropes binding him. As Milo panned the display around Jake, he noticed ants streaming through a break in the wall of fire toward the unsuspecting guards posted around the security chief. Milo slowly lowered the weapon. Realizing what was about to happen, a slow, crooked grin spread across his face.

Jake, realizing he wasn't dead yet, opened his eyes and gave the Captain a questioning look.

Nate looked back and forth at the two security chiefs. "What is it? What am I missing?"

Milo handed the rifle off to his Captain. "I recorded the targeting feed. Look at the ants."

Nate replayed the feed. The group gathered around him saw his face change from sorrow and concern to amazement. "How is this possible? From what I can see the ants haven't touched him and are trying to get clear of the chief."

David looked down at the ground then up at Nate. "We're under the protection of Pateras. That doesn't mean we'll never get hurt, believe me, I can attest to that. It just means he can and will protect us if he chooses to."

Before anyone could respond, one guard cried out in pain and danced about erratically. Two more complained and swatted at the insects crawling up their legs. The remaining three quickly moved away from Jake fearing they would be next. They were right—and too late to protect themselves. Several early arrivals were crawling on the men's shoes. They quickly made their way inside the shoes and made their presence painfully known. The six guards took off running for the river on the back side of the ridge. It was about a half mile away, but the men were now desperate to rid themselves of their painful passengers.

King De-Marion had settled in to watch his carefully crafted drama unfold. When it fell apart before his eyes, he stood angrily. "I RULE HERE! ARCHERS! KILL THEM ALL!"

The archers drew their bows and took aim at Jake.

PATERAS SPEAKS

The ground shook, causing the side of the mountain to crack, pop, and crumble. The crew and miners were only a few yards from the mine entrance at the base of the mountain when the landslide that started early yesterday by the drilling resumed.

"Captain, we need to get away from the mountain!" Braxton hastily warned. The miners were terrified as they watched the rocks and boulders sliding toward them. A crevice in the side of the mountain split open. The tumbling debris collapsed into the crevice. Most of the miners were too terrified to even move. The crew members tried pulling them away from the foot of the mountain and the crewmen who had portable shield generators slid them on to protect themselves and the miners. The landslide stopped before it reached the men and women standing at the base of the mountain, leaving the cavern they had slept in during the night filled with monstrous rocks and boulders. If they had still been inside, they would have all died.

Jake continued to pull and strain at his bonds. He had watched nervously as the ants seemed to crawl off his body and head straight toward the fire. Although he wasn't very familiar with insects, their behavior seemed odd to him. The insects had also clustered onto the ropes binding him. Jake stopped watching the curious creatures when he saw David take aim at him with the laser rifle. He closed his eyes and waited for the end. The end seemed to take a long time in coming. He also noticed he hadn't been bitten yet. Jake opened his eyes to find out what he was missing. When the guards reacted to the ants, Jake noticed the small gaps in the surrounding fire. The ants were crawling through the gaps and attacking the guards. From the reaction of the guards, Jake was glad he hadn't been bitten. He relaxed—Arni did have things in hand, just as he promised.

Jake heard the King get angry and begin to shout. The King was too far from his bracelet for a translation to be relayed to his earpiece. He looked around and saw the archers draw their bows and take aim at him. His case of nerves returned. He quietly asked, "Arni, you still got this, right?"

The ground shook and most of the archers eased the tension on their bow strings without releasing their arrows. One younger, less experienced archer released his bow string and sent his arrow flying toward Jake. The shaking of the ground and the anxiety of the archer caused the arrow to just miss the security chief's chest. It planted itself firmly in the ground mere inches from his body. Jake swallowed hard as he looked at the arrow. He dropped his head back onto the ground. Breathing a sigh of relief, he whispered, "Thanks, Arni."

Jake raised his head again to look at the mountain. He watched in horror as the rocks seemed to cascade toward his friends and co-workers. He wondered why they didn't run from the rolling disaster. It seemed as though the entire thing lasted an interminably long time, but from the beginning of the quake to the moment the last boulder rolled into place was less than a minute. A thick cloud of dust covered the area.

Jake pulled at his bonds again. The ropes frayed and snapped. Seeing the progress on the ropes, he pulled one more time. The ropes tying his hands snapped completely. Jake shook the remnants from his wrists, then scooted down to untie his ankles. The cloud of dust was still thick enough to hide him from the others around him. Now free, Jake jumped across the narrow fire barricade, recovered his clothing and raced toward the last place he had seen the Captain.

David was concerned, not so much by the mountain's collapse, but by the fact they no longer had any place to go if the King ordered his archers and troops to attack. The miners and crewmen were on open ground with no shelter. An unstable mountainside at their backs prevented any type of retreat, and a large contingent of soldiers in front of them prevented their escape. Their weapons could take on a direct advance, but the larger number of archers who could take refuge behind the trees and other natural formations would not be easy to combat.

Out of nowhere, Jake came bounding in. "Captain, we need to get these people to safety, while no one can see."

Before the words were out of his mouth, a strong wind cleared the dust. King De-Marion wiped the dust from his eyes, drew his sword and ordered, "Prepare to attack and kill them all on my command!"

David touched his comm link. "Commander, launch the shuttle and protect the city. No one gets in or out until I say otherwise. Advise Lt. Holden the Chief is currently alive, well, and back on duty."

Silas issued similar orders. The two crews worked together to protect themselves and the miners. There were five shield generators between the two crews. David assigned Jake to configure the shields and handed the other four generators off to Dr. Henry Oliver, Aulani, Elize, and Lazaro. Those with portable shield generators formed a line and linked their controls together. Jake orchestrated the shields with his now reacquired bracelet to form an energy wall. Those who didn't have shield generators ushered the miners in behind the wall of protection.

Nate, David, Silas, Milo, Deka, and Braxton took defensive positions behind the miners and near the perimeter of the shields with their sidearms or laser rifles.

Realizing he had lost control of the situation, King De-Marion was near total mental collapse. He ranted angrily and pace maniacally. Not all his words were discernible through the translators. As he drew closer, David caught his demands.

"I am King here. You will drop your weapons and bow down to me. I rule here, not you. Face your punishment like men, not spoiled children."

When David heard his last sentence, he stood from his crouched position and laughed robustly. He looked at Nate. He decided to use Nate to translate instead of his bracelet.

"Nate, translate this for me. Tell the King I said he is the spoiled child who throws angry tantrums when he doesn't get his way. Pateras has easily bested him, and now he wants to destroy the entire game because he didn't win."

Nate glanced at David nervously. "You realize we are outnumbered, and the guy is crazy enough to do whatever pops in his head."

David grinned. "I know."

Nate scowled. "You also know we are in a nasty spot strategically, right?"

David nodded. "I know, and so does he. It will make him even angrier."

Silas kept his eyes focused on the troops in front of him. The conversation between the two Captains had him concerned. "I thought the idea was to calm the King down, not make him angrier."

David didn't want to take the time to explain his actions. "Nate, trust me. Give him my message and say whatever you think will anger him even further. I want his focus on us, not on killing children in the city."

Nate wasn't sure about David's strategy but conceded nonetheless. "King De-Marion, my friend Captain Alexander, believes you are a spoiled child who has been bested and now wants to destroy the game so no one can play again."

The translation came through to David and he scowled. "Nate, I know you don't believe this, but you have to tell him Pateras beat him."

Nate looked annoyed. "Really? Is it that important?"

David pointed at the mountain. "Do you really think I did that? Yes, it's important. If it helps, tell him my Ruler is Pateras, not the Commonwealth and Pateras has destroyed the mine."

Nate was still annoyed, but he stood and shouted the message to the King.

King De-Marion sheathed his sword and grabbed a spear from one of his guards. He launched the weapon expertly into the air. His anger fueled his throw so much that the spear sailed cleanly above their heads and easily missed the huddled group. Seeing his error, King De-Marion grabbed his sword again and rushed the group. His bodyguards hesitated, then followed. The King stopped just short of the shield and swung it at what appeared to him to be little more than a glass window. Jake hastily altered its configuration to run an electrical charge through the shield. The charge was sufficient to grab the sword and hold it, and the king in place. The King stood there twitching, unable to release his sword. His guards tried to pull their King away but found themselves caught as well. The third and fourth guards looked at their King and their fellow guards. One tried to rush around the end of the shimmering glass and attack those who were causing the problem. Milo promptly dropped him with a Tri-EMP. The fourth guard wasn't sure who or what to attack. Every option seemed to be a losing proposition. The archers held back for fear of injuring their King.

David nodded at Jake. Jake released the charge. The King and his men collapsed onto the ground. The men continued to writhe and moan painfully.

The fourth guard rushed to the King's side and raised the King's head and torso onto his lap. The King muttered something unintelligible. He repeated his utterance, only this time they could make out the words, "My son."

The Commander of the Guard watched closely to see if his King would die. The King had given orders to slay all male children within the city if he died. His orders included being taken prisoner or ordering them to stand down. The orders hadn't included instructions on what to do if the King were injured attacking the men from the stars.

The King got control of his arm enough to point toward the original mine entrance. Every head turned to see what the King was looking at. The young Prince was walking slowly toward them. The Commander of the Guard hastily sent four men to retrieve the Prince. They pulled him behind the nearest barricade. He knew King De-Marion would never forgive him if he allowed his son to be used as a hostage.

The King's troops moved quickly to tend to their young monarch. The King's personal bodyguard drug the King behind the nearest barricade.

David kept his eyes on the situation beyond their own barricade. "Jo-Na, is the prince a reasonable man?"

Jo-Na moved closer to David. "Yes, definitely. He is young and inexperienced, but he is nothing like his father. I do not know if he will challenge his father's authority, but perhaps he can reason with him."

David glanced at Nate and nodded again. "Prince Ca-Litana, your father sought to destroy us, and all the male children, on your account. We've done nothing but try to find you and all those trapped in the mine. We mean you and your people no harm. Can we have a truce?"

As Nate relayed David's request, the group waited breathlessly for the Prince's response. The Prince looked toward his father who had regained control of his faculties. The man struggled to get to his feet. He leaned heavily on his guards and the barricade. "No! There will be no truce! You have mocked and taunted me in front of my son and my men. I will punish you even worse than before! Commander, send your men into the city and bring all the male children out of the city and slaughter them here in front of these wicked, prideful men. They have not humbled themselves before me, so I will humble them in their own eyes."

David lowered his weapon and stood upright quickly. He glanced at Nate to be certain he would still translate for him. "Wait! King De-Marion, we have followed your rules. We have not attacked you or your men. You attacked us. Pateras brought your son back to you alive and well. Why would you punish your own people like this?"

The King quickly retorted. "My people would gladly give their lives to serve me. I am their KING!"

"So, you would kill all the male children in the city, including those in your own household, and that of these who guard you?" David pushed the man a little harder. "You have your son back, but you still wish to take theirs from them? You are no King, you are a spoiled child. You don't deserve to rule over even a flock of sheep."

Nate hesitated before relaying the message. He knew David was trying to push several people's buttons. He wasn't sure he wanted his crew or the miners in the middle. David gave Nate a reassuring nod. Nate shook his head, then relayed the message. He was sure David was going to get them all killed.

"Surrender yourselves to me, and I will spare the children." The King demanded.

David dropped his weapon down beside him. "Your Highness, I will give you my life in exchange for the lives of these and the children in the city. If Pateras allows you to take it from me, then so be it. I am the one who has defied you and taunted you. Let me be the example."

Nate again resisted, and this time Jake balked as well. "Captain, you can't!"

Braxton glanced over at Jake. He agreed with Jake's impassioned plea, but there was more going on than that. He said the only thing that made any sense to him, "Can it, Jake. The Captain knows what he's doing."

Nate rolled his eyes this time and relayed the message. He carefully rearranged the pronouns so there was no mistaking who was offering their life to whom. Nate didn't want to get caught up in this accidentally.

The King narrowed his eyes as he weighed the Captain's offer. It would allow him to re-establish dominance. Captain Alexander seemed to be the one who could make him the angriest. "I will accept the offer if your people swear on your own deities that they will not exact revenge for your death."

David wasn't going to let this go too easily. "Swear on the life of your son Prince Ca-Litana that when Pateras chooses between you and me, no harm will come to any of your subjects, my people, or Captain Weiseman's people."

"Pateras does not rule over me!"

"Pateras rules over all. If he chooses to let me die by your hand, then I will accept it without hesitation. If he stops you from killing me, then you have to accept his rule over you."

King De-Marion glanced at the mountain. He was concerned this man had something up his sleeve, yet he wasn't willing to give up this one minor victory. He feared that if he didn't win even a little, his people would no longer respect him. "So be it! I swear to you on the life of my son Ca-Litana, no harm will come to your people or my subjects. Let this Pateras decide between us who will rule these people. It will not be you. Have your people swear on whatever gods they serve they will not interfere or exact retribution on me or my people."

David looked to Braxton. "Lt. Commander, swear to him, and if I fall, you're in charge. No retribution."

Braxton lowered his weapon and raised his right hand. He swore his oath, "In the name of Pateras, no harm will come to you or your people if our Captain falls by your hand."

Nate raised his own hand and took a similar oath, only his oath was in the name of the Commonwealth.

David moved slowly out from behind the barrier. "Now let Pateras decide who should rule this place. You are an evil man who cares for no one but himself. It's time for another to take your place."

David put his hands up in a gesture of surrender and moved toward the King. King De-Marion was still too shaky to draw his own sword. He ordered a nearby guard to slay the Captain. The guard looked up at the mountain, then back at Prince Ca-Litana. He shook his head and retreated. "No, Your Highness, I do not wish to anger his god. He is too powerful. I would not survive his wrath."

The King angrily spat, "And you think you will survive mine?" The King grabbed his own dagger, though considerably smaller than his sword was still a formidable weapon. He started toward the fearful soldier.

David called out to the King. "King De-Marion, you gave your word none of your subjects would be harmed."

This time, his anger burned even hotter. The King, fueled by his raging temper, walked steadier and more determined. He stomped toward the Captain. The two met on middle ground. He swung the dagger viciously at David. David easily dodged him, focusing on his movements carefully and waiting for the proper opening.

A half-dozen swings later, the opening came. King De-Marion gave a broad swing across his body. David jumped back to avoid the swing then lunged at the King, taking them both to the ground. He pinned the arm holding the dagger. David found a pressure point in the King's hand. The King cried out in pain and dropped the dagger. David grabbed it and placed the blade against the King's throat. The King's eyes grew wide in fear. He stopped struggling and froze in place. He had never been in this position before. Even when he sparred with his trainers, they had never taken obvious openings to get this close.

The King tried again to shake the Captain off him. "How dare you touch me in this manner! Get off me! Release me!"

David shook his head. "Not until you yield. You will step down as ruler and hand your kingdom over to your son."

"Never! I will not yield to you. Commander, fulfill your orders. Send your men into the city…"

David pressed the dagger more firmly into the man's neck. "Do you want to die? You attempt to break your word and I will stop you… permanently."

David was losing his temper now. He pressed the dagger so tightly against the King's throat, the outer layers of skin were cut. A single small drop of blood rose to the surface and slowly rolled down his neck. Prince Ca-Litana ran forward. "Father, please surrender to him."

His son's obvious fear embarrassed King De-Marion at the same time he realized his situation was not currently winnable. "Alright, I yield. I will abdicate my throne. You have won. Release me!"

David stood cautiously as the King touched the cut on his neck. He pulled his hand away and stared at the blood on his fingers. David tucked the dagger into the back of his belt under his jacket. He reached down and offered the King a hand up. "I'm sorry I cut you, Your Highness. You aren't the only one with a temper."

The King slapped Captain Alexander's hand away. Prince Ca-Litana stared at his father's resentful behavior with fresh eyes. David stepped away from the King, turning his attention toward the miners and crew. "If King De-Marion is a man of honor, everyone is free to…"

"Captain! Look out!"

King De-Marion allowed Prince Ca-Litana to pull him off the ground. He berated his son angrily. As he dusted off his clothes, he discreetly pulled a knife from a sheath attached to his calf. "You are a disgrace to me! A king's son should never show weakness! I will never turn my throne over to such a pathetic son. I should kill your mother for bearing such a weak son. One of your younger brothers will now inherit my throne!"

The King grabbed his son and swung the knife at him. Prince Ca-Litana reacted quickly enough to grab his father's hand. The two wrestled for control of the knife. David whipped around to see the two struggling. He raced back toward the King. King De-Marion twisted in time to miss being hit by a spear. The King stopped struggling. He looked the direction the spear had come from. The Commander of the Guard was standing there. His posture indicating he had thrown the spear. His eyes pointed at his intended target—King De-Marion. As realization set in, the King's eyes grew wide. The man he trusted to protect him for years had just tried to kill him. The King released the knife slowly. A dull pain in his head grew sharper. His face went blood red. He released his grip on his son. His eyes drifted from the Commander to the sorrowful look on the face of his son, to the spear sticking in the ground. The pain in his head forced itself to the forefront of his mind. He grabbed the side of his head and dropped to his knees. He tried to stand again, but staggered, dragging one foot behind him. With a stricken look on his face, he reached for his son. His arm refused to cooperate. His vision went dark as he fell to the ground.

David reached the King's side. He pulled out a scanner and set the scanner to transmit the data directly to Dr. Adams. He hailed the Doc to let him know the information was coming. The doctor studied the data coming through. In a moment, he returned his grave diagnosis. "Captain, the King is dying. He's having a massive stroke. I've never seen one this bad. I doubt I could save him if he were lying here in front of me."

David looked at Prince Ca-Litana and shook his head. The Prince looked at the ground. He was conflicted by the events just thrust upon him. The Commander of the Guard moved forward. He drew his sword and approached Prince Ca-Litana. David and the Prince stood as David pulled his sidearm and prepared to defend the Prince.

The Commander turned his sword and offered the hilt to the Prince. He knelt in front of his new King.

"Your Highness, I have attempted to kill the King. I offer myself to you for retribution." The man bowed his head in submission to wait for justice to be served.

Prince Ca-Litana raised the sword and placed the tip of the blade against the side of his neck. "Why did you attempt to kill my father?"

"Forgive me, your Highness. Your father was a wicked, selfish man. He cared for nothing but himself. When he attempted to kill you, I could stand it no longer. You have always shown yourself to be a wise and caring man. He was still the King, and even though I did not harm him, I have done a great wrong." The man explained simply. He showed little emotion.

Prince Ca-Litana had another question. "Do you wish me dead?"

"No, your Highness, I only wished your father dead."

The Prince looked over at David. "Would you also have killed my father if he hadn't yielded?"

David's guilt was obvious on his face. "If he had given me no other choice... yes, I would have. I'm sorry. It's not what I wanted to happen."

"When you fought my father, you said Pateras would decide between you, did you not?"

"Yes, Prince Ca-Litana. I hoped he would stop your father so I wouldn't have to."

Prince Ca-Litana looked down at the man kneeling before him. "It appears he has. Pateras has chosen between us all. Commander, my father was a condemned man. You have done no wrong. I forgive you. Return to your duties under one condition."

"What is it, my King?"

"Serve me as faithfully as you did my father. If I begin to follow the same path he traveled, give me your word you will warn me. If I should fail to correct my behavior, then remove me from my throne by whatever means you see fit."

The man looked up and scowled at his new King. "Your Highness, I could only make one such mistake in my lifetime. I could not..."

The Prince pressed the sword point into the man's neck. "You chose right when you stopped my father from killing me. If I cannot count on you to choose wisely beyond today, then I have no further use for you. Can you not protect our people from their own monarch any longer?"

The man looked around again. He struggled with how to answer the brash young man. "If that is truly what his Highness desires, then you have my word. I will do as you ask."

The new young king returned the sword to his Commander of the Guard. He turned to the Captain again. "Is he gone?"

David nodded. "I'm sorry, your Highness. You have my condolences on your loss."

Prince Ca-Litana looked at the knife on the ground. "I'm not sure I've lost as much as I thought." His eyes yielding both pain and anger.

The young man who appeared to be no more than twenty years of age seemed to age ten years in the last few minutes. He stepped confidently into the place he had been groomed to fill. "Commander, prepare a stretcher for my father. Place the stretcher in his carriage, and I will ride back into the city beside him."

"You... come forward."

One of the King's personal servants came forward and knelt before his new young King. "Yes, your Highness. How may I serve you?"

"Take one wagon down to the river and fetch some water for the workers to clean themselves up before they return to the city. Send some of the other servants to bring food the King brought for himself to feed the miners and those who came from the stars."

The servant kept his eyes glued to the ground beneath his master's feet. Prince Ca-Litana quickly became annoyed with this posturing. "I am not my father. I expect you to look at me when I speak to you. Tell the others I expect the same things from them."

The servant slowly raised his head. Each moment expecting to be slapped for his insolence. He looked into his new master's eyes and saw a calm reassurance that he had acted appropriately.

"Go about your duties." The Prince quietly admonished him.

The servant moved to do as he was told. His heart quietly rejoicing over this sudden strange development.

The Commander of the Guard had his men working on the stretcher and returned to protect his new King. The young man would not officially be King until his coronation ceremony, but the Commander already viewed him as his beloved King.

Prince Ca-Litana nodded his approval as the Commander moved to his side. He turned toward the group of miners and space travelers who were now milling around. Some were exhausted, some in shock, and some were back to doing business as usual. "Jo-Na-fandrassin, approach me!"

Jo-Na looked at David and Nate sadly. "Thank you for rescuing the workers. I believe it is time for me to account for my failures. It has been a pleasure working with you."

Jo-Na moved forward and knelt humbly before the young Prince. Jo-Na was prepared to pay the price for his failure in the mines. "Your majesty, I have allowed great harm to come to you and many others. I am prepared to offer you my life as payment for my failure."

"Jo-Na, you discouraged me from entering the mine, did you not?"

"Yes, my Lord, I did."

"Why did you consider the mine to be so dangerous?"

David whispered to Nate. "He isn't going to punish him for the collapse in the mine, is he?"

"He could. These people have been living under a harsh and unforgiving example." Nate returned quietly.

Prince Ca-Litana's face was difficult to read. The Prince asked the Commander of the Guard for his sword. The Commander drew his sword and gently handed it to his King. Prince Ca-Litana placed the flat side of the blade on Jo-Na's shoulder. "Jo-Na-fandrassin, are you prepared to pay for the harm you have caused in the mine?"

"Yes, my King." Jo-Na steeled himself for the blow of death. He closed his eyes to wait.

There was a pause where Jo-Na waited for the blade on his shoulder to lift before striking him. It didn't move. Jo-Na felt the blade lift, then touch him just under his chin. "Before I pronounce your sentence, look me in the eye and tell me what went wrong in the mine."

Jo-Na lifted his head and looked the young man in the eye as requested. He swallowed hard before answering. "The—The demands for the black rock came so fast, I did not have sufficient time, supplies, equipment, or workers to secure the tunnels sufficiently. I knew the mine was not safe, and I allowed the workers into it anyway. Forgive me for endangering them and you, your Highness."

"Who made these demands of you, Jo-Na?"

"King De-Marion placed one of the Prefects over me to run the mine. Prefect Odo-Ishan is assigned to oversee the mine."

"His demand for the black rock continued to increase until we could not meet the quota required. The Prefect took my daughters to serve as slaves in his household until I met the quota. He plans to take my wife and sons in three days and sell them all in the slave market if I do not produce the product he requires. There was no time to place adequate supports in the mine. Forgive me, my Lord."

Prince Ca-Litana knew his father had ultimately created the demands for the rocks. "If there were sufficient workers, supplies, and time, could the mine still produce a profit?"

Jo-Na nodded. "Yes, my Lord. The mine is capable of producing a nice profit, but it will take time. I imagine with the amount of rock we have removed to free the miners, the rubble itself would yield large quantities of the rock."

Prince Ca-Litana eyed the man cautiously. "If you could do something differently without fear of retribution, what would you do?"

In all earnestness, Jo-Na answered, "I would have secured those tunnels weeks ago. The braces were too few and too far between. This should never have been allowed to happen. The workers should not have been in there. It hasn't been safe for weeks."

"I see." Prince Ca-Litana placed the blade of the sword back on Jo-Na's shoulder. "Swear to me you will never knowingly place another man's life in danger."

Jo-Na glanced around nervously. "I do not understand. I cannot put anyone's life in danger if I am dead."

Prince Ca-Litana didn't blink. "You are not dead, yet. Are you incapable of swearing this oath to me?"

Jo-Na decided understanding was probably unnecessary right now. "I can swear this oath to you. Your Highness, I will never knowingly endanger the life of another, and certainly not for mere profit."

The Prince lifted the sword off Jo-Na's shoulder and handed it back to its owner. "Jo-Na, your mistake is forgiven, and it will stay forgiven as long as you keep this oath. I return your life to you and entrust you with this mine. Take three days to rest before returning to the mine to work. Your workers may rest for three days as well."

"Commander, post guards around the mine. No one goes near it until Jo-Na says it is safe to do so. When we reach the palace send two squadrons to the Prefect's house and release Jo-Na's daughters along with all the slaves in his household to return to their own families. They are free, and their families no longer owe the Prefect anything. Their debts are forgiven. Put the Prefect and his family in chains and bring them before me in my courtroom. I will deal with him personally."

"Jo-Na, all that belonged to the Prefect is now yours. You will run this mine as you see fit. See that no one enters it until it is safe."

Jo-Na stood abruptly and, without thinking, made eye contact with Prince Ca-Litana. "My Lord, I don't understand." Remembering his posture, he quickly lowered his head. "Forgive me, my Lord."

"You have shown yourself to be wise and caring by staying here until they freed every miner. Even once they were clearly safe, you could have run for your life, but you didn't. You stayed and offered your life to me. I trust you to handle the Prefect's responsibilities more than the Prefect. Continue to act wisely and I will reward you appropriately. I will send another squadron of guards to secure the mine and keep people out until you deem it safe to enter. Today, go home and be with your family."

"Thank you, my Lord. You are too kind. You have given me more than I deserve. Thank you, thank you." Jo-Na repeatedly bowed as he withdrew, then raced to his home.

While the Prince began to assert himself, Nate and David tied up some loose ends of their own. They each had their shuttles stand down and sent for a Surf-ve to pick them up. Nate and Silas quickly checked on the condition of their wives.

Although David knew Jake was alive and well, he wanted to check on him. "Chief, are you alright?"

"Yes, Captain, I wasn't stung at all."

"Bitten, not stung," Silas interjected. "Ants bite, they don't sting. They inject an acidic substance when they bite, and in sufficient quantities, it can kill. You were lucky."

"Luck had nothing to do with it. The only way he survived was by being under Arni's protection." David knew Silas didn't want to hear that, but he couldn't let it go.

Jake silently agreed but wasn't ready to be as straightforward as the Captain. Jake was still adjusting to the idea of a Supreme Being running things. "How do you know so much about insects?"

"It's always been a hobby of mine. I got some specialized training in it when I joined the mission." Silas had been interested in entomology since boyhood. The mission gave him a legitimate way to indulge his inner child.

"Chief, how did you get free?" David asked.

"I'm not exactly sure. The ropes just snapped. I'd like to examine those ropes again." Jake headed toward the spot of his intended execution.

David and Silas were equally curious and followed him. Jake picked up the ropes and studied them carefully. "The tears are in different places on the individual strands. There's no real continuity to where they snapped. Do you suppose the ants chewed through them?"

Silas shook his head. "Ants don't do that either, at least not exactly. They do, but not like that. I mean this isn't typical ant behavior. There are differences between species, but this is just not normal ant activity." Silas pulled out his scanner and scanned the ropes and some of the remaining ants. He looked back and forth at the ants, the ropes, and his scanners. His brows knit tightly, then raised in amazement and disbelief.

David's curiosity reached its limit. "What is it, Commander Asher?"

"This... This acid is particularly virulent. It seems to have burned through the strands of rope. The ants must have bitten the ropes, leaving the acid behind. Chief, by my estimate, about twenty bites would've made you really sick, and forty would have killed you. I'm guessing there were at least a couple hundred ants dumped on you. The heat from the fire should have driven them to bite you. You weren't bitten even once?"

Jake shook his head. "No, not once."

Silas looked at David. "How did you know not to shoot him?"

David wanted to be totally candid with the man. His promise to Nate still applied. "You already know the answer to your question."

The servants had returned with the water from the river. David moved to go clean up a bit. He didn't care much for the idea of cleaning with what had to be germ infested waters. He didn't want to appear ungrateful to Prince Ca-Litana. Nate was already cleaning up. Prince Ca-Litana kept his distance and didn't attempt to clean himself up. He approached Captain Weiseman.

"Captain Weiseman, were there any losses in the mine? Is your crew... uninjured?"

Nate finished drying his hands and face. He gently laid down the towel. "No one died except your father. There have been numerous injuries. Your personal bodyguard was one of the injured. Several of my crew suffered minor injuries. My wife… is… gravely injured. She is alive, for now. Captain Alexander's doctor has healed all injuries except hers. Her injuries are far too extensive."

"I am so sorry, Captain Weiseman. Can this Pateras not heal her?" The naïve Prince queried.

David overheard the conversation and answered for his friend. "Prince Ca-Litana, although Pateras could heal her, he is considered the enemy of the Commonwealth. If Captain Weiseman asks Pateras to heal his wife, it will guarantee his own death and his wife's. The Commonwealth would find them both guilty of treason."

Nate gave David a look of pain and appreciation. "Thanks for understanding, Davie." Nate stepped away to pull himself together again. His mind had been preoccupied with the events occurring around him. The reminder of his wife's precarious position returned her to the forefront of his mind.

"Prince Ca-Litana, may I ask you a question?" David inquired.

"Yes, of course." Prince Ca-Litana seemed eager to talk with him.

"How did you survive the cave-in? You are as dirty as the rest of us, but you appear to be uninjured."

The Prince looked down at his appearance. It was rare for him to appear as unkempt as this. He grinned slightly at his own disheveled countenance. "A large man, a very large man, shielded me with his body until the rocks stopped falling. His skin and clothes were so bright, it was brighter than the brightest day. He spoke to me of many things while I was trapped in there."

David's eyes widened. "Did he tell you his name? Was his name Gabe?"

Nate turned slightly to listen to the rest of the conversation.

"Yes, he told me to listen to you and to trust you. He told me you had things to teach me. We're all tired and should rest today. May I come to your… your flying… What is it called?"

David smiled. He understood the young man's struggle. "We call it a ship. The name of our ship is the *Evangeline*. It is also our home. You can use whichever term you like. You're welcome to visit us any time of the day or night. We always have someone awake, and I can talk with you whenever you want. I would like a shower and a nap first, if that's possible." David's translator beeped a warning at him. The word shower didn't translate. The hole in his sentence left the Prince with a questioning look. "I want to go home and get cleaned up," David corrected. The Prince smiled, and his confusion cleared.

"Of course. I should warn you, though. The Commonwealth is the enemy of Pateras. Captain Weiseman is duty-bound to report you if you choose to follow Pateras. Tomorrow he will be required to attempt to arrest me or report me if I remain here."

The Prince looked at the two men in their identical uniforms quizzically. Nate turned and gave the conversation his full attention. He interrupted before Ca-Litana could ask the obvious questions. "Your Highness, please allow Captain Alexander and me to talk privately before agreeing to meet with him. He is right to warn you of the danger, but perhaps we can come to an agreement of sorts."

The Prince nodded and dropped the matter for now.

He promised to give them the time they requested. He informed the Captains he would be tied up with his father's funeral arrangements, his own coronation, and other affairs of state for a time as well. The Prince took his leave of the Captain, cleaned himself up and began his long, slow ride back into the city to proclaim his father's death.

Nate pulled David aside. "Would you really talk to him about Pateras, knowing I'll have to report it? You'll only get these people killed, and we've worked incredibly hard to keep them alive."

David shook his head sadly. "Have you already forgotten our conversation from yesterday morning? Nate, my crew and I have to disappear from this planet, and after you leave here, you'll need to disappear too. If you show up near any Commonwealth facility or ship, you'll be shot down, arrested, or executed!"

Silas walked up in time to hear David's comment. "What are you talking about? Captain, what's he trying to tell you?"

Nate balked at the idea of going into the matter right now. "Can we talk about this later? I'd really like to see my wife."

"I will gladly wait to get into this, under one condition. You cannot report our presence here. It will certainly get us killed, but it will get your people killed as well. Don't let the Commonwealth know we're here until we've talked. Your entire crew deserves to hear the truth. I told you we could pick up where we left off, and I meant it. If you decide to report us after we've talked, I will turn myself over to you and send my crew away. Are we good on this point?"

This time it was Silas who balked. "You don't get to set terms for us. You're nothing but a bunch of weak-minded traitors. We..."

"That's enough, Silas. It's what I agreed to, and you are going to need to hear what he has to say as well. No one contacts the Commonwealth until I say so. We'll hear him out later when everyone's had a chance to get some rest. We don't have to believe him, but he's not going to rest until he has his say." Nate tried to settle his Commander down, unsuccessfully.

"But sir..."

"You have your orders, Mr. Asher. We're going to get some down time and wait for clearer heads to prevail. So, drop it for now. All comms go through me. Let's go. Our ride's here."

The two Surf-ves arrived with Lexi and Gennie at the helms. The two crews piled into their respective vehicles, except for Nate and Milo. Nate wanted to go to the *Evangeline* to check on Stephanie, but Milo and Silas weren't about to let him go alone. Nate sent his own Surf-ve back to the *Emissary* to let his own people get some down time. He advised Silas to adjust the duty roster, keeping only one person on duty as a watch officer.

Before going their separate ways, Silas pulled David aside. "Captain Alexander, in deference to your rank and friendship with Captain Weiseman, I'm going to ask you—

politely—not to take advantage of my Captain's current weakness. Don't try to sway him to your cause, please."

David turned to face the concerned Commander. He weighed his words carefully. "Silas, I doubt you'll believe me, but I'll say it anyway. Pateras doesn't force himself on anyone. I walked away willingly because it was the right thing to do. I can't and won't force Nate to do anything he doesn't want to do. I came here to warn him about a genuine danger to you and your crew because I care about him and Steph. I have proof of the dangers and I will share the information with you. You have my word, I'm not going to assault him with it. I'm going to provide the information to all of you. If he asks, I won't withhold it, but this is certainly not the right time and place to pressure him. Just promise me one thing, Silas. Promise me you will not disobey his orders and bring the Commonwealth into this. It will only get all of us killed. I can promise you that."

Jake popped his head out of the vehicle. "Captain, is everything alright?"

"Yeah, Chief, we're good. I'm coming." David glanced back at Silas. "Nate is safe. You have my word as an officer. Are we good?"

Silas stared at the Captain. He wasn't sure he could trust him. "I suppose, if you keep your word."

Silas climbed aboard his own Surf-ve and sat down. "Gennie, you can head back to the ship at your leisure." He spent the brief trip sitting there sullenly, staring at nothing in particular.

David climbed aboard his own vehicle and sat down near Nate. He seemed equally sullen. Nate finally asked, "My Commander giving you problems?"

David gave Nate a weak smile. "No, not really. He's just worried about you."

"So, what's bothering you?"

David hesitated. He wasn't sure he wanted to answer that question. "He's going to ignore your orders and contact the Commonwealth."

"He told you that?" Nate stiffened visibly.

"No, but I know he's going to. I'm just worried about your people and mine. I can't take on the entire Commonwealth. My one little ship can't even do more than run away from the Pacification Fleet, and that's assuming we see them coming."

"It's just your gut telling you he's going to disobey my orders. Right?" Nate proffered.

David winced. It wasn't, but he wasn't sure how far to take the conversation. "Maybe, maybe I'm just a little nervous. It's not like this is anything the Academy prepared us for."

A TRUCE ENDED

The Surf-ve pulled up the ramp extended from the back of the ship and parked in the bay reserved for it. The crew climbed out wearily and paused to see if the Captain had orders for them. David realized he had failed to take advantage of the ride back. He glanced around at his tired crew.

"With the exception of Lt. Flint, all of you have at least six hours of downtime, get something to eat, shower, sleep, drop by the Infirmary if you need to. Lt. Flint, could you escort our guests to the Infirmary? I'll catch up with you in a few minutes, Nate."

David stayed behind and kept Jake with him. Jake knew he was in trouble — again. "Captain, I'm sorry I jumped the gun and..." He tried to beat his Captain to the punch.

David wasn't about to let Jake stop him from venting. "Chief, just stop. Did Arni tell you to do that?"

"Uh... No, not really. I just... well I... uh..."

David rubbed his tired, grimy face. "Just tell me why. You're about to be a father. Do you really think it was fair to Marissa and your son to put your life at risk unnecessarily?"

"But, Captain, it was necessary."

"How do you figure that?" David countered.

"Captain, I wasn't trying to get myself killed. I swear I wasn't. I knew it could happen, though. How much trouble am I in, sir?"

"I'm not even going to venture to tell you how much trouble you're in with your wife. As far as I'm concerned, that remains to be seen. I still need some answers, Chief."

If this had happened six months ago, David would've put the Chief on report. His patience was surprisingly intact.

"Captain, we're in uncharted territory here. You're too important to our new mission. This crew would fall apart without you. I knew you would offer your own life to save the Lt. Commander. I couldn't let you do that. The crew still doesn't have much trust in me. They do trust you. I guess the answer to your question is I owe you my life several times over. The crew and I need you to stay alive more than they need me to stay alive. I'm sorry if I disappointed you—again." Jake looked down at his soiled hands and saw more stains than were physically present on his hands. His guilt over their recent past weighed heavily on him.

"You didn't disappoint me, Jake. You frustrated me, but you didn't disappoint me. Thank you for trying to protect me, and the crew, and the civilians. Next time, let me make the command decisions, please."

Jake looked up, slightly confused. "Sir?"

"You're right. We're in uncharted territory here. Don't second guess me. Let me make the command decisions, and if I order you to your death, then you can go. I was doing my best to keep all of us alive. Arni has been trying to teach us to call on Pateras in these situations. That was my plan. My plan wasn't to offer myself. That was the last resort. Give me your word this won't happen again."

Jake was confused about why the Captain wasn't yelling at him or confining him to his quarters. He studied the Captain's face for a moment. Captain Alexander was clearly tired, but his concern for Jake was abundantly clear. "You have my word, sir. No more jumping the gun. I will wait for your orders."

"Thank you, Chief. The crew will get past their distrust of you. It's just going to take some time. Go present yourself to your wife then get a shower, a meal, and some sleep. I may need you later."

Jake turned to go. "Yes sir, thank you, sir. Um… can I ask you a question?"

David nodded.

"How did you know not to shoot me?" Jake asked as the two headed for the elevator.

David was careful not to smile. "I didn't know. I just wanted you to suffer a little while for your insubordination. I didn't know Arni was intervening on your behalf until a few minutes later."

Jake nearly gave himself whiplash. "What?! Are you serious?"

The corner of David's mouth twitched then gave way to a grin. "Arni told me to wait. The scope display didn't show any bites on you. I saw the ants massing on the ropes and streaming away from you on the ground. I knew Arni had things under control. Chief Griffin nearly took you out himself when I didn't."

"Wow, I really am living on borrowed time. Thanks for not shooting me, or letting Milo shoot me." Jake marveled.

"You might still be a walking dead man. I told your wife I wasn't bringing you back in one piece. You walk in here unscathed after leaving her that farewell message, she may just take your head off herself."

Jake considered the Captain's words for a moment then reached into his belt and pulled his knife out. He offered the hilt to David. "Do you suppose you could nick me just a little? Maybe Marissa will have mercy on me if I'm bleeding just a little."

David grinned and shook his head. "Oh no, you're on your own mister. It was nice knowing you."

The two stepped onto the bridge to check in with Brynna and Marissa. David quickly excused Jake and Marissa from the bridge for a few minutes. He updated Brynna on the current situation and its surprising resolution. He warned her about the impending end to their truce with the crew of the *Emissary*. The implications were that the crew could come under fire from the crew of the *Emissary*. The understanding was that the truce would remain intact until tomorrow morning. David hoped the crew of the *Emissary* would not violate the truce. The two discussed security measures to put into place to keep themselves on a heightened state of alert. They also discussed Stephanie's situation which quickly rabbit-trailed into a trip down memory lane.

When Marissa returned a few minutes later, her eyes were red from crying, but she was smiling with relief. David stopped to offer her a few encouraging words before excusing himself to get a much-needed shower.

"Lt. Holden, Jake was brave, selfless, and proactive. I can't fault him for that. I do have his word that from now on, he'll wait for my orders. He won't do this again. You have my word and his. Don't be too hard on him, okay?"

Marissa gave the Captain a weak smile. "Thank you for bringing him back to me, Captain. If he ever does anything like this again, I may kill him, myself."

David patted her on the shoulder and laughed. "There may be a line for that."

David swung by his quarters to wash his hands and face. He really wanted a full-blown shower but was too worried about Stephanie and Nate. When he reached the Infirmary, Jason was explaining the extent of Stephanie's injuries.

"Captain Alexander, I was just telling Captain Weiseman what kind of treatment his wife is going to need. These ships don't have the facilities to treat injuries this extensive. The reconstruction to her lower body is going to take state-of-the-art cloning technology. I can save her life, but she would lose her legs if I tried to work on her here. If I could get into a more advanced facility I could do it, but not in one of our ships."

Nate stared at his wife's face through the window in the stasis chamber. "Can we move her back to the *Emissary*? Is it safe?"

Jason gave Nate a reassuring smile. "As long as she's in the stasis chamber, she's safe. We can simply swap this chamber out with one of yours."

David stepped up to object. "Jason, we'll need to change out the chambers."

Jason looked confused. "That's what I said."

David shook his head. "The serial number of the chamber is linked to our ship. If Nate shows up at any Commonwealth base with our stasis chamber, they'll know we've interacted. He and his crew would face the same things we did on Romajin. She'll have to be moved into one of their own chambers."

Jason scowled. "Captain, every time we disengage the stasis field, her body will deteriorate further."

Milo stepped up quietly behind Captain Weiseman. "What are they talking about, sir?"

Nate tried to dismiss Milo. "I'll explain it later."

"Isn't there a way to alter the serial numbers and swap, just the information?" Laura suggested.

David shrugged. "It's possible. It's also possible they could get her and the stasis chamber in and out of a facility without anyone noticing."

Nate looked at David and knew he wanted to say more. "What aren't you saying, Davie?"

"I gave Silas my word I wouldn't prey on your current weakness. You already know what my concerns are."

"What concerns?" Milo interjected again.

Before Nate could respond David intervened. "Nate, give Jason a chance to look at the options. We can get back together in the morning, provided our truce is still in effect. You and the chief are welcome to the guest quarters or Lt. Flint can run you back to your ship. The sofa in the guest quarters converts to a bed so you can both be comfortable."

Nate nodded his acknowledgment. "Could I have a moment alone with my wife?"

Jason nodded. He set the computer to notify him if anything changed, then followed everyone out of the room.

Nate stood over the chamber looking at his beautiful wife's face. Despite the dirt and grime still on her face and hair, she was the most beautiful woman he had ever seen. He leaned against the bed behind him and spoke plainly to his unresponsive wife. "Stephanie, I don't know what to do. I want to do whatever it takes to get you well, but if Davie's telling the truth, the only place to go is into the arms of our enemy. We've worked long and hard to get where we are. I would gladly throw it all away to get you back, but I would be making that decision for both of us. I don't know if I… What if I do this and you hate me for it? I can choose to throw away my career, but do I have the right to throw yours away with it? What do I do? I don't want to go on without you."

"Nate?"

Nate pulled himself up abruptly. "Brynna, I'm sorry. I didn't hear you come in."

"I'm sorry, Nate, didn't mean to interrupt. I—I thought perhaps you might want to talk. I know you and I haven't known each other as long, but I thought I could offer some insight."

Nate nodded. "Perhaps you can. Could we go for a walk?"

"Sure, do you want Milo to come?" Brynna suggested for his own safety.

"No, give me a moment alone with Stephanie and I'll meet you at the airlock."

Brynna nodded and excused herself. She updated David and grabbed a couple canteens of water before heading to the airlock.

Nate looked back down at Stephanie. "Stephanie, I don't know which way I'm going to go on this but forgive me if I choose wrong. It seems that either choice could cost us both our lives. I love you. I'll be back to see you tomorrow." He rested his hand on the chamber for a moment wishing he could touch his beloved wife for just a minute.

Nate found Milo and David in the dining hall drinking coffee and munching on sandwiches. He told Milo what he was about to do and ordered the man to get a ride back to their own ship without him. Milo objected albeit, not as strongly as Nate expected. Nate assured him, he would stay in contact and return to the ship shortly.

David volunteered to send Lexi to take the Chief back to his ship after he was done with his meal. Nate informed David he planned on taking his walk toward his own ship and wouldn't be back until tomorrow morning. He assured him their truce would still be in effect as long as Stephanie was on board his ship.

Nate met Brynna at the main entrance to the ship. The two walked silently down the steps. Neither said a word as they headed across the field. Once the ship was out of sight, Nate started their discussion. "Was there some particular insight you wanted to share with me?"

Brynna squinted. The sun was high in the sky as it had reached mid-morning. "I'm glad to share whatever insights you need. I've been pretty much where you are."

Nate scoffed. "I seriously doubt that."

Brynna didn't want to make light of his situation, but she had been precisely where he was. She stopped in her tracks causing Nate to stop and turn back to her. "Nate, I have been exactly where you are and in similar situations since then."

"Just how do you figure that? You and David are both alive and well." Nate argued.

Brynna continued walking again, only more slowly. "Nate, before we chose to follow Pateras, we were on our third planet. The world was technologically advanced, yet they were non-space-faring. The world had a very rocky history with the Commonwealth. They arrested, tried and convicted us for war crimes. David... David arranged a plea agreement. He took full responsibility for our crimes and was sentenced to death."

"It must not have been that bad because he's alive and here." Nate quipped. As soon as Nate saw the pain on Brynna's face, he regretted his tone. "I'm sorry, Brynna. Go on."

As Brynna relived the pain, her voice grew soft and strained. "Three days before his execution, six men nearly beat him to death because they thought his sentence wasn't harsh enough. He wouldn't allow the doctors to do more than make him strong enough to walk. I watched him limping to his own execution, the bruises still on his face

and body. I saw him chained to the posts, his face...
covered with a hood."

"Was he granted a reprieve at the last minute?"

Fresh tears rolled down her face slowly. "No, not by
the government. Arni Liontari switched places with David.
No one knew. I saw what I thought was David, what had
been David, take twelve jolts of radiation. I saw his body
get weaker and weaker and I saw him die."

"But it was this Arni Liontari who died. How is that
like my situation with Stephanie?"

"None of us had joined the Liontari forces. Arni
promised me, David wouldn't die. I saw David placed
between those pillars, I saw the hood placed over his head.
Nate, I never took my eyes off him. I told Arni, he would
earn a small amount of trust from me if he saved David's
life. When they removed the hood from his body, we all
saw it. It was Arni, not David and he was undoubtedly
dead. I never told anyone, but when Arni reappeared days
later, I gave him my full trust. I didn't tell anyone because
I knew what it would cost me. I was afraid it would cost
me my husband, and I knew it would cost me my career
and my life. Everyone thought David started this. He
didn't. I was both relieved and excited when he chose to
follow Pateras. If there was one person I knew I couldn't
hide my decision from, it was David."

Nate stared down at the ground while they walked.
The *Emissary* was over two miles from the *Evangeline*. The
two walked silently for several minutes again.

Brynna spoke again. "I suppose my situation wasn't
exactly the same. I didn't make a deal just to save his life.
Arni told me outright, he planned to take David's place.
He was only trying to give me hope. Nate, we lost Marissa
at one point. Arni didn't ask us for anything, he just brought
her back to life. We continued serving the Commonwealth
and Arni did nothing to stop us."

"What's your point, Brynna?"

"My point is, Arni can heal her. Arni is a kind, loving
soul. He can be trusted. David went through horrible
things on Romajin at the hands of Supreme Executor
Hale. He would tell him one thing then go back on his
word. Arni protected his life in so many ways. David was
the one who reported Arni's home world. He's the one

who got Arni's mother killed along with everyone else on the planet. David ultimately blames himself for the six million deaths on Galat III. Arni should have hated David along with the rest of us. He certainly shouldn't have taken his place at his execution. Arni has shown us kindness after kindness that we didn't deserve."

Nate frowned. "You mean a superior alien being created a set of circumstances to make you feel indebted to him, so now you blindly follow him?"

Brynna scowled. "I suppose it could look like that. David didn't choose to follow Pateras just because he felt like he owed him. He does owe him, but that wasn't enough to turn him. It was a two-part decision. When we left our third planet, David hadn't left the Commonwealth, but he did have a profound respect for Pateras. I think if Pateras and the Commonwealth hadn't been in conflict, he probably would have left the Commonwealth sooner. David didn't give up his loyalty to the Commonwealth easily. He left because he saw... he saw the Commonwealth and Luciano Hale for what they really were."

"Which is what?" Nate demanded. "What is so blasted bad about the Commonwealth?"

Brynna scowled remembering David's promise to Silas. She didn't want to break his promise indirectly by assaulting Nate with her propaganda.

"Nate, I didn't come out here to debate the virtues or failings of either the Commonwealth or Pateras. I'll answer your questions if you really want. I came out here because I knew you were in a difficult situation and I thought you might want to talk to someone who could understand. I thought you might need someone who could listen without judging or questioning your loyalty. Your ship's psychologist, your commander and your security chief would do that. It's their job to do that."

Their walk took them alongside the river. As it was nearing the hottest part of the day, Nate meandered closer to the water. The heat, exhaustion, and stress were taking a toll on him. For a time, they walked silently through the shade of the trees adorning the shallow twisting river. Nate stopped at the edge of the river. Kneeling at the water's edge, he splashed some cool water on his face and neck. He stared down at the shallow, placid pool in front of him.

Brynna watched the pained look on his face. "Nate is there something else on your mind?"

Nate rubbed his face. His attempt was to wipe away the evidence of his thoughts which were clearly displaying themselves. He sat back on a rock and continued to stare into the water. "Is it true? What David said about Strabothon? Was everyone on the planet wiped out?"

Brynna still wasn't sure about continuing with the conversation, but she hated to dodge his question. "We haven't seen Strabothon personally. David heard Executor Hale and Admiral Deacons discussing it along with Galat III and another planet. We've seen the destruction on Galat III. We can only assume the situation is the same on the other two planets."

Nate rubbed his face again more aggressively as he paced anxiously. He finally came to rest leaning against a tree. "What have I done?"

"Nate, please don't blame yourself. You did what the Commonwealth ordered you to do. They did this, not you."

Nate started pacing. "You don't understand. We—We marooned two of our ship's crew there. They—they turned. I didn't want to space them. I thought—I thought they could at least live out their lives peacefully. Now you're telling me, I sent them to their deaths anyway?"

The stricken look on Brynna's face only added to Nate's feelings of regret. The shock left her speechless. When she could finally speak again, "Who—Who was it?"

"My ship's psychologist and his wife, Elijah and Aneska Perdy; they—they spent a great deal of time with the religious leaders. They came to me and told me they didn't believe Pateras was as dangerous as the Commonwealth had led us to believe. I thought they'd been turned. I left them behind and reported needing new officers. Aneska was my comms officer. They assigned Henry and Luna Oliver as their replacements. Luna wasn't primarily a comms officer. She's actually a trained psychologist and sociologist. It was too late into the mission to replace both officers with comparable counterparts."

Brynna had crossed paths with Elijah and Aneska during their training. She didn't know them well, but she had liked them well enough. "Did—Did they protest at all?" Brynna knew if they had joined Pateras, they would have been honest about it. If they were merely making honest observations and evaluations, they would have strenuously objected.

Nate looked at her sorrowfully. "I never gave them a chance to protest. I told them I would look into it, then discussed it with Silas and Milo. We agreed not to take chances. I sent most of the crew, including Elijah and Aneska, into town. Milo and I cleaned out their quarters. We dropped their personal belongings along with a few rations outside the ship. When they returned, we separated them from the crew, sedated them and laid them down beside their belongings in the shade of a large tree. I got us into orbit then told the crew what I'd done and notified HQ. Admiral Deacons ordered us to the nearest CIF base where we went through some extensive evaluations and debriefings. They assigned the Olivers to us while we were there."

Nate looked around nervously as though someone might overhear him. He covered the microphone on his bracelet and spoke more softly. "I looked at their personnel files. I get the feeling they have a history in intelligence work. Their files seemed—scripted. I've also had the feeling they were watching us."

Brynna grimaced, "Knowing what I do now. It wouldn't surprise me."

Nate began to pace again. "I know you didn't want to talk about this, but I really need to know. Why wouldn't it surprise you to find out they're spying on us?"

"Executor Hale knows he's no match for Pateras. He blatantly told David he would kill anyone David talked to on Romajin. Strange how the entire base was destroyed the second we escaped. Nate, we didn't destroy that base. Luciano Hale destroyed it so the entire Commonwealth would be driven to hunt us down."

The guilt on Nate's face gave way to doubt. Brynna's explanation seemed far-fetched. "I wish I knew who to believe."

Brynna gave Nate a weak smile. "I wish I could help you with that. Pateras gave us the right to make that choice for ourselves, and Luciano Hale wants to prevent us from making that choice. This choice is yours, and yours alone. All I can do is tell you what I chose and why."

The two began walking again. Their conversation waned as Nate weighed Brynna's words. Just short of the ship Nate stopped to ask one more question. "I'm a little confused about something. I—I haven't seen you, your crew or the people of Strabothon do anything... well, anything I could interpret as dangerous to the Commonwealth. What's... uh... what's so dangerous about followers of Pateras? Why's Executor Hale afraid of him, and of you?"

Brynna knew she was getting into rocky territory. "I... uh... I can go there if you want, but it's going to seem more far-fetched than anything I've said so far. Are you sure you want to hear it?"

"Probably not but tell me anyway."

"The Commonwealth told us Pateras was capable of unexplained phenomena. It's because he's a Supreme Alien Being. What they haven't told us, mostly because no one knows, is that Luciano Hale is also a superior alien being. He's capable of taking human form, and he's taken the form of every Supreme Executor in the last three hundred years. He used to work for Pateras until Pateras exiled him. Pateras used to have the loyalty of all of humanity. Luciano Hale knows the only way to get back at Pateras is through us. Pateras plans to punish Luciano Hale for his crimes. His followers are going to face justice as well. Executor Hale is trying to take as many humans down with him as he can."

Nate shook his head. "Yeah... that's pretty far-fetched. I'm starting to feel like a pawn in somebody else's game."

Brynna understood his analogy completely. She smiled weakly again. "It's more like—a parent trying to reclaim a wayward child, only more intense."

The two talked for a few more minutes within sight of the ship. Nate invited Brynna to come inside to cool off and freshen up for a few minutes. Before she could answer, she heard Arni's voice, "Return to the *Evangeline*, don't enter his ship."

Milo had reached the ship an hour ago and reported in to Commander Asher. Silas was less than pleased to find out Brynna was escorting their Captain back to the ship. He and Claire were eating with Henry and Luna Oliver when Milo reported in. Silas had the same concerns about Henry and Luna as Nate. Silas wasn't about to lose any more crew members. He slammed his fist angrily on the table. "I've had enough of this! They killed ten thousand people on Romajin! I'm not about to let them take this crew down too! Milo, get me a weapon!" Silas stood and headed for the door.

Milo chased after him. "Commander, wait! This is my responsibility. I'll take care of it."

Silas stopped just short of the door. Seeing Milo's resolve, he relented. "Alright Chief, when the time comes you can handle it. Just make sure you don't leave any evidence leading Captain Alexander back here."

Dr. Oliver leaned back in his chair and twisted to face the two men. "If their Commander goes missing and they don't suspect us, they may enlist our help to search for her. It splits them into smaller groups so they can be managed more easily."

"Good idea, Henry. Chief, I'm going to stick her in stasis until I know they don't suspect us. They still have the Captain's wife on their ship. Who knows what they might do to her if they think we had anything to do with their commander's disappearance. I'm going to put a stop to their traitorous behavior once and for all."

Milo acknowledged his orders. He retrieved a weapon for the Commander then promptly went to his station to watch the scanners for Captain Weiseman and Commander Alexander.

Claire watched the exchanges silently. She grew increasingly more distressed by the conversation. She and Aneska had been friends. The crew members she had met from the *Evangeline* seemed to be good people as well. She felt indebted to the mysterious man who watched over her in the cavern. She wanted to stop this before it started.

After finishing their meal Silas and Claire went back to their quarters where Claire finally had time to talk to him about her harrowing experience without her eyesight. "I know Dr. Adams assured me I would get my sight back, but I still had a difficult time keeping my wits about me."

Silas wrapped his arms around his wife and held her tightly. "I know, I could hear it in your voice. I wanted nothing more than to tunnel through that debris with my bare hands to get to you."

Claire smiled appreciatively. "I could hear the fear in your voice too."

Silas pulled her head gently to him. He laid his cheek on the top of her head and kissed her. "I'm sorry you heard that. I was trying to help you stay strong."

Claire pulled back. "Silas, you helped me stay strong. The fear I heard in your voice told me you would do whatever it took to reach me. It also told me how much you love me."

Silas pulled her in close again and hugged her tightly. "Thank you. I don't know what I would do without you. I can't help but be thankful you weren't hurt as badly as the Doc. I don't know how the Captain is still standing." Silas slowly relaxed his grip.

Claire moved away from him sat down on the couch. "Me either. I wouldn't be doing that well if it were you."

The two were silent for a few moments before Claire had the nerve to ask. "Did you meet all the crew of the *Evangeline*?"

Silas glanced casually at her. "I didn't stop and count them all, but yeah, I believe so. Why?"

"Did you meet a man named Arni?"

"Arni? Why? Did you see him?" Silas stopped moving completely at the mention of Arni's name. He knew exactly who Arni was, but Claire had not been present when Captain Alexander told them about him.

Claire snickered slightly. "No, I can't say that I did. He was trapped in the mine with the rest of us. I couldn't see anyone at that time. I was just hoping to get a chance to thank him. I was… I was afraid. I'm not sure how to say this."

Silas' attention was riveted on his wife. "Just spit it out."

Claire gave Silas a sideways glance. She knew something was hitting him wrong. "Never mind, it's not important."

Silas continued to stare at his wife. "No, I want to hear this."

"I was feeling very vulnerable in there. I couldn't see. My ankle was broken, and I was trapped in a cavern with a dozen men who were suddenly faced with their own mortality."

Silas moved closer to Claire. It was obvious he was bristling. "What happened Claire?"

"Silas, what's wrong? You sound angry."

"Did he take advantage of you?" Silas demanded.

"No, that's my point, Silas. I was afraid someone might, but Arni kept me company. He made me feel safe. He was a very sweet man and a comfort to me. I just wanted to thank him. I also wanted to put a face to the voice. What is wrong with you? You don't need to feel threatened by him. My point was, I hated losing Elijah and Aneska. I'm worried about the crew of the *Evangeline*. They seem like normal people to me. I just think we need to think this thing through and not act too quickly. I don't want to lose anyone else."

Silas backed away. "I need to go check on the Captain. We can talk more about this later." The Commander didn't wait on Claire's response. Claire was now annoyed by her husband's odd behavior. She yelled after him, "Don't bother if you're going to act like a jerk."

Silas found Milo on the bridge. Milo reported the Captain and Commander Alexander as being at the edge of the clearing. Silas pulled Milo away from his station and back into the corridor. "Milo, I believe Claire may have been compromised."

"What? Are you sure? What are you going to do?"

Silas had trouble looking his security chief in the eye. "She said she met Arni. Arni is the son of Pateras El Liontari. Milo... I can't..."

Milo knew what his Commander was asking. He swallowed hard. "I understand, sir. Put them both in stasis. It guarantees Captain Alexander won't look at us for his wife's disappearance if one of our people disappears at the same time. I'll take care of both of them together as painlessly as possible. I'm... uh... I'm sorry for your loss, Commander."

Silas put up a wall between his personal feelings and the job to be done. "Thank you. Let's go into the Infirmary and get two chambers ready." The two headed down to the lowest level of the ship and worked out how they were going to get the two women into the chambers. Once they decided on their strategy, Silas tapped his comm unit, "Lt. Commander Asher, please report to the Infirmary."

Milo cocked his head sideways. "Lt. Commander?"

Silas' face showed no emotion. "Claire got ticked off at me a few minutes ago. She won't balk if I call her by her rank. She'll know it's official business."

A moment later Claire entered the room and found Silas and Milo examining the stasis chambers. Her tone was frosty as she reported to her husband and superior, "What can I do for you, Commander?"

Silas glanced at her briefly. He didn't want his face to reveal his plans for her. "Dr. Adams needs to move Stephanie into one of our own stasis chambers, so it doesn't get traced back to the *Evangeline*. How much of this chamber is identifiable? Is there a way to attach a temporary power supply and simply move the patient compartment without losing the continuity of the stasis field? I was looking at the connections under here..."

Silas knelt on the floor and pointed at a juncture in the chamber. Claire knelt in front of him to get a better view of the area Silas was referring to. As soon as she knelt down, Silas grabbed her hand. "I love you, Claire, no matter what. You have to believe that."

Claire gave him a confused look.

Milo shoved a hypo-spray against her neck and pressed the button on it. Claire felt the sting as the sedative pushed into her tissue. She grabbed at the spot on her neck and looked up at her husband. "Silas... what...?" Her vision went black and she fell forward. Silas caught her before she hit the floor. He and Milo turned her gently then lifted her and placed her in the chamber. They closed the chamber and activated it.

Silas stood there a moment looking at his wife. Milo backed off to give him a moment to say goodbye to her. Silas finished his mental farewell then shoved the chamber angrily into its slot in the wall. He turned to face Milo. "Somebody's going to pay dearly for this!"

"Are you sure you don't want to come inside or let me get someone to take you back to the *Evangeline*?" Nate asked.

"No, I need to head back." Brynna turned to leave.

Nate smiled, "Thanks for listening, Commander. I'll see you later when I come by to pick up Stephanie."

"I hope I helped. I look forward to seeing you later." Brynna got only a few steps away when she heard a voice call out, "Commander... Commander Alexander!"

She stopped and turned to see Commander Asher coming toward her. "Yes, Commander?"

Silas told her how he, Claire and Milo had been working on the problem with the stasis chambers. He kindly asked her to look at the chamber with him. Brynna declined and suggested the engineers look at it. She volunteered to send Lazaro and Braxton over so they could look at the problem together.

Silas knew he was going to have to push harder to get her into the Infirmary. "Is there a problem, Commander? Are you concerned about our truce? You know we won't try anything as long as you have the Captain's wife, right?

Or did you think I would disobey orders?" Silas feigned hurt feelings.

"Silas, Stephanie is not a hostage. We wouldn't harm her for any reason." Brynna protested.

"I'm sorry, I guess I do know better than that. I'm just concerned about the complexity of this entire situation. Forgive me. It can wait." Silas turned back toward his ship.

Brynna again heard Arni's voice warn her not to enter the ship. She dismissed it as simple paranoia. "Silas, wait. I'll take a look at it. I'm not sure this is within my scope of expertise, but it can't hurt to look."

Brynna followed him back inside and into the Infirmary. Silas tried to put her at ease by reminiscing about old times. "You know, you and I used to be kinda close. We had some good times together."

Brynna smiled. "Yes, we did. Back then Officer's School seemed like the hardest thing in my life. Looking back on it now, it seems like a breeze."

Silas gave her a disarming smile as he pulled open a panel on the waiting stasis chamber. He set the panel aside and stopped looking at the chamber. "You and I even dated a time or two. Did you ever wonder what would've happened if we had gotten serious?"

Brynna winced at the thought. "For about a minute I wondered, then I remembered our last date. It never would've worked. We don't belong together. You're just a little too high-strung for me. So, what is it you need me to look at here?" Brynna knelt to look through the opening.

Silas palmed a neural inhibitor patch. He laid his hand firmly on her shoulder and neck placing the patch along her spine. "Brynna, I need to ask you a personal question."

Brynna stood up again glancing at Silas' arm which was now resting on her shoulder. This closeness was making her uncomfortable. Something told her she should have listened to Arni's voice. "What is it, Silas?"

"I'm in a position to report your presence to the Commonwealth... or not. How far would you go to stop me from reporting you?" Silas massaged her shoulder gently.

Brynna pushed his arm off her shoulder. "Not that far. I would ask you politely not to and give you as many reasons as I could to convince you."

"You wouldn't want to spend some time together for old time's sake?"

"No, Silas, I wouldn't."

"Not even to save your crew and your husband?"

"I'm going to leave now." Brynna turned and got two steps away when she felt a stinging sensation on her spine. She felt her arms and legs give way. Silas caught her before she hit the floor and placed her gently in the open chamber. As much as she wanted to fight back, she couldn't. She had lost all motor control of her arms and legs. "Silas, what are you doing? We have a truce."

Silas scowled at her. "You broke that truce by trying to convince my Captain to join you. Here's what's going to happen. You're going to contact your Duty Officer and report in. You're going to tell the D.O. that you'll be staying here, maybe for the night working on options for the stasis chamber. At the latest, you'll be back in the morning. No private codes or messages, or I'll shoot you instead of putting you in stasis. Are we clear?"

Brynna glanced at the weapon Silas now brandished. "I—I understand, but you better understand something. I answer to Pateras. My life and death are in his hands, not yours."

Silas glowered at her. "Your life is in my hands, not your imaginary friend's hands."

Brynna's anxiety drained away as a familiar presence cocooned her with calm. "Do you intend to see me dead before the day is over?"

Silas didn't answer.

"Silas, for old time's sake be honest with me. It's not like I will have any conscious thoughts in stasis. Do you intend to have me executed before the day is out?"

Silas forced himself to make eye contact with Brynna. "Milo will see to it early this evening. He'll also be taking Claire. It appears she's fallen under your influence as well."

"Can I ask for one last favor?"

Her calm demeanor was unnerving the man. "What?" He asked brusquely.

"If I survive this day, swear to me you will hear us out. Promise me you'll listen to our side of the story, really listen. Can you do that? If Pateras finds a way to get me out of this, you owe it to me, and to Claire, to hear the truth."

Silas stared at her for a moment then glanced over at the chamber holding his beloved wife.

Incapable of moving anything but her head, Brynna twisted the best she could to follow his gaze to the other chamber. She realized Claire was already confined. "You said Arni was my imaginary friend, but he's both real and powerful. He's more powerful than the Commonwealth. If he proves it to you by saving us, shouldn't you at least hear his side of the story?"

"You've got some kind of secret distress signal, don't you?" Silas was sure Brynna was plotting against him.

"I'm sure there are things I could say to get someone's attention, and I'll even tell you this; if you remove my bracelet without disabling it, an automatic distress signal goes out to the ship." Brynna volunteered.

"That doesn't seem like much of an agreement if you put the odds in your favor."

"No tricks, no secret codes, I'm putting my trust in Pateras alone to get me out of this alive. Do we have a deal?"

Silas still appeared skeptical even though he had the upper hand. "Alright, I don't really have anything to lose. One caveat, I have to be convinced you didn't tip off your crew."

"Fair enough, let me talk to them." Brynna took a deep breath. She didn't want to give away her situation inadvertently. Silas punched the buttons on Brynna's bracelet then held her arm up toward her mouth while pointing his weapon at her temple.

"Commander Alexander to *Evangeline*."

A voice came back, "Ensign Dominick here, go ahead Commander."

"Ensign, I'm going to remain here with Captain Weiseman for a while. If it gets late, the Captain has offered his guest quarters for the night. Just make a note in the ship's log and let the Captain know after he gets some rest. Any questions or is there anything I need to know about?" Brynna didn't want to seem too abrupt. She knew Cheyenne was the one person who could detect a problem just from a casual conversation.

"Just one question, Commander. If he asks about the cause for your delay in returning, what should I tell him?"

"I'm working with the crew on options for getting Lt. Commander Weiseman transferred to one of the *Emissary's* stasis chambers. Have Braxton and Lazaro check in with Commander Asher after they get some rest to see if they can offer any suggestions."

Being her usual inquisitive self, Cheyenne continued to ask questions. "Commander, aren't Captain Weiseman and Commander Asher getting some rest right now?"

"Ensign, do you really think they're going to get much rest with the Lt. Commander's life hanging in the balance? Do you have any other questions before I get back to work?" By this point, Silas was pressing his Tri-EMP forcefully into her temple. His patience was wearing thin.

"No, Commander, I hope you get it worked out. *Evangeline*, out."

Despite Arni's comforting, yet invisible presence, losing the connection with Cheyenne left Brynna feeling alone and vulnerable.

Silas laid her arm back down inside the chamber. He holstered his weapon then removed the power supply from her bracelet. He placed a set of binders on her then disabled the neural inhibitor. As he lowered the lid on the chamber, Brynna closed her eyes. He heard her whisper, "Arni, I'm sorry. I should've listened to you."

Silas held the lid for a second. "What's that supposed to mean?"

Brynna opened her eyes. A small tear rolled down her cheek. "He told me not to come here. I didn't listen to him."

"So, you pay for disobeying a direct order with your life? Nice boss you have there." Silas goaded.

Brynna smiled as another tear escaped the corner of her eye. "I gave him my life to do with as he pleases. I messed up, but he hasn't abandoned me. No matter what it costs me, I will continue to follow him."

Silas shook his head and closed the lid. When the stasis field activated, Silas looked at Brynna's face through the window. She had gone to sleep peacefully. He thought back to Claire's face. She had been unconscious when he had placed her in the chamber. Her face should have been neutral. Was it his imagination or was her face as troubled as it appeared? What was the difference between the two women? Silas knew he had betrayed them both. Why was one seemingly at peace, and the other troubled? If they were both compromised, wouldn't their reactions be the same? Was he wrong about Claire? Doubts moved in and took root. He shook off his doubts and shoved the chamber into its berth.

Milo stepped in and saw him putting it away. "Is it done?"

"Yeah, both women are secure barring interference from Pateras." Silas now seemed distracted.

"Pateras... seriously?" Milo scowled at his commander.

"You know what they've said he's capable of. After what we saw this morning, it's possible he could get them out of even a stasis chamber." Commander Asher conjectured. "Just to play it safe, have the computer monitor the chambers and any activity in the Infirmary until you take them out."

"Yes sir." Milo moved to the computer terminal and programmed it as ordered.

Commander Asher and Chief Griffin discussed the safest way to dispose of the two women. Silas decided not to wait any longer than a couple hours. He and Milo agreed Captain Alexander wouldn't suspect them with Lt. Commander Weiseman still aboard the *Evangeline*. They wanted to keep both women long enough to complicate the time-line.

When the appointed time came, Commander Asher and Chief Griffin woke the two women and escorted them into the Surf-ve. Claire was confused as to why Silas was treating her like this. Despite her impassioned pleas and demands for an explanation, Silas coldly ignored her.

Milo climbed into the driver's seat as Silas buckled the bound women into their seats. Claire gave Silas one last plea. "Silas, please tell me what's going on. Where are you taking us? What did I do wrong?"

Silas fastened the last buckle then laid his hand on the side of her face. He gently caressed her cheek. "I'm sorry, Claire. You've been exposed to the enemy. Arni Liontari is the son of Pateras El Liontari. Please believe me. I love you, but I can't take chances."

"What? Silas, I didn't know. I didn't commit treason, Silas. I swear it!"

Silas turned and left the vehicle with Claire's cries following him every step of the way. "Silas... Silas... please... Silas..."

Milo drove back toward the *Evangeline* then pulled off near the river. He pulled his weapon and unbuckled the two women. He escorted them out to the water's edge. Claire tried to appeal to the security chief. "Milo, I'm loyal to the Commonwealth. I was blind. I couldn't see the man in the cave. He was just trying to help me. Please, Milo."

Milo ignored her pleas. He pushed the women down onto their knees. "Commander, why haven't you begged for mercy?"

Brynna had been silent the entire trip. "I know what I've done and what the risks are. I will serve Pateras as long as I am alive. If that ends here and now, then I will join Pateras in his alternate reality. It's a win-win scenario for me. If you kill Claire though... she's not a servant of Pateras. Her life won't end either. She will pass into the alternate reality, but she won't have Pateras' protection. Please don't hurt her. She doesn't deserve this. Milo, please let her go."

Milo stood directly in front of Claire. "If I were to let you go and word got back to Silas, my loyalty would come under suspicion. You understand that, don't you? Please tell me you understand."

Tears were rolling down Claire's face by now. Her hands, like Brynna's, were bound in front of her. She reached up and wiped them away. "I understand Milo, I just can't believe the Captain would allow this to happen without investigating first."

Milo knelt in front of her. He glanced nervously at Brynna as he placed his hand firmly on Claire's shoulder. "The Captain doesn't know. Commander Asher believes the Captain is blinded by his grief. He hasn't told the Captain about this or his plans to enlist the help of Captain Alexander in finding the two of you when you disappear. Once we get the crew divided into smaller search parties, we can take them all out easily. Their guard will be down. It's too bad you won't be alive to warn them." Milo gazed at the two women. He stood slowly and asked one last question. "Claire, forgive me. I hope you understand. You do understand, don't you?"

Claire sniffed and wiped her nose on her sleeve. She nodded but couldn't bring herself to answer. Milo looked concerned. He glanced at Brynna. "You understand... Don't you?"

Milo glanced down at his bracelet. Brynna's eyes followed his. Realization set in. "You want us to go away quietly. You might silence us, but you can't stop Pateras. I understand very well. Arni can save us if he wishes or he can let us die, but he won't abandon us. I assume since we are by the river, you plan on drowning us?"

"You won't know it. I'm going to stun you, remove your binders, then put you face down in the water. You'll drown while you're unconscious. It's the most humane way I could come up with. Let's get this over with." Milo took off his bracelet and his utility belt and laid them down several feet away. He then removed his over-shirt and carefully laid it on top of the other items.

Brynna maneuvered herself in front of Claire. She reached out and grabbed Claire's hands. "Claire, just hold on to me. Close your eyes." Brynna spoke softly.

Claire closed her eyes then opened them again. She hastily whispered, "Can Arni help me again?"

Brynna smiled. "Sure, he can. He hears all our words and thoughts. Just ask him."

Claire closed her eyes again and whispered. "Arni, please help me. I need you."

The women heard Milo's weapon power up then it fired twice. A deafening silence filled the hot summer air. Milo took a deep breath trying to accept what he had just done. He released the women's binders. The next sound was that of the two women hitting the water.

A TRUCE ENDED

A HOUSE DIVIDED

Milo climbed onto the riverbank. He picked up his over-shirt, belt, and bracelet. He reprogrammed the computer on the Surf-ve to indicate Claire had been driving and that she had activated the Nizer-bots to clean the cabin. Milo adjusted his personal laser to a wide-beam low-intensity setting and swept the driver's seat and controls to make sure his DNA wasn't easily discernible to a scan. A small amount of his DNA was explainable as being from an earlier trip in the vehicle, but he didn't want his DNA to be the most recent or prominent trace.

After he finished destroying evidence, Milo pulled a small craft capable of carrying only one person from the storage compartment in the back of the Surf-ve. He climbed aboard the vehicle aptly named the Whipper. The sleek vehicle was compact and lightweight. It could whip in and out of tight spots with an amazing amount of speed and agility. He powered the vehicle and got quickly back to the ship. Milo drove up the ramp into the cargo bay and parked the vehicle on its charging pad. He cleaned it carefully and went to change out of his own wet clothes. The one thing he didn't plan on was answering his wife's questions.

Gennie was working at the computer in their quarters. "Milo, what happened to you? You look like you've been wallowing in mud."

Milo looked down at himself. "I was... taking care of something for Commander Asher, and I slipped and fell in a puddle." He looked down and his clothes and realized he was wetter and dirtier than one puddle. "Twice..." he added with a look of embarrassment.

Gennie scowled at him. "Milo, you're wet up to your waist."

"I tried to wash the worst of it off before coming inside. Can I go change and get a shower or did you have more questions?" Milo was getting annoyed. He really wasn't ready to explain his actions.

Gennie was taken aback when he snapped at her. She decided now wasn't the time to push him. "Yes, I'm sorry. I didn't mean to keep you standing around in wet clothes. I was just startled. Do you need any help?"

"Actually, I have no idea what kind of micro-organisms might be in these clothes. Can you put them through a deep cleaning and de-ionizing cycle while I'm in the shower? My belt, bracelet, and utility items could stand a good once over too, if you have time."

Gennie shut down her terminal. "Sure, I can do that." The entire crew was under stress and worn out. Gennie decided her husband needed her support more than she needed her confusion cleared up.

As the sun set, Captain Weiseman called a staff meeting. He stepped into the dining hall and glanced around. "Commander Asher, where is Lt. Commander Asher?"

"I'm not sure, sir. She took Commander Alexander back to the *Evangeline* in the Surf-ve a couple hours ago. She hasn't returned and hasn't checked in. I tried to hail her, but she never responded. I was about to contact the *Evangeline* when you called this meeting."

Captain Weiseman's face changed. The weariness he felt was replaced by his determined command face. "Chief Griffin, get on the scanners. I want you scanning for human heat signatures between here and the *Evangeline*. Lt. Oliver, see what you can do about reaching the Lt. Commander on her personal comm unit. See if you can track her bracelet and try to hail the Surf-ve. If you get no response, download the computer files from the Surf-ve and see what you can find out. Noah let's head to the *Evangeline* in the shuttle. I want to take one of our own stasis chambers over and just swap the two out. We can check with Captain Alexander about finding Lt. Commander Asher when we get over there."

Although the crew was moving into a crisis mode, they breathed a little easier as Captain Weiseman took a firm hand on the situation.

Silas was quick to volunteer, "Captain, I'd like to go with you to the *Evangeline*. I've been in touch with their engineers about the stasis chambers. I'd like to check in with them to see if they've been able to make any progress. Maybe they've been in contact with Claire and their Commander."

The captain had intended on leaving Silas behind as the primary duty officer. "Alright, you can go. Lt. Commander Davu, you're in command. I want full weapons and scanners for all personnel. Ensign Evans, you'll pilot the shuttle. Dr. Oliver, Ensign Griffin, I want both of you handling security and pay attention to anything that seems off."

Silas calmly asked, "Do you suspect the crew of the *Evangeline* of foul play?"

"Not specifically, but I have to consider all possibilities. It's possible their disappearance is unrelated to any of the things we've been dealing with over the last couple days." Nate's explanation was vague.

Ensign Griffin knew there were was any number of possibilities. "Unrelated? Like what?"

"It's a little early to speculate, Ensign but it could be anything from a wild animal attack, an accident, a war party from a neighboring community, local criminals… anything. Can we stop the speculation until we have some hard evidence? Get to your stations. Milo, issue the weapons then start your scans. Relay your findings to the shuttle."

The crew broke up and went their separate directions. Silas was the last one to pick up his weapons from Milo.

Milo quietly asked, "How long are you going to keep the Captain in the dark?"

"Until every member of the *Evangeline's* crew is dead or captured. They've cost me my wife. They are going to pay for it and pay dearly."

Milo handed Silas a personal shield generator and a laser rifle in addition to his Tri-EMP. Milo picked up weapons for himself then locked the remaining ones. He again pondered the decisions he had made earlier that day, fairly certain Claire had not changed sides until she was faced with her own demise. He didn't want to tell Silas his own actions had cost him his wife.

As Milo started toward his station, he felt Silas' eyes on him. He stopped in front of the elevator. He turned around abruptly. "Is there a problem, Commander?"

Silas scowled. "I was just wondering that myself. You don't seem like yourself, Chief. Are you handling this?"

"No, I'm not handling this. I've never executed anyone before. I've killed in battle, but I've never killed two helpless women."

"Those women were trained soldiers. They were hardly helpless even with binders on." Silas' tone was acrid.

Milo continued his tirade. "I'm not accustomed to lying to my wife or my Captain. And there's one more thing you need to know. Claire… was still loyal to the Commonwealth until a moment before I fired my weapon. She was so lost and looking for whatever comfort she could find. She called out to Arni for help. You sent me out to kill an innocent woman. You drove her to commit treason."

Silas grabbed Milo and shoved him against the bulkhead. "You're lying! Captain Alexander and his crew did this!"

Milo's eyes reflected sorrow. He wasn't afraid of his Commander. Silas saw the sadness in his eyes and knew he was telling the truth. Milo whispered, "You weren't there, Silas. You didn't see what I saw."

Silas slowly released his grip on his security chief. He seemed to be in a daze. He walked over to the elevator and pressed the button. The door opened, and, in a moment, he was gone.

Gennie came around the corner and found her husband standing in the corridor staring at the door to the elevator.

"Milo... what's with you today? You can't seem to stay presentable."

Milo looked at his wife, "What?"

"Your uniform is a mess. Your jacket is crooked, and all scrunched up. What's with you today?"

Milo quickly straightened himself up. He didn't really have a suitable answer for her. Gennie helped him get his uniform straightened up again then reached for the elevator call button.

Milo reached out and stopped her. "Gennie, I don't think I've told you today how much I appreciate and love you."

Gennie cocked her head sideways. "What's this about?"

Milo shook his head. "I'm not sure I could say. I just know I've had a tough day and despite being gruff with you, you've done nothing but be helpful and supportive. Thank you. I needed that." Milo squeezed her hand affectionately then raised it to his lips and gave it a gentle kiss.

Gennie smiled back at him, her eyes reflecting both concern and love as she stroked his cheek. "As much as I would like to pursue this, we've got people waiting on us. I'm glad I could help though."

Milo released her hand and called the elevator, smiling back at her. The two rode the elevator to the top level where Milo got off and headed for the bridge. Gennie continued to the shuttle bay.

The party headed for the *Evangeline* settled into the shuttle. As Maya pressed the controls to open the bay doors, Captain Weiseman started giving orders again. "Commander Asher, hail the *Evangeline*. Ensign Evans don't approach their ship until I have clearance."

Commander Asher scowled. "Captain, they're criminals. Why do we need their permission to approach?"

Captain Weiseman was annoyed at Silas' challenge. "For the same reason you wouldn't corner a wounded animal. You back them into a corner, you might get bitten."

Silas turned back around and hailed the ship as ordered. The explanation made sense, but it didn't enthuse him. "*Emissary* shuttle to *Evangeline*, come in please."

Lexi was on duty with Lazaro and answered. "This is Lt. Flint of the *Evangeline*, go ahead shuttle *Emissary*."

Lazaro perked up when he heard the call come through. Lexi had immediately put it on an open speaker.

Silas transferred the link to Captain Weiseman. "Lt. Flint, this is Captain Weiseman. I am bringing a team over in the shuttle. I want to get Lt. Commander Weiseman transferred to the *Emissary*, and I need to talk to Captain Alexander right away. I have a problem to discuss with him."

Lazaro stepped over to Lexi's station to take the call. "Acknowledged, Captain Weiseman. Lt. Commander Dominick here. The Captain will be notified of your arrival. What is your E.T.A?"

Lazaro knew the ship wasn't far away, but he expected them to be preparing to load up and go. An arrival time in the five to ten-minute range was the expected response.

Captain Weiseman responded, "E.T.A. is one minute. *Emissary* out."

Lazaro and Lexi exchanged concerned glances. Lazaro slapped a control on the communications control panel. "Captain, the *Emissary* is sending a shuttle and crew over to pick up Lt. Commander Weiseman, and their Captain wants to see you, sir. They'll be here within one minute."

David and most of the crew were sitting around a campfire enjoying the warm summer night. "Acknowledged, Lt. Commander. Stay at your post, and lower the ramp from the cargo bay. Set scanners at maximum range and intensity. Standby for additional orders."

David shut off his comm unit and looked at Jake. "You need to disappear. Lt. Commander Flint, are you armed?"

Braxton stood abruptly. "Minimally, but yes sir."

"Grab a couple laser rifles and a shield generator and disappear too. Doc, you and Laura get inside, and get Stephanie ready to go. Get her off the ship as fast as you can. The rest of you relax and enjoy the fire."

David raced aboard the ship and grabbed a couple more weapons, then headed to the bridge. He hastily gave Lazaro and Lexi some urgent instructions. "Lexi, get to engineering and secure all entrances and exits. No one gets in under any circumstances. Lazaro, continue watching both long and short-range scans. Button the bridge up just as tightly as engineering. Prepare to do whatever you have to with environmental controls if the ship is breached. After Stephanie is clear of the ship, button her up. Be on your guard against sabotage."

"Yes, Captain." Lazaro wanted to ask about their truce, but knew with the shuttle coming in so fast, there wasn't time.

David raced back outside and distributed the weapons and placed one laser rifle outside the circle lit by the fire. It was in a place Jake could slip in and pick it up if he needed to, or someone could disappear into the darkness and retrieve it. David sat back down with the rest of his crew near the fire.

Thane was quick to ask, "Do you think our truce is over?"

David looked up as the shuttle flew over them and started its descent. "I don't know, but something's up. I don't want to put them ill at ease if I'm wrong, but I also don't want to be unprepared. They won't start anything until Stephanie is out of danger. You can count on that."

"Not that I want to use her as a hostage or a bargaining chip, but why hurry her off the ship if she's keeping us safe?"

"I want them to know we aren't trying to hide behind her. They need to know I'm trustworthy until the very end." David squinted as the shuttle stirred up dust around them. The shuttle sat down as close to them as it dared without landing directly on top of them.

When he heard the engine power down, David stood to greet their visitors. He glanced at Thane. "Lt. Ryder stay alert, but stop looking like you're trigger happy."

David glanced at the ramp in time to see the Doc and Laura bringing the stasis chamber to the top of the ramp. "Lt. Ryder, Ensign Ryder, go help them bring the chamber down."

Cheyenne and Marissa stood to greet their guests and see if they were needed in any capacity.

Nate, Silas, and Gennie met David. The looks on their face confirmed his suspicion that something was wrong. "Nate, is everything alright? Is our truce still intact?"

Nate looked down at the ground for a moment. "That depends on how you answer my next questions. Is Lt. Commander Asher here?"

David's brow knit skeptically. "Not that I'm aware of. Why?"

"Could I speak to Commander Alexander?"

David stepped back slightly. "Brynna? I was told she was with you. Nate, what's going on?"

"The two women left earlier this evening in our Surf-ve and haven't been seen in several hours. Lt. Commander Asher isn't answering her comm unit."

David quickly tapped his own comm unit, "Commander Alexander, come in." He waited for a reply and watched the display on his bracelet. The display showed no connection. He tapped his comm unit again and hailed Lazaro. "Lt. Commander Dominick, scan for Commander Alexander's comm unit."

Lazaro set his current scans on automatic and initiated the new scan. In a moment, he reported back. "I'm sorry, sir. There's no sign of her bracelet. I've searched in a five-mile radius. Increasing scan to ten miles."

Captain Weiseman hailed the *Emissary*. "Lt. Commander Davu, have you found anything on your scans?"

Elize quickly answered, "Captain, we haven't located their bracelets or any unidentified heat signatures. We have located the Surf-ve. It's half-way between the two ships along the river bank."

David looked at his friend. "Did you think we had something to do with this, Nate?"

"I only discovered her disappearance a few minutes ago. I hadn't really formed an opinion yet, but I had to consider all possibilities. I'm sure you know that, right Davie?"

"I'll accept that… for now. I gave you my word, and my word is good. What's our next move? I've had Stephanie's stasis chamber brought out to load onto your shuttle. We need to go check out that Surf-ve."

"Captain Alexander, it would alleviate some concerns if you would allow us to search your ship." Silas ventured cautiously.

"Commander Asher, I'm just as concerned about your people roaming around on my ship as you were about my people on your ship. Let's see what we find down by the river. If we can't find any sign of them, I'll allow you to search my ship." David calmly offered. He could feel himself losing patience. He wanted to find Brynna as badly as Silas appeared to want to find Claire.

"You want us to leave, so you can slip her off your ship and hide her somewhere else? Is that it? Where's my wife!" Silas moved menacingly toward Captain Alexander.

David became equally aggressive. "I could ask you the same thing, Commander. I don't have any reason to abduct your wife! You do have a reason to take mine. Are you looking to get a promotion for taking in the most wanted criminals in the galaxy?"

Silas grabbed David and jerked him forward. "Where's my wife? What have you done to her?"

Nate and Thane hastily jumped between the two men and pulled them apart. Nate berated his First Officer and attempted to calm him down. Thane held Captain Alexander back as well.

Jake hailed the Captain privately. "Captain, are you sure you want me to stay out here?"

"Yes, Chief, stay put and keep your eyes open."

Once Silas seemed to have himself under control, Nate turned to David. "Davie, can I ask a favor from you?"

"What?" David asked curtly.

"Can I leave one of my people out here by the fire just to assure Mr. Asher you aren't going to sneak his wife off your ship and hide her elsewhere?" Nate asked calmly.

"You can leave as many or as few outside my ship as you want. I had nothing to do with this." David's tone was still quite terse.

David winced as Arni whispered, "This is mine. You need to let go of it."

David stepped calmly toward Silas again. "I'm sorry, Commander. I know you're just as worried about your wife as I am about mine. You have my word. I'm not responsible for your wife's disappearance."

"What about your precious Arni? Can you say the same thing about him?" Silas retorted.

"Arni doesn't take people by force. He could if he wanted to, but that would defeat his purpose. So, yes, I can say the same thing about him. He knows where she is and what's happened to her. I could ask him if you like."

Silas quickly started back-pedaling, "No, that won't be necessary. We're wasting time. Let's head for the location of the Surf-ve."

Silas was quick to suggest. "Captain, why don't you take Stephanie back to the ship? I can go with his people to check out the Surf-ve."

"Get her on board the shuttle. Noah, you and Maya take her back and get her properly tucked in. David, may we hitch a ride with you to the Surf-ve's location?" Nate countered unexpectedly.

Silas was certain the Captain would've escorted Stephanie safely back to the ship before leaving her side. "Captain, I would really feel better if you went with the Lt. Commander back to the ship, just in case. I would also like to get Milo out here to help with the investigation."

Nate turned to Noah. "Chief Evans, you and Maya get Stephanie back. Maya, take Milo's place and send him out here."

"Yes Captain." Noah and Maya acknowledged.

Silas simply fumed. He was certain his Captain didn't have it in him to rid them of these traitors.

David asked Thane to pull the Surf-ve out. He hailed Braxton and Jake and told them his plan to join the search for the *Emissary's* Surf-ve. He discreetly told the two to hold their positions and stay alert. David ordered Lazaro to stay on duty even though his shift was coming to a close. He quietly told Marissa to scan the replacement stasis chamber thoroughly before allowing it on board.

Nate ordered Gennie Griffin to stay with David's crew to stand watch. His orders were simple. "I honestly don't think this is an issue, but watch all the exits from their ship to be certain. Oh, yeah, and watch your own back."

Thane pulled the Surf-ve out of the cargo bay and pulled up next to his waiting passengers. Cheyenne pulled Captain Alexander aside while the others were climbing aboard.

"What is it, Cheyenne?"

Cheyenne glanced around to be sure no one was close enough to hear her. "Captain, Commander Asher said something that's been bothering me when you told him Arni knew where the women were and volunteered to ask him. He seemed disturbed by that. I got the feeling it wasn't because we were talking to the enemy." Cheyenne glanced around again. David waited patiently for her to finish. "Captain, I think he knows where the women are, and he doesn't want anyone to find out. He seemed more concerned that you had a way to find out what happened to them."

Cheyenne could see David bristling again. Her eyes grew wide, as she worried he would start another altercation. "Ensign, you're with me." He turned to see Jason and Laura returning from stowing Stephanie's stasis pod aboard the shuttle. "Doc, get aboard the Surf-ve! Lt. Adams, keep our guest company. Don't interfere with her orders, but don't allow her access to my ship. Ensign Ryder—surf-ve!"

The crew jumped quickly to do as they were told. Aulani wondered why the Captain had changed his mind about leaving her and Cheyenne behind. She didn't bother asking, but quickly climbed aboard. She placed herself strategically in the back row of the vehicle. Jason sat near the center. Nate and Silas were sitting in the first two seats near the door. David sat down across the aisle from Nate and Cheyenne sat to David's left. Henry Oliver was sitting across the aisle from Jason.

David looked over at Nate, "Would you care to assign someone from your crew to take the second chair?"

Nate glanced at the empty co-pilot's seat. "Dr. Oliver, take co-pilot's position."

Henry moved into position as ordered. He silently continued to evaluate the crew dynamics at every juncture. David had noticed the man kept to himself. He wondered if it was related to his job or just a personality quirk.

With everyone in position, Thane headed toward the coordinates of the missing vehicle. Now that the sun had set, it was extremely dark outside. The planet's moons weren't up yet leaving only the stars and the Surf-ve for light. Thane used an infrared scan with a heat signature overlay displayed on the front window to guide him as he drove. Dr. Oliver used the same data to watch the peripheral areas for signs of the women.

Thane stopped the vehicle approximately a hundred yards short of the Surf-ve.

"Why are you stopping so far away?" Silas snapped.

Thane turned around purposefully to face Silas. "I didn't want to disturb any clues or evidence of what happened to our two, missing people... sir." A glint of insubordination slipped through in his voice.

David unbuckled and stood up. "Good thinking, Lieutenant, but watch the attitude. I think I have enough bad attitude for both of us."

Thane grimaced. "Yes sir. Sorry, sir. It won't happen again."

Silas glared at both men as he unbuckled. He punched the button to open the door and climbed out of the vehicle.

David climbed out and quietly told Cheyenne to keep an eye on Silas and his interactions with his own crew.

The two crews spread out in a line and advanced slowly toward the abandoned vehicle. Scanners and recorders blanketed the entire search grid. They continued toward the edge of the river.

By the time they had completed an initial grid search, Milo had arrived riding the same Whipper he had left on earlier that evening.

Thane found impressions in the sand and dirt a few feet from the water. "Captain!"

Being accustomed to answering to the title, both Captains responded. "What is it, Lieutenant?"

Thane squinted. He pointed the light from his bracelet at the spot on the ground where the women had knelt. "This spot shows signs of being disturbed, and I've got trace DNA."

Jason quickly knelt at Thane's side running scans of his own. He glanced up. "There are multiple traces of DNA. One of them matches Commander Alexander."

Milo suddenly got nervous. "What about the other DNA traces?"

Jason punched a couple more buttons on his scanner then scowled. "I have a copy of Lt. Commander Asher's DNA from treating her in the Infirmary. Give me a minute to sync the files."

"Um... I seem to have something akin to a wild boar." Jason continued to watch his display.

If the mood had been lighter, someone may might have joked about Claire's resemblance or lack thereof to a wild boar.

Jason scowled again. "I have two distinct rodents and Lt. Commander Asher's DNA. She was here."

David quickly asked, "Does it give any indication... were they alive and well?"

Jason continued to stare at his display. He seemed a little disturbed by the readout. When he finally looked up, his gaze landed on Milo. When he realized what he had done, he moved his gaze to Captain Alexander. "I can only speculate on that. The DNA is from dead skin cells and hair."

"So, they're dead?" Silas interrupted.

Jason shook his head. "No, that's not what I'm saying. We shed hair and dead skin cells all the time. I'm not finding blood or tissue, which could indicate that they're dead. The cells I found could be from a living human or a corpse. I'm saying I don't have definitive proof. I just know they were here."

Silas wanted to push Captain Alexander to split the group up, so he could move up and down the river and take them out two or three at a time. He wasn't concerned with finding the women or their corpses. He was ready to punish Captain Alexander and his crew for forcing his hand in having his own wife executed.

David glanced at Jason and Cheyenne. Cheyenne had another one of those looks on her face. "Doc, Lt. Ryder, start from this point and scan in an expanding spiral pattern. See if you can trace their movements. Nate, we need to check out the Surf-ve."

Commander Asher, Chief Griffin, and Ensign Dominick followed the two Captains to the Surf-ve. The five ran scans before entering the vehicle. Each one compared their scans. "The vehicle is totally clean," Nate announced. "Milo, check the vehicle logs."

Milo climbed into the driver's seat and powered up the displays. He perused the main logs. "Claire's log-in was the last one input. It appears as though she activated the Nizer Bots just prior to exiting the vehicle. There doesn't appear to be anything in the communication logs. No indication of any problems." Milo powered up the engines. "No signs of mechanical issues."

Silas opened one of the rear storage compartments. "There are no weapons in the weapons storage locker." This time Silas looked genuinely concerned.

Captain Alexander stepped out of the vehicle and walked toward the riverbank. He folded his arms across his chest and stared into the darkness. In a moment he turned slightly and called out, "Ensign Dominick, a word, please."

Cheyenne walked up behind the Captain. "Yes, Captain?"

David gruffly answered her. "Is that how you were taught to report, Ensign?"

Cheyenne hastily moved in front of him and reported formally.

David glanced over his shoulder and saw Silas and Milo having a whispered yet intense discussion. He turned back to Cheyenne and quietly ordered, "See how much you can record of that conversation going on behind me. You'll have to boost the gain and turn slightly to show me something on your display."

Cheyenne realized he had chastised her inappropriate report to get a less obvious position for eavesdropping. She began recording both audio and visual. The two men finished their conversation and continued their perfunctory search.

Even though their conversation was over, David continued looking at Cheyenne's bracelet display. He quietly asked, "Was there something else you wanted to tell me from a few minutes ago?"

"Nothing concrete, it just seems like Commander Asher is angry. It's almost like he knows his wife's situation and is more concerned with getting revenge. He isn't looking for her. He's looking to blame someone for whatever's happened to her."

Jason walked up in time to hear Cheyenne's answer. David turned his attention to the doctor, "Do you have something, Doc?"

"Yes, but I thought it best not to let everyone know what else I found."

David was getting antsy. "What did you find?"

"I had a third…"

David's comm unit chirped at him. He held his hand out to stop the Doc from continuing and answered the hail. He heard Marissa's voice coming through his earpiece. "Captain, this might be nothing, but I thought you should know. When I scanned the stasis chamber, I found traces of human DNA. I compared the scan with the medical records. It belongs to Lt. Commander Asher. Standard Operating Procedures call for these units to be cleaned and sanitized after every use. I checked the logs on this unit. It was used for several hours this afternoon, but no one engaged the cleaning cycle. If the data is accurate, Lt. Commander Asher was in this chamber for about four hours this afternoon."

David got quiet as he tried to make sense of the information. After what seemed like an interminably long silence, he heard Marissa's voice again, "Captain, are you there? Captain?"

"I'm still here, Lieutenant. Have everyone stay on at a high level of vigilance. Lt. Holden, station yourself at the top of the stairs with a laser rifle to watch Laura's back. When we return, get yourself back inside the ship to help with the ship's defenses."

Jason scowled. "What's happened, Captain?"

David relayed Marissa's report on the stasis chamber.

Jason glanced around at the *Emissary's* crew who were examining the area around the vehicle. "That's not good considering the third strand of DNA I identified."

David took a deep breath. "You were about to tell me about that. Whose is it? Silas?"

Jason stepped slightly closer to his Captain. "Captain, just don't go off and lose your temper. If we want to find out the truth, we need to play this out carefully."

David clenched his teeth. "Whose is it, Jason?"

"Chief Griffin." Jason braced himself to block the Captain from attempting to harm the security chief.

David forced himself not to turn around. He didn't want to give away their information. "Jason, take Lt. Ryder and Ensign Ryder to search the river bank about fifty yards in both directions then head back to the Surf-ve. Watch your backs. Cheyenne let's see what we got on that audio-visual record. Play it back in both our ear pieces."

The first thing heard was Silas' voice saying, "... the Captain will know that's a breach in protocol.

"I didn't log the weapons into the ship's weapons locker. As far as he's concerned, we have two missing women and two missing weapons. It looks like the women took the weapons and were in some kind of trouble when they took them." Milo quietly explained.

"You should have told me about this." Silas griped.

"It's better this way. Your reactions are more authentic." Milo countered. "We need to move on and keep looking for evidence."

When David and Cheyenne finished listening to the discussion, they simply stared at each other. Cheyenne finally whispered, "Captain, I know we haven't seen much of Arni since we landed. Knowing what he wants is not easy, but I know he's trying to teach us. Think long and hard before you make your next move."

David nodded. "Thank you, Cheyenne."

The accumulating evidence was now strongly pointing to foul play by two of the *Emissary's* crew, and David's wife was one of the victims. He was now wondering if they had harmed her or merely detained her somewhere. The thought of her being harmed was interfering with his ability to think and make decisions.

David looked around into the darkness. "Arni, please protect Brynna and bring her back to me. Show me how you want me to handle this. I'm lost and distracted."

David thought back to the day they launched the ship and started their first mission. Admiral Deacons had asked him if he would be able to sacrifice his wife if he had to. He hadn't liked the thought at the time, and he liked it even less now. It reminded him where his heart and mind needed to be.

David snapped out of his haze. "Crew of the *Evangeline*, back to the Surf-ve, on the double."

Nate looked around at the sudden increase in activity. He met David half-way to the vehicle. "Davie?"

"I need to protect my crew, Nate. Please don't get in my way. I think you need to pay attention to what your crew's been up to while you've been worried about Stephanie."

Nate looked dumbfounded. "What are you saying? Are you accusing my crew of something?"

"We had a truce, Nate. I'm not holding you personally responsible, but our truce has been broken. I need to get back to my ship and protect my people. No harm will come to Ensign Griffin." David stepped around his friend and trotted back to their own Surf-ve leaving the *Emissary's* crew to take their own vehicle.

Nate stared after David. His crew gathered around him. Nate heard Silas's voice from behind him. "Where's he going?"

Something told Nate he should keep quiet for now. "We need to get Ensign Griffin back. It appears our truce is over."

Milo glanced at the grim faces around him. "He wouldn't hurt her, would he?"

Nate shook his head. "No, he wouldn't. He might leave her outside alone though."

The group promptly climbed into their own vehicle. The crew pulled up in time to see David recalling two of his crew from the perimeter and filling them in on the situation. Ensign Griffin was standing near them looking concerned. As the vehicle got close to the crew, two of the crew took up strategic defensive positions.

The vehicle stopped, and the four crewmembers kept their seats for a moment as they studied David's posturing. Nate knew David felt like they backed him into a corner. He didn't know why, as yet, but he intended to find out. "I want everybody to get out of the vehicle slowly and carefully. Keep your weapons holstered unless you're being physically threatened. Stay near the front of the vehicle."

Neither his security chief, nor his first officer cared for the Captain's plan. Nate shut them down quickly. "David has evidence of foul play, and it seems my crew is involved. I intend to find out who's responsible and why."

Nate got out of the vehicle first and kept his hands where David could see them.

"Keep your crew in the vehicle, Nate."

"Davie, I asked them to get out. We'll stay right here by it, and our weapons are staying in their holsters. I want them to hear what you have to say. You found something, Davie. What was it?"

"Ensign Griffin, please rejoin your crew. Nate, we found two other DNA signatures. The stasis chamber you brought us had Lt. Commander Asher's DNA in it, and the logs indicated it had been used for approximately four hours today." Ensign Griffin walked slowly toward her crew as David continued. "The other trace of DNA was found down by the river. Another member of your crew was down there with my wife and Claire."

Gennie stopped walking. She stared at her husband, Milo. She turned halfway around. Before she could speak,

Milo called out to her, "Gennie, you need to come over here, now."

Gennie looked at Captain Weiseman then Captain Alexander. "It was Milo, wasn't it?"

Nate took a step forward. "What makes you ask that, Ensign?"

Milo stepped forward and gave her a discreet head shake.

Gennie looked at her husband, wondering what he had done. Nate stepped toward her again. "Ensign, answer the question!"

"M—Milo, came back to our quarters this evening. He was wet from the waist down with muddy water. H—He said he was doing something for Commander Asher." Gennie didn't mention Milo saying he fell. She suspected he had lied to her.

Milo was now afraid Captain Alexander would be gunning for him, and his own wife was directly in the line of fire. He inhaled sharply to ask his wife to please come to the Surf-ve.

Before Milo could say anything, David spoke up, "Ensign, please rejoin your Captain. Nate, she's right. The trace DNA we found at the river belongs to Chief Griffin, and I also have proof that he was under the direction of Commander Asher."

"That's ridiculous. You can't have any such proof. We've done nothing wrong." Silas kept his hands still visible. A menacing red dot materialized on his shirt and on Milo's.

Nate felt like he was caught in the middle of a rushing river and trying to stop the current. "Davie, I'll get to the bottom of this. I swear. Please ask your men to stand down."

"I can't do that, Nate. You and your crew need to leave. I would like to know what's happened to my wife though." David responded firmly.

Gennie slowly joined the crew but stood resolutely away from her husband. She was torn between being angry and frightened.

"I have one more question, Davie. How do you know those two were in collusion?"

David pressed a couple buttons on his bracelet and replayed the recording of the conversation between the two men. Commander Asher and Chief Griffin looked at each other. The evidence was indeed damning. "Would either of you two gentlemen care to tell me what you've done with my wife?"

"And my chief engineer?" Nate added. Nate moved cautiously over in front of Silas blocking the laser sight. "Silas, where is your wife and Captain Alexander's wife?"

Silas clenched his jaw tightly. Keeping his voice low, he answered his Captain. "They're gone... dead. Milo executed them for treason early this evening."

Nate swallowed hard. "Why? Why would you do that? That wasn't your call to make." The anger in his voice grew louder with each sentence.

David couldn't hear what was being said until Nate got angry. He quickly hailed his crew. "Nobody fires a shot unless your life is in imminent danger."

"Captain, Claire changed sides. Milo can verify that." Silas protested.

"She didn't change sides until I put a gun to her head. She didn't have a clue what was happening to her or why." Milo interjected.

Nate glared at Milo. "Crew! Attention! Nobody speaks or moves until I say so."

The crew was out of practice at snapping to attention, and the hour was getting late. They roughly got into position.

Nate paced angrily in front of the ill-formed line of crewmen. He finally stopped in front of Silas again. "Silas, why Commander Alexander? We had a truce. We owe them."

"She broke our truce, sir."

"Just how do you figure that?" Nate persisted.

"When she walked back with you. She was influencing you while you were compromised by Stephanie's injuries."

"Were you eavesdropping on our conversation, Commander Asher?" Nate demanded.

"No, sir, but it was pretty obvious..."

Nate got right in Silas' face. "And how was it obvious? Have I been acting inappropriately? Have I done something to suggest my allegiance has changed?"

"No sir! Nothing like that, sir. Captain, I was just trying to protect the crew. We've already suffered a loss. I didn't want to take chances that you might be compromised. I was trying to…"

"Trying to what?" Nate demanded.

Silas glanced over at Dr. Oliver. Nate stepped back as it suddenly dawned in on him what Silas was afraid of. "I see." Nate paused to decide his next course of action. Without looking up, he calmly ordered. "Ensign Griffin, Dr. Oliver, get into the passenger compartment of the Surf-ve. The two quietly did as they were ordered."

Nate walked over to Milo and asked, "What was your part in this, and don't tell me you were simply following orders?"

Keeping his eyes straight ahead Milo quietly answered. "No sir, I was doing my part to protect the crew."

"You two know this is half a step short of mutiny, right? I should leave the two of you here to let David take whatever justice he sees fit."

Silas broke his stance and turned his head. "Captain, you can't be serious. Dr. Oliver would report this, and you'd lose your captaincy."

Nate got back in his face again. "It would seem I've already lost it. You two have taken over my job. Commander Alexander was doing nothing more than consoling me during my grief. She wasn't trying to compromise me. She was doing her best to avoid topics she believed would violate our agreement. I think at the very least you two should tell Captain Alexander what happened to his wife. I'm fairly certain he already knows though. You'll be lucky if I don't kill you myself for this. Let's go. After his help, the man deserves to know the truth."

Nate turned to face David. "Captain, may we approach?"

David nodded. Jake and Braxton lowered their laser rifles. Nate led the two men forward. "Davie, I'm so sorry. I let things get out of control. Commander Asher…"

"Captain Alexander, I regret to inform you that I orchestrated the execution of Commander Alexander earlier this evening. I believed her to be in violation of our truce. I found out that Lt. Commander Asher had been in direct contact with Arni Liontari. I took steps to see that no more of our crew were unduly influenced. My intentions for this evening were to split your crew to search for the two missing crewmembers. I planned to execute you and the rest of your crew during the search. I may have been errant in my thinking. I am sorry for the loss I caused you. I may have inadvertently caused my own loss."

As Silas spoke, though it was cold and clinical, flashes of Brynna's face ran through David's memory. Mentally, David cried out to Arni. His greatest plea was, "Can I shoot him?"

Arni reliably said "No."

David bartered his request progressively down to, "Can I at least hit him?"

Arni answered with, "I need you to forgive him."

In a moment, David turned his back, and tears formed in his eyes. He tried to blink them back, but they stubbornly refused to be dismissed. His hands balled into fists. He forced them to relax. His fingers fidgeted nervously. David called out over his shoulder. "Commander Asher, was it done humanely?"

"Yes sir, as humanely as we could make it."

David's voice was almost inaudible as he spoke this time. "Thank you for telling me."

Nate nodded at Silas to leave.

Milo stepped forward. "Captain Alexander, I—uh—I volunteered to handle this detail, and I need to explain why."

Nate tried to cut him off. "That won't be necessary, Chief. He just needs to know what happened to his wife."

Milo nodded and started to add his information when Lazaro interrupted via all comms. "Captain Alexander, we have a ship in orbit. It appeared out of nowhere, sir."

A NEW BREED OF SOLDIER

"Can you identify the craft? Is it military or civilian?" David barked into his comm unit.

An interminable silence preceded Lazaro's reply. "It's not in our database, but it looks like a larger version of our ship."

David's eyes darted back and forth as he contemplated his next move. Before he could cement his plans, Lazaro interrupted with another update. "Captain, they've launched a shuttle. It's coming in fast... It's... It's vanished! That shuttle has some serious stealth tech."

"Shields up! Power the laser cannons, but only fire if we're fired upon first!" David ordered. "No matter what happens to us out here, don't take those shields down. Sacrifice the engines if you have to. Only lower the shields if you can get our own people inside without compromising the ship. Braxton, Jake, go dark and get clear."

Each man acknowledged their orders. They kept their comm lines open to know what orders David gave the rest of the crew.

"Jason, Laura, Aulani, and Cheyenne, get aboard the Surf-ve and get it into the cargo bay."

Jason and the women climbed quickly into the vehicle. Aulani pulled the door shut. "How are we supposed to get the Surf-ve aboard the ship with the shields up?" She asked as she climbed into a seat.

Jason powered up the Surf-ve. "Each Surf-ve is programmed to match the shield harmonics of its own ship. We just have to move slowly."

No sooner were the words out of his mouth than Jason punched it forward knocking Aulani into her seat. Aulani hastily buckled up sensing Jason's actions were going to be sharp and fast until the moment they merged with the ship's shields.

"Davie, do you know who that is?" Nate asked.

"From the Intelligence reports I got, Executor Hale has ships assigned to hunt us, and the other eleven crews down. I'm assuming that's who this is."

David and Thane drew their weapons and took a position to watch each other's backs as they searched the dark sky for any sign of the approaching shuttle.

Nate and Milo pulled their weapons as well. David turned and pointed his weapon at Nate. "I will do what I can to protect you and your crew, but they need to believe you're good Commonwealth soldiers. The truce is over. Take cover!"

Nate looked at the weapon David had aimed at him. He pulled Milo back to the Surf-ve. The *Emissary* crew turned their vehicle to head back to their own ship. Nate hailed Lt. Commander Elize Davu. "Lt. Commander, secure the ship, and raise the shields immediately. Those shields only come down on my orders. There's a ship of unknown configuration in orbit and a shuttle coming in fast using stealth technology. We're headed back. Defend my ship until I get there."

Elize acknowledged the orders and started giving a rapid-fire list of orders to her shipmates.

David and Thane headed for some nearby trees to take cover. A soft, high-pitched whine and a forceful blast of hot air hit them causing them to dive for cover. Thane looked at David, "Was that as close as it felt?"

David saw the trees they were headed for were blowing wildly back and forth as though a turbine were right above them. "Probably not, but it's still too close for my comfort. Let's get moving!"

The two tried to get to the second group of trees. They wanted to stay clear of the direction Jake and Braxton had disappeared. Before they could reach the second group of trees, a laser fired from behind them and took down the trees. The blast of air passed over them again. David and Thane watched as a new beam fired at the *Emissary's* escaping Surf-ve. The vehicle lost power and rolled to a stop. David turned to see if his own Surf-ve had made it into the cargo bay. The Surf-ve was slowing to approach the shield and ramp.

David holstered his Tri-EMP and pulled the laser rifle off his back and fired blindly into the space above his Surf-ve. Several of the shots vanished harmlessly into the distance. Thane pulled his own laser rifle and followed the Captain's example. One pulse contacted the invisible shuttle. It did enough damage to disrupt the camouflage, temporarily revealing the shuttle's hull. It wasn't enough to stop the shuttle from firing a pulse disabling the second Surf-ve. David's heart sank as he saw the vehicle roll to a stop and its lights go out. He tried to continue firing at the mysterious craft. A couple more laser blasts made the same inconsequential contact. The ship appeared to make a wide circle around the area blowing the trees and other vegetation as it passed overhead.

David hastily tapped his comm unit and ordered, "Jason, get everyone out of there. Split up and disappear. Jason… Jason, do you copy?"

Thane shook his head. "They must be jamming our communications."

David didn't need to worry. The crew reacted appropriately. When the vehicle lost power, Aulani unbuckled and dove for the manual control for the door. Cheyenne pulled her weapon. The second the door was open; she bolted through it and covered the others as they followed her out. Aulani was a mere second behind her. Laura and Jason followed them out. Jason ordered Cheyenne and Aulani to head east and find cover. He and Laura headed north.

The *Evangeline* had landed in a large open area of hard ground because of its size and weight. An area meeting those criteria meant there was not much around for them to use as cover.

Aulani and Cheyenne found a small crevice in a rock formation as the ground sloped downhill. They slid into the shallow crevice and crouched down to stay out of sight. The two searched the perimeter for any signs they had been pursued. The further they got from the campfire, the harder it was to see. Seeing nothing on their scanners, Cheyenne whispered, "Should we try to get further out?"

Aulani debated her question. If they went further out and were needed, they wouldn't be able to get back quickly. Ensign Ryder realized the Captain wasn't trying to set up a line of defense. He had been trying to protect the crew. He wanted them out of harm's way. "We probably should get as far from here as possible. I think the Captain was trying to get us to safety."

The women checked their scanners one more time. The scan revealed nothing more than small indigenous life forms. Aulani scanned the perimeter with her eyes, just in case. She saw nothing and heard little more than crickets and frogs from the nearby river. The invisible shuttle had moved to the other side of the clearing. Aulani decided it was safe to move. Cheyenne stood watch as Aulani raced across the field.

Cheyenne saw Aulani get halfway across the field then tumble headlong onto the ground. She rolled a couple times before coming to a stop. Cheyenne paused and held her breath as she waited for Aulani to get up. When she didn't move, Cheyenne visually scanned the perimeter before running to her side. She rolled Aulani over and quietly tried to rouse her. Aulani didn't respond. Cheyenne was about to activate her scanner when a noise above her got her attention.

Ensign Dominick looked up to see an extremely large dark figure floating down toward the ground. She remained frozen in place kneeling by Aulani. She was torn between the desire to flee and the desire to stay and protect her companion. Her training kicked in and overrode her emotions. She raised her weapon to fire at the looming figure. The gigantic humanoid creature was now standing on the ground a few feet from her. Although he was over nine feet tall, her posture, small stature, fear, and the imposing darkness made him seem immensely larger. Cheyenne decided the lowest setting on her Tri-EMP wouldn't do enough damage to the monstrous figure in front of her.

Without taking her eyes off the figure, she slid the setting to level two. The figure seemed to wait on her to make her move. She used the opportunity he offered her. She fired. The charged pellet grabbed onto her would-be assailant. He looked down at his chest, a helmet obscured his face with a dark face shield. A small flickering light danced on his body armor where the pellet had attached itself. The ominous creature reached down, pulled the pellet from his chest, and flicked it away like an annoying insect. He slowly raised his own weapon and pointed it at her. Cheyenne dropped her weapon and raised her hands in surrender. The creature walked silently around behind her. Cheyenne's hands began to shake. Why hadn't he spoken? Who was he and what did he want? She got the distinct impression he was purposefully tormenting her. She shuddered as she heard his weapon power-up behind her. She berated herself for giving up so easily and assuming his weapon was powered up to fire. She carried other weapons and could have attempted to protect herself and Aulani with those.

The one question she didn't have an answer to was, how effective would her other weapons be, since the Tri-EMP had been so ineffective? What she failed to realize was, her attacker was toying with her. He had powered his weapon down for the sheer pleasure of watching her fear escalate as he powered it up again. He was enjoying tormenting her. The urge to cry welled up in her. The one thing that prevented her tears from flowing freely was the Captain's repeated admonition for her to not give her enemies the satisfaction of seeing her cry. She swallowed the lump forming in her throat then spoke to her adversary. "Whatever you're going to do, do it, and get it over with."

Her words seemed to anger the giant soldier. He grabbed her arm and threw her to the ground beside Aulani and fired. Cheyenne convulsed and lost consciousness. The figure holstered his weapon and grabbed the two women by the back of their collars and drug them roughly across the ground back toward their ship.

Jason and Laura weaved their way toward the denser population of trees and the riverbank. Jason watched the tops of the trees for movement to give away the location of the shuttle. In his preoccupation with the shrouded vessel, he and Laura failed to notice the dark figure on the ground in front of them. Jason was nearly on top of the figure before he noticed it. He stopped quickly. Laura, not realizing Jason had stopped, ran into him. The doc lost his balance and pitched forward. The figure in front of Jason, caught him, disarmed him, and threw him to the ground in one swift move. Laura screamed, "JASON!" She knelt at her husband's side and raised her weapon to defend him. As soon as his head cleared, knowing something severely outmatched them, Jason raised up and tried to get her to stand down. "Laura! No!"

His warning came too late. The giant backhanded Laura and sent her flying. She landed just beyond Jason's reach. Jason glanced at his attacker to be sure the man wasn't about to attack him again. The man motioned with his own weapon for Jason to move toward Laura. Jason scrambled to her side and mumbled, "Pateras, please let her be alright."

The gargantuan figure grabbed Jason pulling him to his feet. He placed one large hand firmly around Jason's throat cutting off his air supply. Jason grabbed frantically at the man's thumb. The thumb was the weakest part of the hand, but the doc was no match for this man's incredible size and strength. At this close range, Jason could see the man was wearing full tactical gear. The gear was almost an exact match for their own Commonwealth tactical gear. Jason was accustomed to reading his patient's faces to determine whatever they weren't comfortable verbalizing. He wished he could see into the eyes of his attacker. The window to this one's soul was draped with a dark reflective visor revealing only a reflection of Jason's own face and his own fear.

The man pulled Jason close to him. "Never speak that name again!" His voice was deep, and his message slow and deliberate, as though his anger threatened to override his orders. Jason sensed if he spoke again, the man could easily snap his neck with his one hand. The man, seeing he had made his point with his prisoner, tossed him back on the ground. Jason coughed and sputtered, taking in deep breaths and expelling the accumulating carbon dioxide. He rubbed his now aching throat then turned to check on Laura. He was relieved to find she was breathing easily. He reached for his bracelet to scan her for injuries. Before he could activate it, the voice behind him spoke again. "Remove all your weapons, your bracelet, and utility belt, and drop them on the ground. Remove hers after you've finished with yours."

Jason looked at his attacker with pleading eyes. "Please… let me see to her injuries first."

The man pointed his weapon at Laura. "You can do as you're told, or I can see to it her injuries are no longer relevant."

Jason held up his hands in surrender. "Okay, we'll do this your way." Jason slid his bracelet off then removed his utility belt and other weapons. He carefully moved to Laura. When he finished, he looked up to see what his captor planned next for them.

"Pick her up and carry her back to the campfire." The man ordered.

Jason hesitated. He still didn't know the extent of his wife's injuries. He decided the risk to his wife was less if he cooperated. Jason carefully picked her up and walked slowly back to the far side of the ship.

Braxton watched the sky trying to see any spatial distortions that would indicate the presence of the shuttle.

As the shuttle came near him, he saw a slight distortion in the stars overhead. He watched as the distortion changed course above him. He knew the scanners had picked him up. Remembering their visit to Tudoren and their attempts to find the Captain inside a burning building, he decided a fire could help hide his presence. Braxton adjusted his laser and fired at a nearby pile of dry leaves. He also ignited a dead tree then moved closer to it to hide his heat signature. Braxton shut his bracelet completely off and removed the power supply to keep from being tracked. The knowledge gleaned from the situations they had faced over the last year served him well, a little too well. The men pursuing him had trouble locating him although they knew someone was definitely in the area. Four of the men converged on the area trying to locate the troublemaker. The blaze spread creating a wall of fire. Braxton coughed as softly as he could when the smoke began to overwhelm him. The heat was becoming too much as well. He wondered if his decisions had been the correct ones. The men hadn't found him, but soon there might be very little left to find. Braxton looked around and whispered, "Arni, I need some help."

Arni's reply was not what Braxton wanted to hear. His quiet voice whispered, "Surrender."

Braxton's immediate mental argument was, "Are you kidding? I just worked really hard to escape being caught, and you want me to turn myself in."

Silence was the reply. Braxton knew Arni meant it. He was still having trouble bringing himself to do what was asked. Arni pushed again, "Surrender now!"

Braxton didn't know why he was pushing so hard. Deciding he better listen, Braxton raised his hands in the air, walking away from the fiery area. Stepping between two trees, they greeted him by the business end of three weapons. He looked past the weapons aimed at him and saw three enormous men in combat gear. One man spun Braxton around and slammed him against a tree, bloodying his nose. The man removed Braxton's utility belt, bracelet, and weapons. He placed binders on Braxton's wrists before spinning him back around. The men pushed him toward the ship. Braxton noticed a fourth man toss a large oval-shaped device into the center of the burning brush. The device exploded and covered the area including the treetops with a glowing shield. The *Evangeline* carried similar smaller devices which power themselves off the heat of the fire and produce a temporary shield covering a fire. The shield seals the area preventing oxygen from getting in to continue fueling the fire. As the fire uses the oxygen and goes out, the shield eventually dissipates. Braxton had heard about larger devices but had never seen one personally.

One of his guards shoved him to encourage him to move faster. "One more minute and you would have been suffocating with that fire." The guard informed him.

Was it his imagination or did his guard sound disappointed? At least he knew now why Arni sent him out of the fire.

Jake found a rock formation to slide into. It unnerved him slightly to climb into it not knowing what wildlife might already inhabit this hole in the ground. He was hiding near the path, which supposedly qualified as a road by the primitive standards of the locals. He saw the *Emissary's* Surf-ve get hit and come to a stop. It was about a hundred yards from him. He debated about checking on the passengers to be certain they were safe when Arni's voice spoke clearly yet silently to him. "Jake, stay put until I tell you to come out."

Jake, being the last one to follow Arni, should have been the least confident in recognizing his unspoken voice. Somehow, his practice at ignoring and rejecting Arni's voice made it easier for him to recognize and accept it. When he understood what was expected of him, Jake scooted as far back into his hole as possible and waited.

Captain Weiseman and his crew tried to restart the Surf-ve. When it failed to restart, they used the manual control to get out, but they kept their distance from David and his crew. The crew took defensive positions around the vehicle. They heard the shuttle fly overhead again then land in an adjacent field. Three members of the incoming team approached the crew of the *Emissary*.

The *Emissary* crew was equally amazed at the size of these new intruders. When the shuttle powered down, it became visible, including the large Commonwealth emblem on the side. Remembering David's warning to behave as loyal Commonwealth Soldiers, Nate pointed his weapon less aggressively at the visitors. "In the name of the Commonwealth Interstellar Force, identify yourselves."

The three men stopped their advance but didn't lower their weapons. One man lowered his but didn't put it away. He took two steps forward. "Lower your weapons, and I will escort you to my Captain. He'll answer your questions."

Nate was reluctant to lower his weapon, but decided it was the safest course of action for now. A fleeting thought ran through his head; perhaps Pateras' protection of the *Evangeline's* crew might carry over to him and his crew. Nate holstered his weapon and nodded to his crew to follow suit. The other four crewmen did as they were instructed and slowly came forward. Nate motioned for the one who spoke to lead the way. "After you."

The man walked past Nate and led the group toward the campfire. The man's companions holstered their weapons, but they stayed purposely behind Nate and his crew. They approached the man who had just landed the shuttle. The Captain of this new crew was similar in stature as his comrades. It appeared their sizes varied by several inches from one to another like any other human beings only bigger. The man stopped and saluted his Captain. Neither said anything, but he stood there facing his Captain for what seemed like an eternity. The Captain nodded. His lieutenant, as denoted by the rank on his uniform, stepped aside. The new Captain removed his helmet, handed it to the nearby lieutenant then folded his arms across his chest.

"Captain Weiseman, I presume."

"Yes, and you are?"

"My name is Captain Magnus Doherty of the Commonwealth Interstellar Ship *Talon*. Why are you here with Captain Alexander and his traitorous crew?"

Before he could answer, several of his men walked into the light of the campfire bringing their prisoners. The one bringing the two unconscious women dropped them unceremoniously on the ground. Jason came forward and gently laid Laura down. He sat down beside her and did as much as he could to assess her condition. He watched Cheyenne and Aulani carefully until he could see they were at least breathing. Captain Doherty recognized Jason from his CIF personnel file. When he saw the doctor studying the women, he interjected, "I gave my men orders to capture each of you alive if possible. The women are only stunned... and bruised."

Jason's captor rousted him. He pulled his hands behind his back and placed a set of binders on him then shoved him back on the ground.

Four men entered from the southeast escorting Braxton. They shoved him onto the ground near Jason. Braxton looked at the three unconscious women. "Are they okay?"

Jason looked at Braxton's bloody nose and what appeared to be first-degree burns on his face. "I think they're just unconscious. Are you okay?"

Braxton nodded. "Yeah, thanks to Arni."

Before Jason could warn him about mentioning the Liontaris, one of their guards jerked Braxton up and punched him in the abdomen. "Never speak that name!" came the familiar order.

Braxton collapsed on the ground as he tried to catch his breath. Jason winced and stared at Braxton as though he could heal him with his stare. Braxton rolled back and forth wheezing as he tried to force air into his lungs. His bloody nose wasn't helping matters and his eyes began to water. The surrounding voices sounded distant, and the darkness was creeping closer. He heard Jason calling his name. Jason was trying to keep him focused. Braxton knew he was near losing consciousness. He forced himself to concentrate on Jason. He managed to draw one long hard breath. The burning in his lungs subsided. As he continued to push himself to breathe, his hearing and eyesight slowly cleared. He was able to relax enough to lie still for a few minutes.

Aulani had come to by the time Braxton could see again. Cheyenne was stirring as well. Aulani looked over at Braxton. "Is he okay? What happened?"

Jason glanced at him then carefully worded his answer. "There are two names you probably shouldn't say, and they are the names of the Commonwealth's most prominent enemies."

Captain Doherty walked over between Jason and Aulani. He squatted down and gave the two a frigid explanation, "That would prevent unnecessary pain and keep you alive a few minutes longer."

He looked at one of the guards. The two appeared to be having a conversation though neither one spoke. The guard nodded then jerked Aulani up, removed her utility belt, bracelet, and weapons. He placed binders on her then grabbed Cheyenne and did the same. A second guard rolled a still unconscious Laura over and placed binders on her. The movement caused Laura to regain consciousness. The guards shoved each one into seated or kneeling positions around the fire.

Captain Doherty returned to deal with Captain Weiseman and his crew. "Captain Weiseman, you never told me why you were here fraternizing with the enemy."

Nate folded his arms across his chest. "Do you mind telling me why you're questioning me and my actions?"

Captain Doherty reached into his pocket and pulled out a data crystal. "Here are my orders. This comes from Defense Minister Hamilton Payne, and his orders come directly from Supreme Executor Hale."

Nate plugged the data crystal into his bracelet and downloaded the file. He reviewed the data then handed it back to Captain Doherty.

"Everything seems to be in order. In answer to your question, I wasn't fraternizing with the enemy. Captain Alexander and I had been friends, years ago. There was an accident in the mines over toward town. We agreed on a temporary truce for old times' sake because half my crew was trapped in the mine. He helped rescue my people. The agreement was that he wouldn't mention his new benefactor to my crew or me. He broke our agreement. I brought part of my crew out here to either place them under arrest, execute them, or sabotage the ship so they couldn't escape the planet."

Captain Doherty didn't look convinced. "I see. So, if I start executing his crew, you won't object?"

Nate shrugged. "I'd rather not watch. I don't enjoy seeing good soldiers die, but I won't try to stop you, if that's what you're asking."

Captain Doherty looked at one of his soldiers. The man nodded. He walked slowly behind each member of the crew.

David was watching every move from his hiding place. He couldn't make out what Nate was saying, but he hoped it was the right things. When the guard started walking around the crew, David knew his time was up. It would only be a moment before they would force his hand. David looked around and whispered. "Arni, I need you, and my crew needs you. Nate's crew needs you too. Please tell me what to do. Where are you? What do you need me to do?"

Thane took his eyes off the scene by the fire for a moment. "What did he say?"

David frowned, "Nothing yet. I really wish he wouldn't wait until the last moment to tell me what to do."

Thane pondered the situation for a moment. "Maybe he doesn't want you to do anything different than what you would do normally, so there isn't a reason to say anything yet."

David looked sullen. "You might be right. Just for the record, I'm going to have to surrender in a minute."

Thane nodded. "I know. I'll probably be right behind you."

"I'll try to cover for you. Stay hidden as long as you can. My understanding is they plan to execute all of us."

Thane gave David a puzzled look. "Why stay hidden? What good is a few more minutes?"

"The longer we're alive, the greater the chances of finding a weakness or a way out of this."

"What if this is it? What if we don't get out of this?"

"Then we'll get to see Pateras, face to face." David smiled at the thought. "Whatever happens, it will be a good ending to this day."

"Yes sir." Thane wasn't as confident as his Captain, but he trusted him.

"CAPTAIN ALEXANDER! I know you are close enough to hear me." Captain Doherty announced loudly.

David remained silent and watched Captain Doherty search the darkness for him. Most of the soldiers with him stood around the outside of the perimeter looking out toward the darkness. The men guarding the prisoners were now keeping their visors pulled up. Nate looked around gathering intelligence of his own. He realized the helmets were equipped with night vision technology.

Captain Doherty turned toward his lieutenant and nodded. The man took three long steps and grabbed Aulani, jerked her roughly to her feet, and brought her to his Captain.

Aulani gathered strength from her recently developed relationship with Pateras. She tried to jerk away from the man dragging her forward. "Stop IT! I am quite capable of walking!" Despite her courage, she felt dwarfed by the monsters lording over her.

Captain Doherty looked down at the puny human female in front of him. "You aren't afraid of us?"

Aulani planted her feet firmly and stood as straight and tall as she could, which made little difference compared to her captors. "No, I'm not. You're the ones who should be afraid. You can hit me if you want, but Pateras is the one in control here, not you."

Captain Doherty gave her an amused smile. He looked away and out into the darkness. With fire in his eyes he looked back at her. The smile disappeared from his face, and an icy darkness took its place. Aulani braced herself for what she knew was coming next. "As you wish, Ensign." Captain Doherty raised his hand and swung it forcefully, striking her. His large hand covered most of her face and head. Aulani landed forcefully on the ground.

Captain Doherty's cohort picked Aulani up. The hit had made her quite woozy. This time she did need help standing and walking. Her face quickly began to swell and bruise. Her lip was split in two places and bleeding. Her ear felt like it was on fire. She shook her head to clear it. The Lieutenant moved Aulani to a spot a few feet in front of his captain. He pushed her roughly onto her knees.

The swelling in her jaw was quickly making it difficult for her to speak. "This—doesn't ch-change anything. He-He's still—in charge. Even if you k-kill us. You can't st-stop him."

The man raised his weapon and pointed it at her. Thane was already seconds away from tearing through the trees with his bare hands and attacking the men for hurting his wife.

David grabbed Thane and stopped him. "Stay here! I'll stop this."

Captain Doherty called out again. "Captain Alexander! Turn yourself in right now, or I will shoot Ensign Ryder just to prove to you how serious I am. If you don't turn yourself in, then I will take the next crewmembers and torture them to death one at a time until you do. You have until the count of three."

David was already moving stealthily and quickly. He didn't want to announce his previous location since Thane was still hiding there.

As soon as he got as close as he could without losing the last few trees for cover, he shouted back to Captain Doherty. "I'm here. What happens to my crew if I surrender?"

"They get to live a few more minutes without pain."

David knew from the man's reply; their fate was sealed, and the only difference was how painfully they died. "Alright, I'm coming in, unarmed."

Captain Doherty looked disappointed as David approached with his hands in the air. "Captain Alexander, you didn't even let me start counting."

"I'm no fool. I know what's got to happen here. Why waste your time and mine?"

The two perimeter guards nearest to Captain Alexander approached him. They searched him. Unlike the rest of the crew, they kept his hands in front when they placed binders on him. The men removed his utility belt but left his bracelet in place. They escorted him the rest of the way in and presented him to their Captain. Aulani was moved back by the other prisoners, and David was forced to his knees in her place.

Captain Doherty folded his arms across his chest. "Well, capturing you was easier than I expected. I was told you were a formidable foe."

David smiled. "I'm not dead yet. Even if I were, I've been there before. Death's only temporary."

Captain Doherty squatted in front of him. "You seem awfully confident. I hold all the cards, Captain. I may not have all of your crew yet, but I will, one way or another."

"Who are you? Did he send for you?" David nodded toward Nate.

"I'm Captain Magnus Doherty of the CIF ship known as the *Talon*. I suppose you're wondering about a little more than my name. Supreme Executor Hale created us as an elite force. We're known as the Nefil Force. We do special jobs."

Captain Doherty leaned in closer to David and whispered. "I'm told you know the true nature of Supreme Executor Hale. Is that true?"

David smiled. "You mean his parentage, or the lack thereof?"

Captain Doherty smiled. "You might say, he's our uncle. We're cloned hybrids from some of his… relatives."

David looked around at the twelve giant specimens. "You certainly make an impression, initially."

"Initially? We are twice what you are. We are bigger, stronger, faster, more intelligent and we have state-of-the-art equipment. What makes you think we lack something?"

"It took twelve of you to capture six of us, or should I say it took twenty-two. I suppose you'll get the rest of my crew eventually, but so far the odds are still in my favor." David glanced at Nate and his crew.

Captain Doherty stood up. "Twenty-two? I'm afraid I'm not following you."

"Ten of the *Emissary's* men and twelve of yours. I'm sorry, are there more than twelve of you?" David was now toying with the man. He was also digging for information.

"Executor Hale created us to take the place of his twelve faulty teams. We cannot be corrupted. We are twelve teams of twelve and we will thwart the prophecies in the Ancient Texts. Our mere existence will convince anyone who believes those prophecies that they are a myth. Our existence proves the Ancient Texts to be nothing more than a storybook designed to frighten children."

David laughed outright. "Is that what he told you? His deception knows no bounds. What other great fantasies has he filled your heads with?"

"Captain, I thought you didn't want to waste time."

David was still amused despite the gravity of the situation. "Oh, I'm not wasting my time, just yours."

Captain Doherty was losing patience. He jerked David up and wrapped his hand around his throat. "Enough of your prattle. You will cooperate with me, or I will hurt your crew."

Captain Doherty's control over his own temper was better than that of some of his crew. He squeezed David's throat just enough to make it difficult to breathe and impede the circulation to his brain causing David's head to pound. Magnus slowly released his grip on David's throat. "First question, where is your wife?"

David coughed, cleared his throat then glared at Nate. "Ask him."

Captain Doherty stared at David for a moment. He turned his gaze to Captain Weiseman. "Care to explain, Captain Weiseman?"

Nate stepped forward. "I'm afraid Commander Alexander was… put down… earlier today along with one of my crew members."

Captain Doherty scowled. "Where are their bodies?"

Captain Weiseman glanced back at his crew. Milo quickly stepped forward to volunteer the information. "I put them into the river." Milo held back one piece of information. The plan had been to put the women into the water face down, so they would drown in their unconscious state. He couldn't prove the women were dead, and technically, he couldn't even say he had seen them dead.

Captain Doherty was not amused. "Well, Captain Weiseman, it seems you are good at following your orders. You've proven yourself twice now. I have just one question for you. You had orders to return to the nearest CIF base and report in. Why haven't you followed those orders?"

Captain Weiseman stood his ground. "Perhaps you weren't aware, but my orders were to complete my current mission, then report in. We had just started our mission on this world when we received those orders. We are about a week away from completing this mission. I haven't disregarded my orders or even stretched the limits of them. Admiral Deacons and Admiral Garcia are both aware of our status."

Captain Doherty stared at the man looking for some glimmer of deception. He was concerned their stories were too convenient. The facts seemed to add up, but his gut told him something wasn't right.

"Lt. Commander Oliver, you've seen the enemy firsthand when you were on Mara. Has the crew of the *Emissary* become adversely affected?"

Nate was rightly offended that Captain Doherty had usurped his authority among his own crew. He wisely kept silent although he made sure Captain Doherty could read his dissatisfaction in his body language.

"It would depend on your definition of adverse. Commander Asher has just lost his wife. He hasn't mourned as yet. It will affect him negatively although he has shown an uncanny ability to separate himself from his own grief. It also took a substantial amount of strength and resolve for him to turn her in instead of offering her a second chance."

Captain Doherty studied the ship's psychologist's words carefully. "What about the rest of the crew?"

"To be honest, I am truly amazed. Captain Weiseman's wife is in a stasis chamber, in dire need of medical care, yet he has wasted no time in ending the truce when the crisis was over. I would have expected him to feel indebted to Captain Alexander and his crew. He's treated the temporary truce as a necessary evil, a means to an end."

"What about Chief Griffin?"

"Chief Griffin volunteered to put the two women down. He was looking out for the well-being of his Captain and Commander Asher. He knew this would be a difficult task for either man. Yes, the crew will be negatively affected, but they will get past any difficulties. I'm quite certain of it."

Captain Weiseman turned irately to Dr. Oliver. "So, they sent you to spy on us."

Dr. Oliver smirked. "Of course, I was. Did you really think otherwise?"

Captain Weiseman shrugged. "No, not really."

David continued to listen closely to glean as much information as he could. The fact he found most interesting was Dr. Oliver's reference to Mara.

"Captain, I know you have one more man out there for certain. Get him in here, now. You know what happens if either of you doesn't cooperate."

David twisted his wrists and hailed Thane. "Lt. Ryder, it's time for you to come in."

There was a brief pause as Thane took a deep breath then responded. "Acknowledged. On my way, sir."

Thane came in fairly quickly. He left his laser rifle leaned against the *Emissary's* Surf-ve. He dropped his Tri-EMP, utility belt, and knives behind as well.

Two men went out to meet him. They scanned him, bound him, and roughly pulled him in. They deposited him next to Aulani.

"Now that we're all here," Magnus gloated. He looked over at a nearby Ensign of his own. The man turned to face his Captain directly and stood there staring at him. In a moment, the man saluted and walked toward Captain Weiseman's Surf-ve. Magnus turned his attention back to Nate. "Captain Weiseman, are the rest of your crew aboard your ship?"

"Yes, Captain." He answered. Nate knew these men were extremely dangerous and not to be trusted. He found himself trusting David's instinct more than he cared to admit.

"My Ensign is getting your Surf-ve working again. Please take your people back to your ship. I won't make you watch any of this. I do need to meet with you and your entire crew after I'm done here. Take your Surf-ve back and get some sleep. I'll meet with you in the morning."

Captain Weiseman turned to lead his people away then stopped. "Captain Doherty, your crew seems to know what you want them to do without being told. Do you have telepathic abilities?"

Captain Doherty smiled. "That would be a nice trick, indeed. No, we aren't telepathic, not in the traditional sense. We have the next generation in the nanite technology. The nanites can read my thoughts and transmit them through the comm units in our own bracelets. We can control much of our equipment the same way. My men used them to control the anti-grav units on their belts when we landed."

Captain Doherty gave another silent command, and one of his men launched himself into the air and floated there for a moment then mentally changed the settings of his anti-grav units bringing him gently to the ground.

David piped up. "I knew those things were dangerous."

"Be silent!" Magnus hissed at him. "You open your mouth again, and I'll have your crew's nanites activated and make you watch your crew kill each other."

David smiled again. "Good luck with that."

Captain Doherty frowned. "You haven't used the nanites, have you?" He mistakenly believed David was gloating over his foresight in avoiding the nanite usage.

David was smiling because he had given Nate a vital piece of information. The two had been playing off each other the entire time digging for information. Captain Doherty was so confident in his situation, he hadn't tried to hide anything.

Captain Doherty glared at David, then decided it didn't matter. The nanites would have provided him with some sadistic pleasure, but the outcome would ultimately be the same. "Captain Weiseman, take your leave or you will see this crew die."

Nate turned to go again. He didn't want to leave, but he wasn't sure how to help his friend.

David twisted around where Captain Doherty couldn't see his wrists. "Nate! Listen carefully! You know he's coming for you next! Don't do this, Nate! We were friends! I helped save your crew! Nate! Don't abandon us like this! Nate! Nate!"

Nate stopped and turned around one last time. "Davie, you brought this on yourself. I'm sorry, my friend. I appreciate your help in rescuing my crew. You should've left when you had the chance. I'm sorry."

Nate turned coldly back around and walked back to his vehicle. Noticing the items left behind by Lt. Ryder, he picked them up and tossed them casually into the vehicle. The Ensign sent by Captain Doherty to repair the Surf-ve was just finishing his work. He watched the Captain seem to pay little attention to the gear. The large man decided this Captain was merely cleaning up the prisoner's mess and dismissed the information from his mind.

The crew loaded up, and Nate instructed Milo to run scans of the vehicle and Gennie to run diagnostics on the Surf-ve before moving it. They stalled as long as they dared before powering up and moving.

Captain Doherty turned his attention back to Captain Alexander. "That was pathetic, Captain Alexander. Begging your friend to save you."

David grinned again. "It will make him think twice though."

Captain Doherty sighed. This man wasn't as pathetic as he first thought. "I don't suppose any amount of torture is going to get you to order the rest of your crew members to leave your ship."

David looked up sullenly. "Probably not."

David glanced over at his frightened crew. "What happens next?"

Captain Doherty was accustomed to giving his orders mentally, but he wanted to enjoy tormenting his prisoners as long as he could. "Gentlemen gather more wood. The Captain's fire is dying. We'll also need lots of wood to dispose of these bodies properly. I, for one, do not plan on digging graves."

Each one of the crew took turns looking toward the bridge of the ship. They knew Lazaro and the remaining crew were watching the drama outside unfold. The ship represented safety and was a mere fifty yards from them. It might as well be on the other side of the galaxy.

David sat back on his heels and stared at the ground. His crew was losing hope. His wife was gone. He was again forbidden from speaking the names of Arni and Pateras.

A NEW BREED OF SOLDIER

THE ELEVENTH HOUR

The Nefil soldiers moved about gathering firewood the size of small trees and tossing it onto the small campfire, then they placed David near his crew. He doubted it was with the intent of allowing them to say their farewells—surmising it was simply to make guarding them easier.

David noticed Captain Doherty was staring into space. He guessed the man was "talking" to his crew and his equipment. He decided the man needed more things to do and think about.

"Captain Doherty."

The man blinked twice then turned toward Captain Alexander. "What do you want?"

"You seem to have your plans well in hand. I just wondered how you plan to get to the rest of my crew. I know it's only a matter of minutes before you execute me and the crewmen you've captured. Your confidence tells me you aren't worried about the rest of my crew escaping."

Captain Doherty knelt in front of David and laughed. "I can see right through you, Captain Alexander. I know your people on the inside are probably watching and listening. If I tell you what I have planned for them, they may find some way to thwart my plans. I will clear up one misconception though, Captain. My orders are to put you and your wife in stasis and bring you both back alive. I will, unfortunately, only be able to comply with half of that order. You are going to watch your entire crew die, then I will put you in stasis and deliver you personally to Supreme Executor Hale. I suppose if there is another female member of your crew you'd like to lay claim to, I could arrange it right after I have the male members of your crew executed. How about it Captain Alexander? Have you had your eye on one of them?"

David was torn between giving an angry retort and a cutting remark. "Knowing what Luciano Hale probably has planned for me and whoever you bring back, it's better if I go alone. I wouldn't wish that on my worst enemy." David turned his head and looked Captain Doherty in the eyes. "Actually, maybe I would."

Captain Doherty sneered at his adversary. "Duly noted, Captain."

"Do you plan on putting Captain Weiseman and his crew in for a commendation for the murders they've committed?" David egged the man on.

Captain Doherty leaned in and whispered. "Not that it matters to you, but I suppose it's only fitting. It will have to be awarded posthumously though. I plan to destroy his ship right after I destroy yours. Their loyalty and service are appreciated, but we can no longer take chances."

"Why? They've more than proven their loyalty. What chances are you taking?" David tried hard to stifle his anger.

"He and his crew have been exposed to your vile, oppressive system of beliefs too many times. He's already lost three of his crew to the Timeless One. It's only a matter of time before the rest of them fall. It's a shame to lose the Olivers though. They've proven to be excellent operatives against Pateras. Executor Hale's new campaign needs a scapegoat. The blame for the deaths of the twelve crews is going to fall on you. The entire galaxy will know your name shortly."

Captain Doherty stood to let the information sink in. David was too stunned to continue trying to stall and distract his adversary.

Captain Doherty had to add one last evil jab. "By the way Captain, I am doing you one favor. Executor Hale ordered a specific method of execution for your crew. He wanted you to watch your crew die by the same method your Aunt Abigail died."

A stricken look crossed David's face. Imagined visions of his grandparents, mother, and Uncle Rob watching his Aunt Abigail bleed to death ran through his head and was promptly transferred to the faces of his crew.

Captain Doherty smiled knowing what had probably just run through his mind. "I think that's good enough. That sort of death is particularly messy. I had already decided to disregard that particular order. Just knowing what he wanted for you is enough." Captain Doherty went back to work.

David tried to study what he was doing, but he was clearly distracted. The pictures Captain Doherty had drawn for him, the losses he had already faced, and the ones he was about to face were quickly overwhelming him.

"Why are you listening to him?"

David heard the voice and the question, but somehow, he wasn't sure who said it, what it meant, or whom it was addressed to.

"Captain... "

It was Cheyenne's voice.

"What? I'm sorry, what did you want Cheyenne?" David forced himself to pay attention.

"Captain, why are you listening to him?"

David stared at the young woman feeling lost. He was a ship's Captain. He was supposed to be in control of his faculties and his ship and crew. He had lost nearly all control. It wasn't in his nature to complain or confess weakness.

"I–I'm not sure I can do this. I can't stop this. I don't have any fantastic rescue plans."

The rest of the crew, except for Cheyenne, now looked scared. Cheyenne's youthful innocence and exuberance led the way. "Captain, you need to listen for Arni's voice. This isn't about us. It's about him."

Thane, the handsome young pilot who enjoyed thrill rides and taking chances, now spoke with unexpected maturity. "She's right, Captain. Even if we don't make it through this day, Arni promised to always be with you. Whether we live or die is Pateras' call. This isn't about your success or failure. Captain -"

"It's David."

"Sir?"

"We aren't in the Commonwealth anymore. We're equals as far as Pateras is concerned. Right now, he's using you to speak to me. Don't call me Captain. Call me David."

Thane frowned. "That just feels wrong."

David glanced at each expectant face around him. "You are my friends, my brothers and sisters. If this is the last time I see you, then please call me by my name."

Thane still looked hesitant, but he honored the man's wish. "David, I don't regret coming down this path. If it ends in my death, then so be it. I chose right. Since we're on a first name basis, David, don't dishonor my death, even for a minute by blaming yourself."

Braxton joined in. "I agree with Thane, sir."

Cheyenne, Laura, and Aulani chimed in with their agreement as well.

Jason glanced around to see how close their guards were. None appeared close enough to overhear. "David, none of us want to die right now, but I think we could handle it better if we knew this wasn't going to overwhelm you. We need to know you'll keep fighting the Supreme Executor and working for Pateras. It's what Brynna would have wanted."

Cheyenne resumed her tutelage. "Captain, Arni said he was trying to teach us how to depend on the power of Pateras. He wouldn't bring us into this without giving us a way out of it."

"What?" The assault of evil on David's soul and consciousness subsided as he listened to Cheyenne's counsel.

"What good is it if we learn something, then don't have time to use it?" Cheyenne persisted in her explanation. "Arni wouldn't spend all this time trying to teach us just to take us out of the game."

Jason and Thane enjoyed playing "Zone," a ball game several crewmembers frequently played in the gym on board the ship. The analogy was certainly not lost on them. They gathered strength from her thoughts.

Braxton and Laura hadn't completely lost hope, but they took their cues from David. They clearly empathized with his loss and it clouded their focus like his. Aulani was caught somewhere in between all of them.

David realized he had taken on the posture of one who was already defeated despite some of his witty remarks to their captors. He looked around at the giants moving about. Most had taken their helmets off, and those nearest the fire had shed their warm, cumbersome tactical gear. David grinned. "Thank you, Cheyenne, and you too, Thane. They've dropped their guard. They think this fight is over."

David scooted in closer to his crew. He pushed himself off the ground and onto one knee. Looking toward the sky, he spoke to the one who was not limited by time nor space. "Pateras, we need your help. I need your help. I can't get my people out of this, only you can. Forgive me. I didn't mean to get distracted and lose my focus. Please tell us what you want us to do."

The crew moved in close together and took similar postures. They knew their captors would not take kindly to David's actions. They were right.

One of those assigned to watch the prisoners saw the subtle commotion and moved closer to the group. "What do you think you're doing?!" He demanded.

David grinned. "Planning our victory party."

The man stood there looking confused. He decided he wasn't going to get a straight answer. He ordered them to sit back down and stop talking and stayed closer to them this time. He was genuinely concerned by their newfound strength and comradery. David saw the man look at his Captain as he silently conveyed his concerns. He saw Captain Doherty cast a concerned glance in their direction.

Captain Doherty walked past David at one point and stopped long enough to leave him a message. "You attempt to cause me any problems, and I will see to it you will watch your crew die the way Executor Hale wanted you to. Are we clear on this?"

David gave the man an honest answer. "I'm not sure I'm capable of causing you any real problems, but I'm not the one you should be worried about."

"If you think Captain Weiseman is coming to your aid, you are severely mistaken. I have scanners trained on his ship. If it so much as powers up, my ship will be on top of him before he can lift off. He and his crew will be nothing more than a pile of rubble."

"No, Nate doesn't have a clue how to defeat you either, but I know someone who does. Pateras will defeat you."

At the sound of Pateras' name, David could see Captain Doherty's blood boil. He grabbed David by the jaw and squeezed tightly. "You know, I can hurt you and put you back together, before I deliver you to the Supreme Executor. You do understand that, don't you?"

Captain Doherty shoved David back onto the ground and walked away.

"Ow." David wiggled his jaw around and tried to massage the pain away.

Jason was wide-eyed at the scenario thinking Captain Alexander's jaw was nearly crushed in the man's gargantuan hand. "You alright?"

David nodded. "Just bruised."

Cheyenne snickered slightly. The crew looked at her. Laura quietly asked. "What's so funny?"

"I was just thinking in those old entertainment files, about the stories of people going off to wars or becoming martyrs for their cause. They always had a battle cry or chant or song they could sing. Does Pateras have songs or mantras or something?" Cheyenne pondered.

Jason, the oldest of them all shook his head. "The only ones I know are Commonwealth songs. I'm not sure those are appropriate to the occasion. You and the Captain know the Ancient Texts better than anyone. Have you seen anything in there?"

Cheyenne squinted. Her expertise was in linguistics, but this was not the things she spent a lot of time on in her career. "There are songs, but they don't translate right. We would need a musician to help rework them."

"Jake is a musician." David offered.

"He is?" Laura asked. "How do you know that?"

David smiled. "I'm the Captain. It's my job to know all your secrets."

Braxton raised an eyebrow. "I thought that was Lexi's job."

"It's my job to know them. It's her job to fix them." David teased.

David turned his attention back to Cheyenne. "Get Jake to look at it with you. It would be nice to have something like that in the future."

Thane's face clouded. Aulani could feel her husband tense up. "What is it, Thane?"

"Nothing." He snapped.

David looked at him quizzically. "Thane, that fire is almost ready, and our time is almost up. Speak up. You might not get another chance."

Cheyenne whispered to Laura. "I thought we decided we weren't dying today?"

Laura gave her a trite, "You've got my vote on that."

David gave the two women an annoyed look then turned his attention back to Thane. "What is it, Thane?"

"Some, or all of us, may die in a few minutes and you want Cheyenne to work with that traitor, who is still hiding in the woods out there, to help come up with a theme song for our wayward band of... whatever we are. Jake doesn't deserve such an important opportunity." Thane's grudge surfaced again.

"Oh, come on, Thane. This really isn't the time." Aulani groaned.

Braxton piped up. "Thane, Jake nearly lost his life once already today. He took a big risk to save those hostages from King De-Marion. The only reason he's alive now is because Pateras protected him."

Thane shook his head. "He'll always be a traitor. He was looking out for himself when he betrayed us. When he finally gave in to Arni, it was because Executor Hale betrayed him. He probably had some self-serving reason to free those hostages. He was probably just trying to earn back some respect from the crew."

Jason stared down at the ground as he thought. "Thane, we're all guilty of something, including betrayal. Jake's betrayal of us was just more obvious. Painfully obvious. We all betrayed our Commonwealth commissions. I'm not excusing Jake. I'm just saying we're all guilty, and I believe he's on board with Pateras."

"So why is he out there hiding and not trying to save us?" Thane quipped.

David kept silent for a moment to see where the conversation went. The topic was not what one would

249

expect from prisoners on death row and several things became clear. The crew, himself included, no longer expected to die, despite the obvious intentions of their captors. Second, Jake was winning back the trust of some of the crew. He hoped Jake was earning their forgiveness as well.

"Jake was trying to earn back the trust and respect of the crew today. He fully expected it might cost him his life to do it, but he was willing to do that." David explained. "Thane, I'm asking as your friend, not as your Captain, give Jake a second chance, please."

The normally lighthearted pilot still looked cross. "If we survive the next few hours, I'll give him a second chance. You have my word."

The fire was now roaring. Captain Doherty grabbed Cheyenne and pulled her over toward the boundary of the ship's shield. The crew tried to rally to protect her but were decisively returned to their places on the ground. Magnus placed his weapon to Cheyenne's head and called out loudly. "Lt. Commander Dominick, I know you can hear me. Lower your shields. You and the rest of your crew surrender peacefully, or you can watch your wife die and her body burn in the fire."

The wind gusted suddenly nearly knocking Cheyenne off her feet. David continued to struggle to get to his feet. He finally shouted loudly to Lazaro. "DON'T DO IT! HE INTENDS TO KILL ALL OF YOU!" The guard, holding David down, punched him in the face hard enough to make his head spin.

Captain Doherty frowned at David. The powerful aroma of rain filled the air. Magnus looked at the sky above him. He knew he wouldn't have much time to do this before the rain put the fire out. He had checked the atmospheric conditions before leaving the ship. There were no indications of rain for a hundred miles in any direction.

As if in response to his thoughts, rain poured down. In a matter of seconds, they were all drenched. The campfire dimmed drastically from the towering inferno it had been minutes ago.

Magnus looked to his lieutenant. David watched as the man snapped to attention. Four men retrieved their helmets to protect them from the rain, then took up positions around the ship. The others rousted their prisoners and shoved them away from the ship. Captain Doherty led the way on a trek into the darkness. He seemed to be quietly seething, and his men did their best to keep out of his sight.

David knew the man's orders were to keep him alive, so once they were just out of sight of the ship, he decided to press his luck. "Captain Doherty! Captain Doherty!"

The big man stopped and turned around. His face clearly displaying the anger he felt. As the rain continued to pour down the sides of his helmet, he answered far more calmly than David expected. "Be silent, or I will start breaking bones, some of them might be yours."

"I just wanted to know where you were taking us."

The man's jaw clenched so tight he had trouble speaking. "If Pateras thinks a little rain will save your crew, he's mistaken. I'm going to let your crew join your wife, downstream."

David clenched his own jaw at the thought. The guards shoved them forward again. The darkness and slick ground made moving with any amount of speed difficult, even for their superior counterparts.

David kept watch and worked his way back and forth in the line headed toward the river. The eight large guards were now only seven. Where had the eighth man gone? Aulani tripped over a rock jutting out of the ground. Thane stopped to help her, but with his hands bound behind him, he could do little more than offer her encouragement. With David's hands bound in front, he was able to help her up before the nearest guard could roughly roust her.

"Spread out. Slow down and stay alert." David whispered the quick message to her and Thane before the guards redirected them.

David allowed himself to drift to the back of the processional again as Thane and Aulani moved forward to share the Captain's message. Two guards brought up the rear and kept pushing David forward.

As they neared the river, the foliage increased, and the storm seemed to get worse for a few minutes forcing the group to stop where they were. The trees were bending and swirling in the wind, and raindrops pelted their skin so hard, it stung. The guards forced their prisoners to take cover up against nearby trees, splitting the entourage into small groups. David was separated from the others in the haste to take cover. He and the two rear guards huddled at the base of a large, old tree, which twisted violently. A loud crack warned them of the tree's impending demise. The three backed away from it hastily, unsure of the direction it was about to fall. One guard dodged to the left while the second one pulled David with him to the right. The second guard chose correctly. The tree collapsed onto the first. As he moved to check on his companion, the second man kept David close to him. The two found the man pinned under the tree. A quick scan revealed he died on impact. The guard tried to send a mental message to Captain Doherty, but frequent lightning made it impossible. The man's attempts to send a verbal message through his comm unit were just as unsuccessful.

The guard pulled David roughly through the storm until he reached the place where Captain Doherty huddled with Braxton, Cheyenne, and the Captain's lieutenant. He reported the loss to his Captain.

Captain Doherty grabbed David by the collar. "I don't care what Supreme Executor Hale says. If any of your people try to escape, I will kill you, slowly and painfully."

David shouted back loudly to be heard over the storm. "I had nothing to do with this! My people haven't tried to escape. You can't blame us for the weather!"

The group stayed huddled for another few minutes until the storm slowed to a light rain. The heart of the storm had moved off, but the sky still flashed brightly with frequent lightening. A loud rumble of thunder overshadowed what should have been a quiet night as the wind continued to rustle in the trees.

Captain Doherty decided it was time to move on. David breathed a sigh of relief when it appeared Magnus had not noticed he was now two guards short. He hoped the reason the first guard disappeared was because that Jake had taken him out.

Captain Doherty wasn't as oblivious as David hoped. He grabbed David by the back of the neck and forced him to walk in front of him and ordered the others to follow suit.

The crew grew more somber as they neared the river. As suddenly as the rain had begun, it stopped. The wind continued to blow and break up the clouds. The planet's two small moons now shone brightly through a hole in the clouds. With the freshly cleaned air, their light reflected brilliantly on the surface of the river.

Captain Doherty unfastened Captain Alexander's binders. He pulled David's arms up around a stout tree branch over his head and reconnected the binders.

The young Captain stood facing the water feeling helpless. The tree branch they secured him to was far too large to escape. It branched out and got larger and higher the further it went. Mentally he called out to Arni who had not been seen since they landed. "Arni, please protect my crew. Don't let them die, not any of them."

Arni appeared at his side. "What if I need them with me?"

Instinctively David worried about his captors spotting Arni. Knowing how they felt about him, they wouldn't react well to his presence. Arni didn't carry weapons, and David knew he could die. He had died on Drea.

Knowing his thoughts, Arni smiled and put this one worry to rest. "They can't see or hear me."

David allowed himself to dismiss this one fear as he watched the large Commonwealth soldiers shove his crew to the edge of the water and force them to their knees. His mind remained clouded with many other fears. He was trained to be a ship's Captain. He knew sacrificing a crewmember was always a possibility, but he wasn't prepared to sacrifice seven crewmen. Why did Executor Hale want him alive? Did he have more terrors planned for his future than those he suffered on Romajin? With his family safely hidden on Drea, half his crew about to die, and Brynna now gone, David wasn't sure he could face Executor Hale again. He was seconds away from losing hope. "Arni, if you take them, take me too. I'm not sure I can face Luciano Hale again. I almost didn't make it last time."

"Never lose hope. David, you are my child. I created you."

David stared hard at Arni trying to make sense of his words. Physically, Arni was the same age as David. He had explained his true nature to the crew. Arni, although the son of Pateras, was a separate representation of Pateras. Pateras was infinite. He had no beginning and would have no ending. Although David's imagination couldn't reach that far, he understood the concept. He did have trouble with a man his age claiming him as his son. It wasn't uncommon for the elderly to call a young man "son", but a man in his thirties calling another thirty-year-old man "son" was just odd.

Arni slowed for David to process his words then continued. "I want what is best for you. Without giving you a way out, I will never put more on you than you can handle. I didn't abandon you on Romajin, or Drea, or Medoris, and I will never abandon you. You know this is true, don't you?"

David winced. He did know it was true, but his fears were causing doubts. He was afraid Arni would allow his crew to die. Even if he had good reasons, David didn't know if he could handle the guilt of being unable to protect his crew. He was afraid he couldn't go on without Brynna. His time on Romajin in the hands of Executor Hale had nearly cost him his life and his sanity. He was afraid he wouldn't maintain his integrity this time if Brynna and his crew were gone.

Arni stepped directly in front of David. Knowing what David was afraid of him he bluntly asked, "Which one of those fears do you think I am incapable of handling?"

David's throat and mouth went dry. "I'm sorry, Arni. I know you can handle all of them. I guess what I'm most afraid of is that our goals are different."

Arni smiled. "You will learn to pursue the things my Father values and see things as he sees them. I have asked you this before. Trust me, with your life and your crew's lives. Don't just trust me for one circumstance or another, but trust me every day under all circumstances."

David glanced at his crew who were all now together on their knees at the edge of the water. He flexed against his restraints. He looked back into Arni's eyes, "Yes sir."

Captain Doherty made a quick visual scan of his surroundings. His eyes landed on David. "Say goodbye to your crew, Captain."

David wanted to give them a reassuring smile, but it wasn't in him. He pulled himself up as straight and tall as the tree branch above him would allow. He wanted to thank them for their service and tell them how proud he was to have served with them. The words wouldn't come. He said the only thing he could, and the smile came with it. "Arni says, 'Trust Pateras'."

Captain Doherty and his crew looked like they were ready to attack Captain Alexander all at the same time. Captain Doherty turned to his lieutenant and kept his orders verbal to get the full effect of terrorizing the crew. "Lieutenant, take Lt. Commander Flint into the water first. Take his binders off. I want the Captain to watch him fight for his life."

The man did as he was ordered being careful not to let go of his prisoner. He forced Braxton to wade into the water. They reached a point where Braxton was nearly up to his waist. His heart was pounding. Was he supposed to fight back? What did Pateras expect? Braxton looked at David.

David's own heart was pounding. He trusted Arni, but he was still afraid it meant losing his crew. His fists balled up tightly. His crew dying didn't feel right. David calmly waited for Arni. He kept his eyes trained on Braxton.

The man grabbed Braxton and forced his head under the water. Braxton sucked in one large quick breath before being submerged. He tried to break the man's grip on him. The man was too large and too strong. Braxton felt his lungs burning as he struggled and fought. The man's sadistic nature displayed itself as he toyed with Braxton. He pulled him out of the water long enough to grab another quick breath of air. The man pulled him up for a third and final breath. The evil giant grinned and said, "Say goodbye."

He started to push Braxton down again when an arrow struck the man's neck and shoulder. Braxton stared wide-eyed at it for a half-second then reacted quickly. He got his feet under him, pushed off the bottom of the riverbed, and launched himself at his would-be assassin. He knocked the man off his feet. The man was torn between wanting the arrow out of his neck and shoulder and holding onto his prisoner. He knew pulling the arrow out was not wise.

Braxton also knew it and purposely grabbed the shaft of the arrow. The man used his now diminished strength and shoved Braxton away from him. With one hand, he grabbed Braxton and shoved him back under the water and dragged him into deeper water. Now Braxton had the current to fight in addition to his attacker. The man released his grip and went limp. Braxton surfaced to survey his situation. The man had a second deadlier arrow protruding from his body. The man stopped moving and sank into the water.

Braxton started to come back toward the shore when David shouted. "Run, get to safety!"

Captain Doherty searched the darkness around him for the source of the arrows. He grabbed Jason and held him in front of him. The difference in their sizes made Jason a poor shield. Captain Doherty activated his own personal shield generator with nothing more than his thoughts. He pulled a knife from his utility belt and held it to Jason's throat. "Captain Alexander, tell your people to surrender, or I will kill each one of these crewmen here and now."

David scowled at the man. "There are two problems with that, Captain Doherty. First, my people all know you intend to kill them. That's not much of an incentive to surrender, but the second thing is what you really need to be concerned about. My people don't use bows and arrows."

It dawned on Captain Doherty that Captain Alexander was right. Although they were trained to use them, they didn't carry them. Magnus reacted decisively. He mentally ordered his men to each grab a hostage and slaughter them quickly. The men looked to their leader as though they were still waiting for orders. A voice came from the darkness. "Captain Doherty, drop your weapons, and release your hostages. You and your crew will be allowed to walk away peacefully."

Captain Doherty sent his order again. His men stood still waiting for instruction. He looked over at David who was now grinning. "I sent instructions the old-fashioned way. I kept my comm line open to transmit. Everything you've told me, they've heard."

The fire in Captain Doherty's eyes was back. He looked at his men and verbally ordered. "Kill them all starting with the prisoners!"

The men went into action. Some activated their shields first while others reached for prisoners.

Cheyenne reacted quicker than the others. She was closest to the water. She did a backward somersault away from the river then rolled onto her feet and headed directly into the water. She narrowly missed being grabbed by one of the guards. The man promptly ended up with a laser piercing the back of his knee, causing him to hit the ground. Cheyenne moved out into the water and headed downstream after Braxton.

Thane tried to run interference for his wife to get away. The soldier nearest them reached for Aulani who was attempting to roll to her feet. He hastily yelled, "Aulani! Run! Don't look back!"

Thane rolled back onto his back and kicked at the man with both feet. He promptly earned himself a backhand to the face then found himself the man's new target. The man pinned Thane against a tree. He pulled a knife with his free hand and reared back to plunge the huge instrument into Thane's abdomen. Thane strained against the man's enormous arm. His eyes widened as the knife came toward him. He closed his eyes and braced himself for the impact. A series of unexpected noises reached his ears before the menacing dagger reached his belly. The sounds included a piece of equipment powering up and cries of pain. Thane opened his eyes. A shield had materialized in front of him taking his attacker's arms captive. When the shield materialized, it formed around the man's hand carrying the knife and around the upper part of the arm pinning Thane against the tree. Thane looked down at his abdomen. The knife was less than an inch from his uniform. His eyes followed the shield to its source. Jake held the shield that was keeping him alive. The pressure of the shield caused the man to lose strength in both arms. The two together forced the man backward, freeing Thane from his grasp. Jake deactivated his shield and fired his Tri-EMP before the man could react. The man convulsed violently then relaxed.

Thane looked at Jake curiously. "Did you kill him instead of stunning him?"

Jake responded flatly, "Yes, we don't have a choice this time."

Aulani was smaller and quicker than the giants. The guard who continued to chase her was nearly on her when she jumped into a tight circle of trees. He reached his long arm between the trees to pull her out. She pulled herself as far away from his grasp as she could, sinking down to the ground where the gaps between trees were smaller. His fingertips brushed her hair. She twisted her head further from his reach. He finally pulled back and reached for the laser on his belt. He stuck his arm back in and aimed the laser sight at her chest. Forgetting the urgency of the situation, he paused to enjoy her fear. His pleasure served only to contribute to his own demise. Someone struck the man behind the knees with a large tree branch throwing him off balance. He pulled his arm back to defend himself. He turned and attempted to activate his shield, but he wasn't fast enough. The pellet from a Tri-EMP contacted his neck causing his laser to fire wildly into the trees. Aulani came out of the trees to find out who her rescuers were. She was greeted by Commander Asher and Chief Griffin. Knowing what they had done to Commander Alexander and Lt. Commander Asher, she wasn't sure if she had been rescued or not.

Seeing the fear in her eyes, Commander Asher released her from her binders then turned her back around. He placed his hand gently on her shoulder. "We won't hurt you. You have my word." He reached for his laser pistol and handed it to her butt first. "Here, you might need a weapon." She took the weapon from him then turned back toward the center of the fray.

Laura ran a few feet in the general direction the arrows had come from before being caught by a guard. Before the guard could cause her any harm, men from Prince Ca-Litana's army attacked him on three sides. The three men caused him to lose interest in Laura and look to his own protection. Once Laura was pulled to safety, four more men joined the fight.

The man who chased Cheyenne into the water limped back only to be confronted by five adversaries waiting to engage him. The five men put him down with surprising ease.

Five men surrounded Captain Doherty looking for an opening. Jason was certain even if they rescued everyone else, his predicament would guarantee his own demise. Captain Doherty seeing his people falling quickly, hung onto Jason. The man glanced over at David. He understood now why Supreme Executor Hale wanted the young Captain alive. He wanted to see the man suffer. Magnus was having the same desires. Just as he entertained ideas of what harm he could still cause the resilient Captain, a random blast from a laser shot through the trees and cut through David's binders, releasing him from the tree. Magnus' eyes widened in amazement then narrowed as he realized who was responsible. He glanced at the sky mentally hurling useless threats and insults at Pateras.

Magnus activated his anti-grav units and increased the radius of his shield to 355 degrees. He would have been happier to have a full 360 degrees, but the safety feature of the item kept the last five degrees open to ensure proper air circulation. It was new technology, so he took comfort in believing his enemies wouldn't be able to exploit the small weakness. His anti-grav units lifted him and the doctor sixty feet into the air.

Seeing the last of his men fall, he looked to David. "Captain Alexander, would you consider a deal?"

David moved as close as he could. "What do you want?"

"Surrender yourself to me, and I will leave your crew alone. I won't even attempt to shoot down either ship." Captain Doherty was willing to be truthful in this bargain, although he did fully intend to send out a distress call the second he got into space.

"What happens if I don't agree?"

Captain Doherty's temper flared. "Don't test me, Captain. I will drop your man head first on the ground. He won't survive such a fall."

"You seem to be on the losing side of things. I will let you walk out of here unimpeded if you release my man safely. If you are afraid I won't keep my word, just fly your little anti-grav bubble to the other side of the river, drop him off, and go about your business." David countered.

Captain Doherty knew he could just walk away and either take Jason with him or kill him and drop his body in the river. He really didn't want to leave empty-handed.

"Captain Alexander, my orders were to bring you and your wife back alive and kill your crew. I will follow those orders to the best of my abilities. My preference is to take you back alive, but if I have to settle for killing only one man on your crew, I'll do it. So which way is it going to be?"

Commander Asher, Chief Griffin, and Ensign Ryder came running through the trees to the riverbank. Milo pulled his laser to fire at the floating bubble. Jake jumped in front of him pushing his hand off target. "Don't shoot! You'll just push him farther away."

Jake grinned as soon as the words were out of his mouth. "Is that jammer still working?"

Milo looked down at his utility belt. "Yeah, why?"

"Shut it off." Milo did as he was told. Jake pressed a couple buttons on his bracelet then whispered into it while Captain Doherty was speaking. Jake closed the comm line then looked at Milo. "Be ready. I don't know how this is going to play out." Jake trotted to a position opposite Milo along the riverbank.

David gave Jake a quizzical look and Jake returned a half shrug. "Alright, Captain Doherty, I'll take the doctor's place. How do you want to do this? Should I just hike back to your shuttle and wait for you?"

"Don't get smart with me, Captain." Captain Doherty snapped. "Swim across the river, alone."

David started wading into the water.

Jason began to wiggle and twist. "I... can't... breathe." He complained. He reached the anti-grav unit clipped to one side of the man's belt and gave it a swift yank. Removing it altered the giant's center of gravity throwing the two of them sideways. As long as the doctor held it, it kept him lightweight and easy to hang onto.

Jake yelled loudly. "DOC! DROP IT!"

Jason did as Jake ordered. It found the five-degree opening in the shield and slipped through. Magnus decided his passenger was now more trouble than he was worth. He dropped his shield long enough for Jason to fall. Jason fell into the shallow area of the river. He heard Laura scream as he hit the water. Jason felt a painful snap as his leg hit a rock and slid into an unnatural position. As he landed, his head contacted another rock rendering him unconscious. David was only a few steps from where he landed. He dashed over to him and pulled his head carefully out of the water.

Milo and Jake were ready for the shields to drop. They aimed their lasers at Captain Doherty's shield generator and second anti-grav unit. Their efforts paid off. The man came crashing to the ground near David and Jason.

Captain Doherty couldn't take any more humiliation. He was a superior being. How dare these insects try to best him like this? He pulled a knife from his belt and began swinging it wildly at David and Jason.

Seeing his predicament, Milo and Commander Asher rushed to extricate Jason from the water. While Jake went to David's aid, several of Prince Ca-Litana's men drew their weapons to prepare to attack this last man. David had no weapons but kept himself between Jason and Captain Doherty. Prince Ca-Litana's men moved in quickly and attacked Captain Doherty viciously. Captain Doherty reached the first of Prince Ca-Litana's men. He yanked the first one in and threw him into the deepest part of the river. A second was just as easily dispatched. The rest of the Prince's men used more wisdom and cunning to attack. They quickly dropped the man face-down in the water. He lay there not moving. The Prince's guard had been instructed on how to remove or find the weak spots in the body armor worn by the soldiers. They wasted no time in using their new knowledge. Captain Doherty and his crew had portions of their armor ripped away from their bodies or gashes in the seams. When Prince Ca-Litana's men decided Captain Doherty was finished, they walked away from him.

The crew and Prince Ca-Litana's guards gathered around Jason. Commander Asher called for a stretcher. He had positioned a Surf-ve a few hundred yards away. Nate, Noah, and Henry grabbed a stretcher and med kit and came down to the riverbank.

David checked in with his crewmembers to be sure each one was unhurt and accounted for. His crew and Nate's dispersed quickly to treat any injuries sustained by the Prince's guards. Surprisingly, only minor cuts and bruises resulted.

David moved to Nate to thank him and the leader of Prince Ca-Litana's guards for their help.

Milo and Nate pulled David aside. Milo still hadn't told David about Brynna's death. At this point, Milo knew he had to tell David the truth. "Captain Alexander, I need to tell you about your wife."

David put his hand on Milo's shoulder. "I appreciate it, Chief. I want to know what happened, but I can't take the time right now."

David turned to walk away from the two, but Nate grabbed his arm. "Davie, you really need to listen to him, and you need to listen now."

David stopped. What could be this important? He decided if Nate thought it was necessary, then perhaps he should too. "Alright, Chief, what is it you need to tell me?"

"Well, Captain, I saw how your people conducted themselves during the rescue operation and how your security chief risked his life to save the lives of the hostages and Lt. Commander Weiseman. The idea that you and your people should be executed unsettled me. It just didn't make sense to me. Then when I saw Jake and those ants... I just didn't know what to think."

David was losing patience. His doctor needed medical care, and it was very late. His crew needed to stand down and get some rest, not to mention the possibility of more incoming Commonwealth ships. "What's your point, Chief?"

"My point is; when Commander Asher seemed determined to execute the two women, I... uh... I volunteered to take care of it for him."

"So far, I am not seeing what couldn't wait until later, Chief." David groused. This wasn't a subject he cared for, and he would have preferred to have this discussion privately.

Milo realized he needed to give the Captain the short version of the truth. "Captain, I volunteered because I wanted to protect them. I couldn't kill them. I faked the whole thing. We were worried about the Olivers being spies. Commander Asher was doing what he could to protect the crew, or he wouldn't have ordered the women's execution. Captain Alexander, your wife isn't dead. She's safely back aboard the *Evangeline*."

David stood there in shock.

"Captain, did you hear what he said?" Captain Weiseman asked.

Brynna's smiling face appeared in his mind's eye. David stepped away from the two men. His gratitude overwhelmed him. He leaned his arm up against a tree. Looking around, David blinked back tears of relief. "Thank you, Pateras. Thank you."

David turned back around energized by the good news. "Let's get moving back to the ship. Is the Doc ready to be moved?" He walked the few steps back to Jason's side quickly.

A movement in his peripheral vision caught his attention. He turned to see Captain Doherty at the edge of the shore roll over onto his side. With shaking hands, he pressed some buttons on his bracelet. Barely able to hold his own head up, he grinned evilly. "It's not over… until… I say… it's over." He laughed, coughed, and gasped one last time, and then his head dropped back down. His eyes stared into the darkness.

David looked around and searched the area including the sky for some indication of what the man had done. Jake moved away from Jason's side scanning the area for everything imaginable. He crouched by Captain Doherty's body and tried to access the data on his bracelet, but he was locked out. David's next thought was the ship in orbit. Before he could issue any orders, he heard Jake sing out. "LOOK OUT!"

Captain Weiseman pushed Milo aside and pulled a knife from his belt. He was moving toward David with purpose. Jake jumped in front of him and attempted to disarm him. David moved toward Nate as Jake continued to wrestle with him. Jake warned his Captain to stay back. Prince Ca-Litana's guards were unsure of how to handle this new dispute.

Nate's focus kept him from making tactical mistakes. Jake was less privileged. He was tired and didn't want to hurt his Captain's friend and new ally. He was more prone to errors in judgment. Nate's moves were cold and clinical. David realized too late that Jake was in trouble. Nate plunged his knife into Jake's side then pulled the blade out and shoved him aside. Jake collapsed on the ground holding his side. David and Thane charged Captain Weiseman taking him to the ground. David looked up in time to see Milo advancing with his weapon drawn. "Milo, stun him! NOW!"

Milo fired at Captain Weiseman as David and Thane released him and jumped clear. Nate writhed and twisted then collapsed. As Captain Weiseman relaxed, David and Thane got up slowly and relieved him of his weapons. They placed a set of binders on him, in case he regained consciousness.

Thane looked around at the startled group. "What was that all about?"

David was the only one of those taken prisoner, who still had his bracelet. He made eye contact with Silas to make a point as he contacted his ship. "Captain Alexander to *Evangeline*."

David's heart skipped a beat when Brynna's voice reached his ears. "This is the *Evangeline*, go ahead Captain."

David was so happy to hear her voice, he had trouble responding. "Commander, we have a cloaked Commonwealth vessel in orbit. I don't know what its orders are or even if it's occupied. Keep your scanners looking for everything, including atmospheric temperature changes in a possible approach pattern. Get the ship ready to launch the second you see any potential incoming vessels. We have medical emergencies coming your way, so try not to take off until we get back, but do what you must to protect the ship."

Commander Asher gave a similar message to his own crew then looked at David. "What do we do about Captain Weiseman?"

David wasn't entirely sure where the man stood in relation to their treason at this point. He decided to play it safe. "My ship is closest. Let's try to get all the wounded, including Captain Weiseman, into my infirmary until we get that part figured out. Can I borrow Chief Evans for a while?"

Commander Asher nodded. "Yeah, let's get moving. Our Surf-ve is over here."

Noah Evans had turned temporary care of Jason over to Laura. He was actively treating Jake. He had the bleeding under control, and Jake could move with help. Thane moved to Jake's side to help him to the Surf-ve. Prince Ca-Litana's men rigged a quick stretcher to transport Captain Weiseman.

Thane helped Jake to his seat in the Surf-ve and buckled his seat belt for him. Jake winced with every move and broke out in a cold sweat. His clothes were still wet from the storm earlier making him even colder. His body was visibly shivering which increased his pain. Thane grabbed an emergency blanket and covered him with it. Thane gave his shoulder a reassuring pat before he moved toward a seat for himself.

"Th-Thane," Jake stammered.

Thane turned back around. "Yeah, Jake?"

"Th–Thanks."

Thane gave Jake a weak smile. "You saved my life. I think I at least owed you a ride back."

Jake tried to smile at Thane's attempt at humor. "I owed y–you."

Thane smiled again. "It's paid in full, man, paid in full."

The Surf-ve was loaded as heavily as possible leaving a half-dozen of Prince Ca-Litana's men without transportation. The men eagerly agreed to go on foot and took off before the Surf-ve even moved.

Chief Griffin drove the *Emissary's* Surf-ve up the ramp into the *Evangeline's* hold. They quickly unloaded all the wounded. Commander Asher hastily ordered his crew back aboard the Surf-ve and raced back to his own ship.

Before David could organize the evacuation of the wounded, Prince Ca-Litana's guards saw to the task. David sent the crew to change into dry clothes and grab a hot cup of coffee or soup. He headed to the infirmary to make certain Captain Weiseman was appropriately handled. To his surprise, he walked in on a lighthearted disagreement among the medical personnel.

"Dr. Adams, if you don't mind, I will give the orders for your treatment. I know this is your infirmary, but right now you are my patient."

David stood there flabbergasted. "Steph?" Dr. Stephanie Weiseman stood in front of him, alive and well. "How did you...?"

"Your friend, Arni, is quite a doctor."

David smiled. "Yes, he is. I'm glad you're well. Do you have everything under control in here?"

Stephanie gave David an impish grin. "So long as your doctor minds his own business, I do. Why is Nate wearing binders?"

"You need to keep him sedated and secured until we can do something about his nanites. He knifed Jake and tried to kill me. I need to get to the bridge as soon as possible. We may need to launch suddenly, so be prepared."

Stephanie glanced at Nate. "He is going to be okay, isn't he?"

David stepped closer to her. He reached over and took her hand. Squeezing it gently, he smiled. "I've got my best people working on it."

The hand squeeze wasn't enough for Stephanie. There had been far too much emotion in play over the last couple days. She grabbed David and hugged him tightly. She whispered softly, "Thank you," then released her grip on him. "I think we both need to get to work."

David smiled warmly. "It's great to see you, Steph."

David glanced at Jason. "Doc, behave... like a patient." David then quickly headed down the hall to his quarters to change clothes. He was so cold and tired, he desperately wanted a hot shower. He checked in with the bridge. The ship hadn't been located, so he grabbed his shower.

Captain Alexander made a fast run through the dining hall to grab a cup of coffee and a meal ration bar. He swallowed one large bite then shoved it into his pocket just before stepping onto the bridge. As the doors opened onto the bridge and he caught sight of his beautiful wife, he had to work hard to suppress the urge to grab onto her and hold her tightly.

The first words out of his mouth were, "Status report!" The first words his eyes conveyed to Brynna were very different. Brynna could see his thoughts were radically divided. She gave him a quick understanding smile then reported as ordered. "Captain, we think we've found the ship. It just materialized on the long-range scanners. We followed a tachyon trail leaving orbit. I think it had to disengage its camouflage in order to engage the tachyon drive. It's leaving this star system."

"Did it attempt to enter the atmosphere at all? Do we know if it sent any signals? Is the *Emissary's* ship okay?"

"Commander Asher just checked in with me. He and his ship are fine. He inquired about his Captain and Lt. Commander. I didn't have anything to report to him about Captain Weiseman. I informed him his wife wouldn't be coming back to him at this time. We prepped the *Evangeline* for launch if necessary. Prince Ca-Litana is in the guest quarters along with a couple bodyguards."

David glanced around the bridge to see who else was present. He had been so focused on his wife, he was barely aware of the others around him.

Thane and Marissa were sitting at their usual stations running the helm and navigation. Aulani was monitoring for any long-range communications signals. Lt. Commander Asher manned the weapons console. David's brow knit at her presence. He gave Brynna a questioning look.

"Lt. Commander Dominick is in engineering, and I wanted someone on weapons." Brynna answered his unasked question.

His brow remained knitted together. "Why didn't she go back to her ship?"

Brynna stopped herself from rolling her eyes. "Captain, her husband tried to have her executed. She wasn't inclined to want to return."

"You know, I think there are a lot of missing pieces in this puzzle. Right now, we need to figure out what to do about that ship out there. If we knew where it was headed, we might be able to cut it off as it leaves the system."

Claire took her eyes off the scanners a moment to offer a suggestion. "Captain Alexander, their shuttle is still sitting out there in the field. You might be able to download its flight plan from the shuttle. You might even be able to control it from there."

"Good idea, Lt. Commander Flint. Ensign Dominick, to the bridge. Ensign Ryder, you're with me." David started to leave the bridge again, but Brynna stepped in front of him. "Captain, I think your place is here. I'll go to the shuttle."

David hesitated. He had lost her and just gotten her back. He didn't want to take a chance on losing her again, but he knew she was right. "You're right. I have the conn. Be very careful though, there could be fail-safes in place."

"I will, Captain." She smiled lovingly at him for a second then moved toward the door.

"Brynna…"

Brynna stopped and turned around to see what he wanted.

David took two fast steps toward her, hugged her tightly then kissed her passionately.

Having nowhere to go yet, Thane's exhaustion and boredom got the best of him. He looked at the other women around him. "Thank goodness. If he hadn't done that, I might've done it for him."

David released his wife but kept his eyes locked on hers, burning her smile into his memory. "That action could result in some dire consequences for you, Mr. Ryder."

Thane grinned. "Yeah, but if you had delayed that any longer, it might've had dire consequences for you."

David pulled back as Cheyenne entered the bridge and took the communications station.

Brynna and Aulani headed out to the shuttle. They grabbed two Whippers to get them out there quickly. They noticed Braxton coming to the Surf-ve still sitting just outside the range of the shields.

Braxton hooked it up to a winch and pulled it aboard the ship into its berth. It was going to take a little time to fix it, but he wanted to get it aboard, so he and Lazaro could work on it when they had time. He secured it then casually started working on it. Lexi joined him a few minutes later. Her secondary skill set was engineering, but it had less to do with her being there and more to do with the fact that she nearly lost her husband.

David had Cheyenne hail the *Emissary* while he waited on Brynna's report. "Commander Asher, I wanted to bring you up-to-speed on our situation. I assume you're tracking the Nefil vessel?"

Commander Asher could just see Claire in the corner of the screen on David's bridge. It was clearly a distraction. "Yes... Captain, we see it. Are we going to attempt to pursue it? We're clearly a long way behind it, and I'm... missing several crew members."

David glanced at Claire who refused to focus on anything but her station screen. David narrowed the video input, so she was no longer visible to him. "Commander, can you have Chief Griffin forward the frequency he was using to jam the nanite signals to my comms officer? I might need it later."

David saw Silas nod to his security chief, and a moment later Cheyenne was nodding to acknowledge she had received it. "Silas, I've sent Commander Alexander and my comms officer to the Nefil shuttle to see if they can break into the computer systems. This could tell us where that ship is headed and possibly recall it. Stay ready to launch at a moment's notice. If it's alright with you, I'll take the lead on this."

Silas looked sullen. He had been so adamantly opposed to the *Evangeline's* presence earlier. He had trouble swallowing his pride despite the fact that his pride had slapped him in the face for the last few hours. "You... uh... you have my full support, sir. I apologize for my attitudes, earlier. I think I am a man without a home right now."

David nodded his understanding. "If we can do this just right, I might be able to get you back in good standing with the Commonwealth. There are no guarantees, but I'll do what I can."

Silas rubbed his tired face. "I think that's something the Captain needs to decide. Do you have any idea when he'll be back to normal?"

David shook his head. "I'm afraid I don't know that yet. I'll let you know something as soon as I have the information."

"Understood."

"Is there anything I need to know on your end?"

"No sir. Captain, would it be possible for me to speak to Lt. Commander Asher?"

David's eyes never moved off the screen to look at Claire who was vehemently shaking her head at him. "I'm afraid she's tied up keeping a close eye on the scanners right now. I would rather not have her distracted from her duties until my security chief is out of the Infirmary. I will make arrangements for her to speak with you as soon as I can. You have my word."

Silas looked dejected. "Yes Captain, I understand. Thank you. Sir, could you tell her I made a mistake, a bad one, and I'm sorry."

"Of course, Commander. I'll contact you as soon as I have more information. *Evangeline*, out."

The screen went dark and Claire whipped around to David. "I've got nothing to say to him."

David understood her pain. He wanted to direct her down a path that would lead to forgiveness and reconciliation. "I can understand that. He almost killed you. I just ask you to think about two things. First, he was trying to protect the crew from Pateras, not you. The second thing you need to realize is, he now knows Pateras isn't the enemy he thought he was. That means you aren't the enemy either."

"I wasn't a follower of Pateras when he tried to kill me." Claire retorted.

"Maybe not, but we were all misinformed about Pateras from the beginning. Supreme Executor Hale ordered us to kill each other if necessary. The Commonwealth is responsible for this, not Silas. Just keep those things in mind when you talk to him."

Claire glared at him. "Who says I'm going to talk to him?"

"I do." A familiar voice came from the front of the bridge. Arni had appeared from nowhere.

Claire recognized the voice as familiar but didn't know who the stranger was. His attire wasn't recognizable, and it certainly wasn't a Commonwealth uniform. "Do I know you? How did you get on the bridge?"

David moved closer to her station. "Lt. Commander Claire Asher, this is Arni Sotaeras Liontari, son of Pateras El Liontari."

Claire's anger dissipated. "You're the one who kept me company in the cavern. The one Brynna said would help me when Milo tried to kill us."

"Yes, I've been quite busy helping a lot of people on this... mission." Arni glanced at the others on the bridge. Each one was glad to see him, and they clearly displayed their gratitude on their faces.

Knowing how dire their circumstances had been, David knew they had certainly kept Arni's attention. He bowed his head in deference to the man's greatness. "Thank you for saving all of us. Forgive me for losing hope. I don't understand why your Father has so much patience with me."

Claire looked back and forth confused by several aspects of the conversation. Captain Alexander had seemed quite in control of his faculties, even when he kissed Brynna on the bridge. It seemed he knew exactly what he was doing. She hadn't seen him lose his temper or act inappropriately at all.

Arni put his hand on Claire's. "Claire, I need you to talk to Silas, but not tonight. Whether you go back to him as his wife is your choice. I would like you to hear him out. Every man and woman has chosen to do the wrong thing at some point, even you. If you choose to return to him, he'll mess up again, but never as bad as this. This is the worst you'll ever see. From this point on he'll protect you with his own life."

"I'll think about it." Claire groused.

Arni smiled. He knew she would return to him, eventually.

Cheyenne interrupted with an update and a request of her own. "Captain, I've been working on the shutdown codes for the nanites. If Captain Doherty used an override code, the shutdown may might not work. Can the Commander search the shuttle databanks for those codes?"

David moved back to his seat. "Check with her and see what she can find."

"Yes sir. Sir, it's also possible we could give them another program. One that would cause them to leave the brain and go someplace where they could be excreted or extricated."

"Do what you can to have it ready, Ensign. We'll make our decision on how to proceed once we have all the information."

David turned his attention back to the scanners. "Lt. Ryder, keep an eye on that shuttle out there. If you see anything suspicious going on with it, sing out."

Thane had a course laid in if he needed to launch. He switched his screen over to scanners and monitored the shuttle as instructed.

"Lt. Commander Asher, any changes at all in that ship?"

"No sir. The ship will clear the last planet in about twenty minutes." Claire reported.

David paced impatiently. If they couldn't stop that ship, it might report the crew of the *Emissary* and this planet as compromised. David looked over at Arni only to find the man gone again. He sighed audibly.

He decided to put one more contingency plan into effect. He sent Lexi and Braxton to their own shuttle and prepped it for launch.

Brynna and Aulani got to the shuttle and started working. They easily established an interface with the ship and downloaded the current flight plan and the flight history. They downloaded the communications logs next. Cheyenne contacted them requesting the nanite override codes. Aulani found the access codes and downloaded them onto a data crystal. Brynna and Aulani tried to override the navigation. They were locked out—nothing they did was successful.

Aulani took her hands off the console and folded her arms resolutely. "The only thing I can think of that we haven't tried is we could either send out a distress signal from this shuttle. It might override the navigation. Our only other option is to initiate the self-destruct sequence aboard the ship."

The computer began to run through a scan. Aulani looked down and saw the scan indicating remote access of system files. It also showed a scan of the *Talon's* crew's life signs. Seeing none, the computer displayed a new message. "Self-destruct sequence activated. Shuttle self-destruct sequence activated." The shuttle went dark except for the one computer display.

Aulani's eyes got wide. "Commander, we need to get out of here, right now!" Aulani tried to open her passenger door. The power to the shuttle had shut down to energize the self-destruct mechanism. The door refused to open. She turned to Brynna who discovered she was having the same problem. Aulani jumped into the rear compartment and ripped open the panel covering the manual override. She pumped the mechanism as fast as she could. The door seemed to take forever to open. A piece of her wanted to look at the countdown to see how much time was left. She forced herself to focus on the door.

Brynna was only a half-second behind her. She tapped her comm unit and alerted the Captain to their situation. David promptly ordered Lexi to launch the shuttle. Lexi tied in the shuttle's translator and broadcast a warning to

Prince Ca-Litana's guards resting by the fire to move under the ship. The guards weren't sure why they were moving, but they sensed the urgency and moved quickly.

Brynna grabbed onto the doors and helped force them open. As soon as they were open just enough to slide through, she grabbed Aulani and pulled her to the doors. The two women slid through and took off running. They jumped on their waiting Whippers and pushed the power output to raise the Whippers high enough to use the wing for propulsion. The shuttle opened the cargo loading doors on top and lowered its back end. The women gave one additional quick burst of power then shut the power completely off as they reached the openness of the cargo area under them. Both vehicles landed roughly throwing their passengers about in the back of the shuttle. Brynna shouted out, "We're in. Go!"

Braxton ordered Lexi to head to the other side of the ship. He told the Captain to activate the ship's shields, closed the cargo hatch on the shuttle, and activated their own shields just as they passed the top of the *Evangeline*.

The *Talon* shuttle exploded shaking the ground. The *Evangeline's* shuttle was still moving when the concussion hit them. Lexi had trouble controlling their trajectory. The shuttle hit the ground roughly. It bounced a couple times before it came to a stop.

A wall of smoke and flame blew toward the *Evangeline*. The men standing under the ship were unfamiliar with the shields. They wanted to run from the fiery wall of death approaching them but knew instinctively it was coming too fast. They stood their ground bravely, each believing they would be dead momentarily.

When the wall of smoke and flame dissipated, and the concussion stopped echoing through the hills, no one breathed or moved. The men under the ship gave a shout of joy when they realized the danger was past and they had survived.

The crew aboard the shuttle took a deep breath then assessed themselves. Aulani had hit something when she landed and was hurting. She started to move and her side rebelled. "Commander, I–I'm injured. I think I broke some ribs when I landed." She started trying to take deep breaths, which were getting harder with every breath.

"I'm… having… trouble… breathing." Her skin broke out in a cold sweat.

Brynna went to her side. She tapped her comm unit, "Captain, we need to get aboard the ship. We have a medical emergency. Could you clear a path for us?" Brynna grabbed a med kit while she waited on David to respond.

"Path is clear. *Evangeline* shuttle you are clear to dock."

Braxton jumped to help Brynna with Aulani. Lexi shut down the shields and powered up the shuttle. She lifted off as smoothly as she could and slid the shuttle neatly into the bay. Braxton didn't take the time to get her onto a stretcher. He simply picked her up and carried her. Brynna escorted them down to the Infirmary.

Stephanie was just finishing up her surgery on Jake. She handed off to Laura to finish up. Jason was lying in one bunk undergoing the bone mending process. Stephanie had closed the surrounding partitions to keep him from getting involved in the surrounding activity. He was not amused by being banished in his own infirmary. Noah was moving back and forth from Jason to the members of Prince Ca-Litana's guard who needed treatment for various cuts, scrapes, bumps, and bruises. He suspected they were hunting for injuries to be treated because they were so amazed by the ship's healing technologies.

Stephanie got Aulani on a table. Her scan, as expected, revealed broken ribs and a punctured lung. Stephanie worked quickly to relieve the pressure in her lungs making breathing easier.

Braxton returned to the shuttle to assess for damage, make sure it got settled in properly, and the bay doors closed. Brynna headed to the bridge to update the Captain and let Thane know what happened.

The nearby explosion temporarily disrupted the scanners Commander Asher was monitoring. He stabbed at the communication controls. "*Emissary* to *Evangeline*, come in. What's happening?"

David was busy handling the emergency on his end. He had raised the shields, kept an eye on his own shuttle, answered the shuttle's distress call, lowered the shields, opened the bay doors, notified the infirmary of the incoming medical emergency, and got reports from the various departments indicating no injuries or damage. Cheyenne answered Commander Asher long enough to put him on standby.

Captain Alexander sent Marissa down to check on Prince Ca-Litana's men. Seeing everything was now under control, he turned his attention back to Commander Asher.

"Commander Asher, sorry to keep you waiting."

"What happened, Captain? We show the ship in space exploded and then our scans were disrupted by a blast here on the ground. Is everyone okay?"

David glanced at Claire. He knew the hidden meaning behind his inquiry. Claire didn't seem as angry this time at the sight of her husband, but she still didn't seem interested in talking to him. "The blast injured one of my people. I don't have any details as yet, but all of your people are unhurt. I sent two of my people onto the Nefil shuttle. It appears they triggered the self-destruct mechanism. Commander Alexander should be joining me on the bridge momentarily."

Stepping onto the bridge, David's look of relief greeted Brynna. He stood abruptly and ordered, "Report, Commander."

Brynna held her hand out with three data crystals. "We got all the navigational flight plans on record. I have the override codes for the nanites and all communication logs. We didn't intend to activate the self-destruct. That was an accident. Ensign Ryder had a rough landing in the shuttle and broke some ribs and punctured her lung. She's currently being treated. She'll be fine. Was the ship destroyed along with the shuttle?"

David smiled. "Yes, at exactly the same time." David turned his attention back to Commander Asher.

"Commander, I will get these nanite override codes to Lt. Commander Weiseman. I'll let you know if it works. It may be morning before I have a report for you. I think we're safe for tonight. I suggest you and your people get some rest."

"Understood, Captain. I'm glad you and your people are okay. I will look forward to your report in the morning. *Emissary* out."

David closed the link and turned to the bridge crew. "Lt. Ryder, catch Lt. Holden and as long as the Prince's men are good, go check in on your spouses. Ensign Dominick, hail Dr. Weiseman to join me in my office as soon as she's free, and I need to see you in there as well. Commander Alexander, if you could join me. Lt. Commander Asher, if you wouldn't mind, can you hang out on the bridge a little while longer? I need you to watch the scanners and man comms. I'll get you some relief as soon as I can."

"Yes, Captain and thank you, sir."

"Thanks? For what?"

"For not ordering me to go back to the *Emissary*."

David moved around in front of her. He knelt and took her hands in his. "Claire, I'm not going to make you leave, but there are a couple of things you need to consider. I'm not sure Silas is the same person he was yesterday, just like you aren't. If you stay here with us, you're putting Nate at a disadvantage. You may not choose to go back to Silas, but they need you aboard the *Emissary*. I have the impression a lot of things have changed in the last day. Please keep an open mind. Arni forgave me for more things than you can imagine. He expects me to forgive others the same way. Can you keep an open mind?"

Claire looked hurt. "He tried to kill me. I'm his wife, and he tried to kill me."

David nodded. "I understand, really I do. He was following the mandate by Luciano Hale to kill Pateras, just like those Nefil soldiers. Silas chose to fight against the Nefil. He should've helped them, not opposed them. I owe him my life. He's clearly sorry and disturbed by the recent events. I'm just asking you to listen to him and give him some time to figure things out. I can talk to him first if you want."

Claire's face was troubled. "Ask me again tomorrow." She pulled her hands away from David and turned back to her station. David smiled. He patted her shoulder as he walked away from her.

Now alone on the bridge, tears formed in her eyes. She quickly wiped them away, so she could see her displays. Arni appeared and pulled up a chair so the two could talk.

THE ELEVENTH HOUR

ANSWERS

As soon as Dr. Stephanie Weiseman released Jason from her medical care, he took the lead in treating Captain Nate Weiseman by asking Cheyenne to use the override codes to rewrite the nanite program. The nanites stopped stimulating the centers of the brain causing Nate to react in a murderous rage at the sight of Captain Alexander. The new program sent the nanites into the cerebrospinal fluid. They gathered into the lowest portion of the spine where Jason extracted them. Once they were safely in a lab container, Cheyenne transmitted a shutdown order and monitored them to be certain they complied.

Nate woke up as though he had just experienced a frightening nightmare. When he found himself in restraints in the infirmary, he realized it was more than a nightmare. Nate felt sick to his stomach. "Davie? I'm so sorry. Chief Holden? Is he...?"

David smiled at his friend and pointed at the Chief who was standing guard by the door... with his weapon in his hand.

Nate gave him a weak smile. "Chief Holden, you have my most sincere apologies. I don't know what happened. I just wanted to kill David, and you got in my way."

David grinned. "You wanted to kill me, and he gets the apology? Thanks, pal."

Nate looked back at David. "I'm sorry, Davie, really I am."

Jason jumped in to rescue the man. "This wasn't your fault, Captain Weiseman. Captain Doherty reprogrammed your nanites. We overrode the programming and removed the nanites. We just needed to be sure your murderous rage wasn't going to continue. Captain Alexander, can I remove his restraints now?"

David nodded, then grinned impishly as he took two exaggerated steps backward.

Released from his restraints, Nate sat up slowly to respond to David's behavior. "Ha—Ha. Very funny. So, what's our status?"

David stepped forward again and gave him a serious answer. "It's very late, and we're all tired. All of your crew is healthy and accounted for. In addition to Stephanie and Noah, Claire is aboard the *Evangeline*. The Nefil ship and shuttle have been destroyed. Commander Asher will expect my report on your condition in the morning. I advised him and his crew to get some rest. Prince Ca-Litana has returned to the city to reassure his people that they're safe. The Nefil shuttle shook the entire region when it blew up. You and Steph are welcome to our guest quarters tonight. It would make us all feel better if you were monitored for a few hours."

Nate nodded. "Understood, Captain. Consider us under house arrest. What about the rest of my crew?"

"They are welcome to stay here in the Infirmary, or there is a sofa-bed in the guest quarters and our quarters. There's also one in Jason's quarters."

Nate scowled. "How did you rate sofa-beds?"

David smiled. "We stole... well scavenged them from another ship."

"I want some." Nate whined playfully.

Stephanie patted his hand. "Take it easy, dear. It's not like we have guests very often."

David nodded his understanding. "Listen, in the morning, we need to talk."

"I know we do. I think I'm ready to listen now, but what if that ship called for reinforcements?"

"It didn't. Arni says we have seven days before we have to leave. We've got work to do before we leave here, anyway."

Jake escorted and secured Nate and Stephanie in the guest quarters for the night.

Nate and Stephanie had a lot to discuss, although she didn't expect his first question.

"Steph, just where did they take those nanites out?"

Stephanie looked at him oddly. "What?"

"They took the nanites out of me, right?"

"Yes, Nate, they can't hurt you anymore. In the morning, Jason's going to take mine out too."

"Where did they take them out though?" Nate persisted with his question.

Stephanie sighed. She wasn't sure what was bothering him, so she answered his question as simply as possible. "They programmed them to gather in the spinal fluid at the lowest possible point. Jason then extracted the fluid from that juncture, filtered the nanites, and re-injected the fluid so you wouldn't get a headache from an imbalance in the cerebrospinal fluid."

"He took them from my spine?"

"Yes. Nate, what's bothering you?"

"What part of my spine?" Nate persisted.

"Your sacrum, Nate, the lowest part of the sacrum. It's not a good place to access spinal fluid, but we wanted to stay as far away from vital organs as possible. He went through the skin, here." Stephanie touched a place on Nate's lower back. "He sent a catheter down into the sacrum and drew out the nanites. Nate, why is this bothering you?"

"Because my butt hurts."

Stephanie laughed. "I'm sorry to laugh at you. When David and Lt. Ryder took you down out there, they apparently broke your tailbone. That's what hurts. We fixed it, but it's going to be sore for a couple days."

David and Brynna spent a couple hours lying in bed talking before they were able to settle down and go to sleep that night. Besides being grateful his wife was alive and well, he was eager to find out how she got back to the ship safely.

Brynna's eyes still reflected her own amazement at being alive. "I was sure Claire and I were dead. I was getting strange vibes from Milo. He sounded like he was trying to tell us something important but was afraid to say things outright. It scared Claire to death. He told us exactly how he was going to kill us. He talked like he was bragging about what he was about to do, but his tone wasn't boastful. It almost sounded like a doctor walking us through a procedure. It seemed odd at the time. Milo fired twice at the ground. I realized when he fired those two pellets, he was making sure if somebody was were monitoring him, it would look real."

Her tale fascinated David. "Sounds like he did a good job. I'm assuming you kept quiet when you figured out what was happening. What about Claire?"

"She took a deep breath like she was about to say something. Milo covered her mouth and motioned for her to be silent. He pushed us over onto the ground so it would give all the appearances that we had dropped where we were, then he took our binders off and carried us into the water to prevent there from being any footprints on the riverbank. He put us down in the water and quietly told us to go downstream, past the ship quite a way before getting out and returning to the *Evangeline*."

David had been lying on his side, so he could see Brynna's face. He rolled onto his back and pulled her closer to him. "How did Prince Ca-Litana get involved?"

Brynna cuddled up next to him and placed her head on his shoulder. "We thought he might be able to smuggle us back past the *Emissary*. He agreed to help us under one condition. Captain Weiseman had to answer some questions. Prince Ca-Litana gave us a place to rest and recuperate until dark. He wanted to wait until nightfall before trying to get us out. The palace was already locked down to prevent the royal family from escaping. I suppose that was a tactical error on my part." Brynna lay there silently for a moment then said, "Twice in one day, that's not a good precedent."

"Twice?" David asked sleepily. The Adrenalin fueling his energy was quickly breaking down and leaving his system.

"Arni warned me not to enter the *Emissary*. Silas goaded me until I gave in. I nearly paid for that mistake with my life."

"Why did the Prince insist on taking you to the one place you were trying to avoid?" David asked as he held his precious bride tightly.

"He wanted to know why Captain Weiseman wanted us dead. He wasn't going to let Nate know we were alive until he got some satisfactory answers. We caught Nate as he arrived back at the *Emissary* from his run-in with the Nefil. Prince Ca-Litana told the Captain our bodies had washed up on shore near town. Nate wasn't in the mood to answer the Prince's questions because he was trying to get back here and save your life. The Prince finally pushed Nate too far. Nate grabbed him and slammed him against his own carriage. He was pretty angry. He told the Prince he hadn't approved the orders, and if he could have prevented our deaths, he would have. I thought the Prince's guards were going to kill Nate on the spot. Prince Ca-Litana asked Nate one more question. He asked him what he would do if he had a second chance. He said he would give Pateras a chance to prove himself. Prince Ca-Litana showed him we were in the carriage. Claire told him point blank Arni had helped her, and she was not returning to the Commonwealth. Nate asked me if Arni would help Stephanie. Prince Ca-Litana, Nate, Claire, and I went in to ask Arni to help Stephanie. He healed Stephanie, and the rest you pretty much know. Nate reloaded his Surf-ve and took off to help you."

David was close to falling asleep. "How did you end up back here?" His words were bordering on slurring.

"Prince Ca-Litana sent half his troops with Nate, and the other half stayed with him. The Prince brought us, and Stephanie, back here." Brynna twisted to look at her husband. His breathing was slow and rhythmic. "Are you still awake?"

"Mm-hmm."

Brynna smiled. "I love you."

David took a deep breath inhaling the love he felt emanating from her. He pulled her even closer and kissed the top of her head. "I love you, too. I didn't know what I was going to do without you. I'm glad he didn't take you away from me."

"You know, that day will come for one of us, someday. Right?" Something in Brynna wanted to know he could survive without her.

"I know, but it wasn't today." David sensed she needed more. "At least, I know now, I can survive. I just won't like it. I also didn't shoot Commander Asher or Chief Griffin. That's good, right?"

Brynna raised her head and looked at him again. "I'm glad you didn't shoot Milo."

David's eyes popped open. "So, I should've shot Silas?"

Brynna scowled. "I'll let you know later. I still don't trust him."

David added one last thing before letting the conversation drop. "For the record, Arni wouldn't let me shoot him or even hit him. He asked me to forgive him."

Brynna didn't move and kept her eyes closed. "It figures." She droned sleepily.

The two drifted off to sleep until the alarm woke them for their turns on watch.

The crew of the *Evangeline* took short watches to get them through the night. The day started much later than normal.

Prince Ca-Litana sent fresh guards in the early hours of the morning to gather up the bodies of the twelve dead giants. They removed their armor, utility belts, weapons, and anything that looked useful and tossed their bodies into the river. The men left the gear in organized piles around the fire and waited for the crew to show themselves before approaching the ship. Prince Ca-Litana had cautioned them about disturbing the tired crew. Once the crew came out to greet them, they extended an invitation to a banquet the next afternoon to celebrate Prince Ca-Litana's ascension to the role of King. Having Arni's reassurance they were safe, David accepted the invitation.

The crew took the gear salvaged from the Nefil. They split it between the two ships and put the items in the ship's stores after carefully scrutinizing them.

Nate was quiet when he got up late the next morning. Jake released him from the guest quarters and escorted him to the bridge where David was on comms with Commander Asher. Glancing up he waved Nate forward and dismissed a reluctant security chief. The three discussed their plans for the day including the banquet for King Ca-Litana.

Commander Asher was still eager to talk to his wife. David assured the man his wife would come around eventually, but she wasn't ready just yet.

They closed out their communication, and David escorted Nate to the Dining Hall. Nate was surprised by the extra kitchen equipment. "Did you scavenge this too?"

David smiled. "Yes, and a few more things. We have some hydroponics equipment in our rec room."

"Really?"

"So, where's Steph this morning?" David asked.

"She's getting her nanites removed. Where's Claire and Noah?"

David shrugged. "I'm not sure. They both had a grueling day yesterday. They might still be in bed. Claire stayed in our spare bed last night, but I was up early this morning."

Brynna came in, grabbed some breakfast, and sat down with Nate and David. She smiled warmly at David. She too, had feared she would never see him again. Noah and Claire came in a moment later. They politely asked if they could join the three commanders. David greeted them warmly.

Noah and Claire were quiet for a few minutes. They seemed to have something on their mind. Nate finally asked them what was keeping them so quiet. Claire, being the senior officer volunteered. "Captain, we didn't ask for your permission about something. I don't think you'll disapprove, but after we did it, we realized it was definitely a breach in protocol."

"What is it?" Nate responded calmly.

Noah wasn't about to let Claire take all the heat if things went badly. "We had Dr. Adams yank our nanites. After what happened to you, we didn't want any part of that."

Nate had the distinct urge to clown around with them and feign a fit of anger. Considering what the nanites had done to him the night before, he decided it might not go over well. Nate grinned at them, "I'll forgive you... this time. I want them out of the rest of the crew too."

After breakfast, Noah excused himself to see if Dr. Adams needed any help straightening up the infirmary after its busy night.

Nate pulled Claire aside.

"Claire, I know you've sought asylum aboard the *Evangeline*. I would like you to consider returning to the *Emissary*. I don't know what our plan is yet. We'll have to discuss all our options. I need you. You can stay in the guest quarters if you need to, but please think about it. We can sit down with Captain and Commander Alexander and Silas to come to some sort of understanding. Would you be willing to do that?"

Claire hesitated.

"For me, please?" Nate persisted.

"Yes sir. I'll discuss it either here or on neutral ground. I won't go back to the ship to talk."

"Done. I'll make the arrangements."

Captain Weiseman's Surf-ve arrived to pick him and his crew up within the next hour. Commander Asher accompanied Chief Griffin to retrieve the crew. The Commander was desperately hoping to talk to his wife or at least catch a glimpse of her.

Claire kept herself discreetly out of sight. She watched him on the external audio-visual feed as he left the Surf-ve. He started up the steps to the primary airlock. He offered Captain Alexander a salute and a perfunctory, "Permission to come aboard?" as though the Captain would never deny his request.

David stepped clearly into his path before offering the counter salute and response, "Permission denied, Commander. She's not ready yet."

Commander Asher eased back down the steps onto the ground. His face clearly reflecting his disappointment. "Could you let the Captain and crew know I'm here and... and tell Claire I asked about her."

David came down the steps and stood beside Silas. "Your crew already knows you're here. They're on their way out. I apologize for being impolite, but neither Claire nor Brynna want to see you. I'm not overly happy with you myself."

"Captain, I'm sorry. Incredibly sorry. I'm sorry for all the attitude I gave you, sorry for attempting to execute your wife, and I'm really sorry for trying to execute Claire. If I could take it all back, I would in a heartbeat." Silas paced aimlessly kicking loose rocks. "I knew when I did it I probably wouldn't be able to live with myself. I can't live with myself now."

Nate was the first one down the steps. Silas stopped his pacing and gave his Captain a salute. He knew Nate wasn't happy with him either. Nate countered the salute. "Silas, she's agreed to talk to you... later. She'll talk either here or on neutral ground with Captain and Commander Alexander present. She's refusing to return to the *Emissary*... for now."

Silas angrily kicked another rock. "I swear I'm not going to hurt her, never again. I don't care where her loyalties lie. I'm not feeling particularly loyal to the Commonwealth myself."

Stephanie came down the steps followed by Noah. Nate gestured toward the Surf-ve. "Let's get loaded. We've got work to do."

Silas led the way and opened the door to the passenger compartment for the Captain and crew. He secured the door after they were inside. He slowly opened the door to the passenger side of the vehicle while watching the ship's airlock for any sign of his estranged wife. Claire zoomed in on his face. Was she reading regret or frustration? She wondered if she should consider forgiving him.

Claire took her troubled thoughts to the gym to get a workout. After a well-rounded workout, she decided to go a few rounds with the punching bag. The longer she punched, the angrier she seemed to get. The bag swung back and forth taunting her punches. She punched harder and faster until her strength was finally exhausted. She collapsed into a heap on the floor, sobbing uncontrollably.

Jake walked in to get his own workout. Seeing her crying on the floor he started to get Lexi, but something stopped him. He turned, picked up a clean towel and a cup of water, then he sat down on the bench near her and waited for her to catch her breath. When she finally sat up, he offered her the towel and cup of water.

Claire looked up at him. She was embarrassed by being caught blubbering on the floor. Seeing no condemnation on his face, she graciously accepted his offerings. "I'm sorry you had to see me like this."

"It's okay. I'm used to it."

Claire wiped her face and neck down with the towel. "Used to it? How's that?"

Jake stared at the ground in front of his feet. "I... uh... I did what any good Commonwealth soldier would do. I reported the crew to the Commonwealth and got them arrested... including my pregnant wife. I betrayed the crew, the Captain, and my wife. They went through grueling tortures because of me."

"But, Chief, I thought you were loyal to Pateras too. You risked your life to save them. I don't understand."

"I am loyal to Pateras, now. A few weeks ago, I wasn't. I tried to protect the Captain and crew from him. I failed. I did the only thing I knew to do. I turned them in and tried to get them re-educated. It was the biggest mistake of my life. When Marissa found out, she was bordering on hating me for a long time. I really don't know why she forgave me. I certainly didn't deserve a second chance although I am grateful she gave me one."

Claire scooted back against the wall and listened to him. She finally muttered, "At least you didn't order your own wife to be executed."

Jake slapped his hand with his own towel rhythmically. "I'm just as guilty as if I had. Executor Hale ordered her execution despite our agreement."

Claire was torn between asking how they escaped, why he did it, and why Marissa forgave him.

Sensing her divisive mindset, Jake spelled out the experience for her. "I can tell you for a FACT, Supreme Executor Hale is a superior alien being created by Pateras. He is a master of deception. He had us believing Pateras was the deceiver and an enemy of the Commonwealth. Even before anyone turned, he had the entire crew afraid of me. The crew nearly spaced me. The only reasons they didn't was I helped them escape, the Captain took up for me, and they didn't want to upset Marissa or hurt the baby."

Claire scowled at him. "Did Captain Alexander send you in here to talk to me?"

Jake shook his head. "No, I just came in to work out the stiffness in my side. This punching bag and I have spent a lot of time together over the last few weeks. It's taken a lot of time, effort, and patience to start earning the crew's trust. I think last night broke the final barriers to our trust issues. For the good of the Commonwealth, I did some terrible things. I don't deserve to be forgiven, but I'm grateful it's happening. I really thought I was doing what was best."

Jake was silent for a moment then added one more thing. "Claire, I had a gun to my Captain's back ready to shoot him for his treason. I couldn't kill him. His actions…

his actions weren't those of a traitor. His actions were those of someone who cared about people. He saved the life of the crew, and he saved my son."

Claire gave him a vexed look. "Why did Marissa take you back? Was it because of the baby?"

"No, definitely not. We were trying to get past it. It wasn't going well, then it went from bad to worse. Luciano Hale showed up in my quarters."

Claire sat up quickly. "Wait! Captain Alexander let him on board? His own security officers let him come?"

Jake grinned. Claire wasn't used to thinking in such expanded terms. "No, Claire, he isn't human. Like Arni, he just showed up. He showed up in my quarters and tried to recruit me back. He tried bribery, and then he tried to threaten me. He took on my form and attacked Marissa. I didn't know what to do. I told the Captain and Lexi what happened. Lexi didn't want to believe me. Captain Alexander did though. I asked the Captain to put me in a stasis chamber until he thought it was safe for Marissa and the baby. The Captain's a really smart man. He made me tell Marissa I was going into the stasis chamber. She realized I wasn't the one who hurt her, and it saved the baby's life again. I think that's what made the difference. Marissa realized I was a different man than the one she married."

"But you didn't put a gun to your wife's head, and you didn't proposition another woman, did you?" Claire retorted.

"No, I never did that. Commander Asher propositioned somebody?" That information surprised Jake.

"Oh yes, he did. Commander Alexander and I had a LOT of time to talk after we got out of the river and walked to Prince Ca-Litana's palace."

Jake still looked lost and surprised. "So, who did he… oh… he propositioned Commander Alexander?"

Claire nodded as her blood ran cold.

"He likes living dangerously."

"Living dangerously? Would Captain Alexander react badly?"

"No, I was talking about her, not him. I've seen Commander Alexander react to unwanted advances. It's not pretty."

Claire smiled at the thought of Brynna decking her husband. Her face sobered again. "Why do you care about what happens between Silas and me?"

"Everybody makes mistakes.... some of us more than others. The Captain, as far as I can tell, has never made a mistake. When I betrayed him, he knew it, even before it happened. Arni told him I was worth the pain and suffering he was about to go through. He went through six days of torture, just to win me over." Jake got up and paced around. The memories were not pleasant. "He could have walked away and left me behind. He didn't. I swear, I don't understand why he did that for the likes of me. Silas is a good soldier. If he believed you were the enemy, like it or not, he had a job to do. He had to protect the rest of the crew. When I did it, I ended up riding high. I was the hero who saved the day. I got a promotion to officer ranks, I was eating in the officer's club, and rubbing elbows with Supreme Executor Hale, Admiral Deacons, and Admiral Garcia. It all came crashing down."

Jake suddenly changed the subject. "What was the last thing Silas said to you? Do you remember?"

Claire stared at the floor as her mind replayed the memory. "He said he loved me, and he really wanted me to believe him."

"Do you remember the look in his eyes? What did you see?" Jake pushed.

"P-pain."

"Claire, he believed the lies we've all been told, and he thought the crew was in danger. He thought he had already lost you. He did his job. He wasn't propositioning another woman, he was testing Commander Alexander to see how far she would go to protect herself and this crew. He's still in love with you."

Claire glared at Jake. "You don't know that. You haven't talked to him!"

Jake squatted in front of Claire. "Neither have you. When he speaks, make sure you listen to what he's saying, and what he isn't."

Claire looked up at Jake. "You sound more like a ship's psychologist than a security chief."

"Our careers do have some areas in common." Jake stood and offered Claire a hand up.

Claire took his hand and got to her feet. "I'm going to hit the showers. Thanks for your advice, Chief. I'll... try... to follow it." She gave him a weak smile then left the gym.

Captain Alexander kept one person on duty at all times just to monitor the long-range scanners. He gave most of the crew time off. He very much wanted to spend the time alone with his own wife, but compromised slightly by working with Brynna. The two reviewed the data downloaded from the Nefil shuttle.

"Brynna, I think this is their home world. The only things logged are starting on Ahnak III, a stop at the Commonwealth Capitol World and then straight here."

"I think I know why they stopped at the Commonwealth Capitol. There's a press release in the comm logs. David, this isn't good."

David scooted closer to her to see her screen. Brynna played a broadcast that had gone out three weeks earlier.

"Citizens of the Commonwealth, I come to you today regarding a very serious matter. The Commonwealth has been at peace for over three hundred years. We've had our share of small skirmishes, and police actions as a new world transitions to a space-faring society. It is the natural process of growth and societal maturation that cannot be avoided.

"The situation I present today has brought our days of peace to an end. When the intelligence reports came to me, I thought the threat was coming from outside this galaxy. New reports indicate this is not the case.

"The Commonwealth government is under attack by a group of subversives from among our own people. This group is led by Pateras El Liontari and his son Arni Sotaeras Liontari. We believed they were invading through the undeveloped worlds. New reports indicate their forces have used those worlds as staging areas to prepare to attack the Commonwealth."

Supreme Executor Hale paused and took a long slow drink of water. David froze for a moment as he recognized the woman who handed it to him. It was Heather Shields; the woman Executor Hale had used to try to manipulate him on Romajin. David had supposed she died with everyone else on the base on Romajin. Executor Hale was keeping her close to him. Why? Did this have something to do with why the Nefil Team wanted to take him and Brynna back alive?

David suddenly realized the images on the screen were frozen. He blinked then gave Brynna a puzzled look.

"You're staring at her."

"No, I'm not... Yes, I am, but not for the reasons you're thinking. I want to know why he's keeping her close to him and why he wanted to take us both back alive."

Brynna didn't seem overly convinced of his motives. He claimed to have very little memory of Heather and no feelings for her, yet he had spotted the woman instantly on the feed. Was he fooling himself? What if there was something there? Supreme Executor Hale had subjected all of them to mental reprogramming protocols. Had he programmed something unexpected into her husband? It had only been six days. How likely was it for the programming to remain?

"Now you're staring at her." David quipped.

"You brought up some very thought-provoking points." She admitted. Brynna pressed the button to continue watching the broadcast.

"A few weeks ago I was on Romajin interrogating agents of the Liontari movement. You heard about the destruction of the base on Romajin and the ten thousand men and women who lost their lives that day. The one thing I didn't tell you was this was an elaborate plot intended to destroy me, and my administration. I was on that very base along with Defense Minister Hamilton Payne and Admirals Garcia and Deacons. If this group of dissidents had succeeded, they would have seriously crippled the Commonwealth's defenses.

"I sent out twelve teams to gather intelligence and establish alliances with the governments on the technologically undeveloped worlds. I–I underestimated the strength and power of the enemy."

Executor Hale was playing his audience, appearing heartbroken as he took another sip of his water, cleared his throat, and spoke again.

"I underestimated them. The twelve teams I sent out have either been corrupted or destroyed. I will not make the same mistake twice.

"Hear me, Pateras El Liontari. The Commonwealth is declaring war on you. You've sought to take the power of the people away from them and force them to choose you or die. I will not let that happen. This galaxy belongs to the Commonwealth and its people. We aren't afraid of you.

"The twelve teams I sent out were young and inexperienced. They were vulnerable. I have twelve new teams who cannot be corrupted. They will not be intimidated. They are genetically engineered. Captain Doherty, please join me."

Captain Doherty and two of his crew stepped out onto the stage near Supreme Executor Hale. Gasps could be heard in the background as the audience was shocked at the incredible size of the men.

"Captain Doherty and his team are known as the Nefil Forces. They are engineered to utilize the best of humanity. They are stronger, faster, more intelligent, fearless, and they are programmed to despise the Liontari and their followers. They will hunt down and eradicate all signs of Pateras El Liontari.

"If any of you believe you have encountered any of the Liontari traitors, please contact your local authorities immediately. Let me be clear about this. These are actual Commonwealth Citizens who have chosen to reject our advanced and civilized ways and take us back to the Dark Times when dictators and power-hungry individuals sought to push their own ways onto the people. They are seeking to destroy all the freedoms the Commonwealth offers. I have sent out bulletins on the original twelve ships and their crews to be on the lookout for. If you spot these ships, notify the authorities immediately.

"We are taking drastic actions against these traitors. If you, as private citizens, are confronted by them and forced to take extreme measures you will not face any legal penalties for these actions. Please use caution though. If they are not truly part of the Liontari movement, you could face legal repercussions.

"If you encounter the Nefil Forces, stay out of their way and give them your full cooperation. These individuals could be anywhere. Your friends, relatives, your former spouses, anyone, could be a Liontari spy. Let's join and show Pateras we are a united Commonwealth force and not to be taken lightly. Long live the Commonwealth!"

A rousing rally cry returned from the audience and the image faded.

In a moment, David sat back in his chair. "You're right. Now he really will have the entire galaxy looking for us. We won't be safe anywhere." His stomach churned nervously.

"You think you won't be safe?" A familiar voice joined the conversation.

"Arni!" Brynna cried out excitedly. She stood abruptly and hugged him. He warmly returned the hug. In a moment, she pulled back. "I'm so sorry I ignored your instructions. Please forgive me."

"It's forgiven. I know it will take time for you to trust me completely. This pertains to all of you. Never forget I know what's ahead of you, as well as what's behind you. David, you and your crew will be safe as long as you trust me. You will die someday. That much has not changed. It is the course of life. I escorted you, unseen, out of the prison on Romajin. Why do you continue to doubt me?"

David stood up. "I'm sorry. I trust you, really, I do. I just keep seeing impossible odds. I stand here and look at you. I know you have great power at your disposal, but... you look like any other normal man. I have to keep reminding myself of who and what you really are."

"Perhaps, before you ask me for direction, you should stop and consider who I am. Then you won't be concerned when I don't answer you at the time you think I should."

A twinge of guilt poked David's conscience. He knew when Stephanie and Jake's lives were on the line he had bordered on losing patience waiting for Arni. "I'm sorry. I'm trained to take control and make decisions. Of the entire crew, I'm probably going to be the hardest one to train."

Brynna snickered.

David gave her a cross look. "What's so funny?"

Brynna grinned. "I just never thought about you and Jake being in the same boat."

David sighed. "Well, if that isn't motivation for me to shape up, I don't know what is."

Arni enjoyed laughing with them.

Later that evening, as promised, Captain Weiseman brought his entire crew back to the *Evangeline* to listen to David's entire story.

Both crews sat casually around the rekindled campfire. The *Emissary's* crew now believed David's message to be worth listening to. The two crews shared their evening meal together and chatted casually until David introduced the intended topic of discussion. He stood to get everyone's attention.

"Nate, thanks for agreeing to listen to me. My crew and I didn't come here to recruit you and your crew. We came here to warn you what the Commonwealth had planned for the twelve explorer ships on this mission. Our evidence was somewhat circumstantial until the Nefil Force attacked us. We now have concrete proof downloaded from the Nefil's computer memory banks."

David played the video on a portable data module. A heavy silence surrounded the two crews as they realized the gravity of their situation. Before they could discuss it any further, David played a second recording for them. When he had surrendered to the Nefil, he had set his bracelet to record and transmit everything to the *Evangeline* and the rest of his crew. David had edited out long periods of silence and the crew's private discussions before their impending executions. He focused on the information gleaned from the overconfident bragging of the Nefil.

The crew of the *Emissary* was convinced of the danger before either of the recordings was played. Captain Alexander gave Captain Weiseman copies of the data for his own benefit. He knew the further they got from the situation, the more they would second-guess themselves. Having a copy of the data at their fingertips would reinforce the gravity of the situation.

David quietly turned off the data module when the second recording finished. The heavy silence continued to permeate the mood.

Dr. Oliver finally broke the silence. "Captain Alexander, this is a difficult question to ask, but how is it you came to change sides? I know you said you didn't come here to recruit us. Why not recruit us?"

David looked skeptically across the fire at Dr. Oliver, the suspected spy. Why would he of all people ask such a question?

Arni walked out of the darkness and sat down on one of the logs scattered around the fire. "Go ahead, tell them how we met."

Henry followed David's gaze. He stared at the man who spoke for a moment then turned his attention back to David.

David saw his actions get Henry's attention. He finally mustered an answer. "I would like nothing more than to have allies. I have been friends with Nate and Steph for many years. My first thought was to warn them about the danger they and their crew were in."

"Were? I think the correct verb is 'are,' not were." Silas sourly interjected.

Silas received several soft murmurs of agreement.

David didn't disagree with them. "My intention was first to save your lives. I guess you saved ours instead. If you were interested in why we changed sides, I had no reservations about giving you that information. I can give you the arguments or tell you what happened to us. It's up to you."

Gennie snuggled closer to Milo. "Stories are more fun."

Nate gave Stephanie a loving glance. He was still amazed she was alive and completely well. He wanted to hear every detail that brought them to this point. "I want to hear your story too."

David repositioned himself to address the group. He told them about their first mission to Galat and the peaceful residents. He described their encounter with Arni on Galat and the discovery that he wasn't human. He told the *Emissary's* crew how Arni warned him not to report his presence on Galat.

David sadly admitted to filing the report despite the warnings. He briefly described their adventures on Medoris and Arni's attempts to befriend them. "He saved my life and the life of Lt. Holden... sort of."

Stephanie gave David a puzzled look. "How do you sort of save someone's life?"

Marissa shifted uncomfortably in her seat, partly because of the topic and partly because of the pregnancy. Jake pulled her closer to him and rested his hand on her expanding belly.

David cast a quick glance at Arni who seemed nonplussed by his discomfort. Arni gave David an affirming nod.

"He didn't save her life. She died. There was no question she was completely dead."

The *Emissary's* crew glanced nervously at Marissa, who grabbed Jake's hand and squeezed it tightly.

Jason piped up before anyone could ask. "She was definitely dead, no question. Every bone in her body was broken." He shook his head as he replayed the memory in his mind.

"Arni restored her to life the next evening." David continued. "He healed her, and he healed me twice."

Jake looked lovingly at his wife. "And that's why she's pregnant!" His happy utterance only caused confusion.

David scowled. "I think I better clarify that. Arni healed Marissa of ALL injuries and imperfections. She and Jake didn't know that, and a month later... SURPRISE!"

Several amused giggles could be heard around the campfire. Jake looked blank. He wondered why everyone was laughing. Marissa turned her head toward him and whispered the explanation to him. His next look was one of indignation. "No... No... this is my boy! Mine!"

The laughter grew even stronger. The mood was getting lighter. Nate encouraged David to continue his tale.

David moved on to their mission to Drea. He guarded his words carefully. "We approached an advanced world known as Drea. The Commonwealth had been there fifty years earlier." As David told the tale of their desire for proof of the Commonwealth's good intentions and the success of their previous missions, Luna and Henry Oliver seemed to pay even closer attention.

"When we arrived back on Galat III, we discovered every human life on the planet was dead, including Arni's mother. Brynna's team went to Medoris. Everything was great there. That was the start of my change in loyalty. The Dreans tried and convicted us of mass murder. I arranged a plea agreement to take the penalty and let the crew go free. I was sentenced to be executed. I was standing there, about to die when Arni took my place. My face was covered, and he just did whatever it is he does. I disappeared, and he appeared in my place. No one knew until after he died that I wasn't there."

Claire sat bolt upright. "So, we've been talking to a ghost?"

David shook his head. "No, he's just as alive now as Marissa is and I am."

Nate looked confused. "You said you didn't die."

David sighed. It was confusing to him, and he lived it. He knew it must be really confusing to the other crew. "I didn't die on Drea."

Brynna scoffed. "It wasn't for lack of trying. There were three attempts on your life while we were there."

Silas scowled. "Okay, so get to the part where you died."

The others were now thoroughly involved in the mysterious tale. David took up the story again. "Arni died in my place. The Dreans didn't know what to make of the situation until the third morning when Pateras restored Arni to life. The Dreans decided to just send us away and forbid us from returning. Arni sent me to visit his father."

The crew was all on the edge of their seats. "You met Pateras El Liontari?" Nate asked incredulously.

"Sort of."

Stephanie scowled, "Sort of again? Did you, or didn't you?"

"I talked with him, but I couldn't see him. He was guarded by these big guys with swords. He was also hidden by a wall of smoke. He told me to go to Mara..."

"Mara? You've been to Mara?" Luna asked.

David hesitated and glanced at Arni. Arni smiled and nodded again. "You're safe to tell them everything, even the name of the Intercessor if you wish."

David nodded. "I would ask you if you're sure, but I know you are."

Silas glanced at the spot where David was looking. "Who's that and how long has he been sitting there?"

Henry stood up and faced Arni. "You're the promised one, the son of Pateras aren't you? I saw Captain Alexander looking to you for support."

David looked around confused. "Wait, you knew he was sitting there? Can everyone see you now?" David kept looking from face to face trying to make connections.

"I have been here the whole time, but not even David saw me until he began his story." Arni explained. He specifically left out part of his explanation.

Henry seemed to stand there in awe of Arni. "I didn't know you had been born. Why didn't Pateras ever tell us?"

Nate scowled at his "Commonwealth Spies." Why did they seem so comfortable and knowledgeable? "Dr. Oliver, would you care to enlighten us?"

Luna looked frightened. "Henry?"

Henry sat back down. He had difficulty taking his eyes off Arni. "Let the Captain finish his story first. I'm eager to hear it."

Arni gave a reassuring smile to Henry and Luna then turned back to David. "It's time to tell them everything."

David paused a moment to gather his thoughts. "Pateras told me to go to Mara and I would learn something important. He wouldn't tell me what I was even looking for. I wasn't sure how we were going to explain a trip to Mara. Pateras arranged for us to get an assignment to pick up three prisoners from Mara and return them to Drea."

Luna grabbed Henry's hand and held on tightly. David had difficulty seeing her eyes, but it appeared she was holding back tears.

"We picked up the last three prisoners still being held by the Commonwealth and returned them to Drea as ordered. What I learned from those three prisoners and our trip to Mara was that over five hundred people had been removed from Drea fifty years earlier. Some were

forced to work for the Commonwealth, most died. My…
uh… my grandparents were two of the prisoners who were
forced to work for the Commonwealth."

Nate leaned forward. He knew David's uncle was
Admiral Robert Deacons. He also knew Admiral Deacons
was significantly older than fifty. David gave Nate a subtle
shake of his head. He wasn't ready for that information
to come out.

Deka idly tossed a stick into the fire. "Is that when
you turned?"

Elize had been scooting closer as the tale became
more inviting. She finally realized it was too hot to be this
close to the campfire. She scooted back then asked, "When
did you die?"

"I chose to serve Pateras just before we reached Drea
the second time. I spent many hours studying the Ancient
Texts. I reached a point of exhaustion and frustration.
I–uh–I acted rashly in various circumstances."

Jake scowled, "He means he shot his own security
chief! I think I still owe you for that one."

David returned his scowl with one of his own. "You
had your shot at me. You also deserved it for disobeying
my orders."

Thane grinned, "At least he didn't shoot you when
the ants had you."

Marissa shivered at the thought. She hated insects. It
was the worst part of this mission. Knowing how she felt
about them, Jake picked up a pebble and lobbed it at Thane
for bringing it up.

Thane jerked and yelped when it hit him.

Gennie was getting frustrated. "Let Captain Alexander
finish."

David sat down on one of the logs. "Several of my
crew were changing loyalties by this time. I really couldn't
say who changed when because I thought it was best if I
didn't know. Some were just sympathetic and upset over
the destruction on Galat III. I volunteered to stay behind
on Drea. Lt. Flint was with me. She chose to be sympathetic
and allowed me to return to the ship. Jake found out later
and nearly shot me, only his weapon was more permanent."

Milo glanced at Jake then back at the Captain. Knowing he had freed the two women the previous day he had questions of his own. "Why didn't you shoot him, Chief?"

Jake shifted uncomfortably. He had nearly killed his own Captain. It was his duty and responsibility. At the time, he was embarrassed at his failure. Now he was embarrassed by the attempt. "The Captain saved all our lives on Drea and mine specifically in an altercation in the prison. He also saved the life of my son. I didn't even know Marissa was pregnant until a couple minutes earlier. I owed him... a lot. I think... oh wow." Jake looked at Arni. "That is some serious strategy."

Arni smiled again. "Don't worry when you have difficult circumstances in the future. My father knows what lies ahead, and he does it all for your good."

Gennie was getting cross. "So, if you didn't die then, when did you die?"

Noah and Maya were tiring of sitting in the same positions. Noah shifted, and Maya settled back in to lean on him. The thought of a baby appealed to her. She lovingly patted her husband's hand as David moved ahead in his tale.

"When Jake graciously allowed me to live, I called a meeting of the entire crew and confessed my change of heart. I didn't tell the crew about my heritage and connection to Drea. I called for a vote. I asked the crew to indulge me and allow me to continue to Captain the ship despite my change in loyalty. Short version is they agreed, and we moved on to Tudoren. Arni protected me when I should've died in a fire on Tudoren."

Noah cocked his head. Captain Alexander's comment was confusing. "You died, or you didn't die in a fire."

"I died on Tudoren, but it was unrelated to the fire. Admiral Deacons arrived to bring us the nanites and anti-grav units. He suspected I had turned. He tricked my security chief into revealing my treason. We went for a walk. He pulled his weapon on me to either shoot me or convince me to change my allegiance back to the Commonwealth."

Nate shook his head visibly. Stephanie knew David's kinship to the Admiral as well. She gave her husband a sideways glance. Nate couldn't keep silent any longer. "I'm not buying it, Davie. What aren't you telling us?"

"I'm not finished. Admiral Deacons couldn't bring himself to kill me, for obvious reasons. He was pretty upset with me, and with himself."

Dr. Oliver looked lost. "I'm not following. Admiral Deacons is very much a by-the-book person. There's no way he wouldn't have executed you."

David took a deep breath. "Admiral Deacons... is my uncle. He tried, but he knew he couldn't face my mother if he executed me. He was going to have to arrest me and take me in. He had me on my knees with his weapon pointed at my back, but he couldn't take the shot. When I stood up, I saw a local with a bow and arrow ready to shoot my uncle. I tried to stop him from firing. I took the arrow in the chest to protect my uncle. Arni knew what choices Admiral Deacons would face. He allowed me to die so my uncle could leave the planet and report my death in good conscience. That's when I died. Arni brought me back shortly thereafter."

David left out the part about his uncle's changing loyalties. His uncle was now the only one of David's family members the Commonwealth could harm. David's father was still out there somewhere, but no one had been able to locate him.

Nate, still the serious-minded Captain, pulled at the loose threads of David's story. "What happened on Romajin?"

Jake looked guilty. "Can we go with the short version? The Captain and crew were captured and tortured for six days, and then Arni intervened and got everybody out safely. Supreme Executor Hale destroyed the base as we left the star system, so we'd get the blame. The end?"

"Jake!" Several voices objected at once. The *Emissary's* crew looked confused.

David stood up again and paced. "Roughly speaking, that is the gist of it. The crew was betrayed and captured. Arni told me we would be freed in six days. The crew was being tortured and subjected to stringent re-education. I was not subjected to the re-education but was tortured repeatedly. They brought my family in to convince me to recant."

David stopped pacing and looked at Arni who nodded again. He glanced around the circle of people. "Do you believe Arni isn't human?"

Each one looked at Arni. Some gave reluctant nods and others gave blank stares. David knew his words were going to sound insane. "Arni isn't human, at least not exclusively. He's more than just a human."

Silas prodded when David paused again. "What's your point?"

"You heard Captain Doherty's statement about his— uh-parentage. Luciano Hale isn't human. Executor Hale and his confederates attacked me mentally as well as physically. They tried to get me to commit suicide. They almost succeeded. Jake knew all the right buttons to push to keep me alive and fighting."

Being a consummate psychological professional, Henry asked, "Who betrayed you? Was it your uncle?"

David really didn't want to make things uncomfortable for Jake. He hesitated again. "My uncle… was definitely… involved."

Claire remembered her earlier discussion with Jake. Without realizing what the Captain was trying not to say, she blurted out, "It was you, wasn't it, Chief Holden?" She had thought the Chief had merely been blaming himself or speaking metaphorically in the gym.

Thane tried to come to Jake's rescue. "The Captain's right. It doesn't matter who did it. What's done is done. Arni asked us to forgive, and that's what we're doing."

Jake gave Thane a grateful smile. "I did it. Everything that happened on Romajin is my fault except the destruction of the military base. I did NOT do that. I changed alliances on Romajin and helped the crew escape. I'm not proud of what I did. I've been working hard to regain the crew's trust."

Thane and Lazaro had been the hardest ones to reach. The two were reaching a point of forgiveness.

David picked the tale up one last time. "Executor Hale swore to me he would destroy anyone I said anything to, rather than see them question him and the Commonwealth. If you have doubts, consider this, the Supreme Executor of the entire Commonwealth took time out of his busy schedule to interrogate and torture eleven soldiers, the highest ranking being a Captain. Do you think for one minute, if this was were that important, he would hesitate to destroy one military base?"

Everyone seemed satisfied by with David's explanation on all levels. Nate turned back to the one loose end. "Dr. Oliver, I believe you have something to add."

Luna grabbed her husband's hand. "Henry, don't."

Henry patted her hand. With his eyes fixed on Arni, he requested a boon. "Captain Alexander, if the situation arises, Luna and I would like to request asylum aboard the *Evangeline*."

Nate looked even harder at his "spies." He knew the CIF had stationed them on Mara for several years. "I'm not sure that's going to be an issue. We're all fugitives, but I won't object if that's what you really want."

David glanced up at Arni. Yep, he had the blank stare again. "I will consider your request, and if I see the need, I will grant it. Now, explain yourself."

"Is Commodore Landon still running the facility there?"

David nodded. "He was looking to retire, but he was there a few weeks ago."

"We were working there with him when there was a fourth remaining prisoner. Commodore Landon shot her and threw her outside in the freezing weather. She wasn't dead- only stunned. The other three remained firm in their commitment to Pateras despite being beaten, imprisoned for thirty-five years, and watching their friend get shot in front of them. Commodore Landon sent to have the woman brought back inside. When she... the way she... died... we just never could come to terms with it. She died of a heart attack outside, but not before she forgave us. We resigned our posts and left a few weeks later. We were involved with the re-education processes. These people couldn't be re-educated. To be honest, it was the worst assignment of our careers. We began serving Pateras before we left Mara. We've kept in touch with Commodore Landon over the years." Henry faced Arni again and knelt in reverence to his esteemed position. "I wish Commodore Landon could have met you."

Jake leaned forward eagerly. "He did meet Arni. I wasn't happy about it at the time though." Jake glanced at Arni. "Sorry, Arni."

Arni smiled and nodded at Henry, dismissing him to return to his seat.

"It's been forgiven. It no longer matters. What matters now is deciding what side of this war the crew of the *Emissary* wants to be on."

Silas had been sitting sullenly by himself. "Do we have a choice? We've just been declared enemies of the state."

Brynna, still having feelings of angst where Silas was concerned, calmly explained. "Of course, you have a choice. You can fight alongside us, you can go into hiding, or you can turn yourselves in as publicly as possible in the hopes that Executor Hale will accept you as loyal. Although I suspect he would have you killed eventually and blame it on us. You never know though, he made Jake a second offer."

Nate turned the conversation back to Henry and Luna. "Wait, wait, you two are telling me you aren't... or weren't Commonwealth spies planted on my ship to test our loyalty?"

Henry and Luna looked at each other nervously. Luna answered for both of them. "I suppose in truth, yes, we were spies. Admiral Deacons and Admiral Garcia assigned us to your ship. They told us what had happened to the previous crew members and wanted us to do a careful evaluation of the crew."

Jake was quick to jump on the change in crew. "What happened to the previous crew members?"

Henry and Luna weren't sure if they were the best ones to answer that question. They glanced at Nate. Stephanie was sitting on a log. Nate was sitting on the ground beside her. She gently placed her hand on his shoulder to offer him support and sympathy.

The rest of the *Emissary's* crew kept quiet and avoided eye contact. Jake followed Henry's gaze back to Nate. "I left them behind on Strabothon. According to your reports, I left them there to die."

Claire looked up. "Elijah and Aneska are dead?" Her face clouded.

David tried to take some of the heat off his friend. "According to the information I got while we were on Romajin, Strabothon suffered the same fate as Galat III. The Commonwealth Pacification Fleet destroyed all human life on the planet."

Claire had mourned losing the couple from the mission, but now she needed to mourn the loss of their lives. Tears formed in her eyes. She abruptly left the group, and headed to the ship but made it no further than the steps before her tears overwhelmed her. Silas watched her go. He wanted nothing more than to chase after her and comfort her. He knew he still wasn't welcome. His eyes landed back on the mysterious stranger. "It's time. Go to her." He heard Arni's voice clear as day, but the man hadn't spoken or even looked his direction. When he questioned what he had heard, Arni turned to look at him. His face clearly said he had indeed instructed him to go after his wife. Silas didn't wait for a second invitation.

Milo went back to Luna's claim to be a spy. "Wait, I'm still confused. How can you be Commonwealth spies if you are loyal to Pateras?"

Luna continued her answer. "No one knew we were loyal to Pateras. Admiral Deacons and Admiral Garcia knew we had experience with trying to re-educate his followers. They knew we could spot the signs of the disloyal. They offered us the assignment. We discussed it and decided it would be a good place to hide. After we left Mara, we made it a habit of changing assignments every two to three years to avoid detection. They put us on this assignment to keep an eye on the crew. We took the assignment to hide our own disloyalty. Logically, your crew would be walking on tiptoes already. If anyone were disloyal, we could counsel him or her on how to hide, and we would have another ally to help cover us. If your crew were as loyal as it appeared, we were still in a position to keep hidden. Our jobs require discretion, so no one would think twice if we had private meetings or seemed aloof."

Milo still looked confused. "But you told us we could take the crew of the *Evangeline* out more easily if we divided them into smaller search parties when Commander Alexander and Lt. Commander Asher went missing, so to speak."

Henry raised a pensive eyebrow. "That was merely an observation."

Milo sat back and huffed. "You've had us all scared to death of you, and all this time you were scared to death of us?"

Henry nodded. "Yes, pretty much. We knew as long as you were scared of us, you wouldn't be prying into our private lives."

The conversation continued to prattle on, unraveling the remaining mysteries of the past events. When Brynna saw Silas chase after Claire, she made eye contact with Lexi and nodded for her to follow the two. Lexi got up quietly and followed Silas.

Silas found Claire sitting on the lower steps up to the ship. "May I sit down?"

"Silas, I'm not sure I can talk about this right now."

"Don't talk about it. I know you and Aneska were close, and you need to mourn her death. I understand that. I'm here to offer comfort. That's all."

Claire scooted over to give him room. Silas moved onto the step beside her. There was a nervous tension between them as they sat quietly side by side. Claire finally looked up into Silas's face. "Silas, I..." She couldn't finish her sentence. Claire began to cry again.

Silas put his arms around her to comfort her. He held her tightly for several minutes as she cried. He looked up as Lexi approached. His eyes pleaded with her not to interfere. Lexi moved over to one of the nearby landing struts and sat on the ground facing them. She was close enough to be of service if needed yet not too close to be intrusive.

Gradually, Claire's sobs subsided. The two talked softly for a few minutes. Silas apologized for his part in the death of her friend. The conversation inevitably worked its way back around to the problem in their own relationship.

"Silas, I want to trust you again, but you tried to have me executed. I'm just not sure I can get past that. You're a part of the reason Aneska is dead."

"I know. I... uh... I may have a way around that." Silas reached in his pocket and pulled out a data crystal. He held it up in the dim light and stared at it for a moment.

This was something that required a great deal of trust. He handed her the crystal.

Claire looked at the crystal as though she could read the data with the naked eye. "What's on here?"

Silas swallowed nervously. "It's the override codes for my nanites."

"Your nanites? I thought Stephanie was removing all the crew's nanites."

"I wouldn't let her remove mine. The codes have been changed and now you are the only one who can program my nanites."

Claire glanced at Lexi who was already sensing they needed her. Lexi approached cautiously as Claire asked. "Silas, why are you giving me this?"

"I want you to feel secure and safe around me. Program my nanites however you like. If I say or do anything that gives you cause for worry, then you can activate them to do anything from giving me nightmares for the rest of my life to shutting down my autonomic nervous system activity."

Claire stared at him in shock, "What?"

Lexi moved even closer. "Silas, are you and the Captain related? This sounds like one of the crazy ideas he would have."

Silas grinned slightly. "You know, I've tried hard to hate your captain, but it gets more difficult by the minute."

Claire looked at him skeptically. "You snuck up on me. I doubt you're going to give me a heads-up the next time you decide to execute me, so I can program a hex on you."

Silas shook his head. "No, Claire, that's not what I'm saying. I'm saying you program it now, so that if it identifies whatever criteria you set, the program kicks in on its own. For instance, if I use the words 'execute' or 'kill' or 'put down' in combination with 'Claire,' 'Lt. Commander Asher,' or 'my wife.' The program would activate, and the nanites would react however you told it them to. I would prefer you would cause me to have a rash or a sneezing fit, just in case there was some kind of misunderstanding. Claire, I MESSED UP... BADLY. This will never... ever happen again. I will protect your life with mine, no matter what. I don't know much about this

Liontari stuff, but I'm willing to do whatever it takes to earn back your love, respect and your trust."

Claire studied the crystal and its implications. If she programmed the nanites, even if he harmed her, she could have revenge. The thing obviously wasn't foolproof.

Silas could see she was considering it. Lexi stood there looking fearful. Silas decided to put it bluntly. "Claire, I was trying to get rid of Pateras, not you. Pateras is no longer an issue. These codes are exclusive to my nanites, no one can override them, not even me. If you're afraid of that, reprogram the override codes yourself. If I hurt you, you can program them to have me shoot myself or throw myself out of an airlock."

Lexi had stayed quiet as long as she could. "Claire, you seriously aren't considering this, are you?"

Claire squinted at Silas, "The Nefil couldn't even use your nanites against you?"

"No, all codes have been overwritten."

"What did the Captain have to say about it?"

"He doesn't know. I convinced the Doc they weren't a threat, so they could remain inside me."

Claire continued to explore the options. "You know, I would want to run a scan and a test myself to be certain you're telling the truth."

Inwardly Silas was disappointed she asked this of him, but he wasn't surprised. "Absolutely, we could run the scan here if you want. I don't have access to the *Evangeline's* systems to program false readings."

Lexi jumped in again, "Claire, could we talk privately for a moment?"

Claire pressed her lips tightly together. "Silas, can you give Lexi and me a moment?"

Silas nodded and walked back toward the fire. He stayed on the outskirts hoping she would quickly call him back.

Lexi moved closer to Claire. "Lt. Commander Asher, please tell me you aren't seriously considering doing this to him. This is not the way to resume your marriage. He would be no better than a hostage or a slave."

"I know." Claire answered coldly. "After what he tried to do to me, he deserves it."

Lexi continued to argue with her and tried to make her see the error in her thinking.

Milo walked quietly up behind Lexi. "Excuse me, ladies, I'm sorry to interrupt, but I think there's something you need to know. Claire, when Silas told me you had been compromised, he was distraught. He couldn't even say the words. I volunteered to take care of it... you, for him. I watched him. You know that wall we all build when we have a job to do, and our emotions get in our way? I've never seen a wall go up so hard and fast. Claire, he was working hard to shut out his feelings for you. He has not been himself since. He loves you, and it broke his heart to have to... well, you know."

Claire stared coldly at Milo. She was thankful he had spared her life but doubted his motivation in speaking up for Silas. "He tried to seduce Commander Alexander in his... grief."

Milo raised his hands in surrender. "I can't speak to that, I just know what I saw. I just thought you should know. The other thing is if you come back to the ship, I'll have your back. I'll leave you two alone to finish your conversation."

As Milo walked away, he heard Lexi start her argument. Claire quickly cut her off. "Lt. Flint, I appreciate your concerns, and I agree with them. I am going to do two things before I decide whether or not to return to the ship. First, I'm going to ask Silas about the Commander. Second, I am going to run those scans to see if the nanites truly are still there and active. If he lied, we're done. If he's telling the truth, I'll let him off the hook. I don't know, I might make him sweat a little first."

Lexi was relieved to hear her decide against using the nanites. "Shall I ask Jason, Cheyenne, and Silas to join us?"

"Cheyenne? Why do we need her?"

"Cheyenne is a computer expert. She could tell if anyone has tampered with the programming. If you want Silas to sweat a little, the more seriously you take his offer, the more he will sweat. I might also need to notify the Captain. Having someone aboard the ship with active nanites is a security risk."

Claire weighed her suggestions. "Let's do this. Let me talk to Silas first."

Claire pulled Silas aside while Lexi discreetly discussed her plan with Captain Alexander.

"Silas, I'm ready to do the scan and reprogram the nanites."

Silas was again disappointed she hadn't simply taken him at his word. He nodded. He took her hand and gave it a gentle squeeze. "My life is now in your hands."

When David heard Lexi's request and explanation, he balked. His reaction surprised Lexi. "Captain, this really sounded like one of your crazy ideas. I'm surprised you're reacting like this."

David stepped away from the others to discuss it further. He scowled. When the entire idea was laid out for him, he realized her line of thinking, but it still disturbed him. "Okay, I'll go along with the scan, but no programming them on my ship. Are we clear? Take whomever you need including Mr. Holden. Don't leave that man alone on my ship."

David returned to the group. His demeanor was obviously different than before his discussion with Lexi.

Lexi pulled Jake, Jason, and Cheyenne away from the group to the steps leading into the ship. Before they entered, she explained why she needed them. The instant Jake realized Silas still carried his nanites, he casually pulled his weapon and kept Silas in front of him.

Seeing what was happening, Stephanie glanced at David with a questioning look. The look he returned told her everything she needed to know. She stood up and nodded toward the ship. David nodded then motioned for Brynna to accompany her.

The diminishing number of crewmembers got the attention of the remaining crew. Nate looked at David, "What's going on?"

David gave a wry reply, "Silas is throwing himself on his sword."

Nate sat up straighter. "What's he doing?"

David told Nate about the nanites and his offer to Claire. Nate shook his head. "Claire doesn't need to use the nanites as her insurance policy. If he tries to execute any more members of my crew, I'll execute him for mutiny. She can count on it. I'll put a stop to this right now."

David waved him off. "Let it play out. Claire's not going to take him up on his offer."

The group began talking again, sharing some of the amazing things they had experienced.

KING CA-LITANA

The hour was getting late. Both crews were ready to say good night and head for bed when the sound of horses reached their ears. The two crews got to their feet and were instantly on alert.

Five horsemen rode out of the dark toward them and slowed as they approached. They appeared to be the King's guards. Two horsemen dismounted and walked toward them.

Due to the lateness of the hour, both Nate and David were concerned. With the King's coronation coming tomorrow, something must be wrong.

David engaged his translator. He tapped Nate to remind him to engage his own bracelet translator. It had taken very little time for him to become accustomed to using the nanites for translation. Now he was going to have to go back to the old way of doing things.

Nate stepped forward to speak to the two men walking toward them. "Welcome, gentlemen. Is everything alright? Is Prince Ca-Litana safe?"

The two men removed their helmets revealing the second man to be Prince Ca-Litana. "I'm fine, sorry to come at such a late hour. I have struggled with a problem and I'm unable to come up with a satisfactory solution. Perhaps you could help me."

Nate nodded. "We will certainly try. Would you care to sit down with us?"

"Thank you." Prince Ca-Litana sat down on one of the logs. His guard remained standing behind him.

The others took their seats again. Silas Asher had been the lead on the ambassadorial team. Prince Ca-Litana had dealt with him more than Captain Weiseman. "Where is Commander Asher?"

Nate struggled with how to explain Silas's current predicament. "He's... uh... getting checked out by the doctor."

"I see. I hope it is nothing serious."

Nate smiled. "I'm sure he'll be much better in a few minutes. What problem has brought you out so late at night?"

The young man sighed. He was clearly not happy about his situation. "It has been the custom of my people when a new King takes the throne to destroy the new King's enemies."

Milo idly tossed a small stick into the fire. "That would seem to be a wise precaution."

"The palace is secured the second the former King is pronounced dead. No one is allowed out except my own personal bodyguards. Others may enter, but no one may leave except for my escorts and me. I was able to escort Commander Alexander and Lt. Commander Asher out because they hid in my carriage. After my coronation tomorrow, all my father's sons are to be executed including those of his concubines. They will expect me to execute my own younger brothers including the infants and small children."

"That's awful." The stricken look on Gennie's face accentuated her words.

Prince Ca-Litana turned to the young woman. "I agree with you. I love my family and do not wish to cause them such grief. If I don't do this, they may perceive me as weak and ripe for someone to try and replace me. My family is currently living in fear of the sunrise. They know they will die by high noon."

"Can you start a new tradition and banish them instead?" Nate suggested.

"I've considered it, but if they were to return and attack the city, my people would turn on me and kill me. I could turn them into slaves. That has been done before, but I don't relish that idea either."

"What reasons would your people accept to keep them alive?" Nate asked.

"I can think of none." Prince Ca-Litana sadly admitted.

David glanced at Arni. "Do your people worship any type of deity?"

"Of course, there are many deities worshiped. None of our deities forbid the killing of one's enemies." Prince Ca-Litana thought he could see where David was going with this.

"I know of one. If you were to establish the worship of a particular god and that god forbid such actions, would that be sufficient reason?" David smiled. Deep down he knew it would. He was excited to see Pateras at work. It had to be Pateras at work.

"I must declare allegiance to a particular deity before I am crowned as King. In declaring that allegiance it determines which priest places the crown on my head and who will be favored during the reign of the new King. What god forbids the death of one's enemies?"

David glanced up at the ship. He silently wished Cheyenne were here. She was much better at quoting the Ancient Texts. "Pateras doesn't forbid killing, but he does forbid murder. If your family swore allegiance to you, they are your allies instead of your enemies. For the young children, solicit an oath from their mothers that they will be raised to follow you as an ally under penalty of death or banishment if they don't comply."

David glanced up to see the previously occupied crewmembers returning from the ship. The last two leaving the ship were Claire and Silas. The two were not acting like David expected. They stopped at the bottom of the steps staying clear of the others. They were pacing back and forth waving their arms about and occasionally raising their voices.

Brynna sat down next to David and just shook her head at him. She managed one quick, "They're... working it out." Seeing the young prince had joined them she asked, "What'd I miss?"

Prince Ca-Litana looked at Arni. "You are the son of Pateras, are you not?"

Arni nodded. "I am."

Milo got concerned. "Wait, how did you know that?"

"His messenger told me I would see him soon. I believe you have spoken to me before."

Arni continued to smile. "I have. I have spoken to all of you at various times in your lives. You will remember those times and my voice soon enough. David, please continue."

"Me? You wrote the Ancient Texts. I'm just now learning what's in them. I will gladly defer to your expertise."

Stephanie had taken her place beside Nate and was trying to catch up on the situation as well. "Hold on, I know I'm a little behind here, but what are these Ancient Texts, and if they're ancient, how could he have written them?"

Arni laughed outright. "My father and I are one and the same. We have always been, and we will always be. My father inspired the men who actually wrote the texts. They are just as relevant as if I had physically written them myself."

Laura piped up. "You have to think 'outside the box.' Arni may look human, but he isn't. Captain Weiseman, I assume you're going to accuse us of trying to keep these people primitive by encouraging deity worship. If Pateras is truly a Timeless One who can create and destroy with a mere thought, does that not qualify as a deity?"

The conversation seemed to take an inordinately long time as each person's comments had to be relayed through the translator.

Stephanie yawned. "I suppose you have a point."

David turned his attention back to the Prince's problem. "There is no… priest to… to place the crown on your head. Each one approaches Pateras himself. You should assign scribes to write down the words of Pateras and share them with the people." David continued to advise him and instruct him with the basic knowledge and goals of Pateras.

Prince Ca-Litana soaked in David's words as fast as David could speak them. It was soon late enough that David advised him to appoint someone to serve as a priest in a lesser capacity. This priest could serve as a teacher, scribe, and visible leader, but not as a ruler or superior.

The thing that now had the Prince concerned was the lack of a candidate to assign as High Priest. He turned to Arni. "Please, you are the only one qualified to serve as the High Priest. I know I do not deserve such an honor, but please be the High Priest my people need."

Arni nodded. "I will serve as High Priest for you. After tomorrow, your people will no longer see me, but they must all learn to seek my face and listen to my voice. Follow David's suggestions. They are wise choices. We have six more days to spend with you then we will need to leave this place. There are many, many more who have believed the lies of the Dark Lord. It is time to set the record straight. I will send another here to be your guide after I've left. It is late, you should get some rest, Prince Ca-Litana. You have a busy day tomorrow. I will protect you and your family from harm tomorrow."

The Prince admitted he was indeed tired. He gave everyone a brief farewell then mounted his horse and rode quickly off into the night.

Silas and Claire had slowly made their way back over to the campfire. They hadn't caught the entire conversation, but they caught the gist of it. Claire smarted off to Silas, "Why didn't you suggest using the nanites to ensure the loyalty of his family?"

Silas bristled. "What? You didn't just say that. I was offering the only thing I could to convince you I was being genuine. I am willing to do whatever I had to. Doesn't that mean anything to you?"

"You tried to kill me, and you propositioned an old girlfriend. Do you really expect me to get over that quickly?"

Silas started to retort angrily. A voice in his head stopped him, "soft answers turn away anger." Silas looked around. His eyes landed on Arni who was conversing with the others near him. Their eyes made contact, and Arni gave him a subtle nod.

Silas took a deep breath and swallowed his pride one more time. He knelt on one knee, took Claire's right hand in his. "Claire, I broke our marriage agreement on two counts. You have every right to no longer consider us married."

The couple was attracting the attention of everyone around. Claire was becoming embarrassed. "Silas, get up. What are you doing?"

Silas didn't budge. "I still love you, and I would like you to return to our marriage. The Captain can reinstate the agreement, and we can restate our vows."

"Silas, stop this. Everyone is staring at us!" She tried to pull her hand away from him.

Silas held her hand even tighter. "Let me finish. I love you, and I want you back. I swear on my life, I will never betray you or our marriage again. You have my word. If that isn't enough, then by all means, walk away. I've done all I know to do to set things right again, except for one thing, which I will tend to as soon as we are done here. I don't know what our futures hold, but I'd rather have a future with you than without you. Please forgive me. If you can't, say so now, and I will walk away and never bother you again."

Claire's temper flared. "Did you just put this back on me?"

Silas relaxed his grip on her hand to allow her to pull away if she still wanted to. "Yes, I did. I'm done fighting over this. I did you wrong. I admit it, and I'm asking for forgiveness. If you can't give it to me, then I need to leave. Please come back to me." Silas resisted the urge to tighten his grip on her hand again.

Claire knew if she walked away now, they were done. She fought the desire to continue punishing him. She looked around at the two crews who were trying very hard not to stare, then looked down at Silas' pleading face.

Arni made his way to Claire's side. "Claire, you asked for my help when Milo was about to execute you. I helped you. I can help you both put your lives back together. Does that help you make your decision?"

Her heart had been cold and hard toward Silas. She looked up at Arni. "He tried to kill me." She whispered.

Arni could feel Silas's heart breaking. "He was trying to kill me, not you." Arni turned to the Commander. "What was the one thing you haven't done, Silas?"

"I wanted to tell Pateras I am sorry for trying to kill his people, and I want to join him. Can you tell him that for me?"

"I am he. You are forgiven, and welcome in my house." Arni rested his hand on Silas's shoulder for a moment then walked on past them toward the ship.

Claire studied Silas's face again. "Did you do that just to get me back?"

Silas stood and released her hand. "No, Claire. I did that for myself. I can see there's nothing I can do to regain your trust. I've done myself more harm than I did to you. Good night, Claire."

Silas stepped just past her when Claire called his name. "Silas, wait… You hurt me, badly. I've wanted nothing more than to hurt you back, over and over. Every time I felt pain, I wanted you to feel it too. It's only been two days, and I'm tired of hurting. Silas, please make the hurting stop."

Silas turned and took her hand again. "Come home with me, and I'll work every day for the rest of our married lives on helping you forget the pain. Please say yes."

Tears formed in her eyes. Claire squeezed his hand, "Yes."

Silas wrapped his arms around her tightly and hugged her. Claire cried again. This time they were tears of forgiveness. The two crews applauded and cheered. Nate gave the order to board the Surf-ve. As David walked past Silas and Claire, he softly informed them, "You know that Liontari marriages are for life, right?"

Silas stopped and blinked for a moment. He looked at Claire and grinned. "I guess this is gonna take a while."

Late the next morning, both crews met outside the city walls. The Surf-ves were just small enough to make it through the city gates and streets. If they took the vehicles into the city, it would be a tight fit and room for little else. The horses and other animals might also get spooked by the vehicles making the potential for mayhem too risky.

The crew exited their vehicles to walk to the palace. The King's palace was located in the center of the city. A few feet inside the gates, several guards invited them to ride in carriages to the palace. The carriages held only a minimal number of people creating a long entourage to carry the twenty-four crewmen and Arni to the palace. The closer they got to the palace, the more crowded it became.

The carriages unloaded their passengers outside a great open hall of stone pillars. Inside the hall, a crowd had already gathered waiting on the coronation ceremony. At the far end of the great hall was a wide staircase leading to a stage with two thrones at center stage. The guards escorted the two crews to a group of seats to one side at the base of the steps where they were placed among a large group of what appeared to be priests from varying temples. The priests fidgeted with their regalia and headdresses, each wondering who would be chosen as the new King's religious preference and thereby the most powerful religious body. When the two crews were positioned among them, their nervous stomachs grew even more nervous. Why would these foreigners be seated with the religious factions unless they sought to usurp the power balance? The crew started getting angry looks. The struggle for power among the religious factions was hard enough. These strangers had no business coming in here upsetting things.

Nate and David were keenly aware of the changing atmosphere around them. They discreetly warned their people to stay alert.

A row of men carrying brass horns marched solemnly onto the stage and stood. toward the back of the stage, two men with two kettledrums moved into place. The roar of the excited crowd decreased as the heralds on the stage raised their horns to their lips and blew a brief two-toned blast on their instruments.

A man standing near the two thrones stepped front and center, "Presenting the royal family of former King De-Marion!" His voice was loud and strong. The acoustics of the hall projected more loudly and more clearly than the crew expected. The crowd dropped to their knees including the surrounding priests. David and Nate quickly took on the same posture. The crew followed the example of their leaders. Arni remained standing. The guards around the perimeter fidgeted nervously. They had been warned to steer clear of the visitors among the priests. Each one feared they would be blamed for Arni's insubordination, but no one was sure how to deal with the situation. Soft murmurs rippled through the crowd as the royal family was escorted into a section of seats in the front and center. An entourage of guards and a sturdy wall about four feet tall on three sides surrounded the family.

David glanced up at Arni who had tears in his eyes. He wondered why. David started to whisper his question to Arni then remembered Arni didn't need his question vocalized.

Arni leaned down and whispered quietly. "These people are afraid they are about to die. The Prince could not tell them his plan, and they fear for their lives. Once they know my father, they will not fear death as they do now."

David nodded his understanding. His own heart ached for the women with their children. King De-Marion had eliminated his own brothers, half-brothers, his father's other wives and concubines, and all their children. When King De-Marion ascended to his father's throne, the only ones who lived to see it were was his own mother, his sisters, and his own wives and concubines. Ca-Litana had been a small child at the time and remembered nothing of the occasion.

The heralds trumpeted again, and the Grandmaster announced, "All Hail Prince Ca-Litana!"

The horns sounded, and the drummers pounded their drums as Prince Ca-Litana marched regally onto the stage and stood formally beside the Grandmaster. The heralds moved down the steps and took up new symmetrical positions.

The crowd chanted, "Hail Prince Ca-Litana."

The Prince and Grandmaster allowed the chanting to continue for a couple minutes. Prince Ca-Litana finally nodded at the Grandmaster who raised his hands to silence the audience. The chant waned as the Grandmaster called out in his loud grandiose voice. "You may rise." The crowd stood as instructed.

"Prince Ca-Litana, with the death of your father his Royal Highness King De-Marion, the rulership of his kingdom and his household falls to you. It is a grave responsibility to govern this these people and this land. Do you accept this responsibility?"

Prince Ca-Litana stepped forward. His response was not what the people expected. "I am not the same man my father was. His priorities are not my priorities. My father did not care for his people. He cared only for himself. Many people taught and trained me. My mother, the Captain of the Guard, several learned scholars, and others have taught me many valuable lessons. This kingdom cannot thrive under the rule of a single man. Barely three days ago, my father would have slaughtered the firstborn sons of the entire city. This is not what I consider the rightful rule of a kingdom. My father was a fool, and Pateras destroyed him for it. I will only accept the responsibility of rule if you, the people of this land will accept me. Do you want me as your King?"

Murmurs and whispers swept through the congregation. The Captain of the Guard, the same man who had tried to kill King De-Marion, was standing near the base of the stairs. He took three steps up and unsheathed his sword. He raised it high in the air, and shouted, "Hail King Ca-Litana!"

His fellow soldiers copied their leader. Jo-Na stood with the other Prefects and eagerly joined the cries. The other Prefects decided there was wisdom in voicing their appreciation of the new King. Their subjects joined the cries until the hall was ringing.

The Prince raised his arms to silence the crowd. "Grandmaster, I will accept this responsibility." The crowd cheered again. The Prince was definitely doing things differently than his father. They hoped this was a good sign. No Prince had ever asked his subjects for permission to rule. Citizens had lived in fear of getting on King De-Marion's bad side.

The Grandmaster raised his hands to once again silence the excited crowd. "Before you are crowned as King, you must choose which god you will serve and who will crown you. Who do you choose?"

The Prince looked down at the anxious Priests around the crew. Each one stood as tall as he could, trying to catch the Prince's eye at the last possible moment.

"Three days ago, one god represented here today saved my life. The people from the stars are powerful people, yet even they could not save me. None of the other gods has ever done anything for me, nor have they even shown themselves to me. I deny their existence. The one true God I serve is Pateras. Pateras saved my life, and the lives of the people from the stars. The son of Pateras is my High Priest, and he will endow me with the power and responsibility of the role of King. Arni Sotaeras Liontari, son of Pateras El Liontari, please come forward and grant me the honor of serving you as ruler over your people."

The surrounding Priests looked like someone had let the air out of their sails. As Arni stepped out and made his way to the stage, angry murmurs were heard around them. David had the urge to join Arni to protect him. He heard Arni's soft voice inside his head. "I don't need to be protected. My Father is in control."

The Priest directly in front of David turned around and asked, "Is this true? Did Pateras save you and the Prince's life? Did he destroy King De-Marion?"

David nodded. "It's very true. That man has saved my life from certain death several times and restored my life from death once. Why do you ask?"

"I would like to serve such a god. I have served one I thought was the most powerful of all the gods for many years, and I have never heard or seen such things. Could we talk later?"

David smiled. "Of course, I'd love to tell you about him."

Arni reached the Prince, and the two whispered a moment. Arni looked at David just as he finished the conversation with the elderly priest who had removed his fancy headgear. Arni's eyes were twinkling with delight. Nate curiously watched the activity unfold around him.

Prince Ca-Litana knelt facing the audience between Arni and the Grandmaster. The Grandmaster had a list of oaths to ask the incoming monarch to swear to. Arni took the lead from him and wrapped the long list into one short oath. "Will you love and pursue the one true god Pateras

El Liontari with all of your might until the end of your days and love your subjects as equally as you love yourself?"

"I will."

"I will hold you to this oath. I crown you, KING Ca-Litana. Do not abandon this path and follow in your father's footsteps, lest I remove you from this position as well." Arni placed the crown on his head and stepped back.

The Grandmaster had been concerned because he and the Prince had not gone over the ceremony with his chosen High Priest. He was afraid the stranger would fumble and appear awkward. Now he felt that same awkwardness. He quickly cleared his throat and shouted, "LONG LIVE KING CA-LITANA!"

Shouts continued across the great hall for several minutes. David glanced at the royal family. Their reactions were expectedly less than enthusiastic. The religious leaders were nearly as unenthusiastic although their reasons were different. The new King had just denounced each of their religions. It was one thing to promote one over another but to denounce all the others was unheard of.

When the strength of the shouts first hinted at wavering, King Ca-Litana raised his hands to silence the masses again. "It is tradition, for the protection of the new king, to destroy any who may attempt to usurp the throne. Pateras does not condone murder. It is forbidden. Anyone condemned to die will only do so after a court has found them guilty and rightly sentenced to death. Some would consider me weak for this. If they believe me to be weak, they are wrong. I am not afraid to go to war to defend my people. This is a war against an evil tradition, and it shall not continue. My family's lives are spared this day. If anyone finds fault with this, let him bring his sword and come forward to challenge me. I will defend my people and my family with my very life!"

The King's eyes searched the mass of people slowly. He scanned the crowd for any obvious signs of dissent or restlessness. No one appeared willing to challenge the brash young King. His eyes finally landed on his family. Seeing their fear, he had compassion on them. "I give you a choice. You can swear your loyalty to serve Pateras and to serve me, or you may leave my kingdom by nightfall.

The choice is yours. Each family will be brought before me and give their oath for all to hear."

King Ca-Litana's mother and siblings were brought forward, and those who were old enough swore loyalty to the King. The King's mother swore to raise her younger children to be loyal to Pateras and to their oldest brother.

Before any more of the late King De-Marion's wives or concubines could be brought before King Ca-Litana, a voice called out. The man was too far away for the crew's translators to pick up. They could tell the man was angry. Another man who favored him followed closely him. David got the attention of the elderly Priest in front of him. "Who is that, and what is he saying?"

David's translator relayed his question far too slowly for David's comfort. The man explained, "He is… was… Prefect Odo-Ishan. He's denying the King's right to rule and demanding to fight the King. The King removed his title and bestowed all his property, titles, and responsibilities upon one of his subordinates. He and his family were sold as slaves to pay his own debts. The other man is his brother."

Captain Alexander started to move to the new young King's aid. Arni caught his eye. He discreetly held up his hand to stop him. David found it difficult to hold his ground. He had already made it two long steps up the aisle before Arni's gesture stopped him. Nate stepped up behind him and gently urged him back to his seat. "Davie, the King will have to maintain control once we're gone. If he's going to do that, he has to prove himself without our help today."

David felt helpless again. "He's not much more than a boy."

"I know, but if his father did anything right, he trained his son to be strong and not back down." Nate tried to calm David's fears while suffering those same fears.

The crews kept casting glances at their Captains waiting for orders. Some knew what had to happen, while others were anxious to jump in and rescue the young man who had saved their lives in the fight with the Nefil.

Jake and Milo were carefully surveying the hall from top to bottom. There was an upper level to the great hall, but it wasn't large enough for more than guards. Jake counted approximately fifty archers with arrows trained on the two men approaching the King.

The two men wisely stopped advancing at the bottom of the stairs. They knew the archers' arrows were trained on them without looking. The one man again challenged the King. "Prince Ca-Litana, I challenge you. I believe you are too weak to be King. You couldn't kill me for failing my duties to the King, and your refusal to kill your own family is more proof. Your father would have killed me for failing him. Instead, you have allowed me to live with shame and embarrassment. I will defeat you and put your father's entire household to death so that none of your family's weakness will be passed on. Be true to your word and accept my challenge."

The young King sighed. He had hoped this wouldn't happen. He glanced at Arni. The two seemed to have an unspoken conversation. The young King had been seated on his throne to accept his family's oaths of loyalty. He stood slowly and spoke loudly, "Odo-Ishan, I spared your life to teach you about justice, mercy, and hope. I see as a ruler, I have made my first mistake. I sent a message to your brother telling him when and where you were going to be auctioned so he could reclaim you and your sons. I kept your wife and daughters here as slaves in my household. I intended to release them to you after I knew you had learned these lessons. I should have sold you to a traveling slave merchant. In the face of learning these lessons, do you still wish to challenge me?"

The man hesitated. His brother grabbed his robe and whispered to him. Odo-Ishan shook his brother off and whispered something back.

"Yes, I still challenge you."

"Prefect Odo-Hiram, is your family present?"

"Of course, your Highness."

King Ca-Litana looked at the Captain of his guard who was standing near the two men. The man was ready to strike the two men down the second the King gave the order. "Captain, escort Prefect Odo-Hiram and his family into the seating area with my family."

The Prefect and his brother now looked nervous. Odo-Ishan voiced his objections. "Leave my brother and his family alone. This fight is ours and ours alone!"

King Ca-Litana removed his decorative outer robe, tossed it onto his throne and laid his crown on top of it. He turned around abruptly and shouted angrily. "I HAVE NO INTENTION OF HARMING YOUR FAMILY! You have sworn to kill my entire family if you kill me. My family is secured there beside you, ready to be slain. As is tradition, the new ruler puts his own brothers and their families to death. I have saved YOU the trouble of rounding them up if you WIN!"

The Captain of the guard turned and pointed at a half-dozen guards who moved swiftly to collect the Prefect's family. The Captain took Odo-Hiram into custody and escorted him into the enclosure.

Odo-Ishan watched as the guards ushered his brother away. The look of shock on his brother's face mirrored his own.

Hiram called out to his brother, "Ishan? Ishan? Don't do this!"

The Grandmaster cleared the platform of all non-essential personnel and equipment, including the large drums.

David caught himself laughing out loud when he heard the translation come through his earpiece.

Nate glanced sideways at him. "You enjoyed that way too much."

David shook his head. "He may be young and inexperienced, but that kid's no fool."

Nate was almost as amused as David. The two waited to see what would happen next.

Odo-Ishan watched as his brother's wives and children were herded into the enclosure. Some of the women wept openly, including the King's family whose second chance at life seemed to be slipping away.

The two families now safely surrounded by walls and guards, King Ca-Litana placed his hand on the hilt of his sword. "Odo-Ishan, the choice is yours. You may withdraw your challenge and leave my home unharmed, or you may continue." The young man looked up at the archers above him. "Archers lower your bows!"

Ishan glanced at his brother who pleaded with him to walk away. Ishan looked back at the bold young King, this child who had shamed him. He glared at him again, pulled his own sword, and raced up the steps. He dropped his outer robe on the steps as he climbed. "I was trained as a warrior before you were even born. I will take great pleasure in destroying you and your family."

The young King was gracious enough to allow the man onto the stage before attempting to cross blades with him. The man charged onto the platform and didn't hesitate. He swung his blade high, then low, then high again. The younger man blocked each one, but lost ground with each blow. Fueled by what seemed to be an obvious advantage, he swung his sword faster and harder forcing his young opponent toward the edge of the steps. Seeing the King's precarious position, Ishan swung his sword again to force him down the steps.

David's fists balled up instinctively. He watched the young man losing ground and began losing heart in equal portions. He glanced at the Captain of the Guard. The man didn't appear worried. Captain Alexander saw the man smirk, then smile outright as King Ca-Litana twisted causing Odo-Ishan to pitch forward onto the steps he tried to force his opponent down. David relaxed his hands. He cocked his head sideways, "Huh... well, I'll be."

Nate glanced at him, "You'll be what? What am I missing? It looked to me like the kid got lucky."

"I don't think so. His instructor doesn't appear worried at all. The kid knows how to fight. He's just sizing up his opponent."

Nate glanced at the Captain of the Guard and saw the same things David had seen.

The swords clanged back and forth noisily for several minutes. Each time seemed to put the King at a disadvantage, and then he would again escape. The two ended up with their swords locked and in each other's face. The older man was sweating profusely. This boy was holding his own although he was no match for the older man's weight and strength. The older man shoved King Ca-Litana straight back causing him to fall onto the floor of the stage. The King rolled hastily to his feet in time to block the next blow although it vibrated his hand painfully.

Seeing his attack had not achieved its intended outcome, Odo-Ishan backed off for a moment. His young opponent took advantage of the opportunity to switch his grip to the left hand for a moment. He attempted to shake the sensation in his right hand but was promptly attacked again. Ishan did not give him the chance to return his sword to his right hand. Ishan assumed he would have the advantage for certain now. He attacked again with a rapid succession of moves. Ca-Litana countered each one with a surprising amount of precision, then made an unexpected swing slicing into Odo-Ishan's tunic, nicking his ribs. The man pulled back surprised. This boy had drawn first blood.

A cold hard fact now became evident. The King carried his sword on his left, and drew it with his right hand as most any man would, but his left was the dominant hand. He had been trained to use either hand. The first half of the fight, the King was using his non-dominant hand... successfully.

Another surprise struck Odo-Ishan. The crowd had been murmuring loudly, yet indistinctly. Now they cheered outright. They had lived in fear of their previous King, and this young man showed signs of being a good ruler.

His minute injury and the added insult of the crowd cheering made Ishan even angrier. He swung more voraciously and less carefully. The spry young man blocked, ducked, dodged, and waited for the right moment. The King narrowly missed getting his head removed permanently. Odo-Ishan was pleased to see he had finally drawn blood from the young man's face. A tiny gash in his jaw dripped blood. The young King didn't take the time to investigate his injury. He kept his eyes focused on his opponent. The young man was proving to be well-disciplined in his fighting skills.

Ishan hadn't fought this hard in a good many years. Fatigue showed on his face. He paused to wipe the sweat from his brow and attacked again.

Ca-Litana heard his Captain yell one quick word of advice. "Wait!" He kept his eyes trained on his opponent.

Knowing the impatience of youth, Odo-Ishan allowed an obvious opening. Ca-Litana heeded his trainer's instruction. He let the opening pass and opted for another. He nicked the older man's calf. The man came at him again. His vigor was faltering. He swung so wildly Ca-Litana could have easily taken several openings and killed the man. Killing him was not the King's goal. When the man reached a point where he was no longer a credible threat, Ca-Litana found his opening. The two locked swords. Ca-Litana swung his own sword in repeated attacks. The last clang sent Ishan's sword flying from his hand. The King hastily used the flat side of the blade to sweep Ishan's legs, taking him to his knees.

The man sat back on his heels in defeat. His eyes fixed on the blade in front of him. He couldn't bear to look the pompous young King in the eye.

The King, however, was adamant about looking into the eyes of his subjects. Using the tip of his sword, he forced the man's head upward. "Odo-Ishan, you have challenged the King and lost. I am within my rights to execute you and your entire family. Have you anything to say?"

The man took several deep breaths before answering. "Forgive me, your Highness. I have wronged you. I have embarrassed myself and my family. Please do not hold my family accountable for my actions. They are innocent. Please punish only me. If you will spare them, they will swear oaths of allegiance to you and serve you well. You have my word."

The King stared hard at the man. Sweat poured from his own brow. "You can assure that from beyond the grave? I doubt that, but could you assure it if you were master of your household? Swear allegiance to me and swear to seek Pateras, and I will grant you your life."

Odo-Ishan looked up in shock. Did this young man intend to embarrass him further? The King leaned in closer and spoke so no one else could hear him. "Ishan, this was supposed to be a day of celebration, not a day of mourning. I do not want to be your enemy. The decision is yours. I will slay you if that is truly your desire."

The man swallowed as hard as he dared with a blade at his throat. "I yield to you. I swear my allegiance to you, King Ca-Litana. My household and I will serve you and seek your new God Pateras."

King Ca-Litana metaphorically took a page from his father's book. He leaned in close again. "You break your oath, it is treason. I will not even need to break a sweat from this moment forward to punish you for it. Are we understood?"

The man nodded nervously. "Y-Yes your Highness."

King Ca-Litana stepped back and lowered his sword. "I grant you your freedom and your life. Rejoin your family. We will continue with the oaths of allegiance." The young King sheathed his sword and beckoned to a woman in an alcove. The woman hurried out to him carrying a pitcher of water and a crystal chalice. Keeping her head down, the woman handed the chalice to the King and filled it with water. She raised her head enough to see Odo-Ishan. Her eyes grew fearful.

Odo-Ishan stood slowly after the King left him. He walked slowly toward the steps. His sword lay on the ground in front of him. He glanced casually at the archers above him. Their attention was not currently on him. He slowly picked up the sword and stared at the blade as it glistened in the daylight. A small smear of blood on the blade dulled its shine, the King's blood. Odo-Ishan turned slightly. The King's back was to him, and his sword was sheathed. The angry voice in his head now taunted him. The King wouldn't be able to react quickly enough. His eyes fell on the slave who brought the King his drink.

The entire auditorium sensed the man's thoughts and held their breath again. Was this over, or wasn't it? As he stood there eyeing his sword and the King's back, the King slowly wrapped his left hand around the hilt of his own sword. Without turning around, he called out. "Consider carefully all that you would lose."

Odo-Ishan looked into the woman's face, her fear blatantly displayed. Ishan raised the hilt of his sword and slid the tip of the blade into its sheath.

Hearing the sword return to its scabbard, King Ca-Litana handed the chalice back to the woman. "Take this water to your husband. You may stay at his side. You are free."

The King's spies and advisers had warned him of Odo-Ishan's anger. They suggested keeping the man's wife and daughters close by.

The woman rushed to her husband's side and gave him the drink as ordered. The man looked at it in fear. Was it poisoned? His wife whispered quietly to him. The man took a cautious sip then a larger drink until he had gulped down the entire container. The King placed his crown back on his head and took his seat again. He was far too hot and sweaty to put his decorative robe back on just yet. He knew his father would frown on his improper attire and smiled to himself. "I am NOT my father."

Ishan looked up in time to see the archers lower their weapons again. He had been in their sights, and their Captain was prepared to give the signal ending his life. He swallowed hard. His mouth was already dry again.

The new King called for several servants. He quietly gave them several orders. The servants quickly scurried in various directions to obey their master. One scooped up the empty chalice, refilled it, and took it once again to the former prefect. Another brought the young King a chalice of his own. A third brought out Odo-Ishan's three daughters who had been kept safely in the palace under the King's watchful eye. He called Odo-Ishan and Odo-Hiram forward along with their families.

"Odo-Ishan, I know the indignities a slave may face. I have kept your daughters here under guard to protect them from those indignities. I now return them to you."

As soon as each gave their oaths of loyalty, the King sent them on their way. He pushed his own family to give their oaths as quickly as possible. The fight had thrown the schedule later than intended. Each one gave a grateful and heartfelt oath. When the last one finished, he admonished them to never forget this oath. He assured them as long as they did they would be safe from him. He gave one stern warning, "Any man or woman who breaks this oath is guilty of treason, and the penalty for treason is death."

The King's speech gave his plans for the immediate future. He introduced them to the data module brought by the *Emissary*. With Nate's approval, David had Cheyenne reprogram the data module to include the Ancient Texts in the native language and to prevent it from contacting the Commonwealth. The modules were intended to spy on the societies where they were planted as well as provide a database of educational material.

King Ca-Litana announced his need for scholars to learn from the data module and pass that knowledge onto others. He also announced his need for scribes to copy and distribute the Ancient Texts.

The speech was brief, and most suspected it was shorter than the young King had originally planned.

The last thing on the agenda was for the King to announce which of his two wives would actually assume the role of Queen. The King called his two wives onto the stage. They each knelt before their King and bowed their heads respectfully. Ca-Litana's marriage to one woman had been arranged to assure peace between their kingdom and a neighboring kingdom. The other woman he had asked his father to provide for him. He cared deeply for the woman. He respected both women more than his father had ever respected any woman. The King's eyes landed on his beloved wife. Either woman would make a beautiful queen and both were trained to be women of stature.

"Both of my wives are trained in the finer arts of diplomacy and manners. Each one would be a great Queen, but I can only choose one. This day I choose La-Reina to sit at my side as Queen. HAIL QUEEN LA-REINA!"

Ca-Litana took La-Reina's hand and escorted her to her throne at his left hand. The crowd chanted as expected. As their chant faded, King Ca-Litana raised his hands for silence. He returned and escorted his remaining wife to a smaller chair recently carried out on his right. "As I mentioned, either of my wives would be a wise selection for Queen. I would be remiss if I did not take counsel from both. Princess Da-Ami will serve as an adviser to me, and to my queen. HAIL PRINCESS DA-AMI!"

The King dismissed the throngs to spend the day in celebration. The crew, priests, and nobles were invited to stay for the ensuing banquet. The group adjourned to the gardens while the great hall was set up for the banquet.

David, Nate, and Brynna took the time to sit down with the elderly priest and talk at length about Pateras. The man decided he would apply to be one of the scribes the King had requested.

"What about the temple you run?" David asked.

"I will dismiss the younger priests and priestesses. I will encourage them to seek Pateras then I will close the temple and destroy the idols. I feel like I have wasted my life. I served my gods with all the fervor any god could ask for, and now, at the end of my days, I learn they are nothing but pieces of stone." The man looked around to see if anyone was listening to their conversation then leaned in more closely to David, Nate, and Brynna. "And they weren't even attractive gods. The carvings are dull... and just plain ugly."

The three grinned at the old man's candor as he continued to rant more sharply. "It's true. You would think if someone were going to worship a god, it would be something nicer than a man with animal characteristics. So, what does Pateras look like?"

David scowled. This would not be an easy explanation. "Although I have been in his presence, I can't really tell you what he looks like. The light coming from him was brighter than any sun and an immense cloud of smoke surrounded him. The first time I was in his presence, he would not allow me to see him for my protection. His goodness was too great for my body to handle. It would have killed me instantly. The second time I was in his presence, what I saw of him is simply more than I can describe."

The crew of the *Evangeline* continued to share information about Pateras with any who asked and with the *Emissary's* crew. The crew looked around during the banquet and saw Arni sitting with the children who were present. He was regaling them with stories about his Father and his life on Galat. He showered them with the love and affection one would expect from a proud father. Brynna told the crew of the *Emissary* about Arni calling her his child. It was a tough concept to grasp, as this man was only around thirty years old. Arni glanced up and smiled at them. He was fully aware they were discussing him.

The great hall was filled with numerous tables, as there were far too many people to sit at one table. The King had invited Captain Weiseman, Commander Asher, and Captain Alexander to join him. The three preferred to sit with their crews but joined the King at his table.

The party lasted late into the night, and the crew moved out into the garden carrying their cups with them. The feast had left them thirsty, and the palace had its own spring bubbling up in this spot in the garden with water that was crisp, cold, and clean. They enjoyed refilling their cups with the refreshing drink.

Stephanie reached in to refill her cup again and caught sight of the time and date stamp on her bracelet. She stopped moving for a moment. Nate cocked his head sideways. "Everything okay, Steph?"

Stephanie stood upright and looked around the circle of Commonwealth crewmen until she located Captain Alexander. "I'm fine, but I'm worried about Davie."

David had been leaned back against a pillar and getting close to dozing off. Hearing his name, he sat up quickly. "Worried about me? Why? I'm fine. I'm just a little tired."

"No, Davie, I don't think you are. You look like you've aged so much… in the last ten minutes."

David continued to look confused. "Last ten minutes?" He glanced down at his own bracelet. A split second later, the realization hit. He jumped to his feet and headed back toward the palace. "I need to go talk to… to take care of… I've got something to handle. I'll see everyone back at the… "

Stephanie giggled and chased after him, pulling him back into the circle. "Oh no, you don't. You aren't going anywhere."

Her sudden burst of activity got everyone's attention. Brynna looked down at the time on her display. She was still lost. Nate looked at his own display. It was late, and he was tired too. It took him a moment to catch on to what Stephanie was getting at. As soon as his mind connected the dots, he laughed robustly. "Live with it, Davie."

Brynna looked at her display again. If it wasn't the time, it must be the date. The date seemed familiar, but she didn't know why. She had known David for less than two years and they had only been close for a little over a year. A little over a year, the date, it finally dawned on her. It was her husband's birthday. They had never celebrated a birthday together. Her own birthday was still a month away. She and David had just started dating when her twenty-ninth birthday came around. Being a new relationship, she didn't want to burden him with by telling him it was her birthday. She had slipped off quietly with some of the ladies in her barracks to celebrate. "David, is it your birthday?"

Stephanie stopped in shock. "Davie, you didn't tell your own wife when your birthday is? Davie is thirty-one as of twelve minutes ago."

It took the tired crew a minute to compose themselves. In keeping with the timbre of the natives, Thane piped up, "All hail, Captain Alexander!"

The crew raised their cups in a toast. "Hail Captain Alexander!"

David whispered into Stephanie's ear. "I'll get you back for this."

Stephanie grinned. "My birthday was two months ago. Sorry, Davie."

"Speech!"

"Speech!"

For once the crew saw their Captain in a way they had never seen him before... embarrassed.

"Aw, come on, guys, haven't you heard enough speeches for one day?"

The crew of the *Emissary* joined in the merriment and cried out for a speech as well.

David climbed onto a bench at Stephanie's urging. He stood there speechless for a moment. He walked back and forth on the bench trying to decide what to say.

Jake laughed at the Captain's loss for words. "There's been a few times you've called me into your office that I wished you were this speechless."

The Captain gave Jake a perturbed look. "Yeah, if you'd been speechless a few times, you wouldn't have been in my office to begin with."

"Ohhh... ouch... I think I've been mortally wounded!" Jake feigned a hit to his chest. He got up from his seat, staggered about, and then collapsed on the ground.

Continuing his wild antics, he crawled to Marissa's feet, "Only a kiss from the fairest of maidens can save me."

Marissa looked down at him and smiled. "Then I guess you're out of luck."

Jake rolled over onto his back, "Oh, the fatal blow!" He moaned painfully and pretended to die with a goofball look on his face.

David tried to sit down thinking his moment in the hot seat was now forgotten.

Thane piped up, "Let it go, Jake. The Captain still has to give us thirty-one things he's grateful for. You can't stop it."

Nate clanked his cup on the bench, "Here, Here!"

Braxton joined him in clanking the metal cup on the stone bench. "Here! Here! Thirty-one things!"

The two crews joined in the cheer then quieted down while waiting on David to begin his speech.

Jake jumped up energetically and sat down next to Marissa. "Sorry, Captain, I tried."

David smiled and nodded. "I appreciate it, really I do."

It was a tradition in the Commonwealth to count one's accomplishments and the things they were grateful for in this life. The Commonwealth's teaching of the lack of an afterlife caused people to base success on lifetime achievements, forcing them to focus only on the moment. Knowing what they did about Pateras, and that their inner beings were not finite, David struggled with the tradition. Brynna softly added her own words of encouragement, "David, I think we've had a lot of things over the past year to be grateful for."

David looked around at the twenty-three people watching him. "I've got twenty-four people right here, that I'm grateful for."

Jake piped up again. "Captain, you can't count yourself!"

"I'm thankful to be alive! I think I can count me. The number of times I should have been dead may allow me to count myself multiple times."

"Cheat! You can count yourself, but only once!" Nate hollered.

The crew quieted down again. David moved to a point on the bench where he could see Brynna straight on. "I'm thankful for this beautiful woman who not only agreed to marry me, but agreed to commit treason with me and remain married to me forever. Thank you for standing by me, my love."

"Is that twenty-five or twenty-seven?" Cheyenne asked.

Several voices hollered, "twenty-five!"

David cast a few annoyed glances after he managed to take his eyes off his beautiful wife.

"I'm thankful for finding Pateras and for everything he's shown us, and the protection he's given us."

"Twenty-six," came the next call.

"I'm thankful my family got to safety." David continued.

"Twenty-seven."

"I mentioned being thankful for both crews, but to be more specific. I'm thankful no one died on this mission. Nate and Stephanie, I'm glad to have had you as my best friends for all these years. Stephanie, I'm glad Arni healed you. No matter what you each decide about Pateras, I'm glad you believed my warning. Henry and Luna, I'm glad you provided Commodore Landon with the support he needed to stay true to Pateras. Milo, thank you for not shooting my security chief, Claire, or my wife and for aiding Jake's well-intentioned, albeit misguided, rescue of the miners. Claire, thanks for giving your husband a second chance. I never deserved a second chance, but Pateras gave me one anyway. Crew of the *Evangeline*, thank you for sticking together and for following Pateras with me. I could not do this alone. I know even the entire crew can't do this alone, so I certainly couldn't do it without you. Cheyenne, thank you for your youthful insight, your words of wisdom, and candor. You thought I forgot about that incident didn't you." David teased.

"Anytime, Captain, anytime." Cheyenne grinned sheepishly as she remembered smarting off at the Captain. He had jumped on her for trying to clarify an order. The Captain had later apologized to her, but her crewmates were sure she was going to end up with a reprimand.

"Jason, thank you for saving my life on Drea. Laura, thank you for what you did in the Infirmary to protect me,

Marissa, and Jake Jr. Braxton and Thane, I heard how you defended my honor with Jake on Romajin. Thanks for believing in me despite the evidence against me. Thanks for all the times you've had my back. Marissa, thanks for trusting me with your life and Jake Jr's. Lexi, thanks for keeping me in check and for not leaving me behind on Drea."

"Captain, you don't listen to my advice." Lexi argued.

David smiled. "Yes, I do. I just hear it in my head before it comes out of your mouth. If you weren't there to give it anyway, I would never even consider it."

Lexi just shook her head.

"Lazaro, thank you for risking your life for me."

Lazaro looked puzzled, "When did I do that?"

"When you sedated Brynna on Medoris." David grinned mischievously.

Lazaro got a serious look on his face. "That was probably the most dangerous thing I've done on this mission. Committing treason was safer."

The *Evangeline's* crew enjoyed the irony of the situation and perspective. Lazaro had to explain to the *Emissary's* crew how Brynna had been injured when she was thrown from a horse. David had ordered him to sedate her and get her back to the ship for treatment, so he could complete their mission without her. Brynna had not been happy with either man over the incident.

"Aulani, your computer expertise and your keen judgment has have saved our hides more times than I can count. You helped me find Lexi on Medoris, you kept the crew alive by helping Jake on Romajin, not to mention keeping Thane in-line on a regular basis."

Thane looked about innocently. "What did I do?"

The crew laughed and groaned at the ridiculous question. Thane was known for being rambunctious and a dare-devil. They all knew Aulani was a stabilizing force for him.

David concluded. "Thank you, all, for being patient with me and most of all, I appreciate each of you going through what you did for Jake. I know we've all been through a lot, but Jake is one of us. He's part of our family.

Thank you, Jake, for saving our lives. Have I reached thirty-one yet?"

Braxton glanced at the others, "I think you put a down payment on next year."

"Here, here!" Nate called out and banged his cup again. The group joined in and cheered. The crew of the *Evangeline* was warmed by the words of praise from their captain. He wasn't the type to offer praise often. Although they never felt like they were being used or taken for granted, it was still nice to hear. They each knew they had made mistakes and it was common for one to focus on their shortcomings. It also made one feel like others saw him or her for what they did wrong instead of what they did right. The crew knew there were a lot of things the captain felt but didn't say. Their appreciation for him rose to new levels.

The two crews got quiet. It was late, and they were getting tired. They decided it was time to say goodnight. They went back inside, thanked the King for his hospitality, and promised to visit him again over the next few days. The two crews had business of their own to conduct with each other. The group rode the carriages back to their vehicles outside the city gate and went their separate ways for the night.

David was glad to see Silas and Claire quietly doting on each other. He really hoped they could put this one unpleasant incident behind them. Henry Oliver would certainly put some effort into helping them.

The next few days both crews worked with Jo-Na to get the mine back into production. As predicted, the loose rubble from the cave-in produced a large easy pay load.

Jo-Na stood there after several days looking at the yield. It was more than he had produced in the last month. He shook his head incredulously. "I don't understand. Why would the Great God Pateras give me so much? I have never served him until King Ca-Litana declared him to be his God of Favor. I do not deserve such kindness from him."

Brynna, Silas, and Cheyenne were surveying the collection of black rocks with him. Brynna smiled and explained, "Jo-Na, none of us deserve his kindness. We've all done wrong in his sight. We were serving the Commonwealth, and Arni pursued us. He showed us many kindnesses that we didn't deserve. Arni may appear to be in his early thirties, but he was with me even when I was a child. I didn't know him then, but he knew me."

Cheyenne beamed. "That's why I am so happy to serve him. He knows how awful we are, and he still wanted us so much he chased us from one world to another and another. His plans are so intricate, and so far beyond us, it's mindboggling. Do you realize he probably caused the mine to collapse on purpose?"

Jo-Na looked vexed.

Brynna took up the tale. "Jo-Na, no one died. Everyone's injuries were healed. Pateras judged the King and removed him as ruler for refusing to care about anyone other than himself. A new and wiser King now rules, Prefect Odo-Ishan was removed from a role he didn't deserve, and he learned a deserved lesson in humility."

Silas found himself in complete agreement although he didn't understand all of it. "The Commander has a point. If that mine hadn't collapsed when it did, we would be gone, lives would have been lost, including yours. King Ca-Litana would either still be under his father's influence or dead. The Prefect would have sold your entire family into slavery, and you would be dead for failing him. I guess we would have been tracked down by the Nefil Team and died in space. Wow, that really is a detailed plan."

The crew of the *Evangeline* spent time educating King Ca-Litana and the crew of the *Emissary* about Pateras. The crew of the *Emissary* took great interest in hearing about what the crew had been through on Romajin.

The last day before they left the two crews sat down together with Arni to discuss what to do next. Nate pulled David aside. "Davie, are you sure about having the entire crew in on this? I don't want to lose control of my ship. It's like asking for a mutiny."

David pondered his answer carefully. "Nate, I understand your concerns more than you can imagine. When I committed treason, I handed my life and my ship over to my crew voluntarily and let them decide what to do with me. I'm not suggesting you go that far."

Nate's eyes grew wide. He wasn't about to go to such extremes.

David continued, "You just need to realize what you are asking them to do. Every member of your crew is a walking dead-man. The second they're discovered they'll be interrogated and executed, either through re-education or actual execution. Their previous lives are over. They are no longer soldiers of the Commonwealth. Their families are now at risk. They can't contact them. They can't go anyplace they've ever been before. I can offer some options, but you've got to let them choose."

Nate was still having difficulty accepting the ugly truth. "I... uh... I see your point."

David gripped Nate's shoulder firmly. "It took a lot of trust in Arni for me to let go. I still try to grab the controls back. You can do this."

"Is... he... going to be here?"

"Physically? I don't know for sure. He will know everything that happens though. Do you want him here?"

Nate gave David an odd look. "I think I do." Nate sensed a need for Arni's reassurance and companionship. It was unlike anything he had ever felt before.

Before David could speak the request, he saw Arni enter the gym. David nodded Arni's direction. "He just walked in."

Arni sat down casually on the floor near the door. The chairs in the gym were arranged in a large circle. The two crews had typically segregated themselves by ship. Today, they were more interspersed as the tensions between them had dissolved over the last few days.

Jake and Marissa walked in past Arni, and her baby jumped and kicked. The assault on her internal organs was sufficient to stop her in her tracks. She gasped and grabbed onto Jake.

Taking one look at her startled expression, he asked, "Are you okay?"

Marissa took a deep breath and relaxed. She grabbed Jake's hand and placed it on her morphing belly. "I'm okay, but Junior's having some sort of fit."

Arni stood, "May I?" He asked before placing his hand on Marissa's belly.

Marissa gladly allowed him to touch her excited child. The baby took one last large jump then settled down. Marissa smiled. "I guess he was just excited to see you. Well, sort of… see… you."

Arni didn't answer. Something in his eyes said that wasn't the situation. Marissa frowned. "You're leaving, aren't you? Jake Junior knows it, too. Doesn't he?"

"Yes, I'm leaving, but you won't be alone." Arni's smile gave her a sense of peace and reassurance.

Jake was not at peace. "Arni, please don't go. We need you. I need you. Marissa and the baby need you. The crew needs you!" His voice got more emphatic as he spoke.

Arni moved his hand from Marissa's belly to Jake's shoulder. "I've hidden your location from him. He won't find you again. He can speak to you, but he can't harm you or Marissa or the baby. You will see your son born, alive and well." Arni knew Jake was afraid Luciano Hale would attack them again.

Jake was still worried. His face refused to release the tension.

"When did you decide to stop trusting me, Jake?" Arni stepped back and clasped his hands behind his back to allow Jake to consider his position.

"I'm sorry, Arni. I trust you, really, I do. I've just never been more scared in my life. As long as you're close by, I'm not worried."

"You won't be alone. We will always be close by. The Father will send an Advocate to guide you, speak for you, and give you access to the Father's power. He will live within you. You will never be alone."

Marissa teared up. She grabbed Arni and hugged him tightly around the neck. After she released him, she slid her arm around Jake and cuddled up under his left arm.

Jake rubbed her arm in a consoling manner. He stuck his right hand out to Arni. "Thank you, for everything."

Arni shook his hand. After Jake released Arni's hand, he gently pushed Marissa further into the room. She moved on without him and wiped quiet tears away as she walked toward the circle of chairs. Jake gave Arni one last desperate question. "Is she going to keep crying like this after the baby comes?"

Arni laughed. "It's just a part of life, my brother. Jason can tell you the particulars. You'll get through this, I promise."

Jake rolled his eyes and walked on. Marissa heard him mumbling under his breath as he approached. "What's the matter, Jake?"

Jake realized he had better word his answer carefully. "I just hate seeing you upset. I would do anything to make you happy."

"Oh, you're so sweet." Marissa smiled at him as they took their seats.

The rest of the group sat down. David started the meeting. "Our mission to Ela Prime was to warn you about the Supreme Executor's orders to destroy you. Our mission here was to see to your protection. We've accomplished that, and our next goals are to find the other teams and warn them. We now have the Nefil to deal with as well. Captain Weiseman has copies of all the information we have.

"Crew of the *Emissary*, whether or not you serve Pateras is up to you. You can't go back to the Commonwealth or your homes or families. Don't even try to contact them. You'll only put them in danger. I can offer you some places to go and hideout if you wish, you can try to hide someplace of your own choosing, pick up a new identity, and stay under the radar. You could make your way back to the Commonwealth and report the rest of your crew as committing treason. You might get back into the Executor's good graces.

"The last option is to join our mission. We would probably need to go different directions, but we would at least have an ally."

Nate looked over at Arni who was again sitting on the floor despite an empty chair being in the circle for him.

"Davie, I know we just got everyone in here and settled, but would you mind giving us a few minutes to talk?"

David nodded and motioned for his crew to step out. Everyone stepped out as ordered and congregated in the hallway.

Arni remained where he was which gave Nate a small amount of comfort. "Alright people, thoughts? The floor is one hundred percent open."

Claire's eyes landed on Arni. "I don't know what all is involved in following Arni, but... it's what I want to do. I also think we need to warn the other ships."

Henry quietly grasped Luna's hand and squeezed it. "I'm tired of hiding my loyalty. Luna and I are with Claire. I'm ready to go on the offensive."

Milo glanced at his wife. "Gennie and I haven't discussed this, but from what I've seen, I'm ready to give Arni a chance."

Gennie reached over and took her husband's hand, "Me, too."

Stephanie looked at her husband. "Nate, I want to join Arni, but the call is yours."

Elize and Deka looked at each other. "What do we do?" Elize asked her husband.

Deka looked around at the others. He finally turned back to his wife. "Your friend, Braxton, he's sure about following this Pateras and Arni?"

"Yes, he is. I had time to talk to him more at the mine. The stories he's told me are incredible. I think it's our only chance." Elize was more outgoing than her husband, but on this, she withdrew and waited for his response.

Deka thought it over then informed the others. "We choose to follow... him." He nodded at Arni.

Nate looked at Noah, Maya, and Silas. "What do you three want to do?"

Silas looked at Claire who got still and quiet. "I am loyal to Arni and Pateras. I'm not about to turn my back on them and risk losing the most precious thing in my life."

Noah was quiet, and Maya was waiting on her husband. She had her mind made up, but she didn't want to influence his decision. Noah finally voiced himself. "I have a question for Arni."

Arni approached the circle. "Tell me what you want to know."

Maya squinted at him. "I thought you already knew our thoughts."

Arni sat down in one of the chairs. "I do, but the rest of you don't. It would be rude and not very helpful for me to answer his question without letting him first ask it."

Maya cocked her head sideways. "Oh… okay… I think."

Noah propped his forearms on his knees. He rubbed his hands together as he struggled to word his question. "I saw Dr. Weiseman's injuries. We don't have the facilities to—to repair that kind of damage. How did you do that? Who… What… are you?"

"I am the creator of all life. I came to pay the debt that man owes to my Father for the evil they have done. I gave life to each of you. Since I created Stephanie, I am capable of healing her. I created every cell that has ever existed. Luciano Hale fell from my Father's good graces, and he has tried to destroy all the things my Father cares about. I'm here to restore humanity to my Father." His answer covered more than Noah vocalized, but it was a more complete answer to the things he didn't fully ask.

"Are… Are you a god?" He added.

"Would it frighten you if I were?" Arni asked.

Noah shook his head. "But gods aren't real."

Arni paused before responding. He knew his reply would be hard for them to swallow. "Most gods are not real, that is true. My Father, the Advocate, and I are all one. You could say we are different manifestations of the same Supreme Being. You may use whatever name you wish. I am known as many things. The things you must know as absolute truth are; first, my Father is all-powerful; second, he is known as the Timeless One because he has no beginning and no end; third, he is all-knowing. Nothing is hidden from him. He is the one true God; there are no others. If that frightens you, then consider which side do you want to be on, his or the deceiver, Luciano Hale?"

Noah had stopped rubbing his hands together and sat there frozen. Arni's words did frighten him. Was this man insane? Before he could go any further with his thoughts, Arni addressed them.

"Noah, if I were a mere mortal making these claims then, yes, I would be considered insane. I am not. Only God could legitimately claim to be God."

It took Noah a moment to realize Arni had read his thoughts, not his voice. He slowly looked up and his own words frightened him. "I believe you. What do you want from me?"

"I want you to follow me."

"I—I don't know what that means, but I do know I don't want to follow somebody who wants me dead. I think... I'm in."

A silence enveloped the room. Nate was waiting on any further questions or comments. He watched his crew as closely as they watched him. He searched their faces for tells of disapproval, dissatisfaction, or a lack of resolve. The greatest negative sign he saw were feelings of loss and a basic resolve to accept Arni as a last resort.

Nate turned to Arni. "Answer this for me. Why should we follow you? What makes you any better than Executor Hale? I mean, I'm looking at my people, and they're turning to you because they have no place else to turn. I know David and his crew trust you. I trust David. Why should I trust you, even if you are as powerful as you say you are?"

"Luciano's plans are to kill and destroy humanity. My plans for you are not to harm you. I have come to find you and to release you from the bondage he's placed you in. He's shrouded humanity in darkness and doomed you to face an eternity of pain. I paid the price with my own life to free you, but only if you choose to accept it. I know my words and these concepts are strange."

David's voice interrupted from across the room. "Nate, the relationship we have is like a parent and child. He's also like a best friend and an adviser."

Nate looked cross. "What happened to our privacy?"

David looked vexed. "Arni asked me to join you."

"Since you're here, tell me why I should join him. I know my choices are limited—run and hide, follow him, or try to convince Executor Hale we're still loyal. Since I doubt that third one is going to work out for me, why choose to join him?" Nate decided hearing from David was just as important as hearing from Arni.

"Everything Arni has done for us has been for our good. He's protected us from things we never saw coming. He's saved our lives more times than I can count. He cares about us. The Supreme Executor only cares about what we can do for him and what kind of satisfaction he gets from keeping us away from Pateras." David gladly explained. He was quietly hoping his friend would choose to join them.

"You see, that's what I'm having a problem with. You said you died. How is that for your own good? You also said your own security chief beat you mercilessly. Brynna told me some guys nearly beat you to death on Drea. How are those things good?"

David sat down in a chair and looked around at the tense faces around him. "I died by another man's hand, so my uncle wouldn't be forced to arrest and execute me himself. The incident with the security chief was more for his benefit than mine. It showed him I was willing to live or die for Pateras, and it also showed Jake what I was willing to do to reach him. The beating on Drea was also to protect Jake and show him what I was willing to endure to protect him. I wasn't loyal to Pateras at that time. If I had called on him, he might've protected me. I don't know for certain, only he could tell you that. The other thing it did was it changed a sequence of events that would have cost me my life and the lives of several other crewmembers. Because of that beating, all of my crew are alive and well, and Marissa is very pregnant."

Henry spoke up. "You know Luna and I have been followers of Pateras for several years now. I've seen you and your security chief working together. You have a good relationship. I know Pateras can do anything, but I'm not sure I would have recovered from such a psychological trauma this quickly. Care to explain that?"

"Jake is—was pretty high-strung when we started this mission. He trusted no one and challenged everyone. He was in my office for disciplinary action more than once in the first few weeks of our trip. When we all joined Pateras, he realized he was outnumbered and had to play along. Yes, he betrayed us, but he was trying to save our lives and our careers. He was also trying to protect his wife and child. He knew what Arni was capable of, but he remained loyal to the Commonwealth until Luciano Hale tried to take away the things he valued the most. Jake values his career, but that would have been all he had left and with the crew about to die... he would have considered his career to be a failure. What kind of security chief allows his entire crew to be conquered by the enemy and killed?"

"That's a fair point." Security Chief Milo Griffin remarked. "So how did you end up with such a good relationship? I think I would have had some pretty hard feelings to get past."

"It's a little hard to explain. We knew at some point Jake would betray us. We just didn't know when or where. Arni told us what was coming, and that it was the only way to reach him. My options were, leave Jake behind somewhere forcing Marissa to make some hard choices, stick him in stasis for who knows how long, or spend six days in Commonwealth custody facing whatever they dished out. I could have walked away. I didn't. I wanted to keep him and Marissa together and part of my crew. I suppose it was more for the chief's good than mine, but ultimately, he's been a better man and a better security chief since then."

Milo shook his head, "He betrayed you, and you now trust him?"

"If it were Jake alone who had gotten us out of there, I might not trust him. Since it was Arni and Jake together getting us out of there, I do trust him. Arni makes the difference." David laughed ironically. "If it were just me without Arni, I might have spaced Jake the second I was well enough to. Arni is what makes the difference in me, and in Jake."

"You really do trust him with your life, don't you?" Milo continued.

Nate moved around the circle, thinking. Hearing Milo's question, he stopped moving and looked at David. "He does, most definitely."

Milo wondered what his Captain was using as evidence. "What makes you say so?"

"The day they arrived, Davie had one man watching his back. It was Chief Holden. If he wanted his Captain dead, or even just out of the picture, he could have easily done that." Nate rotated to face Arni again. "You're the reason he trusts his security chief."

Arni nodded.

Nate considered his options one more time. Going back to the Commonwealth would mean psychological if not physical death through re-education. If they ran, they would be constantly be looking over their shoulders. They'd probably never see their families again. There was no way to feel safe. His friend had risked his own life to come here and try to protect him and his crew. That certainly wasn't safe, but David had never seemed... frightened. He seemed to feel safe with Arni.

Nate looked at Arni. David had followed him, and it cost him his life, but here he stood alive and well. His friend admitted he didn't have all the answers, but he was at peace with his situation. Perhaps sticking with Arni was the only way to be at peace in these circumstances.

Nate finally gave the others his decision. "Arni, I'm ready to follow you. Where do we go from here?"

EPILOGUE

The two ships left the system heading in different directions. A plan was in place to meet again in a few months. They kept their plans committed to memory, and only two people on each ship were given the information of where and when their next meeting would occur. Both Captains felt it would be safest if no one knew. They intended on searching out the other ten ships and bringing the group together at the predetermined time and place.

One day later, the CIF SS *Stalwart*, Admiral Garcia's flagship, entered the system accompanied by two of the Pacification Fleet ships. The Captain of the *Stalwart* reported to the Admiral. "Admiral, we've conducted a thorough search of the system. We've found the remains of a ship orbiting the seventh planet in the system. There is also evidence of an explosion of a Commonwealth ship on the surface of Ela Prime."

"Have you identified the ships?"

"We've positively identified the one from the seventh planet as the *Talon*. It looks as though an asteroid might have struck them as they were preparing to engage their tachyon drive. There are a large number of bradyons present in the area."

"Bradyons?"

"Yes Admiral, the tachyons, once released into space would degrade quickly to bradyons. We detected a bradyon trail leaving the system." The Captain carefully explained.

Admiral Garcia picked up a nearby cup of coffee and sipped on it. "What about the explosion on Ela Prime?"

"We can't identify it from space. Do you want us to send a shuttle down to get detailed scans of the area? The blast radius isn't as big as anticipated for the Explorer Class ships. It's possible they were taking off when they were destroyed. The area shows signs of destabilization. A nearby mountain shows signs of recent cave-ins and landslides, and there's also a river nearby which could have caught some of the debris."

Admiral Garcia stared thoughtfully into his coffee cup.

The Captain waited patiently for orders. When his waiting became uncomfortable, he prodded. "Shall I send the shuttle to confirm?"

"No, I don't think that will be necessary. Just file the report as is." The Admiral finally replied.

"So, what do you think happened, sir?"

"I think Captain Doherty destroyed the *Emissary* and let his ego get the best of him. He didn't watch his back, and an asteroid taught him a lesson he won't recover from." Admiral Garcia didn't care for the Nefil, especially Captain Doherty. He was concerned they would earn the favor of Supreme Executor Hale, and he would lose the Executor's favor. The Admiral had his eye on Defense Minister Hamilton Payne's job.

"What about the *Evangeline*, sir? Reports indicated she might be headed here." The Captain wanted to be thorough. There were too many unanswered questions.

The Admiral looked up. "You mentioned a bradyon trail leaving the system, didn't you?"

"Yes sir."

"I suspect the Evangeline got here too late and has since left the area. Follow the trail of bradyons as far as you can to see if you can find any leads."

The Captain acknowledged his orders and left the Admiral's office. He quietly decided to deploy an observation buoy into orbit around the fifth planet of the system. He didn't want it too close to Ela Prime or too near the outer edge of the system. If the Evangeline hadn't been here yet, or even if it was hiding on a moon in the system, the buoy could spot it and alert the Commonwealth.

Admiral Garcia hailed the Supreme Executor's office to report their findings. The Executor himself greeted him. The Admiral gave Executor Hale only the facts and not his supposition until the Executor asked him for it. Admiral Garcia laced his proposition with numerous ambiguous interpretations. He included the possibility of the Evangeline arriving recently.

Supreme Executor Hale smiled. "I believe I have a new press release to give. I'm going to report that we sent Captain Doherty and the *Talon* out to protect and recover the few remaining ships loyal to the Commonwealth. Captain Alexander must have destroyed both ships. We can turn Captain Weiseman and his crew into helpless victims, and Captain Doherty and his crew will be martyrs. Any thoughts?"

Admiral Garcia grinned. "I like the way you think. I don't know if you are aware of it or not, but Captain Alexander and Captain Weiseman have known each other and been best friends since the Academy. That could really make him seem like a monster."

"It certainly could. I have a couple more surprises for Captain Alexander. I need your help with one of them."

"How can I help?" Admiral Garcia asked excitedly.

"I've found the Captain's father. I need you to bring him to me. Sending you the coordinates and the details now." The Executor pressed a few buttons on his desk.

A moment later Admiral Garcia's display blinked at him indicating the information had finished downloading to his computer.

Admiral Garcia smiled. "I'll get right on this. Do you think this will be enough to get Captain Alexander to surrender?"

"I don't know, but perhaps if his father can't convince him, maybe his son can."

Admiral Garcia's eyes grew wide. "He has a son?"

Executor Hale smiled. His eyes looking colder than ever. "He will have. It seems Miss Shields is expecting a son."

THE DEFENDER SERIES

CONTINUES WITH

BIRTH OF A REVOLUTION
(BOOK 6)

PICK IT UP TODAY
AT YOUR FAVORITE
BOOKSTORE !

Two stories, worlds apart, yet somehow connected. On the backward world of Galat, an inconsequential planet, a young pregnant woman flees for her life. An ancient prophecy predicts the downfall of regimes with the birth of her child. The world is barely past the stone age, yet the child's birth will be felt across the galaxy.

On Juranta, a more advanced world, a former covert ops agent marries an accountant and daughter of two engineering geniuses. Months later, Tristan and Jessica's child is born—the child also heralded by the ancient prophecy—a prophecy his family has been forbidden to speak of.

A mysterious figure schemes to thwart the prophecies. Jessica's brother, the future admiral, Robert Deacons, witnesses the birth of the Galatan baby, and saves the lives of the infant and his mother. He suspects the child belongs to the enemy of his childhood, but he refuses to harm an innocent child. His gut tells him his enemy has already won, even if the battle hasn't started.

Robert returns to meet his newborn nephew, David Liam Alexander, a future Commonwealth captain. How are the two infants connected? What secrets bind them together? Come find out.

The newly promoted captain, David Alexander, takes command of his first crew and starship on a multifaceted mission of diplomacy, intelligence gathering, and dangerous first contacts. He and his crew are searching out a dangerous and subversive new enemy to the Commonwealth, the ruling power in the galaxy. After finding and eluding the enemy on the ship's first contact, David discovers the enemy is now stalking  him and his crew with warnings of impending doom.

A loyal Commonwealth soldier, David resists his enemies' attempts to seduce him to change sides. On his second mission, David finds himself at the mercy of a primitive group of savages intent on killing him. His only hope is his sworn enemy, but what is the price for saving his life?

David learns that his enemy, Arni Liontari, has gone out of his way to protect him and his crew. Could the Commonwealth's Intel be wrong or is the enemy more dangerous than he realized? Get on board the *Evangeline*, now, before it's too late.

DEFENDED

THE DEFENDER SERIES BOOK 2

REGGI BROACH

Captain Alexander and the crew of the *Evangeline* continue their Commonwealth mission to make allies of the non-space-faring planets in the galaxy. Drea III is a technologically advanced world shrouded by a dark and bloody history with the Commonwealth.

Drean officials politely agree to hear the crew's proposal of an alliance with the Commonwealth. A series of heinous discoveries land the crew in jail, charged with several capital crimes. Captain Alexander finds himself torn between his Commonwealth mandates and protecting an entire planet from annihilation.

David throws himself on the mercy of the courts, defending his crew to his last breath. More unexpected revelations cause the Captain and crew to question everything they've been taught.

Discover the 50-year cover-up!

The Commonwealth groomed Captain David Alexander from birth for this mission. When his treason causes a rift among his crew, the stalwartly loyal security chief, Jake Holden, attempts to carry out his duty of executing the wayward captain. Jake is forced to choose between his duty to the Commonwealth and sparing the Captain's life for saving Jake's unborn child.

Captain Alexander confidently moves forward with his traitorous mission against the Commonwealth hoping all of his crew will join him. His loyalty and trust in Pateras is tested when his life and the crew's lives are in jeopardy from a power-hungry Priest and his followers. Most of the crew accept Captain Alexander's treason without question, but if the Commonwealth learns of it, his life will be forfeit.

An unexpected visit from Admiral Robert Deacons, Captain Alexander's uncle, puts a heavily armed Pacification Ship in orbit. If Admiral Deacons learns the truth about his nephew will their familial ties protect David and his crew?

Captain David Alexander and his crew are guilty of treason against the Commonwealth. Security Chief Jake Holden openly opposes the crew's treason. Arni, the superior being who now holds David's loyalty, warns him that Jake will betray him. David knows the cost and the benefits of willingly stepping into Jake's trap.

Alone, imprisoned, beaten, and drugged, David struggles to remain loyal to Pateras and to resist the urge to surrender to Supreme Executor Hale's enticing offers. David is pushed to his limits when his crew is led to believe he betrayed them, and his wife told about a contrived relationship between him and another woman.

Tortured mercilessly, Jake offers him a way out, a syringe with a lethal sedative. The drugs forced on him by his captors wreak havoc with his thoughts. Did Pateras abandon him? Was this the only way out?

Capt. Alexander and his crew have abandoned the Commonwealth in favor of serving Pateras. Pateras' enemy, Supreme Executor Hale, dispatches a fleet of super soldiers to destroy them, and anyone else who gets in their way.

Capt. Alexander needs the crew to forgive Jake's treachery, and he needs allies before the Commonwealth finds them. His best chance is his old friends, Nate and Stephanie, from his Academy days. David seeks the *Emissary*, hoping his friend will listen to reason. To his disappointment, his best friend places him under arrest. Now what does he do?

Mission Abandoned is volume V in the Sci-Fi Defender series. Reggi Broach expertly weaves personal struggles with action and adventure, creating a powerful novel you can't put down. Pick it up now.

BIRTH OF A
REVOLUTION
DEFENDER SERIES BOOK 6

REGGI BROACH

Hunted for treason and haunted by his past, Captain David Alexander attempts to unite the Explorer Fleet against the Commonwealth. The belief that Captain Alexander mercilessly destroyed an entire military base fuels his comrades' desire to turn him in. David has evidence against Supreme Executor Luciano Hale, but it's subjective. Will it be enough to convince the other crews to join him?

The tenuous agreement reached by the Fleet is put in danger when four ruffians, hungry for revenge, kidnap Captain Alexander and Lt. Marissa Holden who is about to give birth. The two are forced into an empty mine tunnel. The odds are not good with four against one and the young lieutenant in heavy labor.

Can Security Chief Jake Holden reach the Captain and Marissa in time? Who is the mysterious stranger stalking them? Can they get off Zulimar before their enemies arrive? Get onboard before the enemy catches you!

The newly formed Pateran Resurrection Movement is severely outnumbered and outclassed. The potential for traitors in their ranks remains high. The *Evangeline* is plagued with a manpower shortage. When his father confesses to being a Commonwealth spy, David is forced to make some hard choices. Can David trust his estranged father?

QUESTIONS OF TRUST

BOOK 7

COMING IN

2023

What else could go wrong? David, the newly appointed Lead Admiral of the renegade Liontari Fleet, was already one of the youngest of the Explorer Fleet captains. His feelings of inferiority to his peers are multiplied when two ships under his command disappear. Personal tragedy adds to the new young Admiral's load.

Executor Hale reveals a secret designed to hurt one person, the new Admiral. How much more can Admiral Alexander take before he cracks under the pressure? The Admiral needs all hands on deck. Join him now, before more tragedy strikes.

REVELATIONS

BOOK 8

COMING IN

2024

After the devastating loss of Captain Talaith Bowen and the revelation of several treacherous Commonwealth secrets, Admiral David Alexander moves forward with his mission to warn the newer worlds about the dangers of allying with the Commonwealth. The ruling officials on Gadola are willing to listen despite the Commonwealth's warnings about the renegade fleet. David and his crew earn the respect of the Gadolan Premier, but not the leaders of the Guilds.

The Guilds take advantage of David's status as a Commonwealth criminal. The Guilds kidnap David's father and Ensign Cheyenne Dominick to force David's hand in destroying the troublesome colonies in the Gadolan system. Elias Soren, a pesky, young Commonwealth reporter also vanishes.

Captain Brynna Alexander tries to present evidence against the Guild leaders but is kidnapped along with the colonial representatives. Will David be forced to choose between saving his wife or his father? Can they make it out of the system before the Guilds summon the SS *Valiant* to arrest him or shoot down his ship?

www.ingramcontent.com/pod-product-compliance
Lightning Source LLC
Chambersburg PA
CBHW030652120726
47905CB00001B/178